NINE LESSONS

Nicola Upson was born in Suffolk and read English at Downing College, Cambridge. She has worked in theatre and as a freelance journalist, and is the author of two non-fiction works and the recipient of an Escalator Award from the Arts Council England.

Her debut novel, *An Expert in Murder*, was the first in a series of crime novels whose main character is Josephine Tey – one of the leading authors of Britain's Golden Age of crime writing.

She lives with her partner in Cambridge and Cornwall.

Further praise for *Nine Lessons*:

'It takes pluck for a crime writer to put an illustrious predecessor at the centre of her novels. But in choosing to invent an afterlife for real-life author Josephine Tey, one of the crime-writing golden age greats, Nicola Upson rises to the challenge . . . *Nine Lessons* is not for the faint-hearted. But with its underlying theme of good intentions having tragic consequences, the story is strong enough to carry us through to a dramatic finale.' Barry Turner, *Daily Mail*

'Intelligent and well-crafted.' *Woman & Home*

'Upson's subtle hand juxtaposes an elegantly descriptive narrative with a thrilling thread of simmering menace, dark, disturbing plot lines and grisly murders that will make your blood run cold.' *Lancashire Post*

'Upson [is] perceptive on the place of women in unenlightened 1930s England.' *Financial Times*

'Upson's novels are always wonderfully evocative of the time period in which they are set . . . Perfect for lovers of classic crime with a contemporary twist.' *Shiny New Books*

'Well-researched flashes of reality add authority and the political subtext is interesting . . . This is a complex, subtle novel in which Upson manipulates her material most skilfully.' *Literary Review*

'Even without knowledge of the first six books in the series, it is clear that Upson has taken the air of mystery that surrounds Tey's private life and blended it smoothly with the few facts available to create a plausible and complex heroine. The blanks of Tey's life – friends, lovers etc. – are filled in with fiction but it's plausible fiction and I felt like the woman coming across in *Nine Lessons* really could be the woman who wrote the golden age classics that I've so enjoyed. Upson's Tey comes across as clever, passionate and sensitive . . . A cleverly plotted, compelling mystery novel.' *Shelf of Unread Books*

---

also by Nicola Upson

AN EXPERT IN MURDER
ANGEL WITH TWO FACES
TWO FOR SORROW
FEAR IN THE SUNLIGHT
THE DEATH OF LUCY KYTE
LONDON RAIN

Nine Lessons

NICOLA UPSON

FABER & FABER

First published in 2017
by Faber & Faber Limited
Bloomsbury House
74–77 Great Russell Street
London WC1B 3DA
This paperback edition first published in 2018

Typeset by Faber & Faber Limited
Printed and bound by CPI Group (UK) Ltd, Croydon, CR0 4YY

A CIP record for this book
is available from the British Library

ISBN 978–0–571–32478–1

2 4 6 8 10 9 7 5 3 1

For the women who survived the real Cambridge rapist,
and in memory of Jill Saward, who did so much to give
rape survivors an identity beyond the crime.

'What is all this love for if we have to go out into the dark?'

M. R. James

1

Detective Chief Inspector Archie Penrose stood by the gate of St-John-at-Hampstead, struck as ever by the strange beauty of its wooded churchyard – quiet, peaceful and rambling, just like the parish it served. He had never warmed to the building itself, preferring the modest grey stone of an English country church to this more ostentatious red brick, but the surrounding land held a fascination which had little to do with worship. Other than Highgate, St John's was probably the most famous burial ground in London, the final resting place of celebrated artists, scientists and actors – or, as his cousins often joked, the most sought-after green room outside of the West End. Many of the more dramatic tombs were to be found in the graveyard's extension on the other side of Church Row, but it was this overgrown, secluded area that Penrose preferred, where the headstones seemed randomly scattered and the ordinary lives of chimneysweeps, bakers and nurses were remembered alongside the achievements of the more famous. He tried to spend time here whenever his work brought him to Hampstead, thankful for a reminder of death in its natural context and the welcome reassurance that not everyone was wrenched screaming from the world before their natural time. Today, that comfort was not to be his.

A blackbird sang overhead, its sweet, melancholy notes offering an eloquent acknowledgement of autumn and the early onset of dusk. Penrose took the meandering path which ran to the left of the church, and soon saw the small clutch of figures standing stiff and awkward by a grave, their dark silhouettes blurred by the mist in a parody of an ill-attended funeral. One of them broke away from the group as he approached, a uniformed constable who seemed anxious, although it was hard to say if his nerves were due to the shock of the discovery or the arrival of a high-ranking detective. He wiped his hand diligently on his trousers and introduced himself. 'Parkyn, sir. We spoke on the telephone.'

Penrose nodded. 'You said you were first on the scene – how long after the discovery of the body?'

'Only a few minutes, sir. A quarter of an hour at the most. Apparently, a couple out walking their dog found him. The slab across the grave's been pushed back a bit and the dog was scrabbling to get in. They fetched the vicar straight away.'

On cue, the vicar glanced their way, and Penrose sensed the unease of someone who was used to being in control of an ordered world. 'And the vicar identified the dead man?'

'Yes, sir, by a ring he was wearing. His name's Stephen Laxborough. Apparently he was the organist here.'

Penrose found himself irrationally irritated by the constable's habit of prefixing every fact with a qualifying uncertainty, but he tried not to let it show. 'And everything is exactly as it was? No one's touched anything?'

Parkyn shook his head. 'Apparently not, sir.'

'Good. I'll have a word with the vicar now and find out what else he knows about the victim. What's his name?'

'Reverend Turner, sir.'

'Take the others back to the church and wait by the gate until back-up arrives. I don't want anyone trampling through here before we've got what we need. Then get a statement from the people who found him.'

'Right-o, sir.'

'And you might put in another call to the Yard and find out where the hell the photographer's got to. We're losing the light, and I want every detail of that scene.'

'I'll get onto it straight away.' Parkyn hurried back to the group and Penrose waited while he ushered an elderly couple with a cocker spaniel and two smartly dressed women towards the porch. He looked around, noticing that he was in one of the very oldest parts of the churchyard; without exception, the headstones were worn and fragile, victims of both weather and age, and there was something poignant about the way in which these once so solid markers of a person's life had faded with their memory. The tomb that had brought him here was tucked away from the main path, sheltered by ancient yew trees and a tangle of branches overhead, and behind it the ground began to slope away towards the boundary wall. It had obviously been restored in recent years, because the flat stone slab was now raised to a height of eighteen inches or so on a foundation of modern bricks. The combination of old and new, red and grey, jarred to Penrose's eye, and he noted that the ivy – the only thing uniting the two – had been roughly torn away. The slab, as Parkyn had mentioned, now lay at an angle to the foundations, partially revealing the horror within. He moved closer and stood silently by the vicar's side, looking down at the flash of grey-blonde hair matted with blood, the clenched fist with its distinctive ring, the fingers scraped almost literally to the bone. The dead man's face was hidden from view, but Penrose didn't doubt that the Reverend Turner's imagination had defied the mercy of the stone.

'Who on earth could do this to another human being?' the vicar asked quietly. Penrose had no answer, and didn't insult the question by trying to offer one. 'I don't suppose I should admit this,' Turner continued, 'but I've struggled to find God in some of the parishes I've been given. He's never let me down here, though. Not until now.'

'Did you know Mr Laxborough well?'

'*Dr* Laxborough. He was always very particular about that.' The vicar moved away from the grave, seemingly glad to pass responsibility for the body to someone more familiar with the violence to which it testified. He met Penrose's eyes for the first time. 'It's funny. I was just wondering that myself when you arrived.'

'And what did you decide?'

'I suppose I'd have to say that I didn't really know Stephen at all, even though we'd worked together for years. He was a private man, neither easy to warm to nor to take against. In fact, now I think about it, I can't remember a single conversation in all that time that wasn't in some way connected to our work.'

'So he'd been here a long time?'

'Oh yes. He was already well established at St John's when I arrived in thirty-two – I gather he settled in Hampstead after the war. The church has an excellent tradition of music going back to Henry Willis, but Stephen was thought to be one of the finest performers we've ever had. He was very well respected.'

But not liked, Penrose thought, reading between the lines. 'When did you last see him?'

'At evensong on Sunday. We'd just moved the service to its earlier time, like we always do ready for the winter, and we were supposed to be sitting down afterwards to discuss the music for the forthcoming month, but Stephen had to cancel. He didn't say why.'

'And how did he seem?'

Turner shrugged. 'Business-like, bordering on brusque, but there was nothing unusual in that. He lived his life like he played his music – precisely, professionally, and with rarely a note out of place.'

The comment was insightful. Most people, when asked to describe the victim of a recent murder, were inclined to exaggerate the positive, and Penrose wondered if the vicar's refusal to sentimentalise his opinion of his colleague said more about him or about the deceased. 'Was he married?' he asked.

'No, he lived alone – except for a housekeeper. She'll be able to tell you more about his life than I can, I expect, and she might be aware of some family. You'll want to tell his next of kin, but I'm afraid I have no idea who that is.'

'Who were the two ladies here with you just now?'

The vicar raised an eyebrow to the heavens. 'Mrs Marchmont and Mrs Willoughby. Flowers and brasses, for their sins – or for mine. They were with me when Stephen's body was found and I'm afraid it would have taken a stronger man than I to keep them inside.'

'Isn't it a bit late in the day for flower arranging?'

'Usually, yes, but we've got a funeral tomorrow morning and the ladies are exhaustingly thorough. Neither will concede defeat by being the first to go home.' Penrose smiled, but Turner looked suddenly uncertain. 'We will be able to go ahead with the funeral, will we? Stephen will be . . .'

He tailed off before the words 'cleared away' could escape his lips. 'Yes, we'll remove Dr Laxborough's body as soon as the photographer and pathologist have done their work,' Penrose said. 'I'll need to keep the area roped off, though, at least for a few days.'

'That's fine. We haven't buried anyone on this side since 1878.' He reddened, embarrassed by the clumsy lack of tact. 'Do you think he was already dead when whoever it was put him in there?'

'No, I'm afraid I don't,' Penrose said, recalling the ravaged hands which had clearly clawed for hours at the stone.

'So why uncover him again? No one would ever have known he was there.'

It was one of many questions running through Penrose's mind, but he had no intention of speculating about any of them, except with the pathologist. A convoy of three cars drew up outside the church gates and he recognised his sergeant, Bill Fallowfield, followed by a police photographer and forensics team. 'You can leave Dr Laxborough to us now,' he said, keen to have the scene to himself for a few precious seconds of peace before science took over. 'But I'd be grateful if you could find me his address.'

'Of course. He was in Mount Vernon, just around the corner. I'll get you the number.'

'Thank you.' The vicar walked off, picking his way carefully over headstones that had fallen across the path. Penrose returned to the body. The slab which now marked a double grave was flecked with moss and scattered with fallen yew needles. Its inscription gave a full account of the original incumbent, but the letters were worn and faded and Penrose could only make out enough to know that the tomb belonged to James McArdell, a London engraver who had died in 1765 at the age of thirty-seven. He took a torch out of his pocket and peered into the grave, but it was impossible to see any more of Laxborough's body without moving the stone further back. As he turned to greet his colleagues, his foot brushed something on the grass by the tomb, and he looked down to see three identical steel padlocks, nestled neatly side by side.

'Jesus Christ!' Fallowfield said, looking over Penrose's shoulder. 'The poor bastard.'

'Eloquent as ever, Bill, but I couldn't have put it better. Someone obviously wanted to punish him, but God knows what for. I'd say the suffering was as important as the death itself, wouldn't you?' He nodded to the photographer to begin his work, and the repeated explosions of light gave the scene an intense, surreal quality that only heightened its horror. 'Get as much detail as you can, and don't miss those padlocks. I've no idea if they're connected yet, but I want everything recorded as it is before we open it up.'

The instructions were unnecessary, and it wasn't like him to patronise officers who were every bit as diligent in their craft as he was, but he realised now that there was a part of him which would happily have delayed the opening of the tomb for as long as possible. The atmosphere in the churchyard had shifted subtly from melancholy to unease, and Penrose had an almost superstitious reluctance to release the violence that lay hidden beneath the stone; none of them, he knew, would be immune to the brutality of this particular death or to the agony of those dreadful hours.

Even Bernard Spilsbury – who had witnessed so much darkness in a long career as Home Office Pathologist that his sanity was nothing short of a miracle – remained uncharacteristically quiet.

'All right, let's get it over with,' Penrose said, when there were no angles left to photograph. He stepped forward to the grave, determined to take the brunt of the task, but the effort of moving a solid slab of stone made him recoil in pain. Wincing, he rubbed his right shoulder, where an injury from a gunshot wound had taken a long time to heal, and the gesture didn't escape the eagle eyes of his sergeant.

'Leave that to us, sir,' said Fallowfield, who had been fussing over him like a mother hen since his return to work. 'You'll set yourself back weeks if you keep going at it.'

Penrose glared at him but stood to one side. 'All right, but just one of you to start with. I want to see if someone could shift this thing on his own, at least enough to get the victim in there.'

'Come on, Wilson, put your back into it,' Fallowfield said, grinning at the burliest of the crime scene officers. There was a sharp grating noise as the stone was moved back, inch by inch at first, then more quickly as Wilson gained momentum. Just as the slab was about to topple to the ground, Penrose signalled to him to stop and stepped forward to look. 'We need some light in here.'

As soon as his request was obliged, he wished he hadn't made it. Stephen Laxborough's body lay face down in its borrowed sarcophagus, his head turned slightly towards the side. Instinctively, Penrose closed his eyes, trying to summon all the reserves of detachment that he had gathered over the years, but his objectivity deserted him. The bloodied and broken fingers that he had noted earlier were just the beginning. Laxborough's face was contorted with agony and fear, his eyes swollen and his skull horribly mutilated where he had beaten it repeatedly against the stone that held him – in a desperate effort to escape, perhaps, or simply to bring on a merciful oblivion. Penrose might almost have convinced himself that the victim had died from blows to the head were it not for an accumulation of signs which bore evidence to dreadful torture. In panic, Laxborough had torn at his face and body until his clothes were all but shredded, and handfuls of hair, wrenched from his own head, lay strewn around the corpse. There were bite marks on his right hand, Penrose noted, but they had not been made by an animal.

In all the murder scenes he had attended, he could not remember a silence as profound as this. Each man stood absorbed in his own private world, defenceless against the power of his imagination. Some words ran unbidden through Penrose's mind, lines from Poe's tale 'The Premature Burial': 'The boundaries which divide Life from Death, are at best shadowy and vague. Who shall say where the one ends, and where the other begins?' It was a story that he had never been able to finish, either as a child experiencing the first frisson of terror or as an adult who admired Poe's macabre power, but he felt that someone had completed it for him now, someone with more evil intent than Poe had ever envisaged. There was no mistake involved in this premature burial; whoever had sealed the tomb had known exactly what he was doing. 'How long would it have taken him to die?' he asked quietly.

'That depends,' Spilsbury said cautiously. 'We don't know yet what state he was in when he was entombed, and it's reasonable to assume that he was rendered unconscious in some way to get him in there in the first place. You wouldn't be tempted to co-operate, would you?' Penrose shook his head, trying to imagine what it would be like to come to and realise the hopelessness of your situation. 'A lot of those injuries are self-inflicted, but they might be hiding something that weakened his resistance and hastened his death. Let's hope so. But in a confined space like this, you're looking at twenty-four to thirty-six hours, perhaps a little more.' He took a few paces back as the photographer began his work again. 'The words "mercifully quick" certainly wouldn't apply. I don't envy you the house call to his family.'

'I don't even know if he *has* a family,' Penrose admitted. 'Usually I'd say there was nothing sadder than leaving no one behind to mourn you, but in this case it might be a blessing. It's hard to imagine a crueller death.'

'Yes, although it's far more common than you might think. He certainly wouldn't be the only one in this graveyard if we looked hard enough.' Spilsbury opened the battered old Gladstone bag which accompanied him everywhere and took out a fingerprint kit, a measuring tape and a pair of rubber gloves, proceeding to place these and various other items on a nearby headstone where he could access them easily. 'I'll tell you something interesting – when they closed Les Innocents cemetery in Paris and moved the bodies out to the Catacombs, they found enough skeletons buried face down to convince them that premature burial was widespread. People were quite literally turning in their grave.'

'Is that supposed to comfort me?'

Spilsbury smiled. 'I think we're beyond comfort, Archie, don't you?'

As the pathologist began to examine the body more closely, Penrose knew that any urgent questions he had would either have to be asked now or go unanswered until later: Spilsbury hated to be distracted while he worked, partly from diligence and partly from a deep-rooted respect for the dead and a determination to give them his best. 'Is it naive of me to wonder that he couldn't get out?' he said, thinking out loud. 'I know he's not as young or as well built as Wilson, but people do extraordinary things when they're desperate and the adrenaline alone might have given him a strength that he didn't know he had.'

'Perhaps that's what the padlocks are about,' Fallowfield suggested. 'The slab might have been weighted down with something.'

Penrose considered the idea. 'That would have drawn attention to the grave, though, and presumably attention was the last thing the killer wanted – at least until he was ready to expose the body. As it is, he ran the risk of someone hearing Laxborough cry out for help. The grave's well away from the main path and that's probably why he chose it, but people wander all over this churchyard.'

'We don't *know* that it was the killer who exposed the body,' Fallowfield said thoughtfully.

'True, but it's more likely than any other explanation. If an innocent man had moved it – for whatever reason – surely he would have alerted someone? Or are you suggesting that Laxborough shifted the stone a little way but didn't have the strength to do any more?' Penrose paused, aware that he and Fallowfield could go round in circles indefinitely without an expert opinion. 'What do you think, Bernard?'

The pathologist gave him a weary glance. 'I think I've said as much as I'm going to say before I've had a chance to examine the body properly.'

Penrose conceded defeat. 'Bernard's right. We're wasting time here when we could be finding out more about the victim. I'll get his address and see if I can track down his housekeeper. In the meantime, Bill, get enough men down here to make the churchyard properly secure. The press will be all over this when they get wind of it, and we don't want any wild speculations flying around until we've got a better idea of what we're dealing with. As it is, we've already got five people who've seen the body, and at least two of them look like they move in some *very* sociable circles.'

'Would you like me to have a word with them?'

'Yes. Find out if there was anyone in the church community who knew Laxborough better than the Reverend Turner. Did he belong to any musical associations or play for any other choirs? Perhaps he gave piano lessons. The man must have had *some* friends or associates, and we need to find out what changed on Sunday to force him to cancel his appointment after evensong. At the moment, that's the last sighting we have of him alive, but his housekeeper might say different. And at least his home should tell us something about his habits and his background.'

Penrose took a last look at Stephen Laxborough's body, then headed to the church to find the Reverend Turner, but Spilsbury called him back. 'Hang on a minute, Archie. You'll want to see this.' He retraced his footsteps and peered at the fragment of paper which the pathologist held out to him – a black-and-white photograph, ripped in half. 'It was in the grave. I thought he might have torn it himself while he was clawing at his clothes, but I can't find the other piece anywhere.'

The image was of a manor house, set in parkland – typically Jacobean in style, and pleasant but unremarkable to look at. Penrose took the fragment carefully between gloved fingers and turned it over, noticing that there was a handwritten inscription on the back; the important letters were missing, though, and all it told him was that the house was a priory whose name ended in 'e', and that it lay in the county of '____shire'. 'That's helpful,' Fallowfield muttered. 'Berkshire? Oxfordshire? Gloucestershire? Couldn't be in bloody Devon, could it?'

Penrose had to smile at his sergeant's lack of enthusiasm. 'Look on the bright side, Bill. It's the most tangible thing we've been offered so far, and think of the satisfaction you'll feel when you've narrowed it down. Thanks, Bernard – anything else?'

'Not so far, but wait a minute while I check his pockets. Turn him over, lads.' Wilson and another officer stepped forward to do as he asked, and Penrose tried to concentrate on how gently and respectfully they handled Laxborough's body, rather than on the injuries which underlined the agony of his final hours. Spilsbury lifted the tattered lapel of what had once been a finely tailored blazer and felt carefully inside the breast pocket, and his smile suggested that they were in luck. Slowly, using a pair of tweezers, he withdrew his prize, and Penrose shone his torch down onto the small piece of parchment paper. '"What is this that I have done?"' he said, reading the single scrawled sentence aloud.

'What the hell does that mean?' Fallowfield demanded, his patience already tested by the photograph. 'Doesn't even sound like a proper question.'

'I can't imagine *what* it means,' Penrose said, 'but I have a feeling that if we find the answer to this, we'll find the answer to everything.'

2

He left his car by the church, preferring to walk the short distance to Stephen Laxborough's house. Setting off up Holly Walk, he was grateful for the encroaching darkness which limited his view of the extended burial ground running parallel with the lane; churchyards, even noble ones, had lost their appeal for him. The air was cold and he turned the collar up on his coat, trying as he walked to sift the facts of the case from the guesswork and speculation that had crowded his mind from the moment the death was reported. Turner, who claimed to know the victim's writing well, had dismissed both the label on the photograph and the enigmatic quotation as being in his hand, and he could offer no enlightenment on the location of the priory or the nature of its connection to his colleague. So what certainties were they left with? A respected musician had been the victim of a particularly sadistic murder – and that was it; everything else was conjecture. Even in the early stages of a case, it was unusual to be fumbling quite so haphazardly in the dark.

'Archie?' The voice sounded uncertain, and he looked up from his thoughts to see a familiar figure walking towards him, her features briefly illuminated by the light from a street lamp. 'It *is* you. I wasn't sure from a distance.'

'Marta! How nice to see you. I thought you'd left Hampstead already. Josephine said you'd sold the house.'

'Yes, but there was a delay at the other end so they gave me a few days' grace. I'm actually leaving tomorrow, so I was just having a last walk round. I'll miss these streets.'

'But no regrets?'

'No, I don't think so. Sentiment, perhaps, but not regret. What brings you here? Are you on your way to see Bridget?'

Archie's lover, Bridget, divided her time between Cambridge and Hampstead, where she rented a studio in the Vale of Health. 'I wish I were. No, this is business, I'm afraid, and about as far from pleasure as it's possible to get.'

'Oh?' She looked intrigued, but was too discreet to ask for any details of his work.

'Yes. If I were you, I wouldn't venture too much further in that direction – not if you want your memories of quiet, leafy Hampstead to stay that way. My lot have rather taken over the church.'

'Ah, I see. Thanks for the tip.' They fell into step, with Marta walking back the way she had come. 'How *is* Bridget? You'd think we'd bump into each other all the time, but I haven't seen her for months.'

'She's very well – working out of town at the moment, so I haven't seen much of her myself. An old friend of hers from the Slade has come into some property in Devon, so they've been working on frescos there over the summer. It's a lot of work, but they're determined to get it done before they lose the weather completely.'

Marta shivered. 'I think she's missed the boat on that one. Autumn's here with a vengeance.'

'Apparently it's warmer in the west.' He smiled. 'And between you and me, she's quite enjoying playing Giotto.'

'So things are all right between you?'

He looked at her curiously. 'Yes, of course. Why do you ask?'

Marta shrugged. 'No reason in particular. I just assumed she'd want to be nearby while you were convalescing. She nearly lost you in that shooting, and I know how badly it affected her.'

'Actually, I encouraged her to go – we needed to get back to normal. Bridget was treating me like a piece of china, and I don't make a very gracious invalid. And it certainly doesn't suit her to agree with me all the time. She was so busy trying not to raise my blood pressure that all we ever talked about was the weather.' He smiled to himself, sufficiently distanced from those dark times now to be able to joke about them. 'And we had our first disagreement on the telephone last night. Admittedly, it was about how many hours I've been working, but it's a start.'

She laughed. 'You *did* frighten everyone half to death, you know. Josephine swears her grey hairs are down to the night she spent with you in hospital. I haven't the heart to tell her they were there long before that.'

The lane narrowed as the graveyard gave way to a terrace of attractive Georgian buildings, and they mingled briefly with a group of stragglers on their way to evening mass at the Catholic church. 'She's coming down to help you get settled, isn't she?' Penrose asked when they were on their own again.

'Yes, she'll be in Cambridge next week. You must come and see us if you've got time.'

There was an awkwardness about the invitation, and Penrose wondered if it stemmed from the fact that he and Marta had once been rivals, even enemies. Marta's love for Josephine had hurt him at first, particularly when it became obvious to him that her feelings were reciprocated, but he thought that those jealousies had been left behind long ago. Before he could answer, she stopped outside a house in Holly Place. The lights were on downstairs, and he could see through the open curtains that the rooms looked bare and deserted. 'I'll be pleased to be gone now,' Marta admitted. 'There's something depressing about a house you've turned your back on. It makes you pay in those last uncomfortable hours.' She smiled, and looked affectionately up at the windows. 'I owe this one a lot, though. It kept me sane, but it's time to move on. Or back. I still can't quite decide which it is.'

'How long is it since you last lived in Cambridge?'

'Twenty years or so. I was there until just after the war.'

'It draws you back, doesn't it? I can't think of any other town that does that, not even Oxford. It's the same with Bridget. Almost all her work is in London now, but she can't quite bring herself to leave Cambridge completely.'

'That's where you first met, isn't it?'

'Yes.' The clock from St Mary's struck the hour, and he smiled apologetically. 'I'm sorry, but I've got to go. Can I ask you something first, though – in confidence?'

Again, there was that awkwardness, but Marta nodded. 'Yes, of course.'

'Did you go to church while you were here?'

She laughed, both surprised and relieved, and he wondered what she thought he had been going to ask. 'No, I can't say I did – not often, anyway. I fell out with God a long time ago.'

'So you don't know a man called Stephen Laxborough?'

'The pianist?'

'That's right.'

'I've heard him play a few times, but I don't know him personally. Why?'

'He lived just round the corner. I thought you might have met him.'

The slip didn't go unnoticed. 'No, I'm afraid not, and it sounds as though I've lost my chance.' Penrose nodded. 'What a terrible shame. He was very good.'

'Will you keep his death to yourself, though – at least for now?'

'Yes, of course.' She took a key out of her pocket and kissed him goodbye. 'I'd better face up to the rest of the packing and let you get on. I've got to the sentimental clutter now, and I can't believe how much of it there is. It's just as well I've had a few extra days.'

He smiled. 'Good luck, then, and I hope the move goes well. Give Josephine my love.'

'I will. And Archie?'

'Yes?'

'I meant what I said about coming to visit. Don't leave it too long.'

'I won't, I promise.' Penrose left her to the mercy of an empty house and continued on to Mount Vernon. The buildings here were uniformly smart – classic, early nineteenth-century terraced townhouses with three storeys and a basement, opening directly onto the pavement and differing only in the colour of their curtains and the amount of attention paid to their window boxes. He checked the number that Turner had given him, but could just as easily have guessed which house was Laxborough's: it was the only one in darkness. He pressed the bell without much hope of an answer, wondering where the housekeeper was and why she hadn't thought her employer's absence significant enough to report. The peal rang defiantly through the empty hallway as Penrose tried again, frustrated to be blocked in his only logical line of enquiry. In vain, he looked up and down the street for a passage or alleyway which might lead to the rear of the property, but the terrace ran in an unbroken line and he suspected that the only way of gaining access to another entrance would be to find the house and garden that backed onto it. As a last resort, he lifted the front door mat, hardly expecting Stephen Laxborough to be the type who left a key where anyone could find it, but there he was wrong. Offering up thanks for Hampstead's honesty and the day's first piece of good fortune, Penrose let himself in.

The hallway smelt heavily of pipe tobacco, and he traced its source to a well-worn tweed jacket which hung on a coat rack just inside the door, obscuring the light switch. He called up the stairs, just in case he was wrong about the house being empty, but the only response was the heavy, hollow ticking of a grandfather clock. There were two rooms on the ground floor, as well as a door leading down to the basement, and Penrose chose the one at the front to search first. He drew the curtains and switched on a lamp; the subdued yellow light fell on a sparsely furnished room, devoted to a single purpose. Most of the space was taken up by a Bechstein grand piano. The instrument was a work of art in itself, elegantly modelled with a black lacquer finish which contrasted dramatically with the pale colours of the walls and carpet. Penrose had no doubt that it would be the envy of any musician, amateur or professional. The lid was open and he played a few notes, appreciating the distinctive tone which transformed even his clumsy efforts into something melodic and beautifully clear. There were no distractions in the room, he noticed – not even a picture on the wall; the only other pieces of furniture were directly related to the piano – a trunk full of printed scores under the window and a decorative Victorian music stand, inlaid with mother of pearl. The stand and the rack on the piano itself were both empty, and Penrose found himself irrationally curious about the last piece of music that Laxborough had played before he died.

The room at the back was smaller, and – by contrast – pleasantly cluttered. It had obviously been used as a study, and Laxborough had placed his desk carefully to make the most of French windows leading out to the garden. A gramophone stood on a table in the corner – an old horn model, scratched and battered and obviously loved – and one of the walls was taken up with the largest collection of gramophone records that Penrose had ever seen. There was an extensive library, too, and a quick glance suggested that the shelves were evenly divided between biography and contemporary fiction. He sat down at the desk and looked through the drawers, but they revealed nothing of any interest except a few financial papers relating to shares and investments, and an appointments book. Penrose flicked back through the last few weeks and saw that a handful of names were repeated at regular intervals – piano lessons, perhaps, or something to do with the church. Noting that the handwriting was indeed different to the two examples found with Laxborough's body, he turned to the entry for the preceding Sunday, trying to find an appointment which would explain why the organist had cancelled his meeting with Turner, but the page was left blank. In fact, the only thing that was remotely useful to Penrose was the record of a meeting with a firm of solicitors in Fleet Street back in July. Feeling increasingly thwarted, he jotted down the name and address and continued his search.

The basement told him little except that Laxborough's housekeeper, whoever she might be, kept a well-ordered kitchen. There was some milk going off in the refrigerator and a half-drunk bottle of claret on the table; the cork had been replaced, and a single wine glass stood upside down on the drainer. Everything else was neat and tidy. Penrose was just on his way upstairs again when he heard the sound of the front door closing and a woman's voice in the hallway. 'Dr Laxborough? Dr Laxborough, are you there?'

He called out to reassure her, not wishing to alarm her any more than he could help, and she looked at him in surprise as he appeared at the top of the basement steps. Stephen Laxborough's housekeeper – assuming he had guessed correctly – was a homely-looking woman in her late forties, with straw-coloured hair under a felt hat and a dark green coat that had not been 'best' for several seasons. She stood just inside the front door, her hand still on the latch, as if she were uncertain whether to stay or go, and Penrose noticed a small suitcase on the floor by her side. 'I'm Detective Chief Inspector Penrose from Scotland Yard,' he said, fishing in his inside pocket for his warrant card. 'This must seem like a dreadful intrusion and I'm sorry to startle you, but—'

The presence of a police officer in the house seemed to confirm something that she had already suspected, and she cut him off before he could finish. 'He's done it, then. I thought he was planning something.'

'Forgive me, but I'm afraid I don't understand,' Penrose said, interested to note that the resignation in her voice was tinged with a genuine sadness. 'Done what?'

'Killed himself. That's why you're here, isn't it? Is he downstairs?' She glanced at the door to the basement, then back to Penrose again, and her hand went to her mouth in horror, distorting her words. 'Dear God, I knew I should never have left him on his own, but he was so insistent. Practically strong-armed me out of the house, he did, and he's never behaved like that before.'

Penrose listened as she blamed herself for a fault which existed only in her imagination, then gently led her into the study and encouraged her to sit down. 'I'm so sorry, Mrs . . .?'

'Pryce. Hilda Pryce.'

'Mrs Pryce. I'm sorry to say that Dr Laxborough *is* dead, but he didn't take his own life.'

She stared at him, confused. 'An accident, then? What happened? Where is he?'

He paused, taking time to choose his words carefully. 'Dr Laxborough's body was found earlier today in St John's churchyard. We don't know exactly what happened yet, but we *are* sure that he was killed unlawfully. That's why I'm here – to look for anything that might help us piece together how he died, and to talk to you about the last few days of his life.' The reality of the situation seemed suddenly to drain all the strength that Hilda Pryce had, and she collapsed into gut-wrenching sobs in front of him. Penrose gave her time to recover, feeling stupid and insensitive for thinking only of a family's grief: he had reckoned without the devotion that often accompanied long service. 'Can I get you anything?' he asked gently. 'Some water, perhaps, or a cup of tea.'

She shook her head and searched in her bag for a handkerchief. 'No, nothing, thank you. I'll be all right in a minute. I'm sorry. Whatever must you think of me?'

'There's no need to apologise.'

'It's just you get fond of someone, don't you, when you've been with them a long time, and he was always good to me.'

The conversation was so different to the one that Penrose had been expecting that he began to wonder if the remoteness between Laxborough and Turner had been down to church politics or personal dislike rather than a general character trait. 'How long had you worked for Dr Laxborough?' he asked.

'Eighteen years, give or take. I started with him as soon as he moved here, and the job saved my life, really. My husband died not long after the war, and I don't know how I'd have managed otherwise.'

'And from what you say, you were obviously happy here?'

She nodded. 'Yes, I was. We got along all right. Dr Laxborough knew how he wanted things and he expected them done properly, but he was decent. Easier to look after than Charlie ever was.' She flushed, regretting her indiscretion with a stranger. 'I shouldn't have said that, but my husband could be difficult. We married in a hurry and we didn't really know each other. After he died, well – it was a relief not to bother about all of that. I knew where I was with my job.'

The conversation had calmed her a little, enough for Penrose to return to more difficult questions. 'Can I ask why you thought that Dr Laxborough had committed suicide?'

'Because he'd tried it before. Last Christmas, it was. I came back unexpectedly and found him downstairs, with the house full of gas.' She paused, reliving the scene in her head. 'He always hated Christmas – it made him morose. People are when they've got no close family, I suppose. I'm not that keen on it myself if I'm honest, though it doesn't seem Christian to say so. But last year was worse. It hit him earlier than usual, and he couldn't seem to shake himself out of it.'

'Do you know what was troubling him?'

'No. He never talked about himself and I knew better than to ask. The only way I ever knew how he was feeling was through the music he played. And I certainly never dreamt what he was planning, or I wouldn't have gone in the first place.'

'So what happened?'

'Well, I'd finished at lunchtime on Christmas Eve, like I always do, and I went off to get the bus to my sister's, but then I realised that I'd left the presents for the little ones in my room and I had to come all the way back for them. There'd have been hell to pay – you know what kids are like. Anyway, it was about four o'clock – I know that because the wireless was on and they were just finishing with the carols. I'll never forget it – all that beautiful music, and there he was, lying on the floor. I switched off the gas and opened the windows, and pulled him away as best I could. Terrible, he looked. It was ages before he came to.'

'But you didn't call an ambulance or try to get help?'

For the first time, Hilda Pryce looked away as she answered. 'No, I didn't, and I know that was wrong but he wouldn't have liked it. As it was . . .'

'Yes?'

'As it was, he never forgave me. Things were different between us after that. We didn't talk as often as we used to.'

'Because he was embarrassed, or because he wanted to die and you stopped him?'

'Both, I suppose. I thought he might get over it in time, hoped he might even be grateful – not because I wanted thanks, I don't mean that, but I wanted him to believe that there were things worth living for, that he'd made a mistake. His music was everything to him, and I hoped it might get him through.'

'But whatever had depressed him didn't go away?'

'It didn't seem to, no. In the end, I felt as though I'd let him down by saving him.'

'Did he leave a note? Anything to explain why he was doing it?'

'Not that I saw. He might have written one and destroyed it afterwards, I suppose.'

'And this time – you said that Dr Laxborough sent you away?'

'That's right. He gave me some time off, out of the blue, as if he'd made his mind up about something and wanted me out of the way. I guessed what it might be, but he was so insistent and there was no arguing with him, so I packed a bag and went to my sister's for a few days.'

'When was this?'

'He told me on Friday and I left on Saturday.'

'And had he seen anybody shortly before that? Were there any meetings that seemed to upset him? Any callers you didn't recognise?'

'No. The only people who ever came to the house were his pupils, and they were a nice lot on the whole. Kids, most of them – he only ever taught people he thought were truly gifted and who would make the most of the opportunity. A lot of the time, he didn't even charge them.'

'So he was wealthy?'

'Comfortable, I'd say, rather than wealthy. And he wasn't an extravagant man.'

'What about post or telephone calls last week? Anything unusual there?'

She considered the question for a long time. 'There wasn't anything particular that I could put my finger on, but now I think about it, it was shortly after I took him the second post on Friday that he told me to go away for a bit.'

'Can you remember exactly what he said? It might be very important.'

'He said that he wanted to be on his own for a while and it would be better if I got away from the house and took some leave.'

'But you told me that he "strong-armed" you.'

'Yes, and perhaps that was the wrong word because I don't mean anything physical. He just said that if I felt any loyalty to him whatsoever, I'd do as he asked. I suppose he knew that was the one thing I would never argue with.' Penrose was about to ask another question, but Mrs Pryce hadn't quite finished answering the last one.

'Anyway, it wasn't so much what he said that worried me. It was the fact that the music stopped.' She saw that he didn't understand, and added: 'There was always music in this house. If he wasn't playing it, he was listening to it. I sometimes used to joke with him that he couldn't hear himself think, and he said that was precisely the point.'

'What did he mean by that?'

She shrugged. 'I don't really know how to explain it. It was like the world saddened him. Perhaps it was the war or perhaps he was just made that way, but he didn't seem to need other people like the rest of us do. My sister and me, we fight like cats over a scrap of fish, but I wouldn't be without her, nor she with me. But Dr Laxborough wasn't like that. He found his refuge in his music.'

Penrose thought back to the quotation that had been found in his pocket – a confession of sorts, a hesitant acknowledgement of responsibility. 'Did you ever get the feeling that he'd done something he regretted, something he felt guilty about?'

'Which of us hasn't? I couldn't answer that. Probably only he could. All I can say is that he was a good man as long as I knew him. I don't mean that in a sentimental way. He wasn't all God and charity, not like some of them at that church, although most of that's for the show of it rather than any genuine piety. No, he said what he thought and he didn't go out of his way to help people unless they deserved it, but he was principled. Do you know what I mean?'

'I think so, yes. Can you tell me anything about his family?'

'There's a nephew, Michael, but he lives abroad – in South Africa, I think. That's it, as far as I know. His parents are long gone and his brother died in the war. I can give you Michael's address if you need it.'

'Thank you, that would be helpful. And the name of his GP, too, if you know it?' Laxborough's body would have to be formally identified, but the last thing Penrose wanted was to put Hilda Pryce through that if he could possibly avoid it; to his relief, she nodded. He thought about the signet ring, worn on the little finger of the left hand, and asked: 'In all the years you've known him, did Dr Laxborough ever have a particularly close friend? Were you aware of any romantic involvements?'

'He wasn't interested in women as far as I could tell – not like that, anyway.'

It wasn't exclusively what Penrose had meant, but he didn't want to offend her by clarifying the question too bluntly. 'He wore a ring on his left hand . . .'

'Ah yes, I *can* tell you about that. His father gave it to him when he got his degree. It had been in the family for years, apparently, and it was a tradition to pass it on at a significant moment.'

'Thank you, Mrs Pryce. Now, if you've no objections, I'd like to take a quick look at the rest of the house. Perhaps you could get me those addresses in the meantime?'

She nodded and busied herself with the appointments book while Penrose went upstairs. The first floor consisted of a bedroom, bathroom and sitting room, all typical of a confirmed bachelor and with nothing particular to distinguish them except for a beautifully crafted antique harpsichord. Apart from a large linen cupboard, the rooms at the top of the house clearly belonged to the housekeeper. He opened the door of her bedroom, feeling every bit the intruder that violent death demanded him to be, and walked over to the dressing table. In spite of all she had said, Hilda Pryce still kept the obligatory photographic reminders of her marriage on display: there was a snapshot of her husband in army uniform and another of their wartime wedding. Penrose looked with interest at the cocky young soldier and his girl-at-home bride – someone to write to, someone to brag about. His view might be coloured by what she had told him, but – to his eyes – the new Mrs Pryce seemed apprehensive, even unhappy, and he was struck by how many silent casualties the fighting had claimed outside of the trenches. His own war was painful enough, but at least he had never felt obliged to make two lives miserable by a hasty and ill-suited match.

The other photographs and knick-knacks only served to emphasise what he had already noticed about the house in general: there was nothing very personal in any of the rooms, and what there was consisted of taste rather than history. Stephen Laxborough's lifestyle and habits were evident in his music and his books, but there wasn't a single clue to his past – no family photographs, no images of friends, nothing to indicate where he had lived or whom he had loved before he arrived in Hampstead eighteen years earlier. Come to think of it, there wasn't even a photograph to show Penrose what the dead man had looked like, and he tried in vain to recall another house that didn't contain a picture of its owner, either taken with a loved one or in celebration of a particular achievement. He thought about Marta and her 'sentimental clutter', and realised how normal that was; here, it was as if Laxborough had just moved in and the important boxes were still to be unpacked.

He went back downstairs, deep in thought, and Mrs Pryce met him in the hallway with the details he had requested. 'Can I get one of my colleagues to take you back to your sister's?' he asked, reluctant to leave her so abruptly on her own.

'No, that won't be necessary. I'd rather stay here.' As soon as the words were out, it seemed to dawn on Hilda Pryce that her tenure was no longer a right and that the man who had made this her home was gone. 'It *is* all right if I stay?' she asked.

'Yes, of course. Ultimately, that will be up to Dr Laxborough's beneficiary, of course, but probate will take some time to sort out. Would you like me to bring someone to you instead? Perhaps your sister could stay here with you, at least for tonight? You've had a shock, and . . .'

Again she refused, more firmly this time. 'No, please – I've got all I need. But thank you. You've been very kind.' She was dismissing him to be alone with her grief. Penrose collected his hat and allowed himself to be shown to the door. 'This will sound funny, but I'm almost glad I was wrong about his death, you know,' she admitted. 'We've had a suicide in the family and it's a terrible thing. You never stop thinking about how much pain they must have been in and how frightened and alone they'll have felt at the end, once they knew what they were going to do. At least this'll have been unexpected. At least it'll have been quick.'

Penrose looked away, unable to give her the assurance she sought that a man she loved hadn't suffered; she would find out, no doubt, but he wouldn't give her those images a moment earlier than was necessary. 'I'll need a formal statement from you,' he said, glad to have a procedure to fall back on. 'Would it be all right if I asked one of my colleagues to call tomorrow and take one?'

If she saw through the change of subject, she was too polite or too fearful of his motives to say so. 'Yes, of course. I'll be here all day.' He opened the door but she put her hand on his arm. 'There *is* one more thing, though. Will I be able to see him?'

Penrose hesitated, remembering Laxborough's injuries. 'I'm afraid that won't be possible,' he said gently, blaming a rule that under any other circumstances he would have broken. Before she could argue or ask him to justify his decision, he bid her goodnight and walked out into the street.

3

'Where do you want these?' Josephine asked, with a weary glance at the plethora of cardboard boxes marked simply 'miscellaneous'. She picked up one of the more interestingly shaped newspaper parcels and unwrapped it. 'Actually, let me rephrase that. *Why* do you want these?'

Marta laughed and took the gilt bronze figure from her hand. 'You and I will never agree on the right side of kitsch, but it's a big house. I'll make sure she stays out of your way.'

'It's not actually the figure I mind – it's that awful marble base they've stuck her on. She looks like she's dancing on a headstone.' Happy to remain oblivious to the rest of the box, Josephine closed the lid. 'I can't help thinking that I might have been more use to you if I'd helped you pack. By the time the removal van drew up outside here, the damage was already done.'

'It *was* a bit rushed towards the end,' Marta admitted, 'but it just seemed easier to shove everything in a box and worry about it later. Now "later" is here, I'm beginning to see the drawbacks in the plan.' She looked round the first-floor room, which somehow managed to appear both sparse and cluttered. 'Anyway, there's precious little point in unpacking very much at all until the decorators have been through the whole house. That'll teach me to rent a place without actually seeing it.' Defeated, she sat down on the bare floorboards and looked at Josephine. 'Are you sure you want to stay here while I'm away?'

'Of course I do. It's lovely.' Josephine pulled Marta to her feet and led her to one of the windows overlooking St Clement's Passage, a pretty paved alleyway which ran between a row of elegant townhouses and one of Cambridge's many churches. 'What could you possibly regret about that? It might need a bit of work . . .' Marta looked at her. 'All right, a *lot* of work, but it's worth the effort.' As if to support her argument, a streak of late afternoon sun brushed the church's pantiled roof, drawing out a rich, autumnal red, and the faint sound of choral music drifted across the passage. 'And anyway,' Josephine added, speaking more seriously now, 'it's the least I can do. You've sold a house you loved just to give us a new start. Why wouldn't I want to stay and make this one beautiful? You won't recognise it when you get back.' She smiled and brushed a covering of dust and flaked paint from Marta's shoulder. 'Let's forget about it for a while and go and get some tea.'

As they were on their way out, a young girl in a nurse's uniform ran down the steps of the house next door and hurried over to the church railings, which were all but obscured by a row of bicycles. She smiled and nodded, then rode out into the traffic, glancing up at the church clock as if she couldn't believe what it was telling her. 'Late for a shift,' Josephine guessed, watching her go. 'I remember what that was like. Have you met many of your neighbours yet?'

Marta shook her head. 'Not really. It's rented rooms on either side and I haven't met the landladies. I think one of them offers digs for the theatre, though, so that might be interesting.'

'Surrounded by nurses and chorus girls, and you're having doubts about the house?'

'Stupid of me, I know. But it makes a change in this town – there aren't many places where the women outnumber the men. It was one of the things I found most isolating about living here last time. Every day seemed to revolve around men and their routines, even the things I loved like evensong and the museums. Then along came the war, and it was as if the town had died. Those glorious buildings, all in darkness. The streets were so empty that the women had no choice but to notice each other.'

Josephine listened, trying to imagine Marta here as a young wife and mother, living in the shadow of an unhappy marriage to a man who abused her, making decisions that would affect her for the rest of her life. The past had brought them together but they rarely talked now of their earlier lives, preferring to concentrate on the present, and she wondered if being in a town which seemed hell-bent on fusing the two would change that. 'Inverness was just the opposite,' she said, remembering the sudden influx of thousands of soldiers sent to the Highlands for training. 'I can still see all those young men marching across Bell's Park.'

'Very romantic.'

'Far *too* romantic. A part of me will always love that music and that spectacle, and a part of me will always hate it.'

'Hate it? Why?'

'Because it made it all too easy. It was so glamorous and so patriotic, and off they all went like lambs to the slaughter. I'd have gone myself if they'd let me. It's a trick I can never quite forgive them for. Your empty streets were much more honest.'

'Yes, they were certainly that.'

They turned into St John's Street, and Josephine stopped outside a tiny newsagent and tobacconist. 'You go ahead and get us a table. I want to see if the new *Film Weekly* is in yet.' Marta gave one of her most infuriating smiles. 'What's that supposed to mean?'

'Checking for an early review of your film?'

Josephine glared at her. Alfred Hitchcock had recently finished filming one of her novels, a project which Marta had worked on, and she knew enough about the director and his disdain for any original source material to dread the results. 'I'm doing nothing of the sort,' she said, more defensively than she had intended. 'There's an interview with Joan Crawford that I want to read. I saw it advertised in last week's issue.'

Marta laughed at the look of indignation on Josephine's face. 'You shouldn't be so uptight about the film,' she said. 'It's really very good. It might not have much to do with—'

Josephine held up her hands. 'I don't want to hear another word until I've suffered the humiliation of watching it.'

'All right, but it still doesn't seem right that I'm off to America to talk about your film while you have nothing to do with it.'

'Trust me – you have my blessing. Now go and order the tea. I won't be a minute.'

The shop specialised in pipe tobacco and smelt faintly of vanilla. It made the most of its tiny floor space, supplementing shelf displays with boxes of biscuits and precariously piled lecture lists, and Josephine was pleased to see an unusually wide range of magazines. She soon found the one she wanted, and flicked idly through its pages while waiting at the counter to pay. Joan Crawford was in typically ebullient mood, she noticed, but she had only got a couple of paragraphs into the article when she found herself distracted by the conversation between the newsagent and the girl in front of her, who was filling out a postcard for the window. 'The sooner you find yourself someone to share that house with, the better,' he said, shaking his head in concern. 'I wouldn't want a daughter of mine living all on her own, not with what's going on at the moment. I've never known anything like it.'

'Oh, I'm not on my own,' the girl said. 'There are people in the flats upstairs, but my friend's just got a bar job in London and she's left me high and dry with the rent on our two rooms. I could kill her, really, but I'd have done the same in her position.'

'Even so, you've got to be careful – that's what I tell all the young ladies who come in here now.' He tapped a bundle of papers on the counter, the early evening edition of the *Cambridge Daily News*, still tied with string, and Josephine tried to read the headlines. 'That's the third attack in a month, and he'll only get braver – you mark my words.' The girl handed him the card and he checked the details before placing it with a block of similar notices in the window. 'It's sixpence a week, but I don't think you'll need any longer. Places like that soon go.'

She thanked him and handed over the money, and he watched her as she walked out into the street. 'There's no telling them at that age, is there?' he sighed, as Josephine took her place at the counter.

'What's happened?' she asked.

'Another girl's been hurt – bad enough to put her in hospital this time.' He cut the string on the newspapers and pushed one across to her. The item in question was a small piece, tucked away in the corner of the front page. 'They're not saying it's the same bloke but it stands to reason, doesn't it?'

Josephine nodded. Marta had told her about an attack on a young woman when she first arrived, but the inference was that a burglary had gone wrong; now it seemed that something far more disturbing was to blame. 'Can I take this?' she asked, adding the paper to her magazine and a bar of Marta's favourite chocolate.

'Of course you can.'

'And a packet of Benson and Hedges, please.' She paid for her goods and carried on to the cafe, deep in thought. The day had grown dull now, and by the time she passed the handsome towered gateway of St John's, lamps had begun to glow in the buildings on either side, filling the irregular leaded windows with a warm yellow ochre. Josephine looked up as she walked, intrigued by what might be going on inside. She had never yearned after learning for learning's sake, rejecting university in favour of a more practical career, but something about those softly lit rooms – so visible and yet so inaccessible – made her wonder what she might have missed.

College buildings were less dominant close to the market square, and Cambridge took on the air of a country town. She had loved the harmonious jumble of Trinity Street from the moment she first saw it – graceful Georgian facades rubbing shoulders with pretty art-nouveau-Gothic and sedate Victorian shop fronts. Matthew's, the cafe which she and Marta had adopted as a retreat from unpacking, occupied the most striking building of all – an

Elizabethan timber-framed and plastered house, much restored over the years and now – if you were to believe the cafe's advertisements – 'a place of quiet refinement'. Marta was seated at a table upstairs by the window. 'I think I might have over-ordered,' she said. 'I suddenly realised how hungry I was and the waitress took advantage of my weakness.'

'What are we having?'

'Poached eggs on toast, Welsh rarebit and a selection of cakes.'

Josephine smiled and sat down opposite her. She looked round the room, which had been decorated with old-fashioned lamps and pewter pots to emphasise the building's original period features, and noticed that all but one of the tables were taken. Without exception, the clientele consisted of genteel ladies in pairs or small groups. 'Nell Gwynn meets Mapp and Lucia,' she muttered under her breath. 'Listen – you know that assault you told me about? Apparently there's been another one, but this time the girl's in hospital.'

'So I gather. I overheard the waitresses talking about it. Where was it?'

Josephine glanced at the front page. 'A cottage in St Peter's Street. Is that nearby?'

'It's further up Castle Hill, on the way out of town.' Marta took the paper from her and read through the report. 'God, this is terrible – well, it is if you read between the lines. It makes me so angry the way they report these things. "Ravished" – what sort of a word is that? We all know they mean raped, so why don't they say so instead of making it sound like something faintly desirable from a bad romantic novel?'

The women on the next table turned in unison to stare at them, one of them looking so shocked that Josephine half-expected her to reach for the smelling salts. 'I think that's just answered your question,' she said. 'Or it could be to protect the girl, of course. The injuries can be treated, but the shame of what's happened to her will be much harder to heal.'

'What's *she* got to be ashamed about? She didn't ask someone to break into her house and rape her.'

Josephine sighed, loving Marta for her fiercely held principles but wishing sometimes that the real world welcomed her more often. 'Of course she *shouldn't* be ashamed, but she will be. That's who she is from now on – the girl who was attacked, the news item. At least they've had the sense not to name her, but her neighbours will know, and the police, and the nurses who treat her in hospital, and the people in court – if it ever gets that far. She won't be a person to them. She'll be a victim. And with all the intrusion, "ravished" might be a word she's more than happy to hide behind.' She paused for a moment while the food was brought to their table. 'What else does it say?'

'Not much, really. There's a vague description of the man – short and stocky, with a local accent. That hardly narrows it down.'

'Nothing more specific?'

'No, she didn't see his face. The lights went out first – that's how she knew that something was wrong.'

'She must have been terrified,' Josephine said, imagining how she would feel at the sudden realisation that a man was in her house and she was powerless to do anything about it. 'That's the worst part for me, somehow. The attack taking place in your home.' She, too, was using euphemisms, she noticed, instinctively reluctant to acknowledge the most intimate and lasting damage. 'It's the one place you ought to feel safe.'

'Oh, don't worry about that,' Marta said, with a sarcastic edge to her voice. 'There's some handy advice here about locking your doors and windows. So that's all right, then.'

She put the paper down and they ate their meal in silence, each of them angered and unsettled by the fate of a girl they would never know. That was the unique thing about this particular crime, Josephine thought; unlike murder or robbery or fraud, it felt personal, no matter how distanced you were from the victim. 'The trouble is, no girl thinks it can happen to her,' Marta continued when their empty plates had been replaced by a two-tiered cake stand, complete with doilies. 'Those waitresses were huddled together in the corner, talking about this as though it were the most exciting thing that's happened in Cambridge for years. That's another reason for honest reporting – it might encourage people to be more cautious.' She gave the newspaper a disdainful prod, and finished the last piece of gingerbread. 'You *will* take care while I'm away, won't you?'

'Of course I will.'

'With a bit of luck the bastard will be behind bars before too long.'

Josephine smiled apologetically to their neighbours and signalled to the waitress for the bill. They walked out into the street and she turned back the way she had come, but Marta caught her arm. 'Let's walk for a bit. The boxes will wait and I love Cambridge at dusk. Do you mind?'

'Of course not.' They crossed the road and took a narrow lane which led down between two colleges to the river. Marta was quiet, and Josephine wondered if she was still thinking about the rape or if something else was on her mind. Once or twice over the last few days, she had caught Marta staring into space, oblivious to anything she had said. Marta had brushed aside her concern, blaming any distractions on the forthcoming trip, but Josephine didn't entirely believe her. She took Marta's arm, sensing that whatever remained unspoken between them was the true reason for the walk. 'There's something you're not telling me,' she said in an even tone, hoping that by sounding unconcerned she could make it trivial. 'What is it?'

Marta looked at her sharply, but didn't try to deny it. 'I'm sorry,' she said. 'I should have talked to you long before now, but I wasn't sure how to. Actually, that's not strictly true – I didn't know if I'd *need* to.'

They stopped on a bridge and Josephine stared out along the river. Marta was right: the town *was* beautiful at dusk, with the outline of towers and chimneys etched clearly against an indigo sky and the first faint suggestion of stars, but just now she would gladly have been anywhere else in the world. She had forced the issue, but she longed suddenly to stop the words tumbling from Marta's mouth, and the vague unease which she had been nursing since Marta first mentioned her trip to America took a form as tangible as the rough, cold stone beneath her hand: it was common knowledge that the Hitchcocks planned to move to Hollywood as soon as he had fulfilled his contract in England, and they made no secret of wanting to take their most trusted employees with them. Her fear must have shown in her face because Marta tried to reassure her. 'Don't look so worried. It's not about us – at least I hope it won't have to *become* about us.'

'Then what is it about?'

'Archie.'

'Archie?' Josephine stared at her in surprise.

'Yes. I saw him last week, just before I moved here. He was in Holly Place, investigating the murder of Stephen Laxborough. You know – the pianist?'

'Of course, I read about it in the paper. But what's that got to do with anything? Archie's all right, isn't he?'

'He's fine, as far as I know. It's just that we were talking about Cambridge and I invited him to come and see us when he had time. I did it without thinking, and then I realised what a mess it could all turn into.'

'Why would that be a mess? Marta, you're not making any sense. Just tell me what you mean.'

'All right – sorry.' She paused to think and Josephine waited impatiently, listening to the dull thud of punts knocking against each other in the river below. 'You remember when I came here in the summer, just to look round and see how I felt about moving back up? Well, I bumped into Bridget at the railway station.'

'Yes, you told me.'

'But I didn't tell you everything. She wasn't on her own.'

It took Josephine a moment or two to understand the significance of what she had heard. 'Bridget was with another man?' she asked in disbelief. 'She's seeing someone here, behind Archie's back?'

'No, although that was *my* first thought, too. She was sitting on her own in the buffet, but there were two cups on the table and she'd obviously come to see someone off. She was so on edge when she saw me – hostile, even. I knew she was trying to hide something and I jumped to the obvious conclusion, but it was even worse than I'd imagined. She wasn't with another man. She was with her daughter. Her daughter, and Archie's.'

'Archie's *daughter*?'

Marta nodded. 'That's right. Her name's Phyllis, and at a guess she's around twenty. I only met her briefly, but she has Archie's smile. I can see that now. And his charm. She was lovely.' Josephine listened, too stunned to say anything. 'He'd gone back to war by the time Bridget found out she was pregnant, and she never told him. Archie has no idea that Phyllis even exists. That's why I couldn't look him in the eye. There I was, inviting him to Cambridge, where the woman he loves has brought up his daughter, and . . .'

'You've known this for months and you didn't think to mention it?' Josephine stared at Marta, the revelation eclipsed briefly by a more personal sense of betrayal. 'How can you stand there and say this isn't about us?'

'She made me promise—'

'You don't owe promises to *Bridget*. You owe promises to *me*.' The tears came from nowhere, part shock and part fury, but she brushed them away before Marta could comfort her. 'And to Archie, too, for God's sake. What the hell were you thinking of? Did you persuade yourself that another few months wouldn't matter when he's been in the dark for years? Or were you just timing it carefully so you could swan off to America and leave me to calm down? If that's the case, I wouldn't come back in a hurry.'

'I knew you'd react like this, but Bridget put me in an impossible position – can't you see that? She *begged* me to give her a chance to tell Archie first. She knows what she's done is wrong, but she also knows that if they're to stand any chance at all, he has to hear about Phyllis from her, not from anyone else, and certainly not from you in some sort of frenzy of injustice on his behalf.'

'And you didn't trust me to understand that?'

'No. If you want me to be honest, I didn't. Was I wrong?' A couple walking arm in arm stared at them as they approached the bridge, and Josephine paused to let them pass. 'Bridget is *terrified* of what will happen when Archie finds out,' Marta said, taking advantage of her silence. 'She loves him, and she loves her daughter, but she knows she might lose them both by being honest.'

'Surely the time to think about that was twenty years ago.'

'Yes, but that's easy to say now. In some ways, I can understand why she did it. It was a wartime romance and she didn't want to be tied down. She didn't even know if he'd come back.'

'Are you *defending* her?'

'No, but perhaps I understand better than you what it's like to be trapped in a marriage.'

'How can you possibly compare your husband to Archie? He did unspeakable things to you, things that Archie would never be capable of.'

'Don't be ridiculous. I'm not comparing them as *men*. I'm just saying that for some women being with *any* man is a sacrifice they're not prepared to make, no matter how nice or how liberated he is.'

'I can't believe you're making decency sound like a character fault, simply to justify siding with Bridget. Don't make Archie a scapegoat for your bad decisions.'

'Oh for fuck's sake, Josephine, grow up. This isn't a scrap in the playground. There aren't any "sides", and people's lives are at stake. There's no going back once it's out in the open. And anyway, if we're talking about ulterior motives, are you absolutely sure that some of your attitude towards Bridget isn't more selfish than you care to admit? Let's face it, it would have been so much easier for you if she'd marched him up the aisle there and then.'

'Why do you say that?'

'Because it would have spared you all those years of feeling guilty for not loving Archie the way he loves you.'

The comment stopped Josephine in her tracks, but she was too upset to address the truth of it. 'You're confusing two different things,' she said, determined not to let Marta lead them into areas that might be even harder to recover from. 'Of course it's Bridget's right not to marry, and if she was strong enough to raise a child on her own then good for her. But not even to *tell* him? To give him no rights whatsoever over his own daughter? The joy of seeing her grow up, even from a distance?' She was going to add that Marta, of all people, should understand that, but stopped herself just in time; using Marta's grief over the loss of her own daughter was something that she would never do, and the fleeting look of pain in Marta's eyes as the unspoken words hung in the air between them dissolved Josephine's anger in an instant. She moved forward to hold her, and they stood together for a long time, allowing silence to heal the rift.

'You're right,' Marta said eventually. 'Archie would have been a wonderful father. Like I said, the whole thing is a mess and I can't see a way out of it.' She shivered and took Josephine's hand. 'Come on, it's getting cold. Let's finish this at home.'

They walked back the way they had come, their footsteps echoing on the narrow cobbled street. 'That must be what Bridget was talking about in Portmeirion,' Josephine said, still trying to make sense of what Marta had told her. 'I've often wondered. We had a strange conversation just after she and Archie met up again, and she asked me if he was still as understanding as he used to be. I told her she'd be surprised by how forgiving he was, and that whatever she was keeping from him would destroy them if she didn't tell him. I think I was wrong, though. It will destroy them either way.'

'*Could* he forgive her, do you think? You know him better than anyone.'

'Perhaps I do, but I still can't answer that. Archie is the most compassionate person I know, but he has a deep sense of right and wrong, and it's got nothing to do with being a policeman.' She thought about it, trying to put herself in Archie's position, but it was impossible to guess at those emotions. 'One of the things that makes him so good at his job is his empathy,' she said. 'He has this knack of understanding why people do what they do, even in the most violent of circumstances. But this is different. Every moment they've spent together has been a lie.'

'Yes, I suppose it has. And I'm guilty of that, too. I'm sorry I didn't tell you as soon as I found out.'

'You were in an impossible position, and you were right not to trust me.' She stopped and took Marta's hand. 'I *do* have to tell Archie. You gave Bridget a chance, but she's had months to do something about it.'

'There was the shooting, though. She couldn't possibly have told him when he was so ill.'

'But he's well now, and she's still avoiding him.'

Marta nodded. 'I know she is. Give her one more chance to do the right thing, though. She can't undo this, Josephine. She can't just apologise and promise not to do it again, so at least try to understand why she's holding back. Perhaps she's hoping that the longer they're together, the stronger they'll be and the harder it will be for Archie to walk away. This is going to tear them apart, but there's more chance of their getting through it if *she* tells him. And if there's the faintest hope of Archie making up for all those lost years, you can't jeopardise that.' Josephine hesitated, knowing that

Marta was right. 'At least go and see her before you say anything. She might listen to you.'

'I don't know about that, but I'll try – and sooner rather than later if you've invited him to come and see us.'

'He told me she's away in Devon at the moment.'

'Then I'll leave a note. That way, I won't be able to lose my nerve.'

'I'm sorry I won't be here for moral support.'

'I'm sorry you won't be here for lots of reasons.'

They turned into St Clement's Passage, and Josephine was astonished by how quickly it had come to feel like home. She smiled to herself, understanding now how foolish she had been to consider even for a moment that Marta would sacrifice so much only to abandon it all. Marta looked at her curiously. 'What's that for?' she asked, unlocking the front door.

'Nothing really. I'm just laughing at my own stupidity.' The harsh electric light flooded the hallway, showing no mercy to the ugly, scuffed floorboards and tired wallpaper, but to Josephine it looked like a palace. 'For a moment back there, I thought you were going to tell me that this American trip was to test the water for something more permanent. I know how much the Hitchcocks rely on you, and I thought they might have made you an offer you couldn't refuse.'

'Oh they did, weeks ago.'

'But you *did* refuse it.' Marta nodded, and Josephine pulled her close. 'That's why I'm smiling,' she said.

4

Penrose had always assumed that his first visit to Cambridge in more than a decade would be to see Bridget, but the invitation, when it came, was extended by a dead man – or rather, by his killer. Faced with numerous gazetteers and county guides, Bill Fallowfield had taken a shortcut and put in a call to the editor of *Country Life*, who offered him three Jacobean priories to choose from: Shorebridge in Yorkshire; Tivendale in Pembrokeshire; or Angerhale in Cambridgeshire. A comparison with the photographic fragment found on Stephen Laxborough's body confirmed that it was the nearest of the three which concerned them, and so, on a beautiful October morning which could easily have belonged to the month before, Penrose took his car and headed north out of London, wishing that Bridget was in town but contenting himself with the thought that at least he could call in on Josephine if he had time.

He considered Stephen Laxborough's murder as he drove, trying to remember an occasion when he had been quite so devoid of ideas. So far, they had spoken to his nephew in South Africa, to various members of the church and musical communities in Hampstead, and to every piano pupil whose name appeared in his diary, but the conversations had been even less enlightening than his own with Hilda Pryce. Laxborough's health must have been good during his lifetime because his doctor was all but a stranger to him, and his solicitor had met him only twice. The will that supplied the business of both meetings surprised Penrose: among the predictable financial bequests to his only surviving relative and the gift of his piano to charity, Laxborough had made one final declaration of gratitude, touching in its lack of sentimentality. Hilda Pryce, the woman who had served him so loyally for nearly twenty years, would never again have to ask for permission to stay in the house on Mount Vernon; it had been left to her, a thank you for an 'act of great kindness', and if Penrose had momentarily considered the legacy as a motive, the housekeeper's obvious shock and disbelief at the news had dispelled any possibility of her involvement in Laxborough's murder. In short, the investigation was no further on now than it had been on the day of that horrific discovery. Even the lurid press coverage and a widely publicised appeal for information had fallen on deaf ears; the only people to come forward so far were a tramp seeking a cell bed on a cold night and a religious fanatic who saw Laxborough's death as a punishment for the growing and pernicious liberalism within the ranks of the Church of England.

He parked at his old college, resisting the temptation to take a nostalgic stroll across the wide lawns and open, neoclassical courtyard, uniquely spacious among the Cambridge colleges and still maintaining something of the edge-of-town feel which it must have had when first built. Out of courtesy rather than necessity, he had made an appointment at the local police station before travelling on to the Priory; it was never politic to turn up unannounced on another force's patch, and, in any case, he was keen to find out as much as he could about the house and the family before arriving on the doorstep. All that Fallowfield's *Country Life* source had been able to tell him was that the property was built in the twelfth century as a religious house dedicated to St Augustine, and that it was currently propped up by the American money into which its owner, Robert Moorcroft, had married. There was no obvious connection to Stephen Laxborough's life or to his death, but given that Penrose had absolutely nothing else to go on, and with pressure from his superiors to come up with some sort of lead before the public started asking awkward questions, he was willing to chance his arm.

Cambridgeshire Police had its headquarters in a handsome building on Regent Street which looked older than it was. He announced himself at the front desk and waited to be called, eavesdropping on the conversations that passed him by as the station went about its business. It was strange, he thought, but no matter where you went in the country, from the bustle and magnitude of Scotland Yard to the smallest of rural outposts, very little changed in the atmosphere of a police station: there was the same shuffling of egos, the same protective camaraderie, the same urgent energy. He stared out into the street, thinking of the countless times he had walked past this building as a student, never once imagining that his life would give him a role inside it. Back then, in the days just before the war, he had been studying medicine, intent on pursuing a career as a doctor, but those years in France – the darkness and the violence and the deaths – had changed all that. Some things could never be healed and he had lost the heart to try, so he abandoned his degree, returning to Cambridge only as a convalescent soldier, nursed in the makeshift hospitals that sprang up in the college cloisters. When peace eventually came, he chose a very different career, one much better served by the sense of injustice that infected him long after the dirt and blood of the trenches were washed away. War had schooled him in human nature at its bleakest and its most brutal, but he saw it still, every day of his working life, and he had never once regretted his decision to treat the sickness rather than the sick.

'DCI Penrose – very good to meet you.' The voice filled the lobby with such self-assurance that Penrose could have described its owner even before he turned round. Detective Superintendent George Clough was a tall, thick-set man in his fifties, with receding grey hair and heavy jowls, and a tight-fitting suit which harked back to younger, less desk-bound days. 'I was interested to get your call. We can talk in my office.' Penrose followed him up a narrow staircase to a small, first-floor room which overlooked the station's back yard. The desk was covered in police reports and various editions of the local newspaper, all opened to articles on the same subject. 'It's a bloody nightmare, I don't mind admitting,' Clough said, noticing his interest. 'Five attacks in three months, and we're as clueless now as we were at the beginning. This time the bastard's used a knife, so we've got no choice but to take it seriously.'

Penrose picked up one of the older papers and scanned the story, a sanitised account of an attack on a young shop worker in her own home. The suggestion was that a burglary had got out of hand, and to Penrose's mind it seemed serious enough to justify police attention, but he was used to the casual way in which some of his colleagues viewed sexual assault and it wasn't his place to argue here. 'I see this one was in August,' he said, looking at the date on the newspaper, 'so you're obviously after a town man and not a student.'

'Yes, but we haven't much more than that to go on.'

'No other patterns?'

Clough shook his head and emptied an overflowing ashtray into the bin, ready to start again. 'No. They're all over the town, at different times of the night, and with no obvious connection between the victims. A couple of them are shop girls but they work in different stores, and then we've had a typist, a hairdresser and a waitress. Some are blonde, some are brunette, some are fat, some are thin. The only thing they've got in common is that they've been on their own in the house when he's struck, even when they share the place with other girls.'

'So he watches them first until he's familiar with the habits of the household?'

'Obviously. I only wish they'd been a bit more attentive in return. Christ, Penrose, they can't even agree on a description, other than to say that he covers his face. His age, his build, his voice – we've had something different from every one of them.'

How unreasonable of a terrified young woman not to take more notice while she was being raped, Penrose thought, but he kept his opinions to himself. 'I won't take up much of your time,' he promised instead. 'I can see you're busy.'

If he had hoped to move on with the business that concerned him, he had chosen the wrong tack. Clough seized on his sympathy and launched into a long list of the various inconveniences associated with the crimes. 'I wouldn't mind, but it's given carte blanche to the timewasters,' he said. 'We've had false alarms all over town – colleges, parks, even the library. Now every time a gas man knocks on a door, the woman phones us in case he's the bloody rapist.'

'People are bound to be frightened until—'

'Frightened? I'll tell you what's bloody frightening – trying to find the manpower to deal with this nonsense as well as all the proper police work. There's a few here who think they could do my job better than me – you'll know what that's like. Much more of this and they're welcome to it.'

He paused to look for his lighter, and Penrose took advantage of the silence. 'You said you were interested to get my call . . .'

'Yes. Quite a coincidence, really.'

'In what way?'

'Angerhale Priory's come up twice now in the last week. I've never had much to do with the place before – never any reason to. Moorcroft, the chap who owns it, is in the papers now and again – mostly sporting stuff. He's an ex-Cambridge man – used to be a cricketing blue, and I've met him a couple of times at Fenner's, but that's all. Then last week we had a call from the Priory to report an intruder.'

'Oh?'

'Yes. One of the servants came down in the morning and there was a window wide open to the front lawn. I sent someone over right away to check through the house, but there was no one there and nothing had been taken, so there wasn't much more we could do.'

'Could the window have been left open by mistake?' Penrose asked, cynically noting that false alarms didn't seem to count as 'time wasting' when class and money were involved.

'No. It had been forced, but that's as much as we know. When your call came through, I wondered if the two things were connected. What's your interest in Angerhale?'

Penrose hesitated, wondering how much to confide. He had intended to be as vague as possible in his enquiries, but he hadn't reckoned on there being anything out of the ordinary in the Priory's recent history; if there *was* a connection between Stephen Laxborough's murder and the reported intruder, he had no right to hold back information. 'I'm currently investigating the death of a man in Hampstead last week,' he began.

'The musician?'

Penrose nodded. 'Dr Stephen Laxborough.'

'Yes, I read about it. What's that got to do with Angerhale? Did he and Moorcroft know each other?'

'That's what I'm hoping to find out. There was a picture of the Priory with the body, and I need to establish why.'

'With the body?' He paused, and Penrose heard the wheezing in his chest as he inhaled the cigarette smoke. 'Were the newspapers exaggerating? It sounded bloody awful.'

'No, I'm afraid for once they weren't. If anything, they didn't quite do it justice.'

Clough shook his head, listening in disbelief as Penrose outlined what had been found at the crime scene. 'Some of them stay with you, don't they?' he said with feeling. 'This Laxborough – what do you know about him?'

'Very little. He kept himself to himself – no family and no close friends, and his past seems to be something of a mystery, although whether that's deliberate or not remains to be seen.'

'And was he up at Cambridge? Could he and Moorcroft have met here?'

'I don't know, but that's easily checked. How old is Moorcroft?'

'Early to mid-forties, I'd say. His wife's younger, but I believe it's a second marriage.'

'Then it's possible that he and Laxborough were here at the same time,' Penrose said. And if it turned out to be true, he thought, then his own college years would also have overlapped; the idea that he might have crossed paths with the dead man, on the playing fields or in the narrow streets, made him more determined than ever to unlock the secrets of his life.

'Are you treating Moorcroft as a suspect?' Clough asked cautiously.

Penrose gave a non-committal smile. 'I wish I could say I'd got that far. At the moment, I'm simply following up one line of enquiry in the absence of any other, but I'll obviously keep you informed of any significant developments.'

'Yes, please do.' Clough stood up and walked to the door with such a sense of purpose that Penrose wondered if he was about to collect his hat from the stand and offer to come with him; instead, he opened the door and boomed down the passageway. 'Webster! Get in here for a minute.' The words echoed down the highly polished corridor, drawing a response before they had even died away. A plain clothes officer appeared in the doorway, broad-shouldered if not particularly tall, with dark blonde hair and a face that was unremarkable except for eyes which were the palest of blues; their youthfulness made his age hard to gauge – early thirties, Penrose guessed, although he could have been wrong by five years either way. He was wearing a trench coat, and an air of suppressed impatience about him suggested that he had been on his way out. 'Webster, this is DCI Penrose from Scotland Yard. He's interested in that business at Angerhale the other day.'

The detective looked at Penrose, understandably curious to know why the Metropolitan Police might be interested in an open window, then turned back to his boss. 'That wasn't me, sir, as it turned out. If you remember, you asked me to go out and check on it, but then we had that false alarm with the woman in George Street and I sent DC Bailey instead.'

Clough tutted with impatience. 'False alarms – that's all I bloody hear these days.' He looked at Penrose. 'The woman came in from the shops and heard someone upstairs, so she called us in a panic. Turned out it was her husband, who'd come home early from work with the flu. They must think we've got all the time in the world. I'm surprised she didn't ask us to call in and get the bloody tissues on the way.' Penrose stifled a smile and caught Webster's eye. 'All right then, Tom – go and find Bailey for me and send him up here.'

'Bailey's on leave this week, sir. That's why we're so stretched.'

'Of course he bloody is. Oh well, I don't suppose there's much more he could have told you.'

'No, probably not.' Penrose stood up, keen to get on with his business. 'In any case, I've got everything I need for now. You've been very helpful.'

'Well, we'll do whatever we can, and by all means take DI Webster with you to see Moorcroft if it would help to have a local man in on the conversation.'

Penrose's heart sank. He had nothing against Webster and didn't want to be rude, but he had been deliberately vague when making the appointment with Robert Moorcroft and wanted to catch him off-guard with the reason for his visit; while he hated pulling rank, there was little doubt in his mind that a call from Scotland Yard about a murder enquiry would focus Moorcroft's attention more effectively if it wasn't diluted by a local officer. To his relief, Webster seemed even less enthusiastic about the idea than he was. 'I haven't really got time, sir. I was just off to the hospital to talk to the latest victim. The doctor says she's well enough to be questioned.'

'Then let one of the women do it – that's what they're here for.

Send WPC Brown instead – she'll probably get more out of the girl than you will.'

Clough's reasoning made sense, even if it was built on a dubious lack of regard for the role of female police officers, but Penrose stepped in to support Webster. 'I'm happy to go on my own,' he said. 'If these attacks were my responsibility, I'd want to question the victims myself and I've taken up enough of your time already.'

'Very well, if you're sure.'

'Quite sure. I'll be in touch.'

Penrose took his leave, and Webster walked down to the front desk with him. 'Thanks for that, sir,' he said. 'I appreciate it. If the Super had talked to some of these girls himself, he might take what's going on here a bit more seriously.'

'I don't think he's treating it lightly,' Penrose said diplomatically, 'but the higher you get, the more you have to play the politician.' Webster looked sceptical and Penrose regretted sounding more patronising than he had intended. 'At least – that's what my boss keeps telling me. One day I'll believe him.' He smiled, restoring the alliance between them. 'Are you walking to Addenbrooke's? If so, I'll come part of the way with you. My car's at Downing.'

Webster nodded and led the way out to the street. 'You sound like you know the town, sir. Were you up at college here?'

'That's right. I came up in 1912. What about you?'

'No, nothing like that. I was here as a boy for a bit, then I moved away and didn't come back until I got my first promotion five years ago.'

'And you've been on these assaults since they started?'

'Yes, back in the summer. The first one was a burglary – he went for the money and thought he'd have a little extra while he was there, but he's really got a taste for it now. Nothing's been taken the last couple of times – well, nothing that can ever be replaced. He's hell-bent on hurting them, and there doesn't seem to be a thing that we can do to stop him.' Penrose listened, wondering if Webster's zeal was simply down to a natural wish to prove himself at a crucial stage in his career or to something rather less cynical; he seemed to be genuinely angered by the crimes he was investigating, and Penrose found himself reminded of his own attitude towards the early cases he was given. 'Do you know what I really hate?' Webster continued. 'Apart from the violence, I mean.'

'The helplessness? The fact that he has all the initiative and you're sitting around waiting for his next move in the hope that he'll make a mistake?'

'Exactly that. And he could be anybody. Somewhere in this town there's a man who has a home and a job, who drinks in the pubs and goes out with his friends, and he's probably so ordinary that you wouldn't look twice at him. The sort of bloke you sit next to on the bus and instantly forget. We could be walking past him right now and we'd never know.'

'Are there really no connections between the victims?'

'Not that I can see, and I've looked at it from every angle I can think of.'

'So how does he choose them? Does he pick a street and watch until he's confident he's found a woman on her own, or do they go to him?'

In spite of his determination not to be distracted, Penrose was becoming increasingly interested in the case and Webster seemed pleased to have a fresh ear to talk to about it. 'Go on,' he said. 'What do you mean?'

'Well, does he have a job that might bring him into contact with them? Is he a taxi driver or a waiter or a barman? Does he take the coats at one of the dance halls or read the meter for the gas board? Anything that might get him into conversation with these women in the natural course of his work.' He smiled at the expression of weariness on Webster's face. 'Sorry. I'm not really narrowing things down for you, am I?'

'No, but at least you don't look at me as if I'm wasting your time.' He shook his head in exasperation. 'And I'm sure the Super's got this one wrong.' Penrose felt duty-bound to argue again, but Webster began to explain before he could object. 'The public can really relate to these crimes. Every one of these girls is someone's neighbour or work colleague. People read the stories in the newspapers and they think about the friend they met for lunch or the woman they talked to while they were queuing for the pictures – it could be them next. If we're not seen to be taking these assaults seriously and doing everything we can, people will start getting angry and it'll be the police in the firing line, not the rapist.' He paused and grinned, embarrassed by his own outburst. 'Is that political enough for you?'

'Impressively so.'

'It's a good idea, though. I've been through the obvious things with the victims and they didn't use any of the same pubs or cafes on a regular basis, but I haven't asked them about taxis or gas men. I'll look into it.'

'It's worth a try.' As they reached Downing College, the sun was shining lazily onto the yellow stone of the porters' lodge. Penrose stopped by the car parked nearby and held out his hand. 'It's been very good to meet you,' he said truthfully, 'and I hope you get a stroke of luck soon. There are people I care for very much in this town, so I know how it feels to worry about their safety, politicians or no politicians.'

'Thank you, sir. And I hope *you* get what you need from the Priory.' Webster touched his hat and walked away, too discreet or too intent on his own mission to ask what that might be.

5

Angerhale and its grounds straddled two villages a few miles to the east of Cambridge. It was set on the edge of remote fen country and, as he drove, Penrose tried to imagine the lives of those early Augustinian monks, isolated here under the vast fenland skies, quietly marking their days from morning prayer to compline. He slowed at the village sign, keen not to miss the entrance, and soon saw the lodge house up ahead, dwarfed by black studded gates and imposing stone pillars. The gates were pulled back and the driveway led him through gentle open parkland, graced now with sunlight and dotted here and there with a giant redwood tree. Half a mile or so on, a pair of smaller gate piers marked the beginning of an enclosed, wooded area, and the densely planted cedars and elm kept the house hidden infuriatingly from view; eventually, at the very last moment, a left-hand curve in the road gave him his first glimpse of the distinctive chimneys and stonework which were instantly recognisable from the photograph found with Laxborough's body.

He parked in a gravelled area on the Priory's north side, dark and forbidding from the canopy of trees. It was still early afternoon, but already he could see lights on through the leaded windows and, as he walked up to the porch, he noticed that several of the interior walls were hung with tapestries in muted colours, giving the rooms a medieval atmosphere in keeping with the original parts of the house. His knock was quickly answered, and a sharp-faced woman whom he took to be the housekeeper invited him in. The entrance hall was actually a long gallery with a vaulted ceiling and five low-hanging lanterns which led the eye to a plain stone spiral staircase at the far end, but he was whisked quickly through to the living room. 'If you'll just wait here, sir,' the housekeeper said, 'I'll tell Mr Moorcroft you've arrived.'

She disappeared, leaving him in peace to appreciate one of the most tastefully furnished rooms he had seen for some time – a light, open space which instinctively married aesthetics and comfort. The room was at the front of the house – the aspect pictured in the photograph – and enjoyed wide-ranging views over the lawns and parkland beyond. Someone in the Moorcroft family was obviously a shrewd collector: among the paintings on the wall, Penrose identified a seascape by Gainsborough and a watercolour which had the subtlety of Bonington, and the rugs and furniture – eighteenth-century chairs and cabinets in a richly coloured walnut – were of the highest quality. In most rooms, the great stone fireplace would have dominated; here, it took its place quietly among the gilded mirrors and pale walls, and the focal point was the fire itself; together with a sun which hung low in the sky, it gave the room a comfortable, drowsy warmth. Penrose walked to each window in turn, soon arriving at one which showed signs of recent mending; a bureau stood within easy reach of it, offering valuable rewards to a burglar chancing his arm – and yet Clough said that nothing had been taken. Perhaps the intruder had been disturbed, or had simply lost his nerve.

'I was expecting you at two, Chief Inspector.'

Penrose turned and glanced defensively at the ornate clock on a nearby cabinet; it was precisely five minutes past the hour, but he decided not to antagonise his host by quibbling. 'I'm sorry to keep you waiting, sir,' he said. 'Thank you for agreeing to see me.'

'Did I have a choice?' Robert Moorcroft might have been a cricketing blue in his younger days, but the intervening twenty-five years had not been kind. He was still a commanding figure, but his height was less noticeable now than the weight of middle age, and his face had a florid puffiness which suggested a liking for the good things in life and the means to enjoy them to excess. His features seemed inclined to petulance, a natural preference which was not improved by Penrose's obvious interest in his windows. 'I'm sure Scotland Yard isn't wasting its time on broken catches now, so let's get on with it, shall we?' he said. 'And it might have been more useful to us both if you'd given me some indication of what you wanted to talk about. That way, I could have prepared whatever you need.'

Or got your story straight in advance, Penrose thought. 'The questions I have are very straightforward,' he said, masking his dislike with a professional civility. 'I don't think you'll find them too taxing.'

Moorcroft frowned at him, trying to decide whether the words were sarcastic or genuine, then sat down on one of the sofas by the fireplace, gesturing to Penrose to take the one opposite. 'I'm investigating the murder of Dr Stephen Laxborough,' he began, raising his voice slightly to compensate for the distance between them. 'He was killed in Hampstead last week, and I wondered if you knew him?'

'I thought that might be it.'

Penrose waited for him to continue, but was forced to break the silence himself. 'So you *did* know Dr Laxborough?'

'I knew *a* Stephen Laxborough, but it was many years ago now. We were at King's together just before the war.' He leant forward and brushed a smudge of ash from the carpet. 'I was a freshman and Laxborough was in his final year, so we didn't have much to do with each other.'

'But you think it was the same man? You've obviously read about his death in the newspapers.'

'The Laxborough I knew was a music scholar, so yes, it's reasonable to assume it was the same man. In fact, that was the only thing that ever brought us together – we were both in the choir.'

Penrose tried and failed to picture the man in front of him as one of the fresh-faced choristers he remembered from his own experience of the Christmas Eve services in King's College Chapel. 'And after university?'

Moorcroft shrugged. 'I went to war in my second year, and I never went back to take my degree. I've no idea what Stephen did when he left.'

'You haven't seen him since?'

For the first time, Moorcroft hesitated. 'Once, just over a year ago, although I fail to see why that might be relevant to your investigation. It was very brief and we hardly spoke to each other.'

'What was the occasion?'

'Monty's funeral. A few of us went.' When Penrose looked blank, he added impatiently: 'Montague Rhodes James? The writer? He was Provost of King's when we were there. A wonderful man and a great supporter of the choir.'

'Yes, I remember him,' Penrose said, feeling stupid for not making the connection sooner. James had been a prominent figure during his own Cambridge years, a respected medieval scholar and former director of the Fitzwilliam Museum. Like most people, though, Penrose had known him for his famous ghost stories, widely read now but originally written to entertain a handful of friends and students in his college rooms on Christmas Eve. Those yearly readings were legendary, and Penrose had been lucky enough to attend one himself at the invitation of a friend. He would always remember the thrill as the writer emerged from another room, manuscript in hand, and proceeded to blow out all the candles but one, by which he seated himself to read. It was the atmosphere he remembered rather than the tale itself, which had been something about an ancient whistle that could summon mysterious winds and a malevolent apparition, and although he had read a few of the stories in subsequent years, nothing could quite match the frisson of fear and dread that the author had managed to conjure in those shadowy, oak-panelled rooms.

'You're a Cambridge man?' Moorcroft asked, and Penrose was amused to note that his presence at a particular university still gained him more respect in certain circles than his rank and impeccable record as a detective.

'That's right. Medicine at Downing, although – like you – I let war get in the way.'

Moorcroft nodded, and Penrose was content to let him find an affinity between them which he doubted would ever exist. 'So you went to M. R. James's funeral. When was that?'

'June last year. He was back at Eton by then, which was where I first met him – he left Cambridge immediately after the war. The service was in the chapel. Beautiful sunshine and all the music he would have loved.'

'Can you remember what you talked about with Stephen Laxborough?'

'We swapped pleasantries, nothing more.'

'And that was the only time you've had contact with him since your college days?'

Moorcroft sighed impatiently. 'Yes, Chief Inspector. I've already told you that. Now – if that's all? I'm really not sure why we couldn't have discussed this over the telephone. A chance connection a quarter of a century ago and a brief meeting at a funeral hardly seem enough to justify your coming all the way from London.'

'I haven't quite finished yet, sir. There *is* a more recent connection that I need to ask you about, and one I find harder to explain. A photograph of your house was found with Stephen Laxborough's body. Can you think of any reason why that might be?'

Penrose was expecting a reaction, but even he was surprised by the sudden transformation in Moorcroft's demeanour. The colour drained from his face, and he stared at Penrose in astonishment. 'A photograph of Angerhale? Of course I can't think of a reason. It makes no bloody sense whatsoever. Are you sure?'

'Quite sure. It's only a fragment, but enough to identify the house without any doubt.'

He took an envelope from the inside pocket of his jacket and got up to pass it to Moorcroft. There was a long silence in the room as he removed the picture and tried to make sense of it, and Penrose let it stretch out between them, undisturbed except for the crackle of a log on the fire and the ticking of a clock. Moorcroft recovered himself eventually, but his immediate reaction could not be entirely erased and, when he spoke again, some of his former arrogance had vanished. 'I'm sorry, Penrose, but I really don't understand why a man I barely knew would have gone to his death with a photograph of my house. I can see now why you wanted to talk to me, but I honestly can't help you any more than I have already.'

'Thank you, sir. I hope you'll also understand now why I have to ask you some rather more delicate questions.'

Moorcroft stood up and took a cigarette from a silver-gilt tobacco box. 'Go on.'

'Where were you on Sunday the fourth and Monday the fifth of October?'

'Where was I? Here, of course, as my wife and household will testify. Surely you don't think that I actually killed the man?'

'I'm not making any assumptions at the moment,' Penrose said evenly, 'but I do need to ask these questions, and the next one is very important, so please think carefully before answering. Is there anyone who might want to harm you? Anyone with a grudge against you who might also have known Stephen Laxborough?'

There was no outburst this time, just a flicker of the fear that Penrose had seen earlier. 'No, Chief Inspector, I can't think of anyone at all,' Moorcroft said, looking him directly in the eye. 'I'll say this once more, and I'll ask you to accept my word. I had no connection with Stephen Laxborough other than the ones I've already mentioned, and, to my knowledge, I don't have any enemies. I'm sorry that Laxborough is dead, but it can have nothing whatsoever to do with me.'

'And yet we have the photograph,' Penrose insisted. 'At its most innocent, it testifies to the connection between you, which is what brought me here. Looked at more seriously, it could be a warning—'

'A warning?' The voice came from behind him, soft with a distinctive American inflection, and he turned to see an attractive young woman who had entered from the other door. She was carrying a baby, and looked anxiously at her husband. 'What's this about, Robert?' she asked.

'Nothing, darling. Go back upstairs and wait for me. Detective Chief Inspector Penrose has nearly finished.'

'Is this to do with the intruder? He said something was a warning and if we're in any danger—'

'I said go upstairs, Virginia,' Moorcroft snapped. 'It's nothing to concern you. Please don't worry – you'll upset the baby.'

She looked unconvinced but did as he asked, and Penrose returned to his line of thought. 'As I was saying, whoever killed Stephen Laxborough might have meant this photograph as a threat. Coupled with the incident here the other night, I would urge you very strongly now to tell me if you can think of anyone who might want to harm you and your family, no matter how unlikely it seems.'

'There's no one, Penrose, but thank you for your concern and if anything occurs to me I'll be sure to let you know.'

He stood up, effectively dismissing his visitor. 'Do you have a photograph of the choir?' Penrose asked, certain that Moorcroft would set enough store by his college days to keep a record of them and wrong-footing him with the question.

'Yes, I suppose so. It'll be upstairs somewhere. I'm happy to send it on to you if I can find one.'

'I don't mind waiting, if it's not too much trouble.'

His tone gave Moorcroft little choice but to oblige. He left the room and returned after only a few minutes, carrying a framed photograph of a group of choristers. 'Here you are.'

Penrose looked with interest at the image, taken on the lawn behind King's College with the chapel in the background. The boy choristers sat cross-legged at the front, some as young as eight or nine, while the tenors and basses stood behind. 'Which is you?' he asked.

'Second from the left at the back.' He moved closer and stood at Penrose's shoulder, staring down at his younger, fitter self. 'And that's Laxborough.'

He pointed to an ascetic-looking figure at the other end of the row. It was the first time that Penrose had seen a clear photograph of the dead man, but he found himself unable to look at his face without replacing it with another, more terrible, image. 'Would you mind giving me some names for the other people in this picture?' he asked.

'Christ, Penrose – it's all so long ago. I really can't remember.'

'Haven't you kept in touch with *any* of them?'

'No. As I said, compared to the war it was a very brief and insignificant part of my life. I could give you a list of all the men I served with, but I could name very few of those boys now.'

'Any you could offer would be a start,' Penrose reiterated. 'You said a few of them had gone to Dr James's funeral, so perhaps you could bring those to mind? I can check with the college, of course,' he added, as Moorcroft still hesitated, 'but it would save time if you could write down the ones you know.'

Defeated by his earlier admission, Moorcroft went over to the bureau and scribbled down five names on a piece of notepaper which carried the Angerhale coat of arms. 'There – that really is all I can give you.'

'Thank you,' Penrose said, and finally allowed himself to be led back to the front door. Moorcroft accompanied him to his car, as if he didn't entirely trust him to leave, but Penrose paused before getting inside. 'Just one more thing, sir – there was a quotation found with Dr Laxborough's body, too. "What is this that I have done?"' He spoke the phrase slowly, making sure that it was understood. 'Can you shed any light on where it might come from or what it might mean?'

Without another word, Moorcroft turned on his heel and went back into the house. As Penrose got into his car and drove away, he didn't need a rear-view mirror to tell him that he was being watched.

6

No one would ever guess that she made her living from a skill with words, Josephine thought as she sat at the desk in what would eventually be Marta's study, trying to write a letter to Bridget that didn't sound threatening or sanctimonious. She read back through her most recent attempt, assessing the tone and predicting Bridget's response: at worst, indignation; at best, a polite enquiry as to why exactly she thought any of this was her business. With a sigh, she confined the sheaf of Basildon Bond to the wastepaper basket and wrote Bridget a simple postcard, asking her to telephone as a matter of urgency as soon as she returned from Devon. By then, she might have decided what she wanted to say.

The house felt empty and strange without Marta. Other than the room they had chosen as a bedroom, which was at the top of the house overlooking the church, there had been no time to put a personal stamp on anything, and Josephine found herself rattling round the hallways like a lodger who had forgotten which door she had the key to. The central staircase, onto which every room opened, reminded her of the Noel Street boarding house she had stayed in while working in Nottingham after the war; the building itself was very different, of course, but there was something in the way that her footsteps echoed on the bare boards as she climbed the stairs, in the old-fashioned bathroom and makeshift kitchen, which recalled the awkward intimacies of communal living. Even now, she could remember her fellow boarders with no effort whatsoever: the amiable Indian student from the university; a raw youth called Ted who was a trade apprentice in the town; the man who knew Inverness inside out and assumed at breakfast each day that she was as interested in Donald

MacKay as he was, just because they shared an accent. The house had been run by a woman and her widowed sister, whose daughter's fiancé was a sweet, smashed-up boy recently returned from the war, and in sharing mealtimes and a sitting room, the lodgers had inevitably been woven into the cheerless fabric of the family's life.

Now, as she had then, she lay in bed at night listening to the sounds outside her window, trying to get used to the rhythms of a new town – the faintly tinny cough of the church clock whenever it struck the hour, the rustle of students and bicycles at the beginning of lectures each morning, the comings and goings of lodgers on either side. During the day, she kept herself busy with an undemanding list of practical tasks that kept a threatening sense of loneliness at bay: she made arrangements with a firm of painters and decorators to work their way through the house, wheedling a half-hearted promise from them to start immediately and be done within a fortnight; she put Marta's name down with a domestic agency in Green Street, whose advertisement promised 'good jobs for good maids' and who could hopefully be relied upon to apply the same principles in reverse; and she made what sense she could of the remaining boxes, leaving anything precious or breakable until the work was complete, but making sure that Marta would at least have somewhere comfortable and functional to come home to.

Whenever she ran out of things to do or tired of domesticity, she simply walked the streets, glorying in the beauty of the architecture and the novelty of the shops and cafes. Perhaps it was the unstructured nature of her days, free from all appointments and responsibilities, or perhaps it was something inherent in Cambridge itself, but for the first time in months Josephine felt inspired to sit down and work. Her early books and plays had been sufficiently successful to give her the right to pick and choose what she did, but while there was something luxurious in a lack of obligation, she suddenly found herself craving a new achievement, measured not by reviews or sales or by the amount of money which a theatrical producer was willing to invest, but by her own satisfaction. Her latest book, a biography of Claverhouse, was soon to be published, but months of researching and writing it – wrestling with a genre that was new to her and longing for the life and breath of fiction – had nearly put her off altogether. Now, though, she was ready to settle to something which would bring her more joy, and she was inclined to think that Cambridge might just give her the ideas she was looking for.

In the meantime, the debt she owed to her friendship with Archie niggled at the back of her mind. It was frustrating not to be able to do something about it immediately, while the shock and anger of Marta's revelation still lingered, but the request to talk was at least a start. She found the address that Marta had given her for Bridget and looked it up on a street map, deciding to deliver the postcard by hand; it was a short walk across town and the knowledge that Josephine had been to her house might just make Bridget more inclined to respond quickly – someone who knew your secret *and* lived on your doorstep was hard to ignore.

Little St Mary's Lane was a quiet, gentrified side street which ran from the bustle of the main road to the river, and was obviously used as a shortcut between the two. At first glance, it appeared to be a narrower, more ancient version of St Clement's Passage, with a church and churchyard on one side and a line of houses on the other whose front doors opened straight onto the street. The buildings here were more varied, though – a haphazard mix of two- and three-storey cottages with attic rooms and basements, distinguished further by an attractive assortment of colour-washed walls and red brick. The lane was mostly residential, except for a striking black-and-white building halfway down; a silver crescent swung on a chain over the door, representing the half moon which gave the inn its name, and this together with the old gas lamps that hung over the pavement brought to the street an atmospheric, Victorian feel which Josephine warmed to immediately.

Bridget's house was opposite the gate to the church. Before she could think too much about it, Josephine took the postcard from her bag and pushed it through the letterbox, listening as it clattered onto the hallway's tiled floor. Even if she hadn't known the number, a closer glance at the house would have given Bridget away. The curtains at the windows downstairs were pulled right back, and Josephine could see into the tiny sitting room beyond. A dramatic landscape painting hung over the fireplace, vast mountains under an angry sky, and she instantly recognised Bridget's style from the pictures in Archie's London flat. She would dearly have loved to press her nose to the glass and take in every other detail of the room, but a group of men turned into the lane from the Trumpington Street end and she moved on, wary of seeming suspicious. Further down, where the churchyard gave way to another row of houses, the road became narrow and tunnel-like, but here it was open to the sky. The clear, nostalgic song of a robin – more conspicuous now that its springtime competitors were absent – drew her over to the railings; she could never resist a graveyard, especially one as tranquil and rambling as this, and she opened the gate and took the path that led round the church. A man in an old corduroy jacket was tidying one of the graves with a pair of shears, adding a regular, percussive click to the birdsong, and a wheelbarrow with a Thermos flask and various other tools stood nearby. He smiled and raised his cap to her, then stood up to stretch his legs. 'Lovely day,' he said, shielding his eyes from the sun with a hand covered in soil and grass stains, a true gardener's hand. 'Have you come to pay your respects?'

'No, not really,' Josephine admitted. 'I'm afraid I'm more of a sightseer. Cambridge is new to me, and I don't think I've ever been to a place with as many churches.'

'There's a fair few, I'll give you that. People talk about King's and the chapel, and they're famous for a reason, but I reckon God's just as fond of the others.'

Josephine smiled. 'I'm sure you're right, although I'm not much of a church-goer. This, though . . .' She gestured towards the winding paths and clumps of autumn crocus, the tombs and headstones decorated with tiny yellow lichen rosettes. 'I can see why people find peace here. Is this a labour of love or are you a gardener by trade?'

'Bit of both, really. I look after this and a few of the other churchyards, then fill in with odd jobs here and there.' His skin had been aged by the sun, she noticed, but his eyes and voice were much younger. 'You're right about the peace, though. Doesn't feel much like work sometimes. Not on a day like this, anyway.'

He took a packet of tobacco from his pocket and she left him to smoke his cigarette in peace, wandering at random through the graves, reading the names which the years had not yet erased and inventing lives for those who had been laid to rest there. A movement in the lane caught her eye, and she stared in surprise as a young woman came out of Bridget's house, carrying what looked like a canvas wrapped in brown paper. Her hair was cut short in a bob, but otherwise she fitted Marta's description to a tee and Josephine wondered why it had never occurred to her that Phyllis might live with her mother. Thankful now that she hadn't put anything more explanatory in her card, she imagined the girl picking it up from the mat and placing it on a hall table with the rest of her mother's post, oblivious to how deeply it concerned her. She moved a few steps closer and watched as the young woman locked the door behind her and walked over to a bicycle by the church railings. Impatiently, she tried to fit the canvas into the basket or balance it on top, but the task defeated her and she set out on foot instead, raising her hand to the gardener, who had begun to hoe a flower bed nearer the main road. She turned left towards the town centre, and Josephine – too curious now not to follow – tried to justify her behaviour by interpreting the abandoned bicycle as an invitation from fate.

Phyllis – if indeed this was Phyllis – crossed the road and took the street opposite, walking with all the energy of youth; Josephine struggled to keep up, reminded suddenly of how many years it had been since she made physical training her profession. By the time they had bypassed the town centre in favour of another, smaller clutch of shops, then cut through a side street to a wide road bordering a park, she was hopelessly lost and regretting her rashness. Even if the girl *was* Bridget's daughter rather than a friend or housemate, she wasn't quite sure what she hoped to achieve by getting into conversation with her; it would only antagonise Bridget if she ever found out, and no doubt it would hurt Archie to know that Josephine had spoken to Phyllis before he even knew of her existence. Worse still, if Phyllis herself were to be harmed by anyone else's meddling, she would never forgive herself. Since Marta had confided in her, Josephine had been so busy debating the abstract rights and wrongs of Bridget's choices that she had almost forgotten the real person who lay at the heart of them – the young woman whose life could so easily be damaged by a careless word or a rash declaration. The thought made her hesitate, but then her new friend fate intervened again: Phyllis left the main road and headed for a building set back on the right-hand side; it was a theatre, the one thing guaranteed to give them something in common.

According to the posters outside, the play for the week was Emlyn Williams's *Night Must Fall*, scheduled to open the following evening. Josephine knew the piece well from its original production in the West End – a psychological thriller in which a number of unsuspecting women fall victim to the charms of a psychopath. It was, she thought, an unfortunate choice for a town under siege to a serial rapist, but at least it had the advantage of being topical. She tried the public entrance to the foyer but it was locked, so she followed in Phyllis's footsteps down an alleyway at the side of the building to a rear entrance which presumably functioned as a stage door. Inside, she was offered two choices – a second door, heading for the pit steps and stage, or a corridor which ran round the back of the auditorium; she chose the latter, unable to think of an excuse which would justify her presence backstage, and cautiously opened one of the pale green doors that led to the boxes. Other than some striking art deco glass panels at the front, the theatre's unassuming facade had in no way prepared her for the character of its interior; she looked round in delight at an exquisite Georgian playhouse. The horseshoe auditorium, split over three levels and decorated in a traditional, rich colour scheme of reds and creams, had all the atmosphere of the original Theatre Royal, and a coat of arms on the proscenium arch suggested that this building, too, had once laid claim to royal title. It captivated Josephine instantly, as historic theatres always did, and she longed suddenly to see a performance there.

'Can I help you?'

Phyllis had come out from the wings and stood on the stage, looking curiously at her unexpected visitor. 'I'm so sorry,' Josephine said, 'but I was just walking past the theatre and I saw the posters. It's a play I like very much so I thought I'd pop in and buy a ticket.'

'We only sell them from here on the night, I'm afraid. The theatre runs on a shoestring, and we can't afford the staff to open the box office during the day.'

'I should have left as soon as I realised you were closed, but once I was inside I couldn't pull myself away. I had no idea that it would be this beautiful. It's a real gem.'

'It *is* lovely, isn't it?' Phyllis said, visibly pleased by Josephine's admiration. 'It gets most people that way the first time they see it. It's not the sort of thing you expect to find on a dreary stretch of road leading out of town.'

'Well, it was definitely worth getting lost for.'

'You don't know Cambridge very well, then?'

'Hardly at all. A friend of mine has just taken a house here, but she's away at the moment so I'm looking after it for her.'

'I hope you're better at watering the plants than I am. My mother's off on a painting holiday and I'm house-sitting for her,' Phyllis explained, dispelling any lingering doubts that Josephine might have had. 'I'll be pleased to get back to my own flat, if I'm honest. I've lost two African violets and a jasmine already.'

'God help the dogs.'

It was a slip, showing more knowledge than she should have had, but Phyllis only laughed. 'Oh they've gone with her, and anyway she's trained them to be self-sufficient. Come to think of it, she and I have got along much better since I started to fend for myself.' The comment was made in jest, but Josephine couldn't help wondering what sort of relationship Bridget had had with her daughter over the years. 'You can buy advance tickets for the show from Miller's,' Phyllis added, and then, as Josephine continued to look blank: 'It's a music shop in Sussex Street, near the Dorothy Ballroom. Anyone will point it out to you once you're back in the town centre.'

'Thank you. I'll call in on my way home.'

'Feel free to have a look round now, though, while you're here.'

'Are you sure you don't mind?'

'Of course not, although I should warn you that if you stand still long enough I might put a paintbrush in your hand. I'm desperately in need of some backstage help and the company will be in soon for a rehearsal.' She looked at her watch and frowned. 'But you know what it's like – if you want something done . . .'

'What *do* you do? Stage management? Or are you part of the company?'

'A bit of everything really, but mostly behind the scenes or front of house. Assistant stage manager, assistant box office manager, assistant wardrobe manager . . .' She smiled while she dragged some furniture onto the stage, arranging it according to a diagram taped to the floor. 'Assistant to anyone who needs one, I suppose. It's the business of the whole theatre that I love, not the acting or the writing. That's why helping out here is such great experience – you get to do a bit of everything, and the shows are always different. A thriller one week, Shakespeare the next, ballet the week after – you soon learn what people like and what they'll pay to come and see. That's what I'd like to do one day – run my own theatre.'

Josephine listened, thinking about Archie's love of the stage and the numerous people he knew who had made it their profession: his cousins, Lettice and Ronnie Motley, who were arguably the most sought-after costume designers in the West End; writers like herself, or the actors and actresses whom he counted as personal friends. Suddenly, the joy and pride that Bridget had denied her daughter and her lover seemed more costly than ever, and Josephine had to bite her tongue to prevent herself from saying something to Phyllis that she would instantly regret. She left the box and walked down to the seats in the pit, where she was closer to the stage. 'This place must have seen such a lot of history,' she said, keen to return to safer territory. 'How old is it?'

'1800-ish, I think, or thereabouts. William Wilkins built it – the architect who did Downing College and the National Gallery.'

'Not a bad portfolio to have.'

'No, I don't suppose it is. Terence Gray had it for a few years – that was when I first started to come here.'

'Really?' Josephine had heard both good and bad things about Gray, a pioneer of *avant-garde* theatre who was famous for staging the experimental work that the West End wouldn't touch.

'Yes. It was a mission hall when he took it over, with pews instead of seats and slogans daubed all over the galleries, but he bought it and put it back to its original use. He called it the Festival Theatre and did some extraordinary things with the stage and lighting, but even he ran out of money in the end. It was dark and run-down for a few years, but some of us thought it was worth giving it another go.'

'It's certainly not run-down now.' Josephine looked round at the immaculate paintwork and lovingly polished steps. 'You've given it a new lease of life without losing any of the past.'

'I'm glad you like it.' Phyllis jumped down from the stage and walked over to where Josephine was standing. 'We've had to beg and borrow everything,' she said, pointing up at the auditorium lights, 'but we've had some luck along the way. Those candelabras came from the old Alhambra in Leicester Square.' Sensing a fellow disciple, she began to explain some of the more detailed technical changes that had been made in Gray's time, so caught up in her story that Josephine was able to study her face intently without seeming in the least bit rude. She looked for a resemblance which would confirm that Archie was the girl's father, finding him less in her features than in her enthusiasm, in her knowledge and passion, and her eagerness to share them. In all the years that she and Archie had been friends, Josephine had always envied his ease with people, the instinctive way in which he found a common ground with everyone, and she saw now that it was a gift which his daughter shared. That, and his smile – sudden and disarming, transforming a face that was naturally serious; Marta had been right about that. 'We still can't afford the big commercial shows that the Arts Theatre has,' Phyllis continued, oblivious to Josephine's true interest, 'and we're away from the town centre, but we're hoping to appeal to enough people to keep it open. Dickens came here to do readings, for goodness sake, so we can't just let it go to wrack and ruin.'

She climbed back onto the stage and began to unwrap the package she had brought with her. 'I'd better let you get on,' Josephine said, picking up her bag. 'I'll look forward to seeing the theatre in action, though.'

'Good, and bring some friends if you can. The week's looking a bit quiet, and it hasn't helped that the film's just opened at the Regal with some of the original West End cast.'

'I'm sure you'll be fine,' Josephine said, thinking back to her first big success with *Richard of Bordeaux*. A clash with another opening night had led to a disappointing first performance and fears for the play's future, but the box office telephone had begun to ring at lunchtime the following day and hadn't stopped for fourteen months. 'Some of the most successful runs start quietly.'

Phyllis looked at her curiously. 'It sounds like you know what you're talking about. Do you work in the theatre?'

Josephine hesitated, wanting to be honest with her but knowing that she couldn't risk saying anything that might reveal who she was. One day, she hoped to sit down and talk to Phyllis properly, but that was a long way off. 'No, not really,' she said, feeling shabby now for her part in the deception. 'I just try to hope for the best.'

'Sometimes I think that should be our motto.' The girl cast the torn brown paper to one side, revealing the paintings that had prevented her from using her bicycle. One was a still life of orange tulips in a vase; the other was a portrait of a soldier in uniform, young and fresh-faced but instantly recognisable, and Josephine watched in disbelief as Phyllis hung the image of Archie on the wall. 'At least there are *some* advantages to having an artist for a mother,' she said, standing back to make sure that the picture was straight. 'Meals are never on time, but you can always borrow something to make a stage room look convincing. What do you think?'

'Who is he?' Josephine asked, keeping her voice as level as she could.

'My father, but I never knew him. He died during the war.'

'I'm so sorry.'

'Thank you,' Phyllis said, misunderstanding the apology. 'And do let me know what you think of the play when you've seen it. If I'm not around out front, ask anyone to come and find me. My name's Phyllis.'

7

Penrose drove back into Cambridge and prevailed upon his colleagues in Regent Street for an office and a local telephone directory. If any of the men on Moorcroft's list still lived in the area, it made sense to pay them a call while he was in town, but a quick look through the phone book suggested that they were either ex-directory or had moved away. He charged the police constable on the front desk with talking to the operator and checking for the names in local files or newspapers, then turned his own attention to King's College. Part of him didn't trust Moorcroft not to have sent him on a wild goose chase with a selection of false names or convenient misspellings, and he wanted an official list of choral scholars in 1913, the year that the photograph had been taken. A quick call to the bursar's office got him the promise of just that, with only the faintest whiff of curiosity, and he set out on foot to collect it.

It was funny, but no matter how often he saw King's College Chapel, it was always as if he were looking at it for the very first time. There was something in its Gothic splendour, in the spiritual aspiration of those tall, narrow proportions and distinctive turrets, that never failed to move him, and which – even as an undergraduate – he had never taken for granted. Unlike most college chapels, it stood apart from the other buildings in the courtyard, as if the King who laid its foundation stone had somehow known that its importance would far surpass the handful of priests and scholars for whom it was originally built. Penrose paused on King's Parade to enjoy the interplay of sun and shadows on the limestone, admiring the way in which the building dwarfed a sprawling horse chestnut tree whose magnificence in any other setting would have been unchallenged. He was pleased to find that a London life, surrounded by the finest, most extravagant architecture, had not made him immune to its grace.

At the porters' lodge Penrose was directed to an austere, classical building on the opposite side of the court, a perfect foil to the chapel's exuberance. He had expected to collect the list from the clerk who had taken his call, but instead was ushered through to an elegant set of rooms overlooking the lawns down to the river and introduced to the bursar himself. 'We don't often get a call from Scotland Yard, Chief Inspector,' Lawrence Crouch said, as soon as they were seated. 'Naturally I'll help you in any way I can, but the information you've requested seemed a little incongruous. May I ask why you need it?'

'Of course. I'm investigating the murder of a former Kingsman, Dr Stephen Laxborough. He was a choral scholar here just before the war.'

'And I'm sure he's been many things since. What makes you think his King's years are relevant?'

Penrose suppressed a smile. He could have predicted the tone, if not the actual words – the guarded civility common to institutions as various as the Church and academia, the government and the BBC, the top ranks of his own profession. 'It's one of several lines of enquiry,' he said, matching it note for note. 'Another man is linked to the crime scene, and the only connection we've found between them so far is that they were both in the choir here.'

Crouch nodded and slid a piece of paper across the desk. 'The starred names are the lay clerks. The rest are choral scholars.'

'Lay clerks?'

'That's right. These days, the choir is made up entirely of undergraduates and boy choristers who attend the King's College School in West Road, but that wasn't always the case. The original Founder's Statutes stipulated that the older members were to include stipendiary lay clerks. Back then, some of them would have been college servants and others from a trade in the town, but that had changed by the time that interests you. By then, the lay clerks were professional musicians who came from cathedrals or other musical establishments and stayed at King's for a few years. There were six of them in 1913.'

'So I see. Why did the system change?'

'I suppose you could say that there's a much greater interest now in the quality of the music. Lay clerks held the position for life, no matter how badly their voices deteriorated, so there was no replacing them – other than by what might be called natural wastage.'

'I imagine the war helped with that,' Penrose said wryly.

'Yes, but even so the last one hung on until about ten years ago.'

Penrose looked down at the list. There were eight choral scholars, including Robert Moorcroft, and he was interested to note that the names Moorcroft had given him were accurate. 'Do you know where these men are now?' he asked.

'I had a feeling you might ask me that, so I looked them up. A lot of our alumni keep in touch with the college – some come back regularly to dine, others have made very generous donations. These are the men we're still in touch with from that list, together with the most up-to-date contact details we have for them. They're all fairly recent – within the last five years or so.'

There were seven addresses in total, including one for Moorcroft but not for Laxborough. 'What about the Kingsmen who died in the war?' Penrose asked, keen to eliminate as many names as possible before starting to contact the rest. 'Do you have a list of those?'

'There are various war lists drawn up by the university, but it's probably quicker to look in the chapel. There's a roll of honour there for our chaps.'

The telephone rang and Crouch excused himself to answer it,

giving Penrose time to study the list of fourteen names in more detail. The lives of the men in Moorcroft's photograph had, for the most part, taken a predictable path after their Cambridge days: the clergy, the Home Office, law and academia. One name – Simon Westbury – was familiar to him from his own work. Westbury was a shrewd, experienced barrister, notorious for defending high-profile murder cases, and they had clashed on several occasions in court; most recently, Westbury had come out on top, successfully acquitting a man who had killed his wife, much to Penrose's anger and disgust. It would give him the greatest pleasure to continue his enquiries at Westbury's door. 'We've lost touch with several of them, I'm afraid,' Crouch said, swiftly dismissing his caller and returning the receiver to its cradle, 'but I can help you with one more. Alastair Frost stayed on as a Fellow here when he took his degree, but he's on an extended sabbatical and we don't expect him to return.'

'Why not?'

'Cancer, poor devil. The last time I saw him was a couple of weeks ago, and he looked as if he'd already long outstayed his welcome in the world.'

'Where is he?'

'I don't think I want to tell you that, Chief Inspector. Whatever days or weeks he *has* got left – well, I'd like them to be peaceful.' Penrose didn't argue; if absolutely necessary, he could return and force the issue but he had plenty to occupy him for the time being. 'Do you want names for the boy choristers from that time as well?' Crouch asked. 'The records for those are held at the school but I can have them sent over.'

'Thank you, but no. It's Stephen Laxborough's contemporaries who interest me.'

Crouch hesitated, and Penrose knew he was debating whether or not to voice the question that concerned him most. 'Do you *really* think one of the others killed him?' he asked eventually.

'I've got no evidence to suggest that,' Penrose said firmly, correctly anticipating the expression of relief on the bursar's face, 'but I do want to speak to them as soon as possible, if only to make them aware of the situation with Dr Laxborough. Until we've established exactly what the motive was for his murder, they would all be wise to be vigilant. Nothing can be ruled out at this stage.'

Crouch sighed. 'I suppose you're right. And now, if that's all, I'll take you over to the chapel.'

They walked out into Front Court and Penrose did his best to picture the rooms he had visited that Christmas Eve, but his memory failed him. 'Did you know M. R. James?' he asked.

'Monty was before my time, I'm afraid, although his legend still lives on here.'

'Is there anyone at the college who would remember him well?'

Crouch thought about it. 'The Dean knew him, of course. I don't know how well, but I believe it was Monty who persuaded Eric to take the position just before he resigned as Provost.'

'Eric . . .?'

'Eric Milner-White. He was chaplain here before the war and became Dean shortly after returning from the Front. If you want to know anything more about the choir, Eric's your man. It was he who introduced the Festival of Nine Lessons and Carols, you know – without it, I doubt that our service would be as famous as it is.' Penrose was interested in knowing more about the Dean, but Crouch moved on before he had the chance to ask. 'You could also try Sydney Cockerell at the Fitzwilliam Museum. He took over the directorship there from Monty, but they knew each other long before that – something to do with buying medieval manuscripts for William Morris. I believe he saw Monty at Eton shortly before he died. If you want me to put you in touch with him, just let me know. He often dines here.'

'Another time, perhaps,' Penrose said reluctantly. He probably had enough now to convince his boss that Laxborough's Cambridge past and King's associates were worthy of further investigation, but wasting time on a dead ghost story writer – no matter how legendary – was pushing his luck too far. 'At the moment, it's little more than personal curiosity. I went to one of his Christmas Eve readings, and I wish I'd taken more notice. All I really remember was the atmosphere – that, and the camaraderie afterwards.'

'Yes, Monty had a genius for friendship – I remember Sydney once telling me that. His kindness was much missed when he left us, I gather.' He glanced at Penrose and gave a wry smile. 'Kindness isn't a particularly common trait among successful academics. Nor, I suspect, among successful policemen.'

'Let's just say it's not encouraged beyond a certain rank.'

They were at the north door to the chapel by now, and Penrose followed the bursar inside. Instinctively, after just a few steps, he stopped and looked round in wonder, forgetting for a moment that he was there on business. Crouch watched him, and spoke unguardedly for the first time. 'It gets me like that, too. Every time, even now. Magnificent, isn't it?'

'It certainly is.' The chapel's interior was breathtaking – long and high and perfectly proportioned, with a glorious fan-vaulted ceiling which was surely one of the most precious architectural jewels that England had to offer. The light through the windows played its customary trick, a feat which had always fascinated Penrose: from the outside, the building stood solid and majestic, weighted to the earth by the genius of the master masons and the sweat of those who had lifted each stone into place; inside, especially on a bright autumn day like this, it was surprising how little of the wall was actually solid but occupied instead by a feast of glass and colour which shone with a luminous intensity. 'I'm afraid I don't have any great faith,' he admitted, 'but whenever I walk in here, I thank God for the people who do. I suppose you could call that someone up there having the last laugh.'

Crouch smiled. 'Perhaps, although the roll of honour might

persuade you that your first instinct was the correct one. The college suffered the most appalling losses. I know we weren't the only ones, but when you see the names laid out like that, it makes you wonder.' He glanced at his watch, then pointed towards the altar. 'The Memorial Chapel is in the south-east corner. Do you mind if I leave you to look on your own? There are some things I need to attend to before the end of the day.'

'No, of course not. And thank you for your help – I appreciate it.'

'Not at all.' The bursar walked away, leaving Penrose alone with the vastness of the chapel. He walked up the nave, below the great organ and past the screen which divided the ante-chapel from the choir stalls, unsettled by the profound emptiness of a place which he had only ever known as part of a congregation. The two side chapels were invisible until he was nearly at the altar, and after the overwhelming beauty of the main building, the small, sparse Memorial Chapel was strangely restful. As Crouch had intimated, the college's contribution to that fated generation was significant, almost unbearably so; the names of the dead covered an entire wall and included graduates, undergraduates, choral scholars, college servants and soldiers who had been boy choristers, running, Penrose guessed, to two hundred or more. The engraving was as scrupulously egalitarian as the sacrifice, and yet two names stood out: Rupert Brooke, who was listed among the Fellows, and whose poetry and tragic death from blood poisoning had made him a national hero; and Ferenc Békássy, another poet – a Hungarian – whose work Penrose knew and who was remembered here as the sole name engraved under the heading 'Pensioner'. He looked at the inscription, which sat conspicuously apart on the adjacent wall, wondering how much of a dilemma it had been for the college to include a Kingsman who had died fighting *against* the allies, and admiring them for their decision.

He went through the lists that the bursar had given him, and crossed off three of the lay clerks whose names appeared on the wall. The choral scholars, it seemed, had been luckier: only Jeremy Bairstow appeared on the roll of honour, leaving him one man to trace from scratch if necessary. Satisfied that he had done all he could, he put the sheets of paper back in his pocket and turned to go, only to find that he had company. A man in his early fifties was standing just outside the door to the side chapel, apparently unsure of whether or not to interrupt. 'I don't want to disturb you, Chief Inspector,' he said, although the dog collar suggested that it was Penrose who was the intruder, 'but Lawrence told me you were here, and why. What a terrible thing to happen. I'm so sorry.' Perhaps he was fooled by the collar or by the voice, which was rich and warm, but to Penrose the words sounded genuine rather than political. 'I'm Dean here,' he added, holding out his hand. 'Eric Milner-White.'

Penrose introduced himself, although it was obvious that the bursar had beaten him to it. 'You're not disturbing me at all,' he said. 'Do you have a few minutes to talk?'

'Of course. Lawrence said you were asking about Monty, and I never need much encouragement on that subject. I owe him such a lot. We can go to my rooms if you prefer? It might be more hospitable than a draughty chapel.'

'I don't mind staying here, if that's all right?'

'Perfectly. We've got a while before people start arriving for evensong.' He offered Penrose one of the chairs that ran along the wall and sat down himself.

'I gather it was Dr James who encouraged you to take the post?'

'That's right. He was one of the main reasons for my coming back here, then he left shortly after I accepted. I could cheerfully have throttled the man.'

'You've been here a long time, though – you must have forgiven him.'

'Of course I did. It was impossible to stay angry with Monty for long. He was one of the most good-natured men I'd ever met.' He nodded towards the roll of honour and spoke more seriously. 'I think this is why, you know. He couldn't bear Cambridge without its youth. He thrived on young company, and we'd lost so much. He always blamed his departure on the politics of the college, and of course he loved Eton, too – it was where he'd started out, after all. But I think the truth was simply that Cambridge after the war was too painful – and sadness didn't suit him.'

'You were here before the war, though, weren't you?'

'Yes. First as an undergraduate, then as chaplain.'

'Did you know any of these men well?'

He handed over the list and the Dean took some time to read through the names, but eventually shook his head. 'No, I'm afraid not. We met at the services here, of course, and sometimes at dinner or drinks – but I wouldn't have remembered them if you hadn't prompted me. Except for Robert Moorcroft, and that's only because he still comes here regularly. I wouldn't choose him as a friend.'

The tone surprised Penrose as much as the words; until now, there had been a gentleness to Milner-White's demeanour. 'You don't like him?'

'My colleagues wouldn't thank me for saying so because he's a *very* generous donor to the college – but no, I don't.'

'Why not?'

'He's an arrogant bully – you can see it in the way he behaves at table – and those are qualities I despise. There are a few like that in every year group, and they rarely grow out of it. I imagine he was exactly the same as a young man.'

'But you don't know that?'

'No.' He gave Penrose a self-deprecating smile. 'I'm afraid it's based on a little observation and a healthy dose of irrational prejudice.'

'Could he be violent, do you think?'

The Dean hesitated, clearly aware that his answer might have serious repercussions. 'I've never known him to be physically violent,' he said cautiously, 'but neither could I say that I believed him incapable of it, if pushed.'

'And you don't recall any animosity between Laxborough and Moorcroft during their time here? Or Laxborough and anyone else for that matter?'

'I'm afraid I don't. It was a very long time ago, but my recollection of those years is one of the calm before the storm.' He glanced at the wall opposite. 'Perhaps I just want to remember it in that way because of what came afterwards, but it was an innocent time, and a happy one.'

The answer didn't help Penrose but neither did it surprise him. The Dean's memories might be coloured by nostalgia and self-deception, but so were his own. That was the trouble with trying to be honest about life before the war: all the petty jealousies, disputes and acts of spite which could so easily escalate into something more serious had been washed away by a far greater evil until it was difficult to remember how much they had hurt at the time. Thwarted again by a lack of information, Penrose began to wonder if he should go back to the drawing board with Laxborough's death and look for another line of enquiry altogether. 'People must have come to you for advice and guidance when you were chaplain,' he said, trying one more question before conceding defeat. 'Do you remember anything at all unusual from those years?'

'You might have to be a bit more specific.'

Penrose smiled, acknowledging his own vagueness. 'I wish I could be. I suppose I mean any upsets that were out of the ordinary. Anyone whose behaviour was out of character. Anything that disturbed the peace of college life.'

'I'm not sure about that. The confidences that most people shared with me were more self-centred – doubts over their work, loneliness away from home, and the occasional bouts of bullying, as I mentioned. I imagine you've heard a lot more confessions than I have, Chief Inspector.'

'Then I won't take up any more of your time.'

He stood to go but Milner-White remained seated, staring thoughtfully out of the window towards the fountain in the Front Court. 'There was one thing, now you mention it,' he said. 'I don't know if it's relevant to you, or how you would even go about determining whether it is or not because I can't tell you very much, but Lawrence said it was 1913 that interested you?' Penrose nodded. 'Monty was troubled that Christmas. It was the only year I ever knew him not to finish a new story in time to read to his friends. He read an old one instead – the one about the Punch and Judy men. None of us minded because it's one of his finest, but it was unusual and he was distracted even in the reading of that.'

'Did you ask him what was wrong?'

'Yes. He said he was worried about somebody, but he wouldn't tell me who it was. Then he asked me if I would counsel the person concerned if he could persuade him to confide in me. I assumed it was an undergraduate, and of course I agreed, but no one ever came forward. Monty obviously couldn't persuade him to share what was distressing him, and the issue wasn't raised again. To be honest, I haven't given it another thought until now.'

'Could it have been Stephen Laxborough?' Penrose asked, thinking about the quotation found with the body.

The Dean shrugged. 'It could have been anyone. I really couldn't say.'

'And did Dr James have much to do with the choir?'

'Oh yes. He was Dean for several years, and then – as now – everything to do with the chapel came under his jurisdiction – the building, the services, the college school. It was always more than duty, though. He *loved* this place. I can still recall one morning when I was an undergraduate – he showed a group of us in here and brought to life the stained glass of each of the windows in turn.

No one told a story like Monty, whether it was one of his own or borrowed from the Bible.' He looked up again at the Memorial Chapel windows, and Penrose imagined that he could hear his mentor's voice as if it were yesterday. 'And he was *kind*, Chief Inspector. People saw that instinctively, whether he was auditioning nervous young choristers or inventing Christmas entertainments to stop the boys from missing their families during the holiday. They have to stay up for the services, obviously, and he always used to devise a play for their amusement which he'd put on at the ADC Theatre with some of the other Fellows. He wrote one of his ghost stories for them, too, I believe.'

'Oh? Which one?'

'I think it was "A School Story" – the spirits of two children taking revenge on an evil schoolmaster. And he presented a copy of his first collection to the college school as soon as it was published. His association with the choristers brought him a great deal of joy – and they were devoted to him. They trusted him, I suppose, and I have to say – if I had something to confess, I'd happily lay the burden at Monty's door.'

Through the open side chapel door, Penrose could see that someone had begun to light the candles for evensong. 'Did you go to Dr James's funeral?' he asked, knowing that the meeting would soon be brought to an end.

'No, sadly. I had business here which couldn't be avoided, but we held a memorial service for him in the chapel. And speaking of services . . .'

'Yes, of course. I must let you get on.'

'Thank you, but please feel free to get in touch if you think of anything else. Will you stay for evensong?'

'I wish I could, but I have to get back to London.' The Dean walked back down the nave with him, and Penrose took the opportunity to ask him something of personal interest. 'The bursar told me that you were responsible for introducing the Festival of Nine

Lessons and Carols to Cambridge – did you have any idea that it would become the moment that starts everyone's Christmas?'

Milner-White smiled. 'No, and I think the BBC might claim most of the credit for that. But I did know we needed something different that year. Everyone in the congregation had been touched by the war, and I thought that the Christmas Eve Service should acknowledge that somehow. And Monty had a hand in it, you know, even though he'd left by then. He was great friends with Edward Benson, who went on to become the Archbishop of Canterbury – but when Benson was the Bishop of Truro, he devised a series of nine lessons interspersed with popular carols to get his parishioners into the church and out of the public houses.'

'That sounds about right,' Penrose said, laughing. 'I'm from Cornwall myself, so I understand exactly where he was coming from. How interesting, though – I had no idea that something so important all over the world was inspired by the West Country's weakness for ale.'

'You can be rightly proud of your heritage. But Monty knew the service well and he showed it to me. I devised some changes to make it more coherent and added the Bidding Prayer, written in a language that I knew would strike a chord with those who had lost a husband or a brother or a son. We've kept it to this day.'

'Remind me how it goes.'

'"Let us remember before God all those who rejoice with us, but upon another shore, and in a greater light, that multitude which no man can number, whose hope was in the Word made flesh, and with whom in the Lord Jesus we are for ever one."'

'It's very powerful,' Penrose said, struck by the quiet sincerity with which the words were delivered.

'It's very simple. I seem to remember that was what we all longed for when we came back. Simplicity.'

'And not much chance of that now, judging by the state of affairs in Europe.' Penrose looked back down the length of the chapel, noting the way that the candlelight softened the forbidding dark wood and cast dancing shadows onto the floor. 'Thank you, Reverend. It's been a pleasure, as well as a great help.'

He walked back across the court to King's Parade, wishing he had time to enjoy the evening service and the beauty of the music, but he had stayed much longer than intended and his plans to call in on Josephine would also now have to wait. The sooner he could contact the remaining choral scholars, the sooner he would either learn something to his advantage or be able to rule out the connection altogether. There was a large antiquarian bookshop in St Edward's Passage, next to the Arts Theatre, and the owner was taking in crates from outside, ready to close for the day. His window held a fine collection of special editions, but it was the modestly bound book in the top left-hand corner which caught Penrose's eye, a collected volume of M. R. James's ghost stories. 'Am I too late to buy that?' he asked, pointing to the book he wanted.

'No, you're not too late. Good time of year for it, too, with the nights closing in.'

'Yes, I suppose it is.' Inside, the shop was gloriously untidy and Penrose could happily have lost himself for hours among the overstocked shelves. He waited while the book was fetched from the window and paid for it at the counter, hoping that his fifteen shillings might just buy him something more significant than a ghostly chill by a roaring fire.

8

'I've got something here that'll interest you, sir,' Fallowfield said, with his usual cursory knock at Penrose's office door. 'It's about the vicar on the list.'

'Giles Shorter?'

'That's right.'

'Go on,' said Penrose. 'I'm glad you're having more luck than I am.' After the formalities of Laxborough's inquest were over, he and his sergeant had divided the list of former choral singers in half and set about contacting each of them in turn. So far, his own shortlist of names was proving particularly unfruitful: Simon Westbury was on holiday and not expected back in chambers for another week; Richard Swayne hadn't responded to either of the messages left for him at the Home Office; and to add insult to injury, Rufus Carrington – now a medieval scholar at Oxford – was at present halfway through a six-month research sabbatical at Corpus Christi College in Cambridge, barely a hundred yards down the road from where Penrose had been just two days before. Any good news that Fallowfield had to offer was more than welcome.

'Well, as we found Laxborough's body in a churchyard, I thought I'd start with the vicar . . .'

'There's some sort of logic to that, I suppose.'

'. . . so I phoned the vicarage in Finchingfield and asked his housekeeper if I could make an appointment to see him.'

'And?'

Fallowfield paused, and Penrose could see that he was quietly excited about something. 'That's going to be a bit difficult, as it turns out. The Reverend Shorter died a couple of months back.'

'Giles Shorter is dead?'

'Yes, but don't get your hopes up until we've had a look. The verdict was accidental death, and it certainly sounds like an accident – no agonising final moments or strange bits of paper as far as I can tell.'

'So what happened to him?'

'He fell down the stairs and broke his neck.'

'So it might *not* have been an accident.'

Fallowfield grinned. 'I thought you might say something like that. Worth checking out, don't you think?'

'Bloody right it is. The woman you spoke to – was she there when it happened?'

'No – she lives in the village. She came in one morning at her usual time and found him lying at the bottom of the stairway. She thinks he must have stumbled in the dark.'

'How very convenient,' Penrose said. 'Am I reading too much into this, Bill?'

Fallowfield shrugged. 'Not from where I'm standing, sir. Laxborough's murder and the business with Angerhale Priory might be a coincidence, but two suspicious deaths from that same group of boys in as many months? We'll have to prove that this one *is* suspicious, of course, and God knows how we'll do that. But not to put too fine a point on it – what else have we got to go on?'

'You're right,' Penrose agreed, both heartened and deflated by the reasoning. 'Call her back, will you, and ask her if we can—' The telephone rang and he snatched up the receiver. 'Yes, I'll take it. Put him through now.' He covered the mouthpiece with his hand and spoke quietly to Fallowfield. 'Things are looking up, Bill. It's the clerk from Westbury's chambers. Perhaps he's come back early.'

'Can't wait to get some other vicious bastard off the hook, I suppose,' muttered Fallowfield with feeling, but Penrose held up his hand; the voice on the line was faint and hesitant, entirely different from the brusque arrogance which had brushed his enquiry aside that morning.

'Detective Chief Inspector Penrose?'

'Speaking.'

'It's Geoffrey Bradford, from Goldsmith Chambers. We spoke earlier.'

'How can I help you, Mr Bradford? Has Mr Westbury returned unexpectedly?'

'No.' There was a pause at the other end, and it seemed to Penrose that the clerk was struggling to hold his emotions in check. Suddenly he knew what the next words were going to be, even before they were spoken. 'No, he hasn't returned,' Bradford continued. 'Someone from the Suffolk police has just telephoned. Mr Westbury was found dead in his hotel room this morning. He was murdered, but I'm afraid that's all I know at the moment. I thought you'd want to be told straight away, though, just in case it has some bearing on what you wanted to speak with him about.'

'The Suffolk police?' Penrose repeated in surprise; somehow, he had imagined that Westbury would have taken his holiday somewhere further afield and considerably more exotic. 'Where was he staying?'

'At the Bath Hotel in Felixstowe. He goes there every... he *went* there every year, for the sea air and for the golfing.'

'Did he go with anyone?'

'No, always alone, although I believe he entertained friends and clients while he was there.'

'Excuse me a moment, Mr Bradford.' Penrose covered the receiver again and put Fallowfield out of his misery. 'Westbury's body's just been found in the Bath Hotel in Felixstowe, and there's no suspicion of an accident this time. Get onto the Suffolk force and tell them we're on our way. Use that native Suffolk charm of yours and don't take any arguments. If they show the slightest sign of wanting to keep this one to themselves, get me the Chief Constable straight away.'

'Right-o, sir.' Fallowfield left the room with a spring in his step, and Penrose wondered for the thousandth time at the peculiar nature of a job in which people were energised and motivated by violent death. 'Mr Bradford,' he said, returning to the telephone call, 'I'm sure someone from Suffolk has already spoken to you at length and I'm sorry to ask you to repeat yourself, but do you have any idea who might have done this?'

'They did ask, and I'll tell you what I told them. Simon never shied away from publicity, as I'm sure you know, Chief Inspector – in fact, he lived for it. Quite possibly, he died for it. He made enemies within the profession among people who were genuinely outraged by his principles or simply jealous of his success, and almost without exception, every case that he took on had repercussions of one sort or another. Angry letters or threats from relatives who felt their loved ones had been denied justice by a few clever words. Strangers harassing him outside court because of the "sort" he defended. Women's charities lobbying against him for his so-called collusion in assault and violent crime. He angered people, Chief Inspector, and he took the hostility in his stride. He always claimed that if no one was outraged he hadn't done his job.' Bradford paused, reflecting on what he had just said. 'He never took any of the threats seriously, even though some of them were quite extreme. Usually, he just laughed them off.'

And now it seemed that he had paid heavily for that, Penrose thought. 'Do any of the threats stand out?' he asked. 'Anything that you felt was particularly dangerous, even if Mr Westbury didn't agree?'

'I was uneasy after the Marlowe verdict,' Bradford admitted without any hesitation. 'It attracted an unusual amount of publicity, even for a murder trial, and the victim's brother wouldn't leave Simon alone for weeks afterwards. He threatened to kill him for winning Marlowe his freedom and I don't doubt that he meant it at the time. Whether or not he'd actually go through with it is a different matter.'

Penrose didn't need to ask for details. He remembered Albert Goulding only too well – his grief and horror at the manner of his sister's death; the anger and disbelief when the jury acquitted the husband who had so obviously killed her. 'Thank you, Mr Bradford,' he said. 'You must have a lot to attend to, so I won't take up any more of your time, but I do appreciate your call. There's a chance that Mr Westbury's murder is connected to the business I wanted to discuss with him, and you've saved me a great deal of time by letting me know.'

'I don't suppose there's any point in my asking what that business is?'

'Not until I'm certain it's relevant, but I'll keep you informed. In the meantime, thank you again and please accept my sincerest condolences.'

He put the phone down before the sincerity slipped, and went in search of Fallowfield. 'We got there in the end, sir,' the sergeant said from a borrowed desk in the control room. 'I spoke to the DCS in Ipswich and he's telephoned the Bath Hotel and told them to put everything on hold until you get there. Forensics have already been, apparently, but they're going to leave Westbury's body exactly as it was found until you say it can be removed. I can't imagine that the DI in charge is going to be too happy about it – his name's Alan Donovan and he's a cocky bugger from what they say – but he'll just have to put up with it. The car's waiting downstairs for you.'

'Thanks, Bill. Let's get going.'

'You don't want me to go and see Giles Shorter's housekeeper to save some time?'

'No, I want you in Felixstowe, if only to win over DI Donovan with your natural tact and diplomacy. Giles Shorter's not in a position to do anything but wait for us.'

Penrose let Fallowfield drive and took advantage of the journey to mull over the events so far. 'On the face of it, Stephen Laxborough and Simon Westbury couldn't be more different,' he said, thinking out loud. 'With Laxborough, we've got no suspects at all, whereas Westbury can lay claim to a queue of people who'd happily string him up in return for all the rope he's saved the government. And Giles Shorter is different again, even with the little we know about him. His murder – if it *was* a murder – was made to look like an accident, whereas the other two could hardly be more overt.'

Fallowfield moved deftly in and out of the traffic, finding the fastest route out of the city without recourse to a map. 'I know you and Mrs Christie don't always see eye to eye, sir,' he said out of nowhere, 'but one of her latest was particularly interesting. There was a series of murders in that, too – led Poirot a merry old dance, it did.'

'I expect he triumphed in the end,' Penrose said with a heavy dose of sarcasm, 'but are you going to tell me how that helps us?'

'Well, only one of the killings had a real motive, you see. The rest were a smokescreen, chosen at random to throw the police off the scent and make them think it was all the work of a maniac. In the end, the solution boiled down to good old-fashioned greed, just like most of them do.'

'So what are you saying? That someone is willing to kill a group of men who can all be linked by their past, just to cover up the one they really want to get rid of?'

'Why not? It's clever, and I think the person we're looking for *is* clever.'

'I won't disagree with you there, but the rest of it sounds a bit fanciful to me, even by Mrs Christie's standards. I can't see Hilda Pryce working her way through a list of innocent ex-Kingsmen, all because she wants to get her hands on Laxborough's house.'

'No, neither can I. But I *can* see a casualty of Westbury's work killing more than once to make it look like the crimes are connected to King's College, when actually they're motivated by something else altogether – something far more recent and individual.' Penrose thought about it, surprised by how credible Fallowfield's scenario sounded. 'Or perhaps the one genuine victim is further down the list – we've still to account for an awful lot of names, and three deaths might be just the beginning.'

'If you're trying to cheer me up, you should probably stop there.'

Fallowfield smiled good-naturedly. 'I was only running through some of the possible motives,' he said, 'and Mrs Christie's model seemed a bit more likely than someone with a grudge against choral music.'

They had left the sun far behind by the time they arrived on the outskirts of Felixstowe, and a gun-metal band of heavy cloud greeted them. It was as if the seasons had turned in the space of the journey, with a generous autumn giving way to winter as smoothly as they had crossed from one county to another. Penrose looked with fondness at the familiar seaside town, with its bustling streets and thriving port. It was exactly a year ago that he had last spent time here, looking after Wallis Simpson while she resided in Felixstowe to await her divorce. It was a strange few days, the only time other than the war that he had ever been truly conscious of history in the making, but looking back now he wondered if anyone involved could have predicted the momentous events which were still to come – the crisis over the abdication, the exile of Edward VIII, the outpouring of joy and relief with which the nation had chosen to mark the coronation of his brother. And the story wasn't over yet, that much was obvious: only the other day, several newspapers had carried pictures of the Duke and Duchess of Windsor taking tea with Hitler, overlooking the Bavarian Alps at his picturesque home in Berchtesgaden. As Penrose opened his *Times* over breakfast and stared down at the woman he had grown to respect, if not like, the few days they had shared in this unassuming Suffolk town seemed more surreal than ever.

A tree-covered stretch of coast, signposted Cobbold's Point, jutted out ahead and the main road wound steadily to the left to avoid it. Fallowfield took a right-hand turn into a smaller street running parallel with the sea, and Penrose looked admiringly at the architecture, curious to discover which building was the Bath Hotel. The houses here were grand, distinctive and varied: cream villas in extensive grounds sat next to mock-Tudor facades and elaborate cupolas, and he wondered whose decision it had been to name at least two of them after bishops who had been burnt at the stake for their faith. By contrast, the building they were looking for was something of an anti-climax: the Bath Hotel was little bigger than a guest house, stunningly situated and attractive enough in a modest, bay-windowed kind of way, but undoubtedly the poor relation of the street. Once again, Penrose questioned why a successful barrister who could surely have his pick of holiday destinations would choose to stay here on a regular basis. The golf course must be something quite outstanding.

Fallowfield drew up outside and parked behind a mortuary van, waiting patiently to perform its sombre task. Perhaps it was the pall that the vehicle cast over the street, but Penrose found it hard to recall a more depressing reality to a seemingly idyllic location. In the gaps between the houses, glimpses of a muddy, restless sea did little to lift the landscape and the ships on the horizon sat heavy in the water, dark and vaguely menacing. They left the car and walked over to the front steps, housed in an arch of white trellising which contrasted pleasantly with the welcoming red brick. Long before he had a chance to ring the bell, the door was opened by a man in his early thirties with sandy brown hair, a cheap, ill-fitting suit and an aggressively proprietorial air – compensating, Penrose guessed, for the fact that the most interesting case he had had in years was about to be snatched away from him. 'Good of you to join us, sir,' he said, with a faintly sarcastic emphasis on the last word.

Penrose smiled pleasantly. 'DI Donovan, isn't it? Thank you for waiting. I'm Detective Chief Inspector Archie Penrose and this is Detective Sergeant Fallowfield. I believe your DCS has told you why we're here.' Donovan nodded and stepped back to allow them over the threshold. Penrose glanced round the entrance hall, which seemed to him so typical of a guest house from a bygone age that it might almost have been a stage set: dark wooden furniture and lace embroidery; potted ferns on stands; and, at the bottom of a wide staircase, a large dinner gong, polished to within an inch of its life. The register lay open on a table by the door and he saw Westbury's name in the right-hand column, entered three days ago in a bold, flourishing hand. 'What can you tell me so far?' he asked, turning back to Donovan.

'The victim was smothered in his bed. There's bruising to one side of the head, so we're assuming that the assailant incapacitated him with a blow of some sort, then pressed a pillow over his face. He obviously tried to resist, so the Doc reckons he was conscious immediately before death but too weak to put up much of a fight. Whoever did it seems to have got in and out through the window – the casement on the left was open, and there's a fire escape within easy reach. Westbury's door was locked, and only he and the hotelier had a key. There's a decanter of whisky on the dressing table which has taken a real hammering – that might explain why someone could apparently climb into the room without disturbing him. And there are fingerprints all over the place, as you'd expect. It's going to be a nightmare sifting through cleaners and past guests, but they might give us something.'

The detective's delivery was unexpectedly succinct, and Penrose was grateful for it. 'Time of death?'

'The pathologist says between midnight and 6 a.m., but we're hoping to narrow that down a bit. The hotelier – a Mrs Marjorie Bessall – spoke to him as he was on his way up to bed, and that was just after eleven. They found him this morning when he didn't come down to breakfast.'

'What about the other guests?'

'Two elderly sisters in the room next door – deaf as a post and didn't hear a thing. Some newlyweds on the second floor, and a salesman who was only here for one night and left first thing. We'll check him out, obviously, but the others are hardly prime suspect material.'

'And who would you say was?'

Donovan paused – surprised, Penrose guessed, to be asked an opinion. Most detectives were frosty and belligerent when they were asked to co-operate with Scotland Yard and he didn't blame them for it: there was nothing worse than feeling undermined through no fault of your own. 'Someone he's upset through his work,' he said cautiously. 'His clerk as good as told me that himself. We've been looking into it while we were waiting for you to get here, and I'd say the place to start was with his last case. Apparently, there was a lot of trouble over it.'

Penrose was suddenly aware of a woman hovering at the other end of the hallway. She stepped forward as soon as she saw that he had noticed her, and introduced herself as the hotel's proprietor. 'Shall I show you to Mr Westbury's room?' she asked, as if determined to hang on to normal procedure, regardless of the circumstances.

'Thank you, Mrs Bessall, that would be much appreciated.'

Donovan stepped forward to follow, but Fallowfield intervened. 'Perhaps I could ask you a few more questions, sir, while DCI Penrose has a look at the scene? It'll save us a bit of time in the long run and then we can let you go about your business.'

The detective had no choice but to comply with such a reasonable request, leaving Penrose free to examine the body in peace. He smiled gratefully at his sergeant and followed Marjorie Bessall to a room on the first floor at the back of the hotel. 'He was in number three,' she explained, 'the same one as usual. It's a family room, really, but he liked to have space to work. There's a lovely big desk overlooking the sea, and we don't have much call for family holidays once the colder weather sets in.'

'Mr Westbury stayed with you regularly?'

'Oh yes, he came every year – sometimes two or three times. He always said we looked after him better than anyone.' There was a warmth and a pride in her voice, reminiscent of the way in which Hilda Pryce spoke about her employer, and Penrose was interested to note that these men – no matter how aloof or ruthless they seemed in the wider world – could inspire such affection in the women who cared for them. 'This is it,' she said, stopping outside the door. 'I won't come in, if you don't mind. It was such a shock to find him like that, and I'd rather try to remember him as he was.'

'Of course. I'll come down when I've finished, and there are a few more questions I'd like to ask you if that's all right?'

She nodded and left him to it. The door was slightly ajar, its handle still covered in the telltale grey dust of a police enquiry, and he pushed it wide open to view the room. As Mrs Bessall had explained, it was arranged to accommodate a family, with two double beds, plenty of storage space, and a comfortable sofa pulled up to the fireplace. The wallpaper was decorated with a heavy floral print – a peculiar hybrid of rose and poppy which had no counterpart in nature – and punctuated at regular intervals by a selection of hunting prints; their gentle, rural landscapes struck a jarring note in a room entirely dominated by its breathtaking views of the North Sea, vast and powerful beyond the window. For some reason the space felt familiar, but the harder he tried to tease the likeness from the back of his mind, the more stubbornly it eluded him.

Simon Westbury's bed was the one near the window, and even from the doorway Penrose could see that his body lay twisted and contorted beneath the sheets; if whisky had dulled his senses sufficiently to allow an intruder into the room, his final moments had been all too conscious and he seemed to have fought for his life, struggling for air with the same violent desperation as Stephen

Laxborough. Westbury was a slight man, but the murder – again, like the crime at Hampstead – would have required a certain amount of strength. He walked over to the bed and looked down at the barrister's face, framed by the soft white pillow in a parody of gentle rest. Westbury's eyes – dull and filmy now – were half open, giving his face an expression of sly cunning which reminded Penrose of his manner in court whenever he scored a victory over the prosecution – but that was the only recognisable sign of the man he had known. In every other way, death had performed its customary trick, removing each spark of humanity – of spirit, for want of a better word – and intensifying the physical until what was left seemed artificial and out of place. The skin around Westbury's nose and mouth was unnaturally pale from the pressure used by his killer, but elsewhere his face was livid with colour – the angry, purple bruising at the temple, the clusters of tiny red spots around his eyes where blood had leaked from the capillaries into the skin. His tongue was protruding slightly, and there were traces of blood and saliva on the pillow. It was ridiculous, Penrose thought, but what surprised him most about the man in front of him was the rich, auburn colour of his hair, and he realised that until now he had never seen Simon Westbury without the depersonalising prop of a barrister's wig. His right arm was outstretched across the bed, his index finger slightly extended as if hammering home a point, and Penrose remembered how expressive those hands had been in front of a jury. But now the tables were turned and Westbury himself was the exhibit, useful only as far as his body proved the point for one side or the other.

Outside, the loud, rhythmic pull of the tide on the shingle below was strangely comforting. Penrose looked round the rest of the room, noticing that the sheets on the other bed were also disturbed, bundled up and twisted as if someone had spent a restless night there. Everything else was tidy: Westbury's watch and wallet were placed side by side on the dressing table, next to the decanter that Donovan had mentioned; his clothes – a dinner suit and a variety of golfing outfits – hung neatly in the wardrobe; and the Victorian mahogany desk of which Mrs Bessall had been so proud was troubled with nothing more than a blank blotter and a bottle of ink. The drawers of the desk were empty, but Penrose found the work that Westbury had brought with him in a travel trunk at the foot of the bed, together with a portable typewriter and a couple of Crime Club thrillers. None of the paperwork seemed to have any bearing on Westbury's murder and Penrose closed the lid impatiently, frustrated not to find any clues – no matter how obscure – which might help him link the scene to Laxborough's death or Angerhale Priory. As a last resort, he checked through all the pockets in Westbury's clothes and felt gently under the pillow, but the search revealed nothing of any use. For the first time, he began to doubt the connections which had previously seemed so obvious.

Mrs Bessall was in the room next door, changing the beds. As he came out onto the landing, Penrose could hear the crisp snap of sheets being shaken out, then vigorously smoothed down. 'My ladies have left already,' she explained when she saw him in the doorway. 'They were so upset. Those two sisters have been coming here for years, ever since Mrs Oliver was widowed. I don't expect we'll see them again now.'

Penrose sympathised with her. The Bath Hotel, it seemed, catered for a clientele who wanted the illusion of an unchanging world; they returned again and again, staying in the same rooms, eating the same food, safe in the knowledge that everything would be exactly as it was the year before and the year before that. But death had destroyed the fantasy, bringing with it an inconvenient reminder that there was ultimately no refuge from time, not even in Marjorie Bessall's lovingly created world. 'No one else was staying in Mr Westbury's room, were they?' he asked.

'You mean the sheets on the other bed? No, I can't explain that. He was the only one who slept there.'

'What about other visitors? Did he see anyone while he was here, or meet up with any of the locals? A regular golfing partner from the club, perhaps?'

'He knew a lot of the members, certainly, and occasionally he'd bring one back here for dinner or a drink, but not this time. He did have one visitor, though – yesterday lunchtime, it was, and he was a bit put out about it because the chap just turned up out of the blue. They went to eat at the club in the end. Mr Westbury said he didn't want to put me to any trouble. He was always very considerate like that.'

'Did Mr Westbury mention his name?'

'Yes, he introduced me. Mayhew, I think. Definitely something beginning with an "m".'

'Moorcroft, perhaps?' Penrose suggested hopefully, and his heart leapt when Mrs Bessall nodded. 'Tall, with light brown hair and a ruddy complexion?'

'Yes, that's right. They were gone for a couple of hours or so.'

'And what happened after that? Did they come back together?'

'Mr Moorcroft dropped Mr Westbury off, but he didn't come into the hotel again. Mr Westbury spent the rest of the afternoon working in his room.'

'Did he say what his friend wanted, just turning up like that?'

'No, he didn't mention it again.'

'And how did he seem last night?'

Mrs Bessall thought for a moment. 'Distracted, I suppose. He only picked at his dinner, even though it was one of his favourites. Come to think of it, though, he was like that at breakfast yesterday, too.' She paused again, as if trying to decide whether or not something was important.

'Please tell me anything that comes to mind,' Penrose said encouragingly, 'even if it seems trivial.'

'It's probably nothing, but he always went for a walk after dinner no matter what the weather was like – twenty minutes along the beach, or the cliff path if the tide was in. He said it helped him to sleep and stopped him worrying about his work, but last night he went straight up to bed, even though it was a fine evening. I can honestly say it's the only time I've ever known him do that for as long as he's been coming here. I told the other policeman that, but he was more interested in the night before.'

'Why? What happened then?'

'Mr Westbury went out for his walk as usual but when he came back he was all out of breath, as if he'd been running. I met him in the entrance hall and the bottoms of his trousers were wet and covered in sand, and his hand was bleeding where he'd grazed it climbing over one of the groynes. He said a wave had caught him, but it seemed to me that there was more to it. He seemed . . .'

'Yes?' Penrose said impatiently, wondering if DI Donovan had shared this information with Fallowfield or if it had conveniently slipped his mind.

'Well, he seemed frightened. That's the only word for it. I offered to get him something for his hand but he told me not to bother, and then he stood in the residents' lounge for a long time, just staring back down the beach.'

'As if someone had been following him?'

Mrs Bessall shrugged. 'I don't know. That's what I thought, but I couldn't see anybody out there. Eventually, he gave up and went to bed.'

Penrose listened, intrigued, and suddenly he knew exactly what the hotel and the state of Westbury's room reminded him of. 'I'd like to have a look at the beach, Mrs Bessall. Is there a way down from your garden?'

'Yes, we've got private access going down to Cobbold's Point.'

'Where Mr Westbury walked?'

She nodded and took him out to the garden to show him. 'Is it all right if they come and get him now?' she asked hesitantly. 'I'd like to get the room back to normal – not that we'll be getting any guests, I don't suppose, but for my own peace of mind.'

'Yes, of course.' Penrose suspected that Marjorie Bessall might be surprised by the demands on her rooms when news of her guest's murder hit the papers; a small crowd of onlookers had already been gathering by the mortuary van when he and Fallowfield pulled up outside. 'Tell Inspector Donovan that he's free to go ahead.'

The wooden beach steps were narrow and overgrown, and a bank of teasels caught at his coat as he made his way down to the shingle. It was after six and the light was already fading, bringing a bleak, desolate quality to the deserted beach, the intense melancholy of a seaside town turning its back on another summer. To the south, the twinkling lights of the pier defied the mood a little but there were no lights to the north, just a ribbon of shingle stretching out in front of him, bordered on the left by a low cliff and intersected at close intervals by wooden groynes, dark and sodden from the sea. At beach level, the roar of the wind was relentless; it hurt his ears and he was glad to turn his back on it and walk away from the hotel and up the beach towards the distant silhouette of a Martello tower, hunkered low against the blast. There was a line of upturned rowing boats chained to metal posts, and – wary of being caught by the incoming tide – he watched the waves licking them gently, as if to prove they could take them if they wished.

It was hard going on the shingle and he turned back at the first groyne, but he had seen enough to know that this stretch of coastline and the hotel where Westbury had died provided the setting for one of M. R. James's most famous ghost stories, 'Oh, Whistle, and I'll Come to You, My Lad'. It was the one that he had heard all those years ago at King's and he had read it again after buying the book, a tale of solitude and terror in which a Cambridge professor retreats to a hotel on the east coast, where he unearths an ancient whistle from a sacred burial site and, by blowing it, summons a terrifying apparition with 'a face of crumpled linen'. He was sure that James hadn't actually named Felixstowe in the story, but every detail he could recollect was identical: the lonely stretch of shingle and groynes; the welcoming but old-fashioned guest house; the twin-bedded room with sheets mysteriously disturbed on both beds; the professor's waking nightmares, pursued by the apparition along the beach; and most chilling of all, James's typically understated description of the ghost's face – an unwitting premonition, surely, of the way in which Westbury had died.

He hurried back to the hotel and was relieved to find that Fallowfield had been left on his own downstairs while Donovan supervised the removal of the body. There was no easy way to moot the idea that someone had staged Westbury's murder to echo an old ghost story, but at least his sergeant knew him well enough to make allowances. 'What do you think?' he asked, when he had finished outlining all that he had learned. 'It supports the idea that the murders are linked back to King's College – if not to Dr James himself, then at least to the time that these men were all there. I bet if I go back through that book, I'll find a story that references Stephen Laxborough's death, and probably Giles Shorter's as well.'

Fallowfield looked doubtful. 'That's all very well, sir, but where exactly does it get us?'

It was a reasonable question, but not one to which Penrose had an answer. 'I'm not sure yet, Bill, but Moorcroft is key to all this. He knows a lot more than he's letting on. Why else would he have come here yesterday? He came to see Westbury because he thought they were both in danger or because he needed a good defence lawyer. Either way, we need to speak to him.'

'Or he could have come simply to kill him, sir. We don't know that he went back to Cambridge when he dropped Westbury off here.'

'No, we don't, but he's got an alibi for the Hampstead murder.'

'Only his wife. You're not telling me she wouldn't lie for him, surely? And so would the servants if they were paid enough.'

'But you're forgetting the clues with Laxborough's body. Why would Moorcroft incriminate himself by leaving a photograph of his own house at the scene?'

'Perhaps it was an accident. Did you find any funny stuff like that in Westbury's room?'

Penrose was forced to admit that he hadn't. 'I wonder if he's got a car here?' he said, realising suddenly that he had no idea how Westbury had arrived at the hotel. 'Will you check with Mrs Bessall while I go and tell Donovan where we've got to?'

He returned a few minutes later to find Fallowfield standing in the entrance hall, grinning like the Cheshire cat. 'I take it all back, sir,' he said, holding up an envelope with a London postmark which was addressed to Simon Westbury at his chambers. 'He *has* got his car here and I found this in the glove compartment. What did you say that story was called?'

'"Oh, Whistle, and I'll Come to You, My Lad".'

'Yes, I thought it was something like that. Take a look in there.' Penrose put on his gloves and felt inside the envelope, gently taking out an old police whistle. 'I think someone's having a laugh with us, don't you, sir?' Fallowfield said. 'And it gets better – there's something else in there as well.'

It was another image of Angerhale Priory, an engraving this time, with some words in Latin scribbled across the picture. '"Quis est iste qui venit",' Penrose read out loud.

'What does that mean?'

'It translates as "Who is this who is coming?",' Penrose explained, 'and it's from the same story, inscribed on the whistle that the professor finds buried in the sand.'

'That sounds like a threat,' Fallowfield said.

'Yes, it does.' He turned the envelope over in his hands and noticed that it had been posted in the week of the Hampstead murder. 'Someone is taunting these men before their deaths,' he said. 'We thought that Stephen Laxborough might have been sent something that troubled him – that's when he told Hilda Pryce to leave. And I think you were right, Bill – this is just the beginning. All of the men on that list are in danger. The killer might be one of them or it might be someone else altogether, but if we're ever going to stop this we need to understand *why* it's happening. Simon Westbury's next of kin might be helpful – any friends or family that know about his past. And as Angerhale Priory seems to be at the centre of everything, I suggest we go back there.'

Fallowfield nodded. 'If *I* were Robert Moorcroft, I might just be frightened enough to talk to us now.'

'So would I, Bill,' Penrose said. 'Let's go and see, shall we?'

9

Angerhale Priory was couched in a brooding darkness by the time they arrived, a darkness which not even the myriad stars of a fenland sky could lift. The heavy iron gates had been forbidding enough when they were open; now, locked and chained, they were an impressive deterrent to any intruder and Penrose wondered if Robert Moorcroft had taken other precautions to safeguard his family in the last few days. He got out of the car, struck by the intense silence of the countryside at night, and announced his business at the lodge, then waited impatiently while a skilfully uncooperative gatekeeper phoned through to the house for guidance. Grudgingly, the chains were removed and Fallowfield followed the route that Penrose had taken the other day, the light from his headlamps picking out features of the parkland and gardens like a series of stills from a film. They pulled up by the side entrance, and Penrose noticed that the Jaguar which had been parked there on his last visit was missing.

'Not a bad pile,' Fallowfield muttered as they walked up to the door. 'Not sure I'd want the heating bill, though.'

'It's even more impressive once you get inside,' Penrose said. 'You can see why Robert Moorcroft thinks he's above the laws that govern the rest of us.'

'You've taken quite a shine to this chap, haven't you, sir? I'm looking forward to meeting him.'

But Fallowfield's hopes were soon dashed. 'Mr Moorcroft's not at home,' the housekeeper explained, a statement of fact rather than an apology, 'but Mrs Moorcroft will see you.' She led them past the comfortable sitting room and down a long corridor to one of the oldest parts of the house. 'You've come just as we were serving dinner.'

Her tone was as critical of Penrose's timing as Moorcroft's had been two days before, and he apologised. 'Will Mr Moorcroft be gone long?' he asked, regretting now that they had not telephoned in advance. 'It's very important that I speak with him.'

'That's not for me to say. In here, please.'

The dining room obviously dated back to the building of the original priory. It was a remarkable space, beautifully proportioned, with a vaulted stone ceiling supported by octagonal marble pillars, and a tiled floor whose red-and-black patterns offered a welcome contrast to the pale grey walls. Compared to other parts of the house, the furniture was sparse and restrained, and paid homage to the medieval origins of its setting. A refectory table, fifteen to twenty feet long, was decorated with an impressive collection of silverware, the centrepiece being a large, elaborate fruit bowl whose contents looked sculpted rather than arranged. Candles and the fire itself supplied the only lighting, and the room was so alien to the modern age and had changed so little since it was first built that Penrose could almost see the cloaked, monkish forms huddled in the shadows. Instead, sitting alone at the table was the woman he had seen so briefly on his last visit. She put her knife and fork down as soon as they came in, and something in her expression reminded Penrose of Miss Havisham at her wedding breakfast, still young but already disillusioned. 'I'm sorry to call at an inconvenient time,' he said.

'It's all right. I wasn't hungry anyway.' Virginia Moorcroft pushed the plate disdainfully away from her, the food barely touched, and it was immediately removed. The housekeeper disappeared through another door, leaving the three of them alone in the room. 'I know you wanted to see my husband,' she continued, 'but I'm afraid he's out.'

'So I understand. We weren't formally introduced the other day,

Mrs Moorcroft. I'm Detective Chief Inspector Penrose from the Metropolitan Police, and this is my colleague, Detective Sergeant Fallowfield. When will Mr Moorcroft be back?'

She shrugged, as though she had no more right to question her husband's whereabouts than her housekeeper. 'I don't know. Maybe tonight, maybe in the morning. Sometimes he's gone for a couple of days. It depends if he's on a winning streak or not. Would you care for a glass of wine?'

'No thank you, but perhaps we could ask *you* a few questions now that we're here?'

'Of course, as long as you don't mind returning the favour.' Penrose shook his head and took the seat he was offered while she refilled her own glass. Fallowfield stood by the fire, although the roaring flames seemed to be doing very little to carry much heat beyond the grate. 'That was the only warmth those monks allowed themselves,' she said, as if they were sightseers come to enquire about the history of the building. 'Just one damned fire in the whole of their priory. My husband tends more to excess. Once in a while that works in my favour.'

It was hard to say if her frankness was due to the wine, but she was much more self-confident now than she had seemed in her husband's presence. There was something contradictory about her, Penrose noticed – a strange, brittle strength which was both unsettling and attractive; intelligent eyes partnered a slight twist in the mouth to give her face an expression of wry amusement, as if she found the whole world faintly ludicrous but accepted that the joke was on her. 'I assume from what you say that your husband is out gambling,' he said, 'and not visiting another old college friend?'

His sarcasm seemed to intrigue her, but she gave no indication of understanding what he meant. 'He doesn't often tell me where he goes.'

'So you don't know where he was yesterday?'

'No. All I know is that he came back in a foul temper.'

'What time was that?'

She hesitated, as if weighing up the need to lie. 'Between five and six.'

'You're sure about that?'

'Quite sure.'

'And will your household confirm it?'

'Why don't you ask them?'

Penrose turned to Fallowfield but he had anticipated the instruction and was already on his way out of the room. 'Does the name Simon Westbury mean anything to you?' Penrose continued, and then, when she shook her head: 'What about Stephen Laxborough? Or Giles Shorter?'

'No, neither of them.' In spite of Penrose's refusal, she poured another glass of wine and pushed it across the table to him. 'My husband wouldn't tell me why you were here the other day, Chief Inspector. Perhaps you'll be a little more obliging?'

Penrose paused. He had no wish to alarm Virginia Moorcroft while she was alone and vulnerable in a house which she clearly found uncomfortable, but her husband's absence bothered him, no matter how normal it seemed to her; if Moorcroft wasn't guilty himself, the threats and his recent proximity to Simon Westbury made him an obvious candidate for the killer's next strike, and he needed her to be honest with him. 'Two of the men who were at King's with your husband have been killed in the last ten days,' Penrose said, watching her face carefully in the candlelight. 'Another less recent death might also be connected. According to witnesses, Mr Moorcroft was with one of the men on the day he died. That was yesterday, in Felixstowe, and the victim's name was Simon Westbury.'

'Are you accusing my husband of murder?'

Her tone was hard to read, but to Penrose's ears it leaned towards curiosity rather than indignation and he wondered about the state of their marriage. 'No, certainly not, but I do need to establish why he was there and what they discussed. It might have some bearing on Mr Westbury's death, and I'm also concerned for Mr Moorcroft's safety.' He let the implication hang in the air, but all that he gleaned from her face was that she could sit profitably at the card tables with her husband. 'Could you be any more specific about where he is tonight? It's urgent that I speak with him, for his sake as well as mine.'

'You could try one of his clubs. There's the Pitt Club in Jesus Lane, and a sporting one – I don't know where that is or even what it's called, but it always makes me laugh that Robert's still a member. It's been years since he played any honourable kind of sport.'

'Is it the Hawks' Club?'

'Possibly. You might find him there, but he tends to move on later if he finds the right company.'

Any attempt to disguise her hostility was long gone, and Penrose sensed that it would play to his advantage. 'How important was his time at university?' he asked.

'The best years of his life, he often says. It doesn't say much for me, does it? Or for his first wife.'

'And yet he doesn't keep in touch with anyone?'

'Is that what he told you?'

'Yes. Is it a lie?' Penrose had begun to doubt the claim when he first heard that Moorcroft returned so often to dine at his college; now he wondered if those reunions were more deliberate, used to meet specific people rather than merely to socialise. 'He told me that he was still close to the men he fought with, but that he could barely remember the names of his fellow choir members.'

She threw back her head and laughed, startling him with her reaction. 'Oh Inspector, you've no idea how funny that is.'

'Then tell me.'

'Robert was in the army for less than a month. He avoided conscription for as long as he could, then fell down one of the trench shafts and broke his leg. No one could prove he'd done it deliberately, but he managed to blag his way out of the rest of the war.' She stood up and brought a silver cigarette box back to the table. 'I've had Paris weekends that lasted longer than his time in France. I don't doubt that his comrades remember him, but not for the reasons he obviously implied to you.'

'Are you sure? He left King's without taking his degree.'

'That's because they threw him out. Bullying, I gather – encouraged up to a point, but beyond that not very gentlemanly.' Her subtle American drawl made the words sound every bit as sarcastic as they were meant to be. 'His first wife told me a lot about Robert while she was on her way out and I was on my way in,' she added, sensing his scepticism. 'I only wish I'd believed more of it at the time.'

'And he's never confided in you about any regrets?'

'Other than marrying me in the first place? No, we don't have that sort of relationship.'

Penrose pictured Moorcroft as he had been at their only meeting – sullen, pompous and now, it would seem, a liar – and wondered what had ever persuaded someone as unusual as his wife to look twice at him. 'How did you meet?' he asked.

'Is that important?'

'Indulge me.'

Again she smiled, but this time without any hint of mockery, and he noticed the fine lines around her eyes, unusual in someone so young. 'It was at the races. My father and he share a passion for horses. Robert was in the process of getting a divorce, and he was in the mood to celebrate.' Something in Penrose's expression must have looked sceptical, because she said more seriously: 'Don't misunderstand me, Chief Inspector – it was fun at first. Robert can be amusing when he wants to be and quite charming in his own way – and I wanted a different life, something a long way from Chicago and automobiles. I was young, but I wasn't stupid.' Of that, he had no doubt and would have said so given the chance, but she was still speaking. 'He moved the courtship along rather more quickly than I'd have wanted, though, and I found myself pregnant with my son. I honestly don't think Robert meant to trap me – he isn't that clever – but I *was* trapped. He did the decent thing and my family's money was his consolation prize.'

'And what was yours? Obviously not the house.'

'My children,' she said, without hesitation. 'Teddy's eight now and he goes to the college school. I'm hoping that's the only path he'll follow his father down. Evie's just six months . . .'

'And already like her mother.'

'Having seen her for barely two minutes, you're either very observant or very kind.' She pushed the glass towards him again and this time he didn't refuse. The wine – a Burgundy – was exceptional, heavily perfumed and smoky on the tongue, and it gave him a childish satisfaction to think of how furious Moorcroft would be to know that he had had so much as a sip. 'You said something to my husband the other day about a warning. What did you mean?'

He told her about the photographs of the Priory which both victims had had in their possession, hoping that she wouldn't ask for details of the murders themselves. 'I wanted your husband to take the threat seriously,' he said, 'and that's even more important after what happened yesterday. It can't be a coincidence – not now.'

She leaned forward and put her hand on his arm. 'Be honest with me – do you think my children are in danger? Is my husband *putting* them in danger?'

There was a knock at the door and Fallowfield came back in. 'The staff have all confirmed Mrs Moorcroft's timings, sir. In fact, the gamekeeper can be even more precise. He said Mr Moorcroft came back just after five and went to see him in the gun room. There's a shoot at the weekend and they spent some time talking about the preparations for it.'

Virginia Moorcroft had removed her hand but not before Fallowfield saw it, and Penrose could only admire his sergeant's discretion, even if he would have to answer for it later. 'Until we know more about why these men have been killed, I would advise you to take every precaution,' he said, knowing she had wanted something more tangible, and disappointing both her and himself with the bland formality which had arrived back in the room with his sergeant's company. 'We'll leave you in peace, Mrs Moorcroft, and look for your husband in the clubs you mentioned. In the meantime, if he comes home before we've caught up with him, please get him to contact me as a matter of urgency.'

'Of course.' He put his card on the table and stood to leave. 'And if I think of anything else, Chief Inspector, may I call you?'

'Yes, please do,' he said, softening a little. 'I'll also speak to the Chief Constable and ask him to get the local force to keep an eye on the Priory until we find whoever is doing this. It may not be possible, as they're stretched to the limit with other cases, but I'll do my best.'

'Thank you. I appreciate that. Let me show you both out.'

'Please don't bother – we can find our way.'

'It's really no trouble.'

She walked out ahead of them and Fallowfield took the opportunity to raise a knowing eyebrow. At the front door, she reached up to draw the top bolts and the sleeve of her dress fell back, revealing a circle of faded yellow bruising on her wrist. She covered her arm quickly and stared defiantly at Penrose, as if daring him to draw attention to it. 'Forgive me for being frank, Mrs Moorcroft,' he said, pausing on the doorstep, 'but your husband strikes me as a man who likes to get his own way.'

She held his eye, and once again Penrose was struck by a combination of vulnerability and detachment. 'Now why is it that you understood that so much more quickly than I did, Chief Inspector?'

'What happens when he *doesn't* get it?'

She hesitated, and for a moment Penrose thought she was going to close the door without answering, but he was wrong. 'I can honestly say I've never known that to happen,' she said. 'And I really don't think I want to find out.'

10

Mary Ennis lifted the lid on the gramophone and waited for the scratching of the needle to become music. She turned the volume up as high as it would go, sending the first dancing notes of the clarinet out onto the landing. The freedom of an empty house was so rare that she was almost sorry to be going out, but there was a band on at The Rendezvous and she couldn't let the other girls down. She slipped out of her uniform and hung it carefully in the wardrobe, ready for Monday, then set her make-up down on the dressing table and looked in vain for her lipstick. Hoping that it had simply fallen out of her bag on the way back from the hospital, she grabbed her dressing gown and slipped out into St Clement's Passage, where her bicycle was leaning against the church railings. With the help of a street lamp, she found the lipstick in the basket and hurried back inside to the lively strains of Benny Goodman.

She walked down the landing to the bathroom and turned on the taps, imagining what her landlady would say if she could see the hot water gushing into the tub. With no one queuing or telling her to hurry, she lay back in the bath with a magazine and a glass of ginger wine, but she had only been there for a minute or two when the music came to an abrupt stop. She sat up, knocking her glass off the side of the tub, and, as she reached down to pick it up, she thought she saw a shadow pass underneath the bathroom door. Unsettled now, she got out and wrapped herself in a towel, listening all the time for a noise out on the landing, but the only thing that broke the silence was the steady dripping of the cold tap. Cautiously, she opened the door and went through to the bedroom. The record was still spinning silently on its deck, but the needle had been pulled roughly to one side.

And then the lights went out. Stifling a growing sense of panic, Mary pulled some clothes on, caring little what they were, and fumbled her way out onto the landing. The house was deathly quiet, but the street lamp immediately outside the front door was strong enough to confirm that she was no longer on her own. A figure stood motionless on the staircase, looking up at her, and then, as she watched, he began to climb the stairs. She ran into her bedroom and shut the door, but he was too quick for her – too quick and far too strong. She felt his weight against the wood while she was still fumbling with the lock, and he pushed the door open with such force that she was sent flying back across the room. In a single, frantic movement, he dragged her up onto the bed and pulled the curtains across the window; the room was pitch black now, and as the light from the street lamp vanished completely, it seemed to Mary that the world had turned its back on her. She felt cold metal against her throat, and, as her eyes adjusted to the darkness, she saw that the man was wearing something dark across his face which moved in and out as he breathed. He clamped his hand over her mouth, squeezing her jaw to tell her to be quiet, and she nodded her promise, feeling the sharp edge of the knife catch at her skin.

He stank of beer and cigarette smoke, and the warmth of his breath on her face made her gag. Her body was rigid with fear, every nerve and muscle straining against the inevitability of what he was about to do to her, and she wished now that she hadn't read the stories in the newspaper. The details forced themselves into her mind, mapping out the horror of the next few minutes with a merciless clarity, and she felt the knife sliding down her chest, cutting through her blouse and underwear, then returning to circle her breasts. He lifted his mask a little and she felt his mouth all over her, sucking at her nipple, biting her skin until she could bear it no longer. As he moved his hand away from her mouth to undo his trousers, she wrenched her head to one side and screamed. It was the stupidest thing she could have done. His fist made contact with her jaw and her head snapped back, then he was on top of her again, forcing her legs apart, calling her a bitch for resisting. 'I'm sorry,' she said, feeling the blood drying round her mouth, pulling the skin taut. 'I'm sorry, I'm sorry, I'm sorry.' She had no idea who she was apologising to, but she said it again and again, pouring words into his silence until her body offered up the only atonement that mattered.

When it was over, he stroked her hair and she lay there in the darkness with tears running mutely down her face, trying not to flinch at his touch in case it angered him again. Out of nowhere he whispered her name, and Mary froze, horrified to think that he might know her. Had she treated him in hospital, she wondered – washed him and fed him and nursed him back to health? Or had they simply passed the time of day in a club or a cafe or the queue for the pictures? Had she been too friendly, encouraging him to think that she wanted this? Or too aloof, provoking him to teach her a lesson? For some reason, this casual assumption of intimacy – harmless in comparison with the violence that preceded it – seemed to Mary the greatest outrage of all, and her fear was suddenly replaced by a fury she had never known before. She launched herself at her assailant, screaming obscenities that sounded alien in her mouth, longing to hurt him as he had hurt her. At first he was taken by surprise, but he recovered quickly and she felt the knife cut deep into her arm, a weapon now and not a threat. Still she struggled, daring him to wound her again and caring little if she lived or died, but his anger seemed to diminish as hers grew, and the cold, methodical strength that replaced it was too much for her. Defeated, she lay shivering and half-naked on the bed, feeling the blood seep from her arm, listening while he rummaged through her dressing table and wardrobe. At last, he answered her prayers and left her to her nightmares, pausing only to throw a blanket over her shame on his way to the door.

11

The night air in Cambridge was chilly and damp as the mist drifted up from the river, but it was marginally less objectionable than the smell of paint which lingered long after the decorators had finished for the day. Josephine opened the sash a little wider and leant on the window sill, breathing in the cold, sharp freshness. The house was near the town end of the passage and she watched the comings and goings of a boisterous Friday night, content to soak up the atmosphere and sense of expectation without actually being part of it. Next door, someone had turned the gramophone up to full volume, and the cheerful back and forth of Benny Goodman and his band was just the sort of unexacting company she was looking for.

The telephone rang in the hallway and she went downstairs to answer it, hoping by some miracle that it might be Marta, even though she would still be somewhere in the middle of the Atlantic ocean. 'Archie – what a lovely surprise!' she said, praying that the false note she heard in her own voice was simply her imagination. 'How are you?'

'Fine, just rushed off my feet. There's no let-up in the case I'm working on, and it's moving so fast that I'm always a couple of steps behind.'

'That sounds interesting.'

'It would be if there weren't quite so much at stake, and time is definitely not on my side.'

His tone was animated, in spite of his obvious frustration, and she pictured him sitting at his desk, oblivious to everything but the paperwork in front of him. 'Scotland Yard sounds lively tonight,' she said, listening to the clamour of voices in the background. 'What on earth's going on?'

'Actually, I'm just round the corner from you,' he said, and for a moment she thought she had misheard. 'The case has a Cambridge connection. Bill and I are checking out a couple of the university clubs but I've drawn a blank with mine. I'm meeting him at the local police station in less than an hour, so I haven't got long, but I thought we could have a quick drink if you're free? I'm in All Saints Passage, near St John's, so I can be with you in a couple of minutes.' She hesitated, caught off-guard. 'Josephine? If you're busy, we can do it another time . . .'

'No, Archie, of course I'm not busy. I'd love to see you, as long as you don't mind wet paint. The house is in a bit of a state.'

'Wet paint's fine. And I'll bring a bottle – the Hawks' Club has a very fine cellar.'

He rang off, leaving Josephine to compose herself. She had not expected to see Archie so soon, and the thought of sitting down over a glass of wine, talking about trivial things while the image of Phyllis with his portrait hovered at her shoulder almost made her wish that she had ignored the telephone altogether – but she couldn't avoid him for ever, especially if his work was now bringing him to Cambridge, and an hour wasn't long to fill. As long as Bridget didn't choose this evening to call, all should be well.

He was better than his word, arriving on her doorstep in the time it took her to fetch the corkscrew and do her hair. 'I see what you mean about the paint,' he said, giving her a hug. 'Marta obviously timed her trip to perfection. It's looking lovely, though, and what a nice place to be.'

'Yes, I'm afraid I've found it very easy to make myself at home.' She stopped him from hanging his coat on the peg. 'Come upstairs – they haven't started on the first floor yet, so it's easier to breathe.' She opened the wine and poured two glasses, then sat down next to him on the sofa. 'It *is* nice to see you,' she said, meaning it, in spite of the difficulties. 'Marta said she'd bumped into you in Hampstead. It's very obliging of your work to keep us in touch.'

'I was here the other day, too, and I was hoping to call on you then, but I ran out of time.'

'Here in Cambridge?'

'Yes, on Tuesday. It's strange to be back after so long – strangely familiar, I suppose.'

There was an awkward silence while Josephine thought of Archie being close by while she was doing some detective work of her own, poking into a life of which he still had no knowledge. 'What a shame,' she said at last. 'It would have been nice to have longer to talk.'

'Next time, I promise. Listen – I know this might be a bit of a cheek, but I wondered if you'd do me a favour?'

'Of course, if I can,' she said, then paused, distracted by a noise from outside. 'Just a minute.' She went to the window, but everything in the passage seemed quiet and peaceful. Even Benny Goodman had obviously outstayed his welcome.

'Is everything all right?' Archie asked.

'Yes, it's fine. Sorry to interrupt you, but I think the entire female population of Cambridge is a bit jittery at the moment. There's been a series of attacks on women, and everybody's talking about it.'

'So I gather. I called in at the station the other day while I was here, and they seemed stretched to their limits.'

'Do they really have no idea at all who it might be?'

Archie hesitated – caught, Josephine guessed, between honesty, professional loyalty and a desire to reassure her. 'They're following up all the leads they have,' he said eventually, falling short of at least one of his objectives, 'and they're doing as much as anyone could without more information to go on.'

'In the meantime, I'll just keep the wardrobe doors open.'

'Why?'

'That was the handy advice from the *Cambridge Daily News* yesterday. We're all supposed to leave our wardrobe and cupboard doors open when we go out – then when we come back, if anything's changed, we know there's a rapist hiding among the coat hangers.'

Archie laughed. 'It makes sense, I suppose, although I would have thought reliable locks on all the windows and doors would be a better place to start. That way, he might not get to the wardrobe.'

'Oh, the shops have all sold out of locks. Locks *and* torches, because we're advised to keep one of those by the bed. I wasn't frightened until I read all of that.'

'Being frightened isn't necessarily a bad thing,' Archie cautioned. 'It means you'll take better care of yourself. I'm not very happy about your being here alone at the moment. Couldn't you come down to London for a bit while Marta's away? Or go and stay at the cottage?'

'No, not really. I've rather committed myself to the decorators, and actually I love being here. It's a beautiful town. I've even started to do some work.'

'What on?'

'A new play. I'll tell you more when it's further along.'

'All right, as long as you're happy. But promise me you'll take care, Josephine. I never thought I'd say this, but I'm glad Bridget's in Devon. I know for a fact she'll be blasé about the whole thing, and the more I tell her to be cautious, the more risks she'll take.'

Little did he know there was someone else in Cambridge he should be worrying about, Josephine thought, someone whose age made her a much more likely target. 'So what can I do for you?' she asked, hoping that the favour in question wouldn't involve taking welcome home flowers round to Bridget.

'It's to do with this case.'

Josephine was surprised. There had been several occasions in the past when Archie had talked through his work with her, usually because she knew the people involved, and once or twice she had infuriated him by interfering in things that didn't concern her – but it was rare for him to ask for help out of the blue. 'You're talking about the murder in Hampstead?' she clarified.

'Yes, although things have moved on since then. There's been a second murder, in Felixstowe this time, and another suspicious death in Essex.'

'All linked? No wonder you're busy.'

'Quite. I can't go into much detail, but all the victims were at King's College at the same time. I'd like to find out more about Cambridge back then, and I wondered if you had time to read through some old newspapers?'

'Of course I do,' she said, genuinely intrigued. 'What am I looking for?'

'I have absolutely no idea,' Archie said helpfully, 'and the whole thing might be a pointless exercise, but the only thing we've found that's common to all the victims is that they were in King's Choir just before the war. That's the period you need to focus on, starting with the autumn of 1913. Anything relating to the college or to the choir, obviously, and anything to do with M. R. James.'

'As in ghost stories?'

'Yes. He was Provost of King's at the time, and he would have known the people involved. Are you a fan?'

'No, not really. I've read some of them and they're very good, but I went off ghost stories when I acquired a ghost of my own.' The year before, Josephine had inherited a cottage in Suffolk from her godmother, only to discover that it held more than happy memories and family secrets. 'When your suitcase throws itself off the bed at regular intervals, the figments of other people's imagination tend to lose their power, no matter how well written they are. But why M. R. James in particular? Surely a lot of other people in Cambridge would have known these men as well.'

'I have my reasons . . .' Archie began enigmatically.

'. . . but you can't tell me what they are. All right, I know the routine. Any other obscure references you'd like me to report back on?'

'No, but I will give you a few names to look out for. Have you got a pen and paper?'

She found both and watched while Archie jotted down a list. 'There are four names there,' she observed. 'I thought you said *three* victims.'

'I did. Robert Moorcroft is very much alive at the moment, more's the pity.' Josephine stared at him, surprised by the vehemence of his words as much as the sentiment itself. 'Sorry, but I've just been with his wife and he obviously treats her abominably. God knows why she puts up with it. For the children, I suppose, although I can't help thinking that sometimes it's better to have one happy parent than two who are constantly making each other miserable.'

'That depends on the parent, I suppose.'

'Yes, I suppose it does. And everything I've just said is confidential, obviously.'

'Obviously.'

He smiled and drained his glass. 'Thanks, Josephine. I'd ask for help from the Cambridgeshire force, but the Detective Superintendent has made it very clear that I'm welcome to a desk and a cup of coffee any time I like, but extra manpower at the moment is out of the question. As it is, I've got to beg him to make an exception by keeping an eye on Moorcroft's house. And we're up against it here. I don't think this killer's going to stop at three. Then there are the preparations for Armistice Day. I'm on duty at the Cenotaph this year and I can't believe how quickly—'

'It's all right, Archie,' Josephine said, laughing at the panic in his voice. 'I don't mind at all. In fact, I'm looking forward to it. Just tell me where to send the bill. Am I seconded to Cambridgeshire or to Scotland Yard?'

'Send it to me and I'll settle it personally.' She offered him a refill but he refused. 'Better not – I can't keep Bill waiting and we need to get on. But I'm bound to be back in Cambridge soon and I'll make sure we have time to talk then. Perhaps we could have dinner and go to the theatre or something? You choose.' Anything but *Night Must Fall*, Josephine thought. She had allowed herself to be distracted by the intrigue of their conversation, but Bridget's portrait of Archie came suddenly into her mind again, unbidden and unwelcome, and for a moment she couldn't speak. 'Josephine? Are you sure you're all right? You seem very preoccupied. Is something bothering you?'

She shook her head. 'I'm fine, Archie, honestly. Just missing Marta. It's strange here without her, especially at night.' They talked for a few more minutes, about the house and about Cambridge, but she noticed the distracted note in his voice which always signalled that work was vying for his attention. 'I'd better let you get off,' she said. 'Let me know when you think you might be back here again, and in the meantime I'll see what I can find out for you. And give my love to Bill.'

'I will.' She went to the door and watched him walk away down the passage, feeling suddenly lonely. Their brief conversation had only emphasised how important Archie's friendship was in her life. It was selfish of her, bearing in mind how much else was at stake, but she resented Bridget more than ever for bringing this awkwardness between them; the trust they had always shared might only be the minor casualty of an impossible situation, but she felt its loss keenly. It had taken them years to find this degree of ease in each other's company, untroubled by intense emotions and the different degrees of love that Marta had so rightly referred to; now, she knew she couldn't even sit across a dinner table from him without his knowing instinctively that something was wrong. And when he found out that she had carried this secret, albeit briefly and through no choice of her own, she didn't know if they would ever be able to find a way back.

She went upstairs and put the wireless on, then sat down at Marta's typewriter with another glass of wine. Work had always been something she could retreat to as a distraction from other dilemmas, and she found that her concentration improved in direct proportion to how bad the other problems were; in less than an hour she had written two scenes. She collected the sheets of paper together and began to read back through her work, but was soon interrupted by the sound of the doorbell. On cue the clock in the hallway struck eleven, as if sharing her surprise that anyone might call on her at this time of night: Archie would be on his way back to London by now, and she had no other friends in the town. She hesitated, remembering Archie's words of caution, but the ringing of the bell was immediately followed by a furious banging on the door and she went to the window to look. Perhaps it was Bridget, back early from Devon and complying with her request to the letter. If so, Josephine was ready for her.

The face that looked up at her was streaked with blood and tears, and at first she didn't recognise it. Shocked and horrified, Josephine hurried downstairs and threw open the door with no thought other than to get the girl inside. She helped her up the steps and into the hallway, noticing that her feet were bare and her clothes – an incongruous combination of night- and daywear – had obviously been pulled on in a hurry. Blood was seeping through the sleeve of her cardigan and there were cuts and bruises on her face which testified to a vicious attack. In the uncompromising starkness of the overhead lighting, Josephine recognised the nurse from next door. Instinctively, driven partly by shock and partly by a vicarious rage on her behalf, she turned to go out into the passage and look for whoever was responsible, but the nurse clung to her arm with such fierce desperation that she simply slammed the front door and bolted it.

She led her slowly through to the sitting room and sat her

down, grateful now for the dustsheet which had been intended to protect Marta's sofa from paint rather than blood, then grabbed a clean towel to stem the flow of bleeding as best she could. 'Look at me,' she said gently, her hand against the girl's cheek. It was a strong face, she noticed, handsome rather than pretty, with high cheekbones and a firm mouth; the eyes that turned to her now were the deepest of browns, and Josephine imagined that even in happier circumstances they would give her expression a natural earnestness. 'You're safe now,' she promised, keeping her voice low and reassuring. 'No one can hurt you here. What's your name?'

'Mary,' the girl said, moistening dry, swollen lips with her tongue and wincing at the alien taste of blood. 'Mary Ennis.'

'All right, Mary. I'm Josephine. You live next door, don't you?'

Mary nodded. 'He must have got in while I was fetching my lipstick. The downstairs windows were all locked and I shouldn't have left the door open, but I was only out there for a second or two.'

Her need to justify herself incensed Josephine. 'This isn't your fault,' she said sympathetically, saving her anger for the faceless man who had earned it. 'Whoever did this to you is entirely to blame and you certainly don't need to make excuses for him. All right?' Mary nodded. 'Good. Now let me have a look at your arm. Did he cut you anywhere else?'

'I don't think so. It was all such a blur. I didn't know what to do.' Gently, Josephine peeled the cardigan away from the girl's injured arm; there were several knife marks above the elbow and on her chest and shoulder, but only one of the wounds looked particularly deep. 'All right, hold this towel over the cut and keep the pressure on it. I'm going upstairs to look for some bandages, but first I'm going to call an ambulance and let the police know what's happened.'

Mary looked at her, panic-stricken. 'No, please don't do that,' she begged. 'I can't go to hospital. They all know me there and they mustn't find out what's happened. I don't want *anyone* to know.'

Josephine sat down again and took her hand. 'Somebody's got to look at these injuries and treat them properly – you know that as well as I do, and I'm sure they'll be discreet. You're a nurse, Mary – you wouldn't advise any other girl to ignore what's happened, would you?'

'No, but I can't tell them anything and they'll think I'm so stupid. All those things he did to me, and yet I didn't even see his face. How can I help anyone?'

'That doesn't matter at the moment. The important thing is that you're taken care of by people who know what they're doing. Stay here – I won't be long.'

She dialled 999 and gave the address and a brief account of what had happened to the anonymous voice at the end of the line. Once an ambulance was on its way, she washed her hands and found a battered old first aid tin whose contents had never seen the light of day. 'Lie back a little,' she said, 'and keep your arm up.' She gave the girl a wry glance. 'It should be *you* giving *me* the instructions, I suppose. I used to wear a uniform like yours but that was a long time ago now, so you'll have to bear with me.'

Mary tried to respond, but the cuts to her lip made it too painful and the result was an odd half-grimace. Josephine swapped the towel for a sterile pad from the tin, then wrapped a bandage firmly round the arm to keep the pad in place. 'That's not too tight?' Mary shook her head. There was still blood soaking through the pad and bandage, so she repeated the process with more dressings, maintaining the pressure on Mary's arm until at last the bleeding stopped. 'There – that should do until they get you to hospital.'

Her face clouded again, but she didn't offer any further objections to going. Josephine stood up to fetch her a drink, but was interrupted by a loud banging at the door. Mary jumped and sat up, the fear instantly back in her eyes, and Josephine tried to reassure her. 'It's all right, it'll just be the ambulance.' She looked out of the window to make sure, and saw a police constable and another man in plain clothes whom she took to be a detective. 'Actually, it's the police. Don't worry – I'll stay with you while you talk to them.'

She opened the door and the detective introduced himself. 'Miss Tey? I'm Detective Inspector Webster. You called to report an assault?'

'That's right – on the girl next door,' Josephine said, conscious of the irony in such an innocent phrase. 'Her name is Mary Ennis.'

Webster glanced at the adjoining house and Josephine noticed that the front door was still wide open. 'And she's with you now?'

'Yes. She came for help after he'd gone.'

The uniformed man spoke for the first time. 'Is she badly hurt, miss, or was it just an assault?'

Josephine looked at him in disbelief and was about to speak her mind, but the detective did it for her. 'Don't be so bloody stupid, Patterson,' he said, his voice low with suppressed anger. '*Just* an assault? Do you honestly think it's the knife scars that are going to stay with this girl, or with any of the others? Get next door and out of my sight and make sure the house is secured. And if I ever hear you make another comment like that, you'll have an assault of your own to worry about.' The constable did as he was told, although he didn't seem particularly chastened by the rebuke, and Webster turned back to Josephine. 'I'm sorry about that. It's no excuse, but the boys just aren't used to dealing with something like this. I think what Constable Patterson meant to ask was how badly is Miss Ennis hurt?'

'She's taken one bad cut to the arm, but most of the knife wounds are minor.'

'Good.' He nodded towards the end of passage. 'The ambulance will be here any minute and I don't want to get in their way, but perhaps I could have a quick word with Miss Ennis if she's up to it?'

'Of course.'

She stood aside to let him into the hallway, then showed him to the sitting room, impressed by how sensitively he behaved. 'Miss

Ennis, I'm DI Tom Webster,' he said, removing his hat and sitting down in the chair furthest from the sofa so as not to intimidate her. 'I understand that it will be difficult for you to talk about what happened tonight, but it would be a great help if you could give me a very brief account before we get you safely to hospital. Is that all right?'

'Yes, but I don't think I can help you. I don't even know what he looked like.'

'Let's start with how he got in. Do you have any idea about that?'

'It was so stupid of me,' Mary said, and Josephine sensed that she was close to tears again. 'I was getting ready to go out and I didn't have my lipstick. I guessed that it must have fallen out of my bag while I was cycling home from the hospital, so I went out to look in the basket and I left the door open. That *must* be how he got in, because I'd locked all my windows like they've been telling us to. It was on the spur of the moment and I didn't think anything of it. I was only going to be a minute or two, after all.'

'Did you see anyone hanging around the passage while you were outside?'

'No. Just a group of undergraduates on their way into town. I only had my dressing gown on and I didn't want them to see me so I hurried back inside.'

'And you're sure you shut the door properly?'

'Yes. I bolted it behind me.'

'Then what happened?'

'I ran a bath and got into it. That's when I first knew something was wrong.' Josephine listened, appalled to think that Mary's attacker must have been in the house for some time while she was innocently going about her business. 'The music stopped suddenly, as if someone had turned the record off, and I thought I saw someone on the landing. Just a shadow, really, underneath the door. Then the lights went out.'

'And you were alone in the house, apart from this man?'

'That's right. The rooms upstairs are empty at the moment, and Mrs Walsh – that's my landlady – is away with her daughter until next weekend. I should let her know what's happened, I suppose, but I've no idea how to get in touch with her.'

'All in good time, Miss Ennis. What did you do when you suspected there was an intruder in the house?'

'Put some clothes on and went out onto the landing. That's when I knew I wasn't imagining things. There was a man on the stairs – I could just see his outline in the light from the street lamp outside. He was standing still, looking up at me. I ran back into my room, but he was too quick and I wasn't strong enough to shut the door on him.'

'And that's when he forced himself on you?'

Mary nodded. 'He hit me first, then he held me down on the bed until he'd finished.'

'Did you get any sense of his build?'

'He wasn't particularly tall – about your height, I suppose – but he was strong and well built.'

'What about his voice? Did he say anything?'

'Not much. He swore at me, and he used my name. Just once, but that was what made me struggle with him. It was the worst thing, really – the thought that he might have known me, that he wasn't just some faceless person who'd picked me at random.'

The information obviously interested Webster, but he was considerate enough to confine his questioning to the basic facts rather than tire his witness with endless speculation. 'Is that when he used the knife? When you fought back?'

'Yes. He made it clear it was a stupid thing to have done. After that, I just lay there, praying that he'd leave.'

'Did he go out by the front door?'

'He must have done, because it was unbolted. After he left my room, I heard him moving about downstairs for a while, then it all went quiet. The only other thing I noticed was the rattle of an old bicycle underneath the window, but I suppose that could have been anyone going past. I waited until I thought it was safe – it felt like ages, but I don't know if it was – then I pulled some clothes on and came here. I didn't stop to see if any of the back windows had been opened.'

'And did you see or hear anything during the evening, Miss Tey?'

Josephine hesitated. 'I noticed that the music had stopped,' she said. 'I had the windows open to ease the smell of paint, so I could hear the gramophone earlier. And at one point I thought I heard someone cry out. I went to the window to check, but everything seemed fine. I'm sorry,' she added, turning to Mary and thinking of how different things might have been if she had taken more notice while Archie was still with her. 'I should have been more thorough, but I thought it was students or someone from the inn round the corner. There's often a lot of noise there at night.'

The doorbell rang again and the small sitting room was soon filled with ambulance men and the paraphernalia of an emergency, but Josephine was pleased for Mary's sake that neither of them seemed to know her from the hospital. They began to examine her, and Webster stood to leave them to it. 'Looks like you're in safe hands, Miss Ennis. Thank you for what you've told me. We'll need a full statement from you and I can come to the hospital to take it, or if you'd find it easier to speak to a female officer, I can send our WPC to do it on my behalf.'

He had obviously won Mary's confidence because she didn't need time to think about it. 'No, there's no need to send anyone else. I'll talk to you.'

'All right. I'll come in the morning when you've had some sleep.' It was the first naive thing that he had said, Josephine thought; she doubted very much that Mary Ennis would be able to sleep properly for some time. 'In the meantime, we'll look at your flat and see if we can learn anything more about this man from that. Where are your keys?'

'In my bag. I always keep them there so I can't lock myself out. It's by the dressing table.'

'Fine. I'll make sure everything's locked up when we've finished, and I'll leave the keys with Miss Tey if that's all right?'

Josephine nodded and showed the detective to the front door.

'I made him angry,' Mary said as he was on his way out. 'I shouldn't have done that.'

Webster stopped and turned back to her. 'He was already angry when he got to you,' he said firmly. 'That's why he was there. Don't ever think that you've encouraged him, or that you could have done anything to *dis*courage him. This man is beyond any sort of logic or reason, but we *will* catch him – I promise you that. I'm only sorry that you had to get hurt before we managed it.'

'Forgive me if this sounds rude,' Josephine said quietly in the hallway, 'but I wasn't expecting you to show her that much understanding. From what I've read in the papers, your colleague's attitude is rather more typical.'

'Perhaps I've just seen it more often than they have,' Webster said earnestly. 'Some things stay with you, and you have to do what you can.'

It was the sort of response that Archie might have given, determined and world-weary at the same time, and she watched him go next door. When she returned to the sitting room, the ambulance men were packing up, ready to leave. 'Nice job with the dressings,' one of them said, smiling at Josephine. 'Now – can you walk, miss, or would you like a wheelchair?'

'I can walk,' Mary said. 'I don't want a fuss.' She stood up, as if to prove a point, and Josephine noticed the blood on the back of her skirt and on the sofa where she had been sitting. It was the smallest of marks, trivial in comparison with the staining from the wound on her arm, and yet it was far more disturbing, far more indicative of the real outrage which she had endured. Mary stared down at the dustsheet, and the evidence there seemed to break her. 'I'm sorry,' she said, turning to Josephine. 'I'm so sorry, but he hurt me and I couldn't stop him.'

No matter how many questions she was asked, no one would ever get closer to the truth than that simple testimony. Mary began to cry, and Josephine held her close while the ambulance men hovered awkwardly by the door. 'Is there anyone you'd like me to contact?' she asked gently. 'Your parents? A friend?'

'No, I don't want my parents to see me like this, and anyway, they live away. And most of my friends are either out dancing or at the hospital already.'

'Then shall I come with you?'

The girl looked at her gratefully. 'Would you?'

'Of course. Just let me fetch you a coat and some shoes.'

With the help of an ambulance man, Josephine led Mary outside and down the short walk to the end of the passage. A small crowd of people had gathered around the ambulance on Bridge Street, and Josephine wondered bitterly where all the casual spectators – herself included – had been when it mattered, when they could have done something to help. How instinctively the subtle craft of shame was learned, she thought, watching Mary hide her face until the ambulance doors were firmly shut behind her.

The man riding in the back with them talked constantly throughout the short journey to Addenbrooke's. 'What a terrible business,' he said, shaking his head. 'It's hard to know what to do to help. A colleague of mine has started organising rides home for the girls in the ambulances when we're not too busy – those that don't live in the nurses' hostel, obviously. He sees them to the door and has a quick look round inside to check all the windows and make sure they're safe.'

'That's thoughtful,' Josephine said, resisting the temptation to point out that it hadn't helped Mary Ennis. She looked at the ambulance man and realised that she, too, was falling into the trap of paranoia and suspicion which seemed to be growing in the town. How easy it would be for his colleague to use such an apparently selfless scheme to identify houses where women were regularly on their own and vulnerable, to find the windows with loose catches and weak locks, and then to return another time, masked and anonymous. Everyone was fair game to her imagination, it seemed: one of the decorators was a short, well-built young man, and she had caught herself wondering if any of the victims lived in houses which had recently been painted.

Addenbrooke's Hospital was an extravagant building on Trumpington Street, a Victorian outpouring of buttresses, coloured bricks and imposing colonnades. The ambulance driver pulled up by the front entrance and his colleague leapt out to find Mary a wheelchair. She hesitated when she saw it, instinctively resenting the invalid status it conferred, but the exhaustion of her ordeal was beginning to take its toll and she allowed herself to be pushed passively along corridors which, on a normal day, she would have walked with a spring in her step. As they reached the wards, Josephine noticed that more and more of the nurses on duty were beginning to recognise their new patient; some came forward to speak to her or squeeze her hand in solidarity, others huddled in small groups and talked quietly among themselves, but they had in common an expression that hovered somewhere between pity and horror, an expression which came partly from the obvious distress of someone they cared about and partly from the realisation that any one of them could be standing in her shoes.

Whatever Josephine thought of the building's facade, there was no doubt that its architects had created an interior of real distinction. The wards were long, high-ceilinged rooms, supported by enormous pillars and blessed with tall windows which – in the daytime – would flood the polished floors with sunshine. Now, the lighting was muted, the wards peaceful, and nurses moved silently between the beds, tucking in sheets and administering the final medication of the day.

Josephine waited with Mary while an empty examination room was found, and then she was whisked away. 'Is this what we all fear it is?' A matron stood at her shoulder, looking on anxiously. 'We teach our girls never to jump to conclusions in this job, but I'm afraid we're all guilty of it now.'

'And you're right to in this case, but the fewer people who know the better.' She smiled at her own naivety. 'I suppose that's a ridiculous thing to say, but it's one of the things that's upsetting her the most, I think – the idea that people will treat her differently once they find out what's happened.'

'You're a friend of Nurse Ennis?'

'No, just a neighbour. We'd never met until tonight. She came to me for help after it happened.'

'And did he . . .?' The matron tailed off, unable to finish the sentence, and Josephine nodded. 'What a terrible thing to happen to someone so bright. Ennis is one of the most talented nurses we have – probably one of the most talented we've *ever* had. It all comes so naturally to her. She has a real empathy with people from all walks of life, and you can't teach that.' She seemed suddenly embarrassed. 'I'm sorry – of course it's a terrible thing to happen to *any* girl, but . . .'

'You don't have to apologise. I know exactly what you mean.'

'It's just that I fear for her. In my experience, the best nurses make the worst patients. She'll need time to come to terms with this, and I hope she'll allow herself the same understanding that she shows to everyone else.'

Josephine hoped so too. 'I'd better leave you to get on with your work,' she said. 'Would you tell Mary I'll come back to see her at visiting time tomorrow?'

12

Josephine woke late after a restless night. It was gone three when the taxi dropped her back from the hospital, and she had returned to the house with a mixture of sadness and trepidation, putting the lights on in every room and checking the locks on the windows before eventually trying to sleep. After breakfast, she took the keys that had been deposited through her letterbox and went next door. She knew that Mary lived upstairs, and the ground floor and basement were obviously the landlady's domain. The hall was fussily decorated with floral print wallpaper and a penchant for lace trim. There was a pile of post and paperwork gathered neatly on the console table by the door and Josephine glanced quickly through it to see if she could find a forwarding address or any other means of contacting Mrs Walsh to let her know what had happened, but she was obviously not the sort who expected emergencies in her absence. A single sheet of notepaper was propped against a vase, reminding Mary's landlady of all the arrangements that needed to be made before she went away, and Josephine was impressed to see that everything had been carefully ticked off – newspapers cancelled, milk order halved, Mary's rent collected. She often wrote herself a similar list before coming south, but rarely got round to completing half of it; Mrs Walsh obviously travelled less frequently than she did or was far more diligent by nature.

She went up to the first floor, unable to climb the stairs without seeing in her mind's eye the shadowy outline of the rapist and trying to imagine how terrified Mary must have been in that split-second realisation. The bath was still full, giving the room a faint scent of lily of the valley, and Josephine rolled back her sleeve and reached in to take the plug out, wincing at the coldness of the water. There was a sticky pool of ginger wine on the black-and-white linoleum and she did her best to wipe it away, then picked up the empty glass and discarded magazine and took Mary's dressing gown down from the back of the door. As far as possible, she was keen to remove anything that would serve as a reminder of that traumatic Friday night, and ordinary domestic details were just as likely to bring it all flooding back as any overt signs of violence.

Nothing could have prepared her for the shock of the bedroom. The note which the police had left with the keys made it clear that they had finished with the premises, and Josephine rashly assumed that some semblance of order would have been restored, but she couldn't have been more wrong. The room was a shambles, with every square foot of it testifying to the hatred and violence that had fuelled the attack. The mattress had been pushed halfway off the bed by the force of the struggle, and there were bloodstains on the sheets and blankets – bloodstains mixed with smears of something darker that looked like dirt or coal. On the dressing table, a couple of small ornaments had been broken and Mary's make-up was strewn everywhere, as if the intruder had wanted to smash anything that was pretty or feminine. And perhaps most unsettling of all, the clothes that he had cut from Mary's body lay in tatters on the floor, a stark reminder of how easily he could have killed her. 'Lucky' was a word that Josephine refused to use in relation to anyone who had suffered an ordeal like this, but it was surely only a matter of time before the violence escalated to yet another level. She thought back to what Inspector Webster had said the night before and realised how right he was: even now, in broad daylight and with the perpetrator long gone, the anger in the room was palpable.

Rather than restoring order, the police search of the room had actually made things worse and a thin film of dust now covered all the surfaces. She would have to come back and clean thoroughly, but in the meantime she tidied as best she could – stripping the bed, refolding clothes that had been pulled from drawers, and opening the windows to allow some much-needed air into the room. There was no saving the sheets and blankets, which she piled in a corner ready to get rid of, but at least the blood hadn't soaked through to the mattress and most of the other chaos was simply a matter of straightening and tidying. Mary's jewellery was still on the dressing table, she noticed; if robbery had ever been an incentive for these crimes, the urge to steal had been replaced by something far more violent. It took Josephine less than half an hour to restore the room to a semblance of normality, although she doubted that Mary would ever return to live here; in her position, she would want a fresh start, as far away from St Clement's Passage as possible. Last but not least, she lifted 'Tiger Rag' off the gramophone deck and put it back in its sleeve at the bottom of a pile of other records; it would be a long time before Mary could listen to the Benny Goodman Quartet without being instantly transported back to the worst night of her life.

She looked round again, wondering if the room could offer her a shortcut in getting to know her neighbour. The film posters on the walls suggested that at least they had a love of the cinema in common, but there was very little else lying around that was frivolous. Most of the books on the shelves were medical textbooks, and Mary seemed to be as dedicated to her profession in her spare time as she was while on duty; even the magazine that Josephine had collected from the bathroom floor was the latest issue of a nursing journal. She walked over to the bedside table and looked at a small collection of photographs which showed Mary at various stages of her life: as a teenager with her mother and father; in uniform at her graduation; and – more recently – on holiday with a pleasant-faced young man, who could have been either boyfriend or brother; if it was the latter, he had none of the telltale family traits which so clearly bonded Mary with her parents.

There was a small suitcase on top of the wardrobe and she took it down to pack some clothes, choosing items that were both seasonal and as different as possible from the ones that Mary had been wearing the night before. She opened the wardrobe to look for some shoes, and stopped in horror when she saw the words scrawled in lurid pink lipstick on the mirror inside the door: 'Sleep Tight'. Feeling suddenly faint, Josephine sat down on the bed and stared at her own ashen-faced reflection in the glass. The message screamed out at her, mocking and contemptuous, and it was several minutes before she found the strength to stand up and wipe it off. Why on earth had the police left it there, she wondered? Of course they had more urgent things to do than clean and polish, but surely they must realise the impact of allowing any victim to come home to something so destructive?

She left the house as soon as there was no trace of the lipstick left and closed the door firmly behind her, pleased to lift her face to the sun. Birds were singing in the churchyard opposite, blissfully oblivious to all that concerned her, and she took comfort from the idea that some things could never be tainted, even on the threshold of evil. A familiar wheelbarrow stood just the other side of the railings, and she noticed that the gardener she had met in Little St Mary's Lane had moved on to work his magic at St Clement's. He returned her smile when he noticed her, but without any sign of recognition, then carried on with what he was doing. She watched him for a while, enjoying the sense of peace that always struck her in someone who loved the land, be it a town garden like this or the fields that surrounded her Suffolk cottage, but then she noticed how often he looked up from his work to stare at the houses nearby.

Unsettled, she opened her front door and went inside, but now that the idea had planted itself in her head she found it impossible to shake it off. How easy it would be for that gardener to get to know the habits of a street simply by going about his business, she thought. He could have watched Mary's house for days, getting used to her comings and goings, realising that some of the rooms were empty and watching her landlady leave with a suitcase. She remembered his hands from the other day and thought of the marks on Mary's sheets, then told herself again that she was being ridiculous: you didn't have to be a gardener to carry dirt around with you. But there was something else, too: according to the newspaper story she had read with Marta, the last attack had taken place in St Peter's Street; although Josephine didn't know where that was, it was reasonable to assume from the name that there was a church nearby. The last thing she wanted was to accuse an innocent man, but what if all the rapes so far had taken place in houses overlooking a churchyard? Surely that couldn't be a coincidence. She thought of Phyllis, living alone in Little St Mary's Lane while her mother was away, waving a friendly hello to the gardener as she headed off into town, and suddenly her fears for the girl were more intense than ever.

*

Addenbrooke's Hospital was a different place altogether by daylight. Josephine arrived amid the hustle and bustle of visiting time, and waited while two nurses stood by Mary's bed, taking her temperature and making sure she was comfortable. She watched their no-nonsense kindness as they worked, surprised by how intensely their cheerful camaraderie brought back memories of her own nursing days. By contrast, their patient seemed tired and withdrawn, and Josephine guessed that the night she had passed – the examinations and the endless questioning, followed by another visit from the police – had merely extended and compounded the ordeal of the evening before.

The nurses finished their checks and Mary did her best to smile when she saw her visitor. 'I've brought you some clean clothes,'

Josephine said, sitting down at her bedside. 'You won't want to put the others back on.'

'The police took them, thank God,' Mary said vehemently. 'I don't want to see them ever again. But thank you for thinking of that.'

Josephine nodded, wishing that all the other reminders of what had happened to Mary Ennis could be so easily destroyed. 'How are you?' she asked. 'If that isn't a stupid question.'

'Better now they've let me wash. I must have used up a week's supply of disinfectant, and I can still smell him. I don't think I'll ever feel clean again.'

'Did you remember anything else to tell the police?' Josephine asked quietly.

'Not really. He made me go into the timings in more detail, but I'm not sure it helped. I felt so sick going through it all again, and it took ages for him to write it all down. It was like reliving it all in slow motion, but he was very kind.' She paused, and looked sincerely at Josephine. 'And so were you. Thank you for everything you did last night. I don't know how I'd have coped if you hadn't been there.'

'Anyone would have done the same.' She poured a glass of water from the jug on the bedside table and handed it to Mary. 'Did the doctor say how long they intend to keep you here?'

'A couple of days, apparently.'

'What will you do then? You can't possibly go back to that house on your own.' Mary was quiet, and Josephine guessed that she was still too shocked to have thought about any practical arrangements. 'You'd be very welcome to stay with me until your landlady comes back, but I'd also understand if you never wanted to see St Clement's Passage again.'

'It's not that. I'd love to accept your offer, but my parents are coming to collect me and take me back to Yorkshire. They want me at home with them, at least for now.'

'How did they take it?'

'They were devastated, but no one shouted or cried. We're a restrained family. Stiff upper lip and all that.'

Josephine smiled, trying to imagine how difficult it must have been for Mary to break the news to her parents. 'Well, it's probably best if they take care of you for a while.'

'Oh, they'll do that all right. They were never happy about my leaving home – not coming all the way down here, anyway. Addenbrooke's was my passport to freedom, but I had to work hard to get it. My parents would much rather I'd stayed at home in a tiny market town and married the boy next door, even though I didn't love him and never would.'

'All parents want that, deep down. It doesn't have to be for ever, though.'

'No, it doesn't,' Mary said, although there was very little fight in her voice. 'Where did you do your nursing?' she asked, changing the subject.

Josephine sensed that Mary wanted to talk about anything other than herself, and she was happy to humour her. 'In Inverness,' she said, 'at a place called Hedgefield. It was a military convalescent home. I'd had some medical training at a college in Birmingham, and I was a VAD during the war.'

'Why did you give it up?'

'I didn't love it, and I think you have to love it to be good at it. Teaching suited me better – for a while, at least. What about you?' she asked. 'How long have you been qualified?'

'Two years. And you're right – you do have to love it. I can't imagine doing anything else, and Addenbrooke's is a wonderful place to learn. One day, I'd like to go abroad and really make a difference somewhere.'

'Then promise me that you won't let this stop you.'

Mary said nothing, staring at the glass and running her fingers repeatedly round its rim. 'I thought I was going to die, Josephine,' she admitted eventually. 'I felt that knife at my throat and I really thought he was going to kill me. For a moment last night, I was so happy just to be alive, but all that's gone now and I don't know how to feel. There's just this void, this emptiness, and I can't see a way out.'

Josephine took Mary's hand and spoke as convincingly as she could. 'I know this is easy for me to say, but his hold over you ended when he left the room, and it's up to you to decide how much he's hurt you. You fought and you survived, Mary. Now you've got to find the strength to keep doing it.'

13

A copy of Giles Shorter's post-mortem report was waiting on Penrose's desk when he got in to Scotland Yard on Saturday morning, together with statements from the vicar's housekeeper and the attending officers, and he offered up a prayer of thanks for the efficiency of the Essex police. He sat down and glanced through the relevant background information before reading the reports in more detail: Shorter had been vicar at the church of St John the Baptist in Finchingfield for nearly ten years, having arrived there in 1928 after a spell in London where he campaigned on behalf of destitute ex-servicemen; by the time he got to Essex, his more political work seemed to have been replaced by gentler pursuits – an interest in ecclesiastical architecture, on which he had published a number of learned papers, and a fondness for amateur dramatics. He was a bachelor, said to be popular throughout the parish, with a broad network of friends and colleagues whom he had entertained at the vicarage on a regular basis. According to an effusive obituary in the parish magazine, Shorter's tragic and premature death at the age of just forty-five had deprived his family of a much-loved son and brother, and the village of a wise and sympathetic friend.

By comparison, the findings of the post-mortem report were blunt to the point of brutal. As Fallowfield had said, the vicar died after a fall on the staircase at his home. The accident had taken place sometime during the night of the tenth of August and his body was discovered early the next morning when his housekeeper, Mrs Rogers, arrived to start work. Shorter's injuries were extensive, but entirely consistent with a fall down a flight of stairs: his vertebral column was fractured in several places, and the post-mortem revealed severe damage to the skull and internal organs, but the detail that caught Penrose's eye was an unexplained scratch on his face. While the pathologist refused to speculate on the cause of the fall, it had been noted that there was no evidence of intoxication in Shorter's bloodstream and that the stair rod on the second step from the top was dangerously loose; the most likely scenario suggested at the inquest was that the vicar had tripped on the loose carpet in the dark and fallen the full length of the first flight of stairs. The housekeeper, he was interested to note, insisted that the stair rod had been in place when she swept the stairs the day before, but it was hard to say if her protestations were truthful or inspired by guilt at having inadvertently brought about the accident through carelessness. Either way, there was no suggestion of foul play.

Penrose read through the post-mortem report again to make sure that he hadn't missed anything. Usually a pathologist's meticulous account helped him to recall a scene that he had witnessed with his own eyes, but the habit of creating mental pictures from the precise language of science served him well here, and, as he read, he saw in his mind's eye Shorter's bruised and broken body lying at the bottom of the stairs, clad only in a nightshirt; he saw his limbs twisted at an impossible angle and the livid red scratch on a deathly pale face; and when his imagination got the better of him and left the facts of the report behind, he saw another figure standing in the shadows on the staircase, a figure whose violent intent had taken him to Hampstead and to Felixstowe, but who so far remained stubbornly out of sight.

He picked up the telephone and asked the operator to put him through to the vicarage in Finchingfield. 'Mrs Rogers?' he asked, when a breathless voice finally answered.

'That's right. I'm sorry, but I've just come in from the garden and I'm a bit short of breath. Who is this?'

'My name is Detective Chief Inspector Penrose and I'm calling from Scotland Yard. I wondered if you had time to answer a couple of questions about the Reverend Shorter's death?'

'Yes, of course,' she said, but he could hear the wariness in her voice. 'I did think that was all over and done with, though. I never left that stair rod out of place, I swear I didn't.'

'It's not the stair rod I'm calling about. Actually, I was hoping you might be able to give me an insight into the days that led up to the Reverend Shorter's death. Did he have any unexpected visitors, or seem out of sorts in any way?'

'No, not that I can think of. He was worried about his parents – his father had been in poor health recently and his mother was taking on too much in caring for him – but that had been going on for months. As for visitors, Mr Giles had people popping in and out all the time and he loved that. He certainly wasn't out of sorts.'

'Did he ever have friends to stay? People he'd known from university, for example.'

'He'd collected people his whole life as far as I could tell,' she said, and Penrose was struck by the contrast between Giles Shorter's life and the solitary existence that Stephen Laxborough had apparently chosen. 'I dare say some of the regulars might have been from Cambridge, but I wouldn't really know about that. I just got their meals ready for them and made sure they were comfortable.'

Her tone was increasingly suspicious, and Penrose knew he would soon have to justify his questions. 'What about post? Did he receive any letters that upset him?'

'No, not that I'm aware of. I don't understand why you're asking all these questions now, though. I would have thought the time to be a bit more thorough was when it happened.'

'You don't think that the Reverend's death was thoroughly investigated?'

She hesitated before answering, and Penrose felt the drawbridge being firmly raised. 'I know I didn't leave that stair rod loose. That's all I'm saying.'

'All right, Mrs Rogers,' Penrose said, conceding defeat. 'Thank you for your time, and if you have any more thoughts on the Reverend Shorter's death, or the enquiry into it, please don't hesitate to contact Scotland Yard. I give you my word that any comments you make will be taken seriously. I'll take care of it myself.' There was a silence at the other end of the line. 'Mrs Rogers? Will you do that for me?'

'Take care – that *was* strange, now I come to think about it. I'd completely forgotten, but what you just said reminded me.'

'Reminded you of what?'

'A couple of weeks before he died, Mr Giles *did* receive something in the post that he couldn't make head or tail of. I suppose you'd call it a note, but all it said was "take care". There was no signature, and Mr Giles hadn't got a clue who'd sent it or what it meant.'

'Was there a photograph with it?' Penrose asked, suddenly excited. 'A photograph of a large house, perhaps?'

'No, nothing else. Just a single piece of paper with the words handwritten on it.'

'I don't suppose you've still got it?'

'No. I was in the room when Mr Giles tore it up, envelope and all. But there was a book . . .'

She tailed off, obviously trying to remember something, and Penrose waited impatiently. 'A book with the letter?' he prompted eventually.

'No, not with the letter. It was lying next to him when I found him that morning. I wondered at the time if that was why he'd come down in the first place, to go to the library. It seemed an odd thing to do in the middle of the night but he sometimes had trouble sleeping. Anyway, the book was open as if it had fallen out of his hand, and I'm sure there was a photograph of a house on that page. I didn't take much notice of it at the time, though.'

'Was the book definitely from his own collection?'

'Oh yes, on architecture – he had a lot of those. I put it back in its place on the shelf after they took him away.'

'Is it still there?'

'I suppose so. The new vicar hasn't touched the library yet, as far as I know.'

'Then perhaps you'd do something for me, Mrs Rogers? Would you look through the book and see if you can find the page again? Once you've found the house you remember, perhaps you'd be kind enough to let me know what it's called. I'll leave you my telephone number.'

There was a long silence at the other end of the line and he thought she was going to refuse, but when she spoke again it was with a mixture of sadness and relief. 'I know something's going on and you won't tell me what it is, but I have to ask – does this mean it really *wasn't* my fault? I know in my heart that I didn't leave that stair rod out of place, but everyone seemed so sure about what happened and they've had me doubting my own mind. I could never forgive myself if Mr Giles died because of me.'

'I don't believe he did,' Penrose said firmly, sorry that she had had to nurse this corrosive sense of doubt for so long, 'and I hope to be able to prove that very soon.'

He gave her the number and replaced the receiver, but the telephone rang again almost immediately and he recognised the long-suffering voice of his superintendent's secretary. 'Are you free to come upstairs for a moment?' she asked in the apologetic tone of a prison warder asking the condemned man to step forward. 'He'd like to see you right away.'

'Is there any chance you could have trouble finding me?'

'Not this time, Archie – sorry. I'm happy to help when I can, but he's really on the warpath today and I've always believed martyrdom to be a very stupid quality. I only popped in to catch up on some paperwork, so if it's your neck or mine there's no competition.'

'All right, I'm on my way.' He risked another few minutes to consult the collected edition of M. R. James's ghost stories that had become his constant companion, and turned to the tale he had identified the night before as being potentially relevant to Giles Shorter's death. 'The Stalls of Barchester Cathedral' was unusual in James's work in that the supernatural elements were really just the backdrop to a good old-fashioned tale of murder and revenge, and he scanned the pages quickly to find what he was looking for. As he climbed the stairs to his superior's office, he had a smile on his face for the first time that day.

Percy Savage's door stood open, which Penrose knew from experience to be an ominous sign. 'I've had two complaints about you already this morning,' Savage said without looking up, 'and it's not even twelve o'clock yet. What the hell are you playing at?'

'*Two* complaints, sir?' Penrose said, admitting by implication that he had half-expected one. 'Might I ask from whom?'

'Simon Westbury's widow, for a start. She telephoned first thing to ask – quite reasonably in my opinion – why the person in charge of investigating her husband's death hadn't arrested the main suspect yet.'

'And who does she think the main suspect is?' Penrose asked, although he knew full well what the answer would be.

'Albert Goulding, of course. He's been making inflammatory statements to the press about the justice of Westbury's murder.'

'Already? How did he know about it?'

'*That* is precisely Mrs Westbury's point. You wanted this case from Suffolk, Penrose, and now you're letting the grass grow under your feet on it. You need to get a grip.'

'I still don't think Simon Westbury's death has got anything to do with Albert Goulding – not unless he's also killed two other men with whom he had absolutely no connection whatsoever. As I outlined in my report, sir, both Westbury's murder and Stephen Laxborough's make very clear references to—'

'Yes, yes – we'll come to all that in a minute, but let's get the complaints out of the way before you take us down that road. I know you, Penrose – you can make even the most fanciful scenarios sound plausible if I give you half a chance.'

'Thank you, sir.'

The superintendent glared at him. 'That wasn't a compliment. Now – Robert Moorcroft says you've been harassing his wife.'

'He should know all about that,' Penrose muttered.

'What?'

'There's no question of harassment, sir. Sergeant Fallowfield and I went to Angerhale Priory last night to talk to Mr Moorcroft because a witness told us that he'd had lunch with Simon Westbury in Felixstowe on the day of Westbury's death. I don't suppose he mentioned that, did he?'

'Well no, actually he didn't.'

'Mr Moorcroft was out when we got there but his wife invited us in. We stayed for half an hour, during which time she willingly answered some questions about her husband's past and his connections with the victims. At no point did she express a wish for us to leave or imply that she wasn't perfectly happy to be interviewed on an informal basis. On the contrary, she was extremely helpful.'

Savage gave an exasperated sigh. 'All right, Penrose – why don't you talk me through whatever's going on here, as you see it. We've got two high-profile murders in a short space of time and we need to be seen to be doing our stuff.'

'*Three* deaths I think, sir. I've just had the report through on Giles Shorter.'

'Tell me why you're so convinced they're linked. I didn't understand a word of that fairytale stuff you started talking about.'

Penrose suppressed a smile. 'Well, sir – all three murders echo very clearly various elements of the ghost stories written by M. R. James. James was Provost of King's at the time when the three victims so far – and Robert Moorcroft – were all members of the college choir. He had a lot to do with the chapel and was a good friend to the choristers, so it's reasonable to assume that each man was part of the circle of undergraduates who met regularly in the Provost's rooms and listened to him read his ghost stories aloud. It was quite a tradition – I went once myself, and it was a privilege to be part of it.' He noticed the expression of disbelief on Savage's face and interrupted his account. 'Is something wrong, sir? Something I haven't made clear?'

'No, you're perfectly clear. I just don't like the sound of the phrase "the three victims so far". Go on.'

'Dr James died in June last year. He'd moved on to be Provost of Eton by then, but Moorcroft told me that a number of former undergraduates went to his funeral. As far as I know, that was the last time they met as a group. Now – the murders. I'll go through them in the order we became aware of them, starting the week before last with Stephen Laxborough. As you know, he was buried alive in a tomb and there were three steel padlocks lined up on the grass next to it and a photograph of Angerhale Priory inside. We also found a piece of paper in his pocket with the words "What is this that I have done?" scribbled on it – that's a direct quotation from a James story called 'Count Magnus' which was published in his first collection. It's about a man who travels to Sweden and unwittingly releases the spirit of a long-dead tyrant from a mausoleum – where he's buried in an elaborate sarcophagus, secured by three identical steel padlocks.'

Encouraged by the superintendent's silence, Penrose continued. 'One other interesting thing to note – Laxborough's housekeeper told me that he tried to take his own life, and he chose to do it while the Christmas Eve carol service was being broadcast from King's College. I don't think the timing was a coincidence. For some reason which we haven't yet discovered, that music brought back a great sadness – a great sadness, or perhaps a great guilt.'

Savage looked sceptical. 'That last bit sounds like a leap to me but I agree with you about the references to the story. What about Westbury's murder?'

'That's even less disputable. James set a story called "Oh, Whistle, and I'll Come to You, My Lad" in a fictional town called Seaburgh on the east coast, but Seaburgh was based on Felixstowe. I've done some research and apparently he used to go there every year just after Christmas – the bursar of King's had a house at Cobbold's Point, just to the north of the town. There was an inn there called The Globe and James based the hotel in the story on that. It's gone now – the suffragettes burnt it down, I think – but the guest house where Westbury stayed is on the same stretch of beach. The view from his window matches exactly the descriptions in the story.'

'And what's that one about?'

'An academic from Cambridge goes to the coast on a golfing holiday and finds an old whistle in the sand on an archaeological site belonging to the Knights Templar.'

'Are all the stories about academics meddling in things that don't concern them?'

'A fair few, yes. Anyway, he removes the whistle, takes it back to the hotel, cleans it up and blows it out of curiosity. Later, he's haunted by dreams of being chased along the sand by a strange figure, and when he wakes up the next morning, the sheets on the spare bed in his room are disturbed as if someone else has been sleeping there. The next night, the figure appears in his room – a horrible apparition with a face of crumpled linen.'

In other circumstances, the expression on Savage's face would have been amusing. 'And people like these stories?' he said.

'Oh yes. They're masterpieces of the genre – understated, brilliantly atmospheric, and genuinely frightening.'

'If you say so.'

'Anyway, we're not here to discuss their literary merit. You'll have spotted all the similarities to Westbury's murder, as well as the setting itself – the old-fashioned guest house, the disturbed sheets on both beds, the whistle that he was sent in the post. And, of course, the way he died – suffocated by a pillow is a rather ingenious interpretation of a face of crumpled linen. Whoever our killer is, you've got to give him credit for imagination.'

'And there was something to do with Angerhale Priory there as well?'

'Yes, another picture. This time it had "Who is this who is coming?" written across it. The same handwriting as the note with Laxborough.'

'From the story?'

Penrose nodded. 'There it's inscribed on the whistle. Our killer gave it a more modern twist, I think – that police whistle was meant to taunt us as well as cocking a snook at Westbury's association with the law. The note might as well have said "catch me if you can". He's killed three times now and he's getting cocky.'

'But not cocky enough to make a mistake.'

'Not yet, no.' They were both quiet for a moment, and Penrose guessed that their thoughts were similar: there was something disturbing and inhuman about these rare cases of serial murder, where the only thing that might get them closer to catching the killer was another crime scene and – if they were lucky – another clue. He remembered Tom Webster's frustrations at being so helpless in identifying the rapist in Cambridge, and sympathised with him more than ever; whether it was rape or murder, they both seemed to be bartering with a human life in exchange for a little more ground, a little more clarity.

'So what about Giles Shorter?' Savage asked.

Penrose went succinctly through the details of Shorter's death and the dispute over the stair rod. 'I'm waiting to see if the book was open at a photograph of Angerhale Priory, but there are plenty of other references. The pertinent story is called "The Stalls of Barchester Cathedral", and it's about an Archdeacon who murders his predecessor to get the position. Eventually, the Archdeacon himself is found dead at the foot of his stairs with scratches on his face, having been taunted by voices telling him to "take care". That was the message sent to Shorter a couple of weeks before he died.'

'So the killer gave him a warning.'

'Yes, but one which was far too obscure for him to take heed of.'

'All right, Penrose – you've convinced me. Where do we go from here?'

'For a start, I believe there are other men in danger and we need to make their safety a priority.'

'How many murders are we looking at – potentially?'

'Well, if I'm right about this having something to do with the King's Choir – which, after all, is the only thing that links them – there are eight choral scholars and six lay clerks to consider.'

'Fourteen bloody men to worry about!'

'I think we can narrow that down a bit. I won't bore you with the technical differences between a lay clerk and a choral scholar, but all the men implicated so far are in the latter group.'

'Eight is quite bad enough, don't you think?'

'Yes, but one died in the war and another is terminally ill with cancer.'

'Thank God for that.' He looked embarrassed by the outburst. 'Well, you know what I mean. So three more murders on the cards?'

'Yes, if we include Moorcroft in that. My most immediate concern is a man called Rufus Carrington. He's an academic and he's supposed to be on sabbatical at Corpus Christi College in Cambridge, but when I telephoned Corpus last night to speak to him, the porter told me he left suddenly three weeks ago to go back to his own college in Oxford. The trouble is, Balliol knew nothing of his plans to return and he never arrived. No one knows where he is.'

'So circulate a description and—'

'Already done, sir.' He paused, knowing that the next piece of information he had to impart would be even less palatable. 'The final man on the list is Richard Swayne. He's a civil servant, working in the Home Office.'

'Jesus Christ, that's all we need – a government connection.' Savage rubbed his eyes wearily, imagining the repercussions. 'Have you spoken to him?'

'Yes, but only briefly. I left several messages and he finally returned my call late last night, but he was very dismissive about the whole thing.'

'At least it's on record that you warned him.' He glanced again through the sheaf of crime scene photographs on his desk. 'This is good work, Penrose, but where does it get us in terms of finding out who's doing this?' It was the same question that Fallowfield had asked twenty-four hours earlier, and Penrose still didn't have an answer. 'Could it be one of the others on the list? Perhaps this Carrington chap who's gone missing? Or Moorcroft? You said *if* we include him on the list of potential victims – did you mean he could be a suspect instead?'

'No, I don't think so. Why would he incriminate himself at every crime scene if he were behind the murders? But he *is* different, somehow. It's as if the killer is sending him a message. And he's frightened, too – that's obvious. I'm convinced he knows far more than he's admitting to, but I can't think of what else to try to make him talk – other than harassing his wife again, of course.' He gave Savage a wry smile, which the superintendent ignored.

'Someone's certainly going to extraordinary lengths to make a statement. Why pick these men off one by one, I wonder? Is it because they're all wealthy and successful, and someone who hasn't done so well bears a grudge? Or is it something *they've* done that's coming back to haunt them? No pun intended.'

'I don't know, sir, but there's a good chance it dates back to the time when they were all in Cambridge. I've got someone looking into the local history just before the war.' He smiled to himself, imagining Savage's comments if he ever found out that

Josephine was the newest recruit to his team.

'Good. What about the man who's dying? Perhaps he'll talk to you.'

'On the grounds that he's got nothing left to lose? Yes, perhaps. I'll get back in touch with King's and find out where he is. The bursar was quite keen that he should be left in peace.'

'We'd all like to be left in peace but I think we're beyond that sort of delicacy, don't you? There are three men out there who might be finding peace rather quicker than they'd hoped.' Penrose didn't say anything and Savage looked at him. 'What's on your mind? If there's something else you haven't told me, you'd better spit it out.'

'No, sir, there's nothing else. It's just a phrase that James uses at the beginning of "Oh, Whistle" – he talks about "the person not in the story", and that keeps coming back to me. It's just a throwaway line to tell the reader that a particular character isn't important – but it seems to me that's exactly who we're looking for here. The person not yet in the story.'

'I'm afraid you're losing me now, Penrose. Go out there and get on with it. Speak to the chap on his death bed, try again with Richard Swayne, and keep me posted on the missing academic. And send Fallowfield to speak to Albert Goulding, would you? He's still not completely off the hook for Westbury as far as I'm concerned. Find out how he knows so much about that murder. I can see you haven't got time to go yourself, but I need to have something to say next time Mrs Westbury telephones for a cosy chat about police negligence.'

'But that's a waste of Bill's time, too,' Penrose objected. 'And don't you think Goulding's been through enough? All right, so he's said things he shouldn't, but I'd be tempted to carp in his position.'

'Humour me, Penrose. It's the least you can do. And lay off Moorcroft's wife.'

14

Like many of the town's most distinctive buildings, Cambridge's University Library was identified by a landmark which could be seen from far and wide, in this case a pyramid-capped tower which had the appearance of a squat cigar, standing on end. Josephine crossed the river by the bridge where Marta had first told her about Phyllis, keeping the tower in view as the lane cut between immaculate college lawns which still held the green of early summer. The weather had turned noticeably colder in the last few days, and yet – in the middle of the day, at least – the sun was bright enough to suggest that the autumnal tints of the trees had come before their time, and she was struck again by the ease with which Cambridge always seemed to linger a few weeks or a few centuries behind the present day.

It surprised her that the library was to be found a little out of town, set apart from significant buildings like St Mary's Church and the Senate House, which formed the university's shared ceremonial heart – but she had reckoned without its size. The building that greeted her was a huge, symmetrical expanse of pale russet brick with a low wing on either side of the tower and long, narrow windows running from ground to cornice. It was a recent addition to the landscape, still less than five years old, and to Josephine's eye the overall design resembled a warehouse, which seemed appropriate in its own way; she liked and admired its individuality, but it must have caused quite a stir in the town and she understood now why the people she had asked for directions all spoke of the 'new library' in tones that clearly hankered after the old.

The richly decorated interior made it clear that no expense had been spared. Josephine showed her letter of introduction to the man on duty in the entrance hall and explained what she was looking for. The materials she wanted to consult were naturally held in different rooms, so she decided to execute her promise to Archie first and use whatever time was left for her own research. The attendant directed her up a flight of stairs and through two pairs of heavy bronze doors to the reading room – a beautiful, high-ceilinged space with closely set arched windows and classical details that seemed to belong to a different building entirely from the one she had entered. Earnest young men – interspersed only occasionally with earnest young women – sat at long tables, and every now and then a librarian appeared from a back room with a great pile of books and left them on a central set of shelves ready for collection.

At the enquiry desk, she sought advice on the variety of local papers published in the year before the war and chose *The Cambridge Chronicle and University Journal* as the title most likely to supply the college-related news that Archie had requested. The librarian offered to bring her two months at a time and she settled down at a nearby table to wait for the first batch, noticing that the smell of old books which she always looked forward to in a library was still secondary here to the less nostalgic smell of new carpets; otherwise, the reading room differed little from the others she had been in, and she was pleased to feel so at home in a place that would usually have excluded her.

The papers soon arrived, dwarfing the man who carried them, and Josephine began her search in October 1913 at the start of the academic term. She soon found two of the names she was looking for in the published list of freshmen for King's College; the register of young men arriving in Cambridge for the very first time was poignantly similar to the lists of names which would appear in newspapers all over the country in less than a year's time, but these were more innocent, more optimistic days, and both Robert Moorcroft and Simon Westbury were included among those just embarking upon their university education. An address was given next to each name, and Josephine was interested to learn that while some of the freshmen lived in college buildings, others had rooms in the streets nearby; when she saw how many ordinary houses were occupied by undergraduates, from King's and from the many other colleges, she remembered what Marta had said and understood for the first time the toll that the war must have taken on the life of the town. Moorcroft lodged in St Botolph's Lane and Westbury in St Edward's Passage; she noted down the details and moved on, but, after a promising start, there were very few references to individual students and the only other time she found any of the names mentioned was in an account of a Varsity boxing match which Robert Moorcroft had won with a knock-out punch in the third round.

Towards the end of October, Dr Montague Rhodes James, Provost of King's, was announced as the new Vice Chancellor of the university and sworn in at a service at the Senate House. There were very few details – obviously if you lived in Cambridge you were expected to understand the significance of the appointment – but a portrait photograph took up most of the page and Josephine looked with interest at the author she had known only by his last name and initials. The conventional nature of the photograph made it hard to guess how old James would have been at the time, but she guessed in his early fifties; he had a strong face, with finely cut features and straight dark hair which fell in a broad wave over his right temple; she imagined she could detect an appealing glint of humour behind the round spectacles which defied the formality of the gown and pose. Again, she wondered what this man – the writer or the scholar – could possibly have to do with the case that Archie was working on, but she made a note of the date and the name of the photographer before turning the page.

It took her three hours and four more batches to reach the end of the academic year, and in all that time she found only one general news story involving King's. In April, a man doing building work at the college had died in Addenbrooke's Hospital after drinking what he thought was rhubarb wine from the college buttery; the 'wine' turned out to be an irritant poison used as a wood preservative, and the builder had suffered some agonising final moments in spite of his colleague's best efforts to help him. As tragic as the incident was, even Josephine's more devious imaginings couldn't turn it into something capable of inspiring three modern day murders, but she dutifully made sure of the details and took the name of the head porter who had attended the inquest just in case Archie wanted to pursue it. Most of the other university news seemed to consist of elections to obscure posts and winners of obscure prizes; the only specific reference to King's Choir and chapel was at the beginning of December, when the college celebrated its Founder's Day with a Holy Communion service in the morning and a feast at night; later in the month, the carol service – now so famous all over the world – was not even mentioned.

Although Archie hadn't asked for anything that wasn't related to King's, Josephine made a note of events in the wider town that were potentially scandalous or crimes that had gone unsolved, as much for her interest as for his. She was always on the look-out for an interesting case which might spark ideas for a new book and enable her to build on the reputation of her first two crime novels, but the news simply confirmed her suspicions that, as a rule, real-life sudden deaths were far too absurd to stand up to the scrutiny and cynicism of most detective fiction fans; she could only picture the letters of complaint if she decided to feature the bride who had expired from 'over-excitement' three hours after her wedding, or the chaplain of St Edward's Church who had quietly left the Magnificat during the Sunday evening service to lie down and die on the floor of his vestry. No, the deaths in the newspapers were either too bizarre or too depressingly symptomatic of the harsh social truths that readers turned to crime fiction to avoid: the child buried in a coppice with terrible signs of abuse; the surgeon found dead after appearing in court on libel charges; the man hanged at Cambridge Gaol for cutting his wife's throat while she lay in bed next to him.

There were two exceptions in the stories that she read, both drownings in the River Cam and both involving young women: one had been missing for more than a month when her body was pulled from the water; the other was found by the riverbank near a place called Sheep's Green on Christmas morning. Josephine could happily have spun a mystery from either tale, intrigued by the questions left unanswered in the newspaper accounts. Where had the first girl been in the weeks between her disappearance and the discovery of her body? Why had the second been walking alone in such a deserted part of town when she was supposed to be watching a film at the Empire? Or *had* she been alone? Josephine spent a pleasant few minutes speculating on the fate of these two women, but the rest of the court pages offered a depressingly mundane catalogue of minor assaults, petty theft and child neglect.

When she got to July, she returned the final batch of papers to the desk and started all over again with the *Cambridge Daily News*, but this only offered different accounts of the stories that were by now familiar to her, embellished with a tediously thorough round-up of events in nearby villages. Frustrated by having found nothing particularly tangible for Archie, she returned the pile of papers to the desk and caught the eye of the man who had been helping her. 'Was there no paper specifically for the university before the war?' she asked.

'No, madam, I'm afraid not. We have *Varsity* today, but that didn't publish its first issue until the Michaelmas term of 1931. There's the *Cambridge Reporter*, of course . . .'

'What's that?'

'It's the official journal of the university, but it really deals with the day-to-day business. Lectures, examinations, council decisions, new appointments – that sort of thing.'

'But no news stories?'

He shook his head. 'Is there anything else I can help you with?'

'Actually there might be. Do you hold recent newspapers as well?' He looked disappointed, as if something that could so easily be offered by the town library wasn't really worthy of his time or hers, but reluctantly acknowledged that they were available. 'Then I'll have the *Cambridge Daily News* for the last three months,' she said.

She sat down again and opened her notebook, keen to trace the history of the recent attacks in the city and plot the journey which had brought the rapist almost to her door. Press coverage of the crimes had begun modestly enough, with a small item on page two about a robbery which had escalated into a physical assault; after that, although still not extensive, the news reports gathered pace, including a series of often contradictory descriptions and a brief flurry of excitement about a scarf left at one of the scenes which later turned out to belong to a friend of the victim. She learned that one of the early victims had fought off her attacker, but that he had only moved on to a house in the next street and raped another girl all the more brutally, presumably frustrated at being thwarted in his original plan; that was the first time he had used a knife, and suddenly Josephine noticed a marked change in the newspaper's attitudes to the crimes.

During the lull between attacks, and whenever facts were in short supply, the paper found other ways to keep the story alive. There was plenty of advice to women on their personal safety – the locks and torches that she had mentioned to Archie, together with more imaginative tips like keeping a pepper pot beside the bed and lining the window sills with empty bottles; there was a particularly inflammatory piece headed 'Keep an Eye on Next Door', which asked readers to consider how well they knew their neighbours or the lodger next door, and played – dangerously, in Josephine's view

– on the suspicion of strangers which was already rife all over the country; and there was much discussion of the growing anger in the town at the police's failure to catch the man responsible. She found this inevitable consequence of the rapes almost as disturbing as the crimes themselves; it was easy to see how the anger and fear might escalate, with vigilantes taking to the streets and outbreaks of mob violence that would only distract the police and leave women living alone more vulnerable than ever. People were getting desperate, that much was obvious; the police were relying on luck, and there was even talk of bringing in a clairvoyant. More practically, the Townswomen's Guild was arranging self-defence classes.

Early in October, the suggestion that girls should ask their young men to stay the night had affronted everyone in equal measure: Christian organisations were outraged by the immorality of the idea, and the more 'militant' women's groups were offended by the implication that their safety depended on the male sex. It was true, Josephine thought: this spate of crimes was effectively imprisoning women by fear, robbing them of the independence they had fought so hard to get. Only an hour before, she had been reading about the vibrant suffrage movement in 1913, with countless stories of women battling for all sorts of issues in the town – battling, and winning. It would take them years to claw back the precious freedom that this man – whoever he was – had destroyed in a matter of weeks, and she felt the constraints on her own life grow a little tighter every day that she remained in the town. It manifested itself in the simplest of things: normally she would have had no hesitation in walking the Cambridge streets after dark, enjoying the romanticism of nightfall and the fleeting magic of the dusk that she had experienced so briefly with Marta, but this was denied her now because she was afraid – not of the streets, but of coming back to the house alone. She was afraid, and she resented it.

Perhaps it was this anger born of vulnerability that made her see a more sinister subtext in much of what she read. So many of the stories went beyond the useful function of warning women to be sensible, and as the attacks grew in number, so did the appeals to wives, mothers and landladies to think carefully about the men in their lives and report any suspicious behaviour. It was impossible to know what you would do if a man you loved was out at night when he shouldn't be or jumped every time there was a knock at the door, but surely it was going too far to suggest that a woman who stayed silent in that position was morally responsible for any future attacks? It left a bitter taste in Josephine's mouth to think that women could in any way be held to account for this, the most male of crimes.

When she had got a good sense of the events overall, she went back to the beginning and wrote down all the streets so far where an attack had taken place, unable to get the brutal image of Mary's room out of her head. When she had what she needed to test her theory regarding the connection between the victims' houses and a nearby church, she asked for directions to the rare books room and spent a pleasant couple of hours reading through the precious Culloden papers as research for her new play before hunger drove her home.

On the way, she stopped at the tobacconist's by St John's to buy the latest edition of the *Cambridge Daily News*. 'Close to home this time,' the tobacconist said gravely, tapping the front page as he pushed the paper across the counter.

Instantly suspicious, Josephine was about to ask how he knew where she lived when she realised that he was referring to his own shop, just a stone's throw from St Clement's Passage. 'Yes, I suppose it is,' she said, hating her own paranoia. 'It's hard to imagine anyone stopping him at the moment.'

'He must know this town like the back of his hand, otherwise he'd never be able to come and go so easily. And the police haven't got a bloody clue, if you'll pardon my French – you can tell that from the comments they're making. This one was a nurse, apparently.'

'*Is* a nurse,' Josephine said before she could stop herself. 'That man might come and go as he pleases, but he can't take everything away from these girls. They're stronger than that. She'll pick up the pieces and get on with her life – and that's the best way to deal with what he's done to her.' He passed her change over without another word, and Josephine thanked him and left the shop, embarrassed to have let her irritation get the better of her.

Back at home, she washed the stubborn smudges of newsprint off her hands and made a sandwich, then picked up the paper while she waited for the kettle to boil. Because she had been so close to it herself, the account of Mary's rape seemed bland and uninformed. St Clement's Passage was mentioned, of course, but no house number was given and, although it wasn't a very big street, that at least offered some degree of anonymity. There was a comment from the police inspector who had come to the house which echoed what he had said to her on the night, but which seemed surprisingly outspoken in print: 'The scars on the bodies of these girls will heal. The scars on their minds never will. They are good girls – hard-working and pleasant. Not one of them asked for this or provoked it. They were home alone, and thought they were safe. Whoever is doing this is a frightened little coward who must operate at night to give himself nerve.' The last part seemed rather inflammatory to Josephine, but she suspected that it was a reaction to repeated questions about police inefficiency and she couldn't blame him; if she was tempted to snap at anyone who made a crass remark, how much worse must it be if it was your responsibility to put an end to the crimes once and for all?

She took a tray upstairs to the study, then settled down with her notes and the map. It didn't take her long to see that her wild speculation was exactly that. Of the six assaults so far, only three had taken place anywhere near a church: the two she knew about in St

Peter's Street and St Clement's Passage, and another in St Botolph's Lane – by coincidence, where Robert Moorcroft had had his first-year lodgings. The other victims had lived further out of town, and, as far as Josephine could see, there were no nearby parks, municipal gardens or other public amenities which might require the services of a nomadic gardener. She put down her pen, half-disappointed and half-relieved; if her theory had held water, she had no idea what she might have done about it. As she looked at the marked-up map, though, she was struck by the sheer audacity of the crimes. The tobacconist had been right: the man who was doing this did indeed seem able to come and go all over the town, gaining access wherever he liked and escaping without a single witness, growing into his own notoriety and living up to the various names attributed to him in the press: the phantom; the monster; the beast.

The doorbell rang and she went downstairs with hesitation, under permanent sentence now of a visit from Bridget. She opened the door to a neatly dressed woman in her thirties with a handbag over her arm and an envelope in her hand. 'Miss Fox, I presume?'

'No, I'm sorry. Miss Fox is away at the moment. Can I help?'

'Oh, but that can't be right,' the woman insisted in an accent very similar to Josephine's. 'There must be some mistake.'

'I'm afraid not,' Josephine said, instantly irritated at being told her own business by a stranger. 'Miss Fox is in America and I think I'd have noticed by now if she hadn't gone. Can I ask why you wanted her?'

'I'm from the Domestic Agency in Green Street, and my name is Mrs Thompson. Miss Fox put her name down for a lady twice a week.'

The phrasing was unfortunate but Josephine managed not to smile. 'Oh, I see. Yes, that's right. I registered with the agency on her behalf last week, but—'

'And you are?'

'A friend. I'm looking after the house while Miss Fox is away, but, as I was about to explain, the agency informed me that all its domestic staff were currently engaged and no one would be available for some time.'

'Well, Miss . . .' She tailed off and glanced at Josephine's left hand. 'It *is* Miss, is it?'

'Yes. Miss Tey.'

'Well, Miss Tey – there's been a cancellation. You're in luck.'

That was a matter of opinion, Josephine thought. 'But Miss Fox won't be needing anyone for at least another three weeks,' she reiterated firmly. 'She's in America, and, as you can probably see, the house is being redecorated. Cleaning it would be a complete waste of time.'

She had gestured behind her to emphasise her point, but it proved to be a fatal error. Mrs Thompson took it as an invitation to come in and was over the threshold before Josephine could do anything to stop her. Wondering why any interview for domestic help invariably involved the employer adopting a subservient role, she followed her visitor meekly through to the kitchen. 'Marta – Miss Fox – has only just taken the house on,' she explained apologetically, seeing the shabby facilities through Mrs Thompson's eyes and wishing now that she'd washed up from breakfast and last night's dinner before leaving for the library. 'She'll be making some changes, obviously, but she hasn't had a chance to settle in yet.'

'That's an Inverness accent, if I'm not mistaken?' Mrs Thompson said. Wrong-footed, Josephine nodded. 'Ay, I thought so. Have you been long away from the Highlands?'

'About ten days,' she said dryly. 'I live there.'

'Ah, how nice. And what does your family do?'

'My mother was a teacher but she died several years ago. My father has a fruiterer's shop.'

'Does he now? And where would that be?'

'In Castle Street.'

'Well then, my aunt's bound to know him. She loves a Golden Russet.'

'Your aunt?'

'That's right. Didn't I mention I had family in Inverness?'

'No, I don't think you did,' Josephine said, horrified to have given away so much about herself already. 'You'll have to excuse me, but I was just doing some work and I really need to get on. I'm sorry you've had a wasted trip—'

'Not wasted at all. What sort of work is it that you do?'

'I'm a writer.'

'Well, that's quite a change from fruit, but I expect your father's very proud all the same. Now, you get on with your work while I have a little look round the house. I always insist on that before I take a new position – you wouldn't believe some of the things I've been expected to put up with in the past. I'll be as quiet as a mouse, I promise. You won't even know I'm here.'

Before Josephine could object, Mrs Thompson was climbing the stairs to the first floor and she had no choice but to follow. 'The rooms are actually quite small, aren't they?' the prospective help said, glancing round the study. 'This will be no trouble at all.' She walked across to the desk by the window, where Josephine had been working, and looked at the open newspaper and the map. 'I expect you've had a lot of sightseers past your windows since Friday night,' she said sagely. 'People do so love to talk. My husband's on the agency's books, too – odd jobs and gardening, that sort of thing – and all he's done these last few weeks is fit locks and bolts for single girls. I swear I've never known him to be so busy.'

'Well, I suppose even violent crime has its silver lining,' Josephine said brightly, smiling to take the edge off her words. 'Now, if you've seen enough, we should discuss a date for you to start.'

'Oh, I'll start on Thursday,' she said, as if the decision were entirely hers. 'If that's not convenient, the agency will find me somewhere else and you'll be back at the bottom of the waiting list. Just one more floor, is there?'

'That's right, but surely you don't need to see everything?'

'In a mess, I suppose? No need to be embarrassed about that – we'll have it all shipshape soon enough.' The bed was indeed still unmade, which was shameful enough for four o'clock in the afternoon, but Josephine knew it wasn't that which had caught Mrs Thompson's attention; she was looking at the collection of photographs on the bedside table, which – without exception – were all of her with Marta. They went back downstairs, but there was a new edge to Mrs Thompson's voice when she spoke again. 'My references are all in here,' she said, laying the envelope on the hall table, 'together with my terms and conditions. My days will be Monday and Thursday, nine until twelve, and every other weekend. All financial matters will be handled by the agency, with whom you must also leave a key. Perhaps you could confirm all that with your friend?'

'Yes, of course.' Josephine saw her to the door and closed it firmly behind her, wondering how long it would take the aunt from Inverness to stock up on fruit.

15

After some persuasion, the bursar's office reluctantly gave Penrose the details of where Alastair Frost was living out the last, painful days of his life. The Evelyn Nursing Home was on Trumpington Road and he found it easily among the handsome, desirable residences that lay to the south of the town. A sweeping gravelled drive led him through rows of mature trees towards an old, ivy-covered house and, a few yards further on, a more modern two-storey building with an attractive curved facade. He parked his car midway between the two and looked round, admiring the home's extensive grounds – lawns edged by carefully tended flower borders, with kitchen gardens and a greenhouse to the rear and a sizeable area given over to soft fruits and an orchard. If there was such a thing as a desirable place to be ill, this was obviously it. The gardens were faded now as they headed towards the quiet of winter, but he imagined that they were still a source of great pleasure to the patients – although not to Alastair Frost, it seemed: from what the matron had said when Penrose telephoned to make an appointment, he was arriving just in time.

The sound of wheels on the gravel brought a middle-aged woman to the door, dressed in a matron's uniform and carrying a small dog. 'Miss Cacroft?' he asked, getting out of the car.

'Yes, Chief Inspector. You've made excellent time.'

'I'm afraid I'm a little earlier than we agreed. If it's inconvenient, please just say and I'll wait.'

'No, not at all inconvenient. Would you like some tea after your journey, or would you prefer to see Dr Frost right away?'

'I won't put you to the trouble of tea, but I would like a word with you first if you've time?'

'Of course. Come through to my sitting room, and I'll take you over to the hospital wing when you're ready.'

She put the terrier down and it led the way obligingly down a hallway lined with watercolours to a small room at the back of the house. It was sparsely furnished – Penrose had never been in a nurse's room that didn't show the same respect for stillness and order which her professional life demanded – but everything was chosen with an eye for taste. There were a number of architectural drawings on the wall, early plans for the hospital buildings, and he studied them with interest before taking the seat he was offered. 'You've got a wonderful facility here,' he said. 'It must be a real asset to the town.'

Edith Cacroft seemed gratified by the compliment. 'It's certainly a great improvement on its predecessor,' she said. 'Up until the end of the war, the only private nursing facilities were in a hostel in Thompson's Lane. A black hole with no daylight, someone once called it – and he wasn't far wrong.' She smiled, and pointed to a photograph of the old building to show what she meant. 'It was very basic, to say the least, and even that was under threat – the building was leased from Magdalene College and they wanted it back to cope with the flood of undergraduates coming back after the war. But we were fortunate in finding a benefactor. I don't suppose you know Morland Agnew?' Penrose shook his head. 'No, long before your time, I imagine. He was a Trinity man, and his wife convalesced in the Thompson's Lane hostel after an operation at Addenbrooke's. It wasn't the most comfortable few weeks she'd ever spent, and it made him determined to give Cambridge something better. She was the Evelyn who gives us our name.'

'And you've obviously been here from the very beginning?'

'That's right. I was matron at a hospital in France during the war, then I came back to Cambridge via London. This place has been my life for more than sixteen years, and it's been a privilege to see it grow and develop. We even have nurses working in some of the colleges now – much to the delight of the undergraduates and the horror of the Fellows. But you haven't come to the Evelyn to listen to me. Time is precious. You learn that very quickly here.'

Penrose nodded, grateful for her understanding. 'How long has Dr Frost been with you?' he asked.

'Since early October. He came back to Cambridge after a research trip to Italy, determined to begin the Michaelmas term as usual, but it soon became obvious that he wasn't well enough to care for himself, let alone to teach, so he moved in here shortly afterwards.'

'And how is he now?'

'I would say he has days left rather than weeks, and perhaps not many of those. He's been sleeping a lot, and he's past the stage now when he can swallow anything but fluids. We've made him as comfortable as we can – the morphine helps with his breathing as well as with the pain – but there's very little else that can be done in the final stages of lung cancer.'

'Has he had many visitors while he's been here?'

'Several colleagues, naturally, and some of his students have begun to drop by since they heard the news. I gather he's a very popular member of the college, and not many days go by without someone from King's calling to see him. He has a brother who lives in Scotland. It's hard for him, obviously, being so far away, but he's visited twice and hopes to come again before the end.'

'What about an old friend of his called Robert Moorcroft?'

The matron looked at him in surprise. 'Now how did you know that, I wonder? I'm not sure I would have called him an old friend, but yes – Mr Moorcroft was here recently.'

'And Rufus Carrington?'

'I don't recognise that name.'

'How about Richard Swayne?'

'I'm beginning to think you know my hospital better than I do, Chief Inspector. Mr Swayne came at the weekend, although he didn't stay long because Dr Frost was having a particularly bad day.'

So Swayne wasn't quite as unmoved by the murders as he had made out, Penrose thought; he had obviously been troubled enough to come to Cambridge. 'Did either of those visits seem to disturb Dr Frost?' he asked.

She thought carefully before answering. 'No, I wouldn't say that. On the contrary – he seemed rather amused by Mr Moorcroft's visit. Perhaps "amused" isn't quite the right word, but he was certainly in better spirits afterwards.'

'Do you *like* Dr Frost, Miss Cacroft?'

So far, the matron had afforded Penrose the courtesy of answering his questions without any reference to why he might be asking them, but now she looked at him curiously. 'I couldn't say that I like him, simply because I don't know him well enough to make such a personal judgement – but I certainly respect him. Many of the terminal patients who pass through our doors rail against their illness, but Dr Frost never has. Some are angry at the injustice of it, others are full of self-pity, but not once to my knowledge has he ever complained, and he has borne the severest of pain with great stoicism and dignity. And if you asked the nurses who spend their days caring for him and are in a better position to comment than I am, I imagine that most of them would tell you that they like him very much.'

'How did he react when you told him that I was coming today?'

'He said that you were twenty-four years too late.' She gave him a wry smile. 'I'm tempted to ask what that means, but it suggests that you won't want to waste any more time. Would you like me to take you across to him now?'

'Yes please.'

He followed her back to the door, deep in thought, then across the front lawn to the nursing block. It was an attractive building with a deceptively simple design: repeated groups of French and casement windows alternated with panels of cream plaster and brick. The rooms were all south facing, and those on the ground floor had wide doors to a pleasant terraced area, where beds could be wheeled out in fine weather. 'Handsome, isn't it?' Miss Cacroft said as they approached. 'Sir Aston Webb was the architect. He also designed Admiralty Arch and parts of Buckingham Palace.'

'Then you're in good company.'

'Indeed.' She opened a door at the side of the building and allowed him to go in first. The main corridor curved gently round, following the line of the building, and they walked past several teak doors with gleaming brass handles. 'Dr Frost is in the room at the end,' Miss Cacroft said, stopping outside a nurses' duty room, its entrance flanked by linen cupboards. 'I realise that whatever has brought you here must be important, Chief Inspector, but I would ask you to be as brief as possible with your questions – and please try not to disturb Dr Frost unnecessarily. Whatever time he has left – well, it's my duty to make sure that he spends it peacefully.'

'Of course.'

She knocked softly and opened the door. A nurse left her seat at the foot of Frost's bed, and the matron gestured for Penrose to take her place. 'There'll be someone outside should you need her.'

'Thank you.'

The blind used to shade the room from the sun in summer was pulled low against the gentle autumn daylight, giving the room a muted half-life which was strangely appropriate. Penrose was struck immediately by the clinical nature of the space: there were no personal belongings on the shelves or bedside table to suggest that the room had been occupied for several weeks – no photographs, no books or cards, nothing to taunt the man in the bed with the pleasures he must leave behind or the things he would never finish; the emptiness moved him, as if – for Frost – the real death had already occurred and the physical act of breathing his last was simply something to be endured as efficiently as possible. The room was so quiet and still that he thought Frost was sleeping, but, as he got closer to the bed, he noticed two wide-awake eyes fixed firmly on him. 'Illness turns the strongest of men into frightened children,' Frost said, his voice low and fragile. 'Any sort of company is better than being left alone, even a policeman's.'

Penrose moved the chair closer to the head of the bed so that Frost needn't struggle to be heard. He forced himself to meet the dying man's eyes without revulsion or pity, but it required some considerable effort and he found it hard to believe that he was looking at a man his own age: Frost was desperately thin, and the frail arm which rested on the bed sheet was mottled and bluish from lack of circulation. His forehead was clammy, and – except for the dark rings that circled hollow eyes – his face had the colour of unbleached wax. The skin across his cheekbones was taut and paper-thin, and, as he made the effort to speak again, Penrose had the unsettling illusion of holding a conversation with a skeleton. 'Robert said you'd be here sooner or later.'

'And did he say why?'

Frost nodded. 'I'm afraid you've had a wasted trip, though. I like a good thriller as much as the next man, but the convenient chapter where the dying man confesses everything is always such a disappointment. It's not a part I'm inclined to play.'

'So there *is* something to confess? That's more than I was certain of when I walked in here.' Frost tried to smile but his lips were too cracked and sore to oblige him. Penrose took the glass of water from the bedside table and held it to his mouth. 'This isn't a thriller, though,' he said quietly. 'People are dying – men who were once your friends. What am I twenty-four years too late for?'

'To help any of us. To save us from ourselves.'

'Is that why Moorcroft and Swayne came to see you?' Penrose asked. 'To beg your silence? To remind you of a pact you all made years ago and to point out that they still have a lot to lose, even if you haven't?'

'Something like that. I was surprised at Swayne, but Robert has always been stupid. It hasn't occurred to him that by helping you and speaking out I might just save his life.' Frost's breathing was laboured and irregular now, in spite of the morphine, and he paused to rest. 'And that is precisely why I'm not going to tell you anything, Penrose, except this: what's happening is justice, pure and simple. All of these deaths are warranted, mine included. If my silence ensures that justice will take its course right to the bitter end, then so be it.'

'You can't take the law into your own hands like that,' Penrose insisted. 'If you know who's doing this and you die without telling anyone, you are culpable in part for any future deaths.'

'So I'll burn in hell?' He gave a bitter laugh. 'You don't believe that justice and the law are the same thing any more than I do. Simon Westbury was proof of that. But even if what you say is true, my conscience is clear – on that, at least. I have absolutely no idea who is doing this. If that's your question, I couldn't answer it even if I wanted to.'

'But you know *why* it's happening.'

'Oh yes. We all know that, and we've had to live with it in our different ways. "The mind is its own place, and in it self can make a Heav'n of Hell, a Hell of Heav'n."'

'Milton,' Penrose said, recognising the lines from *Paradise Lost*.

Frost nodded approvingly, as if rewarding a bright undergraduate. 'For a few years – just a few – I thought I could succeed in making a heaven from the hell that we created. I had my books and my teaching, and I honestly believed that by giving those young men something truly worthwhile I could make up for what I did – for what *we* did.' Penrose listened, struck by the similarities between Frost's words and the selfless teaching that had been an important part of Stephen Laxborough's life, the charity work credited to

Giles Shorter. 'But good doesn't cancel out evil, does it? The stain is always there, and it's so much easier to make a hell from heaven than the other way round.'

He closed his eyes, and for a moment Penrose thought he had fallen asleep. In the deep, expectant silence of the room, he watched the sheet move up and down and heard the ominous, low-pitched rattle in Frost's chest. 'If you can't tell me who and you won't tell me why, can you at least tell me why it's happening *like this*?' he pleaded, no longer sure that the man could hear him. 'What have these murders got to do with M. R. James?'

He waited a long time for his answer. 'That's where we went afterwards,' Frost whispered eventually. 'We drank Monty's whisky and smoked his tobacco, and listened while he told innocent stories of horror that were nothing compared to the one we had just lived through. Someone obviously knows that.'

'And did Dr James know what you'd done?'

'No, absolutely not. If he had, none of this would be necessary. We loved him. If he'd seen us for what we were, the shame would have been unbearable. As I said, Monty liked his evil to be innocent, something he could put away at the end of the evening.'

'Is there *nothing* I can say to change your mind?' Penrose asked, although in his heart he had already conceded defeat.

'No. Silence is the one small power I have left on this earth, you see, and I'm clinging to it. And that shows how little I've learned.'

His voice had grown weaker than ever, and now he struggled to breathe. Penrose fetched the nurse from outside and watched as she hurried over to the bed, noticing how desperately Frost's eyes were fixed on her, pleading with her not to abandon him to the terror of an unknown darkness. He turned to the door, an intruder now in these final, most private of moments, but the nurse called him back. 'Excuse me, sir, but I think Dr Frost wants you.'

He returned to the bed and bent low over the dying man, breathing in the nauseating smell of sickness. 'One more thing,'

Frost said, his words barely perceptible. 'There's an order to everything in this world. Swayne will be next.'

'How do you know that?'

But Frost sank back on his pillow, exhausted by the effort, and Penrose left the room. He walked back to the main house, too disturbed by the emotional impact of what he had just experienced to make much sense of what Frost had and hadn't told him. He would have to have another look at the notes that Josephine had sent him on the news stories she had found, but nothing sprang readily to mind as being relevant; whatever 'shame' Frost had been referring to must have remained secret, now and at the time.

There was a police car parked next to his own and he was surprised to see Tom Webster coming out of the house, deep in conversation with Miss Cacroft. She broke off when she saw him, quickly noticing his troubled expression. 'Is everything all right with Dr Frost, Chief Inspector?'

'Yes, but I don't think he has long now.'

'And a nurse is with him?' Penrose nodded. 'Good. I'll go over myself in a moment. Do you know Inspector Webster? He's very kindly come here to talk to my girls about these terrible assaults.'

'Yes, we met when I was in town recently,' Penrose said, nodding to the officer.

'Good to see you again, sir.'

'Apparently, the last victim was a nurse from Addenbrooke's,' Miss Cacroft continued, 'and although we're a bit out of the way here, it's better to be safe than sorry. Thank you for taking the trouble to come out to us personally, Inspector – it's much appreciated, and I'll make sure that all your advice is followed to the letter. Now – if you'll both excuse me?'

She hurried across to the nursing block and Penrose watched her go, wondering if she was already too late.

'Difficult morning, sir?' Webster asked as they walked over to their cars.

'Interrogating a dying man, Inspector. Sometimes I really love my job.'

'That must have been hard. Was he able to help, though?'

'Yes, but that doesn't make me feel any better about taking up the time he has so very little of.'

'Of course not. Is he really that bad?'

'Yes. Right now, I'd happily swap cases with you.'

'Be my guest.'

Penrose smiled, then spoke more seriously. 'I heard about your latest. A friend of mine lives in St Clement's Passage, and the girl went to her for help.'

'Oh, the lady next door? Yes, she was very kind.'

'And are you any further on this time?'

'Honestly? Not really.' He rubbed a hand across his eyes and Penrose noticed how exhausted he looked. 'We've questioned nigh on a thousand men now, and it's got us nowhere. We've pulled in all the petty criminals we know about – the assaults started as burglaries, so that seemed to make sense – and we're doing spot-checks on the street if we see anything suspicious, but still he's eluding us.'

'It sounds more like the scale of a murder hunt. The public must appreciate that, at least.'

'You'd think so, wouldn't you, but it feels like we can't win. The women are angry because we're not doing enough and the men are beginning to resent us because they're constantly under suspicion. One of our boys was knocked about in a pub the other day just for asking a few questions. Still, if we're looking on the bright side . . .'

'There is one?'

Webster grinned. 'Sort of. General crime rates have never been so low. All the usual villains are afraid to leave the house in case they get caught by the extra night patrols.'

'That sort of manpower must be putting a strain on everyone, though.'

'Yes, but several of the lads are putting in extra time now

without pay. We're all doing our bit, even the top brass.'

'Can't you get someone else to take charge of things like this?' Penrose asked. 'I know it's important to get people to take their safety seriously and it saves time in the long run, but anyone could do that.'

Webster flushed. 'To tell you the truth, sir, I've got an ulterior motive.'

'Oh?'

'I've been out a couple of times with one of the nurses here, but she's hardly seen me over the last few weeks so I thought I'd come out myself and speak to them. Besides, I want her to be safe, and you don't trust anyone else with someone you care about, do you?'

'No, I don't suppose you do.'

'Especially now we've got undergraduates offering to watch out for girls living on their own.'

Penrose smiled. 'Isn't that a good idea?'

'I'm not sure about that. Since when has the honour of a student to be trusted? They all think they can do as they like.' He seemed to be genuinely angry and Penrose said nothing, knowing from experience that the resentment between the town and the university was strongly felt on both sides. 'Are you coming in to the station today?' Webster asked.

'I wasn't planning to. I'm needed back in London for the Armistice Day briefing. Why?'

'The Super's been trying to contact you about this.'

He opened his car door and took a newspaper off the dashboard. The headline on the front page read: 'Scotland Yard called in to help floundering local force'. 'I'm sorry, Webster,' Penrose said sincerely. 'I have no idea how they know I've been in Cambridge or why they would think that I'm here to teach you your job.'

'The usual thing, I suppose – putting two and two together and coming up with five.'

'But they mustn't get away with it. Can I take this paper?' Webster nodded. 'I'll telephone the editor as soon as I'm back in London and make sure that he understands the situation.'

'Thank you, sir, but don't jeopardise your own investigation. If it suits you to make them think that's why you're here, leave it as it is.'

Penrose looked at him with respect, but knew how demoralised he would feel if his own efforts were being undermined so publicly without good reason. 'No, I'll make sure they publish a correction as soon as possible – and please give Superintendent Clough my apologies. If it's any consolation, even if the Yard *had* been called in to help, we wouldn't be coping any better than you are with a spate of crimes as unprecedented as this. Call me at any time if there's something I can do to help. I'm bound to be back here soon, so we'll catch up then.'

'Thank you, sir.' He hesitated, then said: 'What *are* you working on, if you don't mind my asking?'

'I don't mind at all, but there's not much I can tell you at the moment,' Penrose said, feeling a little churlish. 'It's a series of murders – three so far – and I'm making about as much headway as you are.'

Webster smiled and got into his car. 'I suppose that's all I'm getting,' he said, winding down the window, 'but if you *do* want to trade those cases, just say the word.'

16

The museum was quiet, and Bridget breathed a sigh of relief to find herself alone in the familiar first-floor gallery. The canvas – a rare landscape by Renoir – hung in the middle of a crowded wall, and yet, as she walked towards it, everything else in the room seemed to disappear until only she and the painting existed. At first, as she always did, she marvelled at Renoir's extraordinary technical skill: rapid, unerring brush strokes to convey the wind in the trees and the movement of the clouds across the sky; a palette of cool greens and blues which gave life to the freshness of the day; blurred edges in the foreground, hinting at a lazy warmth to come. The artist was believed to have completed the picture in a single session. To Bridget, its very existence was nothing short of a miracle.

But that wasn't why she loved it. There was something far less tangible about the painting which always spoke to her: to look at it was to feel the air on her face, to stroll in the landscape it depicted, to be free. The gentle slopes seemed to stretch out indefinitely on either side and the clouds were ever scurrying towards a new horizon, not imprisoned by a canvas but fleeting and transient. Renoir's inspiration had been a hill near Saint-Cloud, to the west of Paris, but the scene reminded her of something much closer to home – the meadows in Grantchester where she had played as a child, where she had lain on the grass with Archie, listening to the dull thud of the guns in France.

From the moment she first stood here, Bridget knew that the freedom and ambition of Renoir's painting would define her life. She had come here when she discovered she was pregnant, hoping that its strange, enduring power would give her the courage to make a decision which she knew in her heart was wrong, and she returned to it now to give herself strength. As she turned away, holding the image in her mind's eye for as long as she could, she was pleased to find that it had not let her down.

17

Josephine woke to the clatter of bottles in the hallway. She sat up in bed, her heart racing, and peered at the clock: it was five past seven, and just beginning to get light. Trying not to panic, she pulled her dressing gown around her and took Marta's dancing statuette from its new home under the bed, a handy storage space which seemed to suit both the ornament's aesthetic appeal and its more practical role as a weapon of self-defence. Feeling braver with the weight of the bronze in her hand, she tiptoed to the top of the stairs and looked over the banisters to the ground floor. 'Hello?' she called out. 'Who's down there?'

'Who do you think it is at this time of the morning?' grumbled Mrs Thompson, rubbing her foot. 'What on earth are these bottles doing here? Frightened me half to death, they did. I could have broken my neck.' Josephine bit her tongue and resisted the obvious retort. 'In future, I'll ask you to leave them in the kitchen and I'll get rid of them when I leave.'

Mrs Thompson was still looking disapprovingly at the bottles when Josephine joined her in the hallway, and she had to agree that the ratio of wine to milk was unfortunate. 'I'm sorry they startled you, but that was rather the point. Not to frighten you specifically,' she clarified. 'They're supposed to warn me if I have an intruder. It was a tip they gave in the newspaper the other day and I thought I'd try it out.'

'Well, you can't be too careful when you haven't got a man in the house,' Mrs Thompson said, looking pointedly at Josephine. 'All *sorts* of things can happen.'

'Quite. Anyway, I was planning to move them before you arrived this morning. I'm sure you told me your hours were nine until twelve.'

'That's right, but I'm early today because I want to get to the market square in good time for the Armistice service. You're not expecting me to vacuum through the two minutes' silence, I hope?'

'No, of course not.'

'Good. Now would you like me to bring you up some tea?'

It was the first time that Josephine had felt in charge of the help situation since Mrs Thompson appeared on her doorstep, but she shook her head. 'Thank you, but no. I might as well get dressed now I'm up. I've got a busy day ahead.'

'All the more reason to have a nice cup of tea before you get started.' She filled the kettle and put it on the hob. 'Now, where do you keep your cups?' Josephine told her, watching as she took two down from the cupboard above the drainer and set them together on a tray. 'And what have you got planned that's keeping you so busy?'

'I'm meeting a friend for coffee at the Dorothy,' Josephine said, struck by how deceptively civilised her meeting with Bridget must sound to anyone who wasn't aware of the tensions involved. 'Then to the market square, obviously.'

'Ay, it's the most important day of the year, I always think, and you can rely on a good turnout. It's not been the same since they knocked the old Guildhall down, of course,' she added, warming the pot. 'It was much more dignified, standing there under the clock when the silence came. Now we all shuffle round in front of those terrible modern buildings on the other side.' She sighed and put the tray down on the table between them, then poured milk into the cups. 'Still, I don't suppose it matters *where* we do it, as long as we do. Will you be remembering anyone special today, Miss Tey?'

'Of course,' Josephine said quickly. 'None of us escaped unscathed, did we?'

'No, we most certainly did not.' She paused, and then – when it became obvious that Josephine wasn't going to engage any further of her own accord – filled the silence herself. 'I gather there was a young man you were quite fond of, but no one seems entirely sure who it was – not even your family.'

The telephone wires must have been red-hot between Mrs Thompson and her aunt in Inverness, Josephine thought, taken aback by the brazenness of the thinly veiled question. 'His name was Jack and he was killed at the Battle of the Somme,' she said. The words sounded cold and matter-of-fact, even to her, but she knew exactly where the conversation was heading and she was determined to nip the speculation in the bud once and for all.

Mrs Thompson was not to be deterred so easily. 'And there's been no one since?' she asked with a practised casualness. 'He must have been *very* special.'

'Yes, he was. I've never wanted to share my life with any other man since Jack died.' Josephine looked her inquisitor squarely in the eye, falling back on a convenient truth which she often used if a conversation became too personal. She watched Mrs Thompson wrestle with the ambiguities of the phrase, enjoying her uncertainty perhaps a little more than she should have. 'Now, if you'll excuse me, I must go and get ready.' Josephine took her tea and went back upstairs; the skirmish had gone her way, but still she was furious that a stranger with no understanding of a love that wasn't black and white should feel justified in making judgements on her life. She dressed carefully, choosing a smart navy blue suit which was appropriately sober for the day and which also gave her the self-assurance she would need for her meeting with Bridget. It was obviously going to be a day of confrontation rather than peace, and she could have done without such an awkward start to the morning: she was happy to take full responsibility for a row at the Dorothy Cafe, but Mrs Thompson wasn't even her daily.

She pinned a poppy to her jacket, replacing the brooch of her mother's which she usually wore there, then removed some of the photographs from the bedside table and locked anything else that was personal away in Marta's desk. 'The decorators will be here at nine,' she said on her way through the hallway. 'Perhaps you'd be kind enough to make them some tea.'

It was far too early to go to the cafe, so she took a circuitous route into town and browsed some of her favourite shops, all the while rehearsing different versions of what she wanted to say to Bridget. She wandered into Petty Cury, a part of town she was particularly fond of, which earned a sort of contrary distinction in Cambridge by being one of the few streets *not* to offer anything architecturally remarkable; instead, the busy thoroughfare was characterised by solid, Victorian buildings with one or two remnants from an earlier age, most notably a grand old coaching inn. The businesses in this street alone could supply everything that Josephine ever needed, and she had already spent enough time in W. Heffer and Sons to be on nodding terms with several of the booksellers. It was a fascinating shop, obviously expanded over time into the premises on either side, and each of the rooms now devoted to books retained a memento of its former identity – old wallpaper and an apothecary's bottles, a chandelier from a hotel bedroom.

Intrigued by the hints that Archie had dropped over his new case, she picked up a collected edition of M. R. James's ghost stories, then found a book called *The Secrets of Handwriting* among the newly published titles. She took her selection to the counter to pay but was distracted in the history section by a familiar dust jacket decked in an understated green tartan; it was the first time that she had seen her new book, *Claverhouse* – a biography of the soldier and Jacobite hero John Graham – on sale in a bookshop, and the unexpected sight of it on the shelves alongside works by famous historians gave her a thrill every bit as intense as the first time she had ever seen her name in lights above a theatre. She picked up the book and read the publisher's notes, which celebrated her success as a playwright and the powerful battle scenes which she had recreated in the book, comparing the final, bloody days of a seventeenth-century hero to the more recent conflict which had taken so many lives. It seemed an appropriate day to see Claverhouse honoured as she felt he should be and she put the volume proudly back on the shelf, amused as she always was to find that – once a book was out – all the pain and frustration of its creation disappeared as thoroughly as if it had never been.

Petty Cury was just a stone's throw from the Dorothy Cafe and Ballroom, and Josephine made her way reluctantly along Sidney Street, cursing the day that Marta had ever walked into the buffet at Cambridge Station and inadvertently discovered Bridget's secret. The Dorothy was obviously a popular venue, with a dance hall on the first floor and a bustling cafe below, and Josephine arrived just in time to take the last free table. She looked round at the other customers, but there was no sign yet of Bridget. 'Are you always this busy in the mornings?' she asked one of the waitresses, who looked run off her feet already.

'Not usually, no – not in the week, anyway. Blame it on that lot over there.' She gestured to the corner of the room, where three men in brown overalls were fiddling with wires and a television set beneath a sign that said 'Courtesy of Miller & Son', and Josephine remembered that the Armistice Day commemorations were being televised for the very first time. 'They're relaying the service from London,' her waitress confirmed. 'That's if they can ever get that blessed thing to work.' She rolled her eyes and moved on to the next table, and Josephine was struck by how ironic it seemed that she and Bridget should be having this conversation with Archie – on duty at the Cenotaph – somehow in the room with them.

When she looked back towards the door, Bridget was on her way over. It was still ten minutes ahead of their scheduled meeting time, and their shared punctuality suggested to Josephine that they were both keen to get the conversation over and done with as soon as possible. It was likely to be the only thing they stood united on, she thought, struck as ever by Bridget's beauty, by the sense of spirit and determination that she managed to convey in everything she did, even in something as simple as walking across a room. Her face was still tanned from months of working outside in the sun and wind, and Josephine felt the familiar sting of inadequacy – of ordinariness – that she had never quite shaken off since meeting Archie's lover at Portmeirion the year before.

Bridget took the chair opposite and looked round at the nearby tables. 'I thought if I chose somewhere that was the very essence of gentility we'd be less inclined to shout at each other,' she said.

'So you know why I wanted to see you.'

'I can guess what your matter of urgency is. After all, Phyllis has been a matter of urgency to me for twenty-one years.'

The waitress brought some menus over but Bridget waved hers away. 'Just coffee for me, please,' she said.

'I'll have the same.' Josephine waited while their cutlery was removed and replaced with coffee cups. 'This must be a sad day for Phyllis,' she said when they were alone again. 'Thinking about her dead father and all the years she's missed.' She had been determined not to let her anger get the better of her, but Bridget's attitude was little short of hostile and she found it impossible not to respond in kind. 'When *did* he die, just out of interest? Before she was born, or did you let her think that he held her in his arms before he went? Does she imagine she remembers him somehow – one of those elusive early memories that we long to believe in but never quite trust?'

'I'm not about to debate the rights and wrongs of the decision I made all those years ago, Josephine, and certainly not with you. What's done is done, and it's none of your business.'

'But it *is* Archie's business, and as you've seen fit to deny him—'

'Who the hell do you think you are?' Bridget demanded,

interrupting her. 'Expecting me to jump at your beck and call. Speaking up for Archie when you know as well as I do that if he suspected for a minute that we were having this conversation, he'd feel as betrayed by you as he would by me.' Josephine opened her mouth to argue but she knew that Bridget was right and the words died in her throat. 'This is *my* life – mine and Phyllis's – and I won't let you or anyone else send us hurtling over the cliff just because I made a mistake.'

'So we do at least agree that twenty years of silence was a mistake?'

'Of course – but what about Archie's silence? Have you thought about that? He could have contacted me at any time after the war. He knew where I was. He came to my exhibitions and bought my paintings, but never – not once – did he so much as send me a note. Does that sound to you like someone who'd lost the love of his life? We met again by accident, Josephine. Neither of us cared enough to look for each other. If Archie had come to me five weeks or five years after the war, I'd have introduced him to his daughter. But now, when it will wreak havoc in her life as well as in his – is it any wonder that I'm having to think about that?' The waitress arrived with a tray, and Josephine tried to remember a time when two coffee cups had taken quite so long to fill. 'And I've had a lot of time to think while I've been away,' Bridget continued eventually. 'Since Marta found out, I've felt as though I had a sentence hanging over me, threatening everything I love. I knew it was only a matter of time before she told you. In fact, I'm surprised she waited so long.'

'Marta gave you the benefit of the doubt,' Josephine said, refusing to let Bridget reopen the cracks that the secret had briefly caused in their relationship. 'She believed you'd do the right thing – foolishly, as it turned out.'

'*I'm* the fool for blithely accepting that you can hold me to ransom like this. All these months I've been so frightened, lying awake at night, inventing a thousand and one different ways to say

I'm sorry. But that's not who I am, and it stops here and now.'

Too late, Josephine realised how wrong it had been of her to assume that Bridget would be repentant. 'What do you mean?' she asked, suddenly fearful of the answer.

'I mean I'm taking control. So far, I've made the mistake of believing that there's only one way for this to end – I tell Archie and beg his forgiveness, and he decides what happens from then on. But that's not fair, Josephine, and being apart has made me realise that I *do* have a choice. I won't apologise for the life I've made, for me *and* for Phyllis. It's been a good life and we're happy as we are – just the two of us. So I *am* going to tell Archie about his daughter, but I'm also going to tell him that whatever there was between us is over.'

Josephine stared at her in astonishment, understanding now that there was an even more destructive outcome to this than the one she had imagined. 'So you're punishing Archie before he can punish you?' she asked. 'And punishing yourself, of course. Why would you give him up so easily when you obviously love him? You surely can't have forgotten how devastated you were when he was shot.'

'Of course I haven't. I *do* love Archie, you're right about that, but love isn't enough in itself. God forgive me, Josephine, but when I was sitting by that hospital bed watching him fight for his life, there was also a tiny part of me that suddenly saw a way out. And I've seen one now – one I'm less ashamed of. I'll tell Archie about Phyllis and give him the chance to get to know her – if that's what *she* wants, too – but our relationship is over. That way, I won't have to spend the rest of my life trying to make this up to him, especially when it's something I'd do all over again without the slightest hesitation.'

'But think about Archie,' Josephine said, suddenly the supplicant in the conversation. 'This could destroy him.'

'I'm not sure that's true – but even if it were, I'm too selfish to put him first.' She finished her coffee, and Josephine thought that the pause which followed signalled that their meeting was over, but she was wrong. 'When I first discovered I was pregnant, I thought it was the end of the world,' Bridget admitted. 'My mother was a brilliant artist when she was young. She painted the most beautiful watercolours from nature, so natural and instinctive, but when my brother came along, and then me, that urge to create deserted her completely. When I had Phyllis, I kept waiting for the same thing to happen to me, but it never did. In fact, my work got better after she was born because for the first time in my life I needed to make a living from it. My parents were wonderful, but I was far too proud to let them support us financially. So Phyllis – far from destroying my painting – gave it substance and meaning, although I'm not sure I've ever told her that.' She smiled awkwardly, and Josephine guessed that she had never intended the conversation to take quite such a personal turn. 'Phyllis is the best thing about me, Josephine, but there's only room in my life for one other love and that has to be my work. It's my best friend. Happy or sad, it's the thing I always turn to and I never have to pretend to be something I'm not. You understand that, don't you?'

Josephine nodded, feeling disloyal to all her best intentions but touched nonetheless by what Bridget had said. 'What about Phyllis?' she asked. 'Aren't you frightened of how she'll react?'

'Of course I am. I know it's a risk, but I'll take it. We love each other, Phyllis and I – even more importantly, we understand each other. She'll be angry and she'll be hurt, but we'll get through it – even if it takes a long time. We're strong enough to forgive each other anything – and realising that was the other thing that helped me make up my mind. I couldn't say the same about Archie and me – and that's not good enough.'

'I hope you're right,' Josephine said sincerely. 'Phyllis seems a lovely girl.'

She had meant it kindly, another small step in the growing reconciliation between them, but she had reckoned without the intrusion to which it bore witness. Bridget looked at her sharply and their brief solidarity dissolved in an instant. 'How the hell do you know what Phyllis is like?'

'I met her at the Festival Theatre.'

'You did *what*? How dare you? This is none of your damned business. What did you say to her?'

'Nothing – well, nothing to do with this. We talked about the theatre, that's all. I didn't even tell her that you and I know each other.'

'Good, because I'll talk to her in my own good time – to her and to Archie. I've had enough of ultimatums, and I won't take any more bullying from you or from Marta or from anybody else.' She stood up and threw some coins angrily down onto the table. 'If you're tempted to go behind my back and tell Archie before I'm ready, just think about what it might do to your relationship when he finds out that you met his daughter before he did. We're all implicated, Josephine, and I won't lose a moment's sleep over telling him that.'

She turned and left without another word. Shaken, Josephine queued to pay at the counter, trying to distract herself by watching a surprisingly clear picture of the solemn preparations at the Cenotaph, but the thought of seeing Archie – oblivious to the pain that awaited him – only made things worse and she was glad to turn her back on history in the making and walk out into the street. Outside, under an elaborate stone carving of the bow of a ship – a strange motif for a building so far from the sea – she was surprised to find Bridget waiting for her. 'I'm sorry, Josephine,' she said. 'That was completely out of order. You're bound to see this from Archie's side. You love him and he loves you – a little too much for my liking, at least in the early days.'

'But I can see your side, too. In your position I'd probably have done the same thing. We're a selfish generation.'

'Yes, I suppose we are.' She smiled sadly and held out her hand.

'Look after Archie, won't you? Perhaps I'm wrong, but once this is done I can't see myself having a place in his life – not for the foreseeable future, at least.'

Josephine nodded and watched her go, then headed thoughtfully back towards the market square. In the distance she could see the retreating banners of a peace society march, on its way to lay a wreath at the war memorial by the railway station, and the town's Armistice Day activities were in full swing. There was a garden of remembrance and pavement portrait gallery running the length of Great St Mary's Passage, and the university was doing its bit for the Poppy Day Fund all over town: undergraduates had been out selling poppies since the crack of dawn, and a taxi rank had sprung up outside one of the colleges, offering cheap fares for the day in anything from an ancient Morris to a car just off the showroom floor; hot dogs from the college kitchens were being sold out on the streets and they smelt wonderful, but Josephine had no appetite. She wandered among the other fundraisers which now surrounded the market place. A lifelike impersonation of Charlie Chaplin was proving popular, as was a tableau portraying the Berlin–Rome axis, with men dressed as Hitler and Mussolini balanced on either side of a seesaw – but the biggest crowds surrounded the 'Dictator Wagon' which had parked by the building site for the new Guildhall. The German and Italian leaders were again represented, but here they were joined by Peace, a figure clothed in white with a laurel crown on her head; an enthusiastic public was buying rotten fruit from the front of the wagon and hurling it at the two dictators, although Josephine couldn't help thinking it an ill but appropriate omen that in shying things at Hitler and Mussolini, many of the throwers seemed to be hitting Peace instead.

As eleven o'clock drew near, people began to gravitate towards the north side of the square, and Josephine had to admit that she and Mrs Thompson agreed on one thing: the college buildings here looked absurdly modern, which meant that in five or ten years' time they would look absurdly dated; in the absence of anything opposite, their stark Portland stone dominated the whole area, demanding attention but not deserving it. The clock of Great St Mary's began to chime, and in the distance she heard the muffled sound of a maroon marking the beginning of the silence. Vehicles stopped and hushed their engines, and the crowds stood stiff and still, young and old alike with their heads bowed; all around the square, windows were filled with solemn faces.

Suddenly, as the echoes of the clock's eleventh note died away, an alarm bell began ringing violently somewhere over to Josephine's right. It shattered the silence with its hammer-like strokes, and she saw in the faces of the veterans standing nearby that it brought back the dark days of twenty years before with a vivid and terrible immediacy. Heads turned as one, tracing the noise to a jeweller's shop on the corner of the square, and everyone seemed mortified by the timing of the intrusion but at a loss to know how to stop it. Then, to a collective sigh of relief, the bell ceased as abruptly as it had begun, leaving behind a deathly stillness. The silence was allowed to continue, disturbed only by a mosaic of faint but familiar sounds – the whirr of pigeons' wings as the birds wheeled above the crowd, the whimper of a frightened child and the rustle of leaves blowing across the pavement. In no time at all, an engine whistle shrilled to signal that the two minutes was up, but before the market place could become its noisy self again, a piercing scream came out across the crowd, also from the jeweller's shop. The distant boom of the second maroon was lost entirely in the ensuing chaos. Suddenly, Josephine was aware of police running from the streets surrounding the square, and the crowd – sensing that something momentous was happening – moved as one to the north-east corner. Josephine was caught up in the flow of curiosity, and there was only one thought on the lips of the people closest to her. For a single morning, Cambridge had forgotten its current preoccupation in deference to another violence, but now it dared to hope that – after months of living under fear and suspicion – the rapist who had held the town to ransom had finally been caught.

The sound of clanging bells drew closer and two police cars and an ambulance somehow managed to inch their way through the crowds down Market Street. The ambulance men disappeared into the jeweller's and a cheer went up as they re-emerged a few minutes later, helping a young girl who was shaken but obviously unharmed. The crowd parted to allow the ambulance through, and everyone waited impatiently for further news. Just as Josephine was beginning to think that the assailant had escaped yet again, the front door of the jeweller's opened and two policemen appeared leading a handcuffed figure dressed entirely in black, his face still covered by a balaclava. The noise that erupted around her was unbearable and the crowd surged forward again, shouting and jeering, arms outstretched towards the small group trying to reach the safety of the police car. She saw a flicker of fear in the escorting officers' eyes as they recognised the anger in the air – a raw, violent anger which knew no logic or reasoning. The inspector who had come to see Mary Ennis stood in the doorway with his colleagues but his efforts to calm the situation made no difference. Objects were hurled at the man in handcuffs – stones and coins and anything else that came to hand – and Josephine noticed that the women in the crowd seemed to be taking the lead in the disturbance, making up for weeks of fear and powerlessness. A broken piece of paving stone missed its target and smashed into the window of the jeweller's, and in the skirmish that developed as the suspect was wrestled to the waiting car, the mask that hid his face was roughly torn off. In the end, it was this which brought some order to the scene: a hush fell over the crowd while everyone stared at the face they had been denied for so long, as if the official silence had been merely a rehearsal for the intensity of this moment. He was just a boy, Josephine thought, staring along with them; just a red-haired, pale-faced boy of about twenty, somebody's son, and now somebody's shame. As they got him to the car and pushed him firmly inside, she thought she could see him crying.

Eventually the crowds began to disperse, leaving a kaleidoscope of red, trampled poppies on the ground as the only physical reminder of the ceremony that had brought them together in the first place. Josephine waited until the market place had returned to normal, numbed by what she had just seen and by the emotions of the hours leading up to it. Her first thoughts now were for Mary Ennis, and, on the spur of the moment, she cut across Market Hill and into King's Parade, making short work of the five-minute walk to Addenbrooke's Hospital. Reporters were already crowding round Inspector Webster and the details of the capture would, no doubt, soon spread through the town like wildfire, but there were some to whom the news mattered more than others and Josephine wanted Mary to know that justice would now be done on her behalf. It wasn't visiting time yet, but if the nurse on duty wouldn't make an exception, at least she could leave a message.

She climbed the stairs to the ward, hoping to see the matron who had been in charge on the night of Mary's admission, but there was no one there whom she recognised. 'I'm sorry,' the staff nurse said after Josephine had explained her business, 'that's wonderful news but Mary was discharged first thing this morning. Her parents and fiancé came to collect her and take her back to Yorkshire.'

'Her fiancé?' Josephine asked, bewildered. 'Mary's engaged? Are you sure?'

'Yes, of course – to her young man from back home. He proposed the other day when he came to see her and she accepted straight away. Isn't that romantic? Now she can really start to put this awful business behind her.'

'But she'll have to give up her job if she marries,' Josephine said, horrified to think that someone as dedicated and ambitious as Mary seemed should consider sacrificing all her hopes for a life with someone whom – only a few days before – she had readily admitted she didn't love. 'Surely she shouldn't be making a decision as important as that while she's still in shock from what happened. She's throwing away everything she ever wanted to achieve.'

'Yes, it's a shame, but I know what I'd rather have.' The nurse smiled, and perhaps it was Josephine's imagination but she thought she saw a glimmer of pity in her face, as if she were talking to someone who was making the best of a life without the things that any sane woman must want, the man and the children and the home which were denied to so many of her generation. 'It was kind of you to think of coming here, but I'm sure Mary will hear the news soon enough. I'll tell the rest of the girls, though – I dare say there'll be some celebrating tonight.'

Josephine thanked her and walked back home, wondering how many of the rapist's other victims were making rash decisions which there was every chance they would come to regret. As she reached St John's Street, the sounds of the Armistice Day fair on Jesus Green were evident in each lull of passing traffic, and she caught the familiar tunes of Scottish pipers on the march, strangely out of place so far from their home and from hers. The newspaper board outside the tobacconist's was already advertising the shocking turn of events to come in the evening edition, but she had no appetite for reading anything more about the morning's developments; she had seen them with her own eyes, and, in any case, the fact of the guilty man's capture offered inadequate compensation now for the lives he had ruined along the way.

18

It was the first time in nineteen years of remembrance that Penrose's mind had been anywhere else but on the Western Front while he stood by the Cenotaph for the Armistice Day service, but as dignitaries and veterans gathered around Lutyens's simple magnet for a nation's grief, his thoughts were firmly with the more recent dead. Over on the north side of Whitehall, where the Prime Minister stood with his Cabinet colleagues beneath the windows of the Home Office, he could just make out the tall, silver-haired figure of Richard Swayne among a group of civil servants. He had made an appointment to see Swayne immediately after the ceremony and this time he was determined to make him talk, even if it meant arresting him on a tenuous charge and facing the consequences later. As far as he could tell, there were only four people still living who knew what had happened in Cambridge all those years ago; one of them – the killer – wasn't giving himself away, and Rufus Carrington was nowhere to be found; somehow, Penrose needed to make Richard Swayne or Robert Moorcroft tell him what Alastair Frost refused to – and the best way to do that was to play them off against each other until one began to crack. From the little he knew of each man, his money was on Moorcroft to weaken first.

As always, the atmosphere was uniquely charged, an awkward combination of public display and private reflection. King George, wearing the khaki service uniform of a Field Marshal, stared solemnly up at the Cenotaph, calm and dignified on his first Armistice Day as sovereign. His brothers – the Dukes of Gloucester and Kent – stood to either side, wreaths in hand, and the Queen looked on from the balcony, a bunch of Flanders poppies pinned to her black dress. Just as Big Ben drew breath to usher in a brief stilling of city life, Penrose was distracted by a movement in the crowd in front of the Home Office. A fair-haired man in a mackintosh stumbled as if he were going to faint, then pushed forward suddenly through the crowds and, before anyone could stop him, broke the ranks of naval ratings and headed in a direct line for the King. Uniformed policemen and security officers moved forward as one, Penrose included, but not before the man's angry cries cut harshly through the silence, alarming and offending those close enough to hear: 'All this is hypocrisy,' he shouted as he was wrestled to the ground just a few yards from the Prime Minister. 'You are deliberately preparing for war.'

As he joined the skirmish, Penrose saw the fear in Chamberlain's face. He put his hand over the protester's mouth, trying to muffle the cries and protect the silence, and some semblance of order was restored to the crowd. The mounted police arrived, forming a protective circle around the small group of men on the floor, and Penrose waited impatiently for the seconds to tick by. When at last the guns boomed forth from Hyde Park, he and his colleagues got the man to his feet and took him between the troops into Downing Street, where an ambulance station had been set up in case of emergency. Fear was turning to anger in the crowd, but, as he glanced back over his shoulder, Penrose noticed that the King and his brothers had stood motionless throughout the uproar, and he admired their courage; when the time came for the national anthem, it was no surprise that it was sung more fervently than ever.

Away from the public eye, Penrose checked the protester for weapons and eventually managed to establish that he was an ex-serviceman called Stanley Storey, whose performance at the Cenotaph reprised an earlier disturbance in the House of Commons. He left the dissenting pacifist in the Colonial Office to wait for Special Branch, then walked quickly back to Whitehall, where the parade had just finished and the crowd was beginning to disperse. If Storey's intention had been nothing more violent than to divert the public's attention from the matter at hand, then he had certainly succeeded: there was talk of little else among the families in the street, although Penrose couldn't help feeling that the shattering of the ceremony would have struck a rather different chord elsewhere in the country, where feelings about events in Europe ran high and the silence seemed less a mark of respect than a scream of collective impotence; many felt – like the man he had just arrested – that there was very little point in paying homage to the fallen when every day the country drifted closer to another war.

By the time he reached the Home Office, he was twenty minutes late for his appointment and Swayne's secretary shook her head as soon as she saw him. 'I'm sorry, Chief Inspector, but Mr Swayne has just left. He's got a briefing with the Home Secretary this afternoon and he really couldn't wait any longer.'

'What time will the briefing finish?' Penrose asked, cursing Stanley Storey and his bid for notoriety. 'It's essential that I speak with him. If I came back later this afternoon, perhaps he could see me then? I'm very happy to wait until it's convenient.'

'It would be a long wait, I'm afraid. He's going straight from the briefing to Sussex for a few days' leave. He won't be back here now until the end of next week. He suggested you make another appointment for the week after, when he's had a chance to catch up.'

Her tone managed to imply without actually saying so that busy civil servants couldn't be expected to organise their lives around tardy policemen, and Penrose tried another tack. 'Do you have an address for him in Sussex?' he asked, and then, when she was about to deflect him again: 'I can't overstress how important this is. I have very good reason to believe that Mr Swayne is in great personal danger, and that there may well be an attempt made on his life in the next few days. Please, for his sake – if you know where he's going, let me have the address or persuade him to give me ten minutes before he leaves.'

She hesitated, clearly unsettled by the force of his request. 'I don't have the authority to do either of those things,' she said cautiously, 'but I'll speak to someone who does and let you know. That's the best I can do, I'm afraid.'

Penrose thanked her and headed back to Scotland Yard without any great hope of a result. 'You're popular this morning,' the desk sergeant said as he walked through the door. 'There's a woman called Moorcroft been phoning non-stop. Don't they have an Armistice in Cambridgeshire?'

'Did she say what it was about?' Penrose asked, too interested to pander to the sergeant's ruffled feathers.

'No, and she wouldn't speak to anyone else either. Just insisted that you telephone as soon as you're back.'

Penrose did as Virginia Moorcroft had asked, but the mixture of relief and distress in her voice when she realised who it was made it hard to understand what she was saying. 'Mrs Moorcroft, please try to stay calm and tell me what's happened.'

'You said to call and I didn't know what else to do. My little boy found him early this morning. He was playing in the grounds with a friend from King's College School. They shouldn't have been there – I've told Teddy time and again that it's too dangerous. Why didn't he listen to me? Finding him like that with no warning. They're just kids, for God's sake.'

'Finding who, Mrs Moorcroft?' Penrose asked, although he was already anticipating the answer. Alastair Frost had obviously been wrong in his prediction: Richard Swayne was still alive and well, but it seemed that Robert Moorcroft's body . . .

'I don't know who he is,' Virginia Moorcroft said, wrong-footing him completely. 'It's impossible to tell. He's obviously been dead for a while.' A few weeks, Penrose thought, guessing now that the body was Rufus Carrington. 'I have no idea how he got there,' she added. 'Please come, Chief Inspector. I don't know what's going on, but my children . . . You *will* come, won't you?'

'Of course, I'll leave now – but first I need to know exactly what happened this morning. Where did your son find the body?'

'There's a derelict mill on the outskirts of the estate, with a house and some old outbuildings,' she explained, her voice much calmer now. 'They used it for grinding cement before the war, but the company went bust and it's been falling into disrepair ever since. All the old machinery's still there – which is why it's too dangerous for Teddy to play in, and why it's too enticing for him to take any notice of me when I tell him that. Anyway, there's a cellar in the ruins of the house, and that's where the body is.'

'Have you seen it yourself?'

'Yes. Teddy was in a terrible state and he was obviously telling the truth, but when I'd calmed him down I went to make sure that he hadn't made a mistake.'

'Are the remains skeletal?' Penrose asked, anxious not to read too much into a corpse which had lain undiscovered for years.

'No, more recent than that. I didn't look too closely – it was worse than anything I could have imagined. In fact, it took me a moment to work out what I was seeing. He's just sitting there, at a table . . .' She tailed off, but Penrose had heard enough to know that the crime scene echoed very clearly another of M. R. James's most famous stories, 'The Tractate Middoth', in which one of the characters – a vindictive, elderly clergyman – chose to be buried in an underground room, sitting at a table. 'This has something to do with my husband, doesn't it?'

'Where *is* your husband?'

'He's in his study, drinking himself to death.'

'And does he know what's happened?'

'Yes, of course. I told him myself, but it was as if he hadn't heard – or wouldn't listen. He just screamed at me to leave him alone and locked the door after I'd gone. He's frightened, Chief Inspector – frightened, and out of control.'

'Have you contacted the Cambridge police yet?'

'No. I had your card, and you were the first person I thought of.'

'Then I'll telephone them now and ask them to send some men out to the Priory to secure the scene until I get there. I'll be as quick as I can. Will you be all right in the meantime?'

She seemed to understand that his concerns for her stemmed more from her husband's potential for violence than from whoever was responsible for the body in the derelict cellar. 'Yes, I'll be fine. I can handle Robert when he's drunk. It's when he's sober that he frightens me. And anyway, I'll be with Teddy. He'd never lay a finger on his children.'

Penrose rang off, then telephoned Cambridge police station and asked for Superintendent Clough. 'I know this is the last thing you need when you're already overstretched,' he began, but was quickly interrupted.

'Looks like we've got him, Penrose. Webster arrested a man this morning. The bastard assaulted a shop assistant during the two-minute silence, would you believe? He's not talking yet, but it's early days. So what can I do for you?'

'I need you to send a couple of men over to Angerhale Priory right away,' Penrose said, and explained why.

Clough listened without any interruptions, then said a little peevishly: 'Can't imagine why she didn't call us first. I suppose this *is* connected to your earlier interest in Moorcroft?'

'Without a doubt,' Penrose said firmly.

'Do you think Moorcroft did it? And the chap in Hampstead?'

'I'm not making any assumptions until I've had a look at the body for myself – and it's vital that I see the scene as it is, without any—'

'Don't get yourself worked up about it, Penrose. No one's going in until you get there – I'll make sure they understand that.'

'Thank you. I'll be with them in a couple of hours, and I'd be grateful if they could also make sure that Robert Moorcroft doesn't leave the house. From what his wife tells me, he's in no fit state to go anywhere, but if he tries anything they have my full authority to arrest him.'

'Very well. I'll make sure they know what's expected.'

Penrose thanked him and left instructions for Sergeant Fallowfield to follow on with Bernard Spilsbury as soon as the pathologist could make himself available, then headed for the fens by the now familiar route. This time, Virginia Moorcroft opened the door to him herself. She was even paler than usual, her skin bone-white in the shadows of the hallway, her lips a slash of crimson. 'Thank you for coming, Mr Penrose,' she said, as if he were fulfilling a social obligation, although the way she took his hand was less formal. 'This is beginning to feel like a very bad dream.'

She led him through to a drawing room at the back of the house, more intimate than the room he had questioned her husband in, with oak panelling in the Jacobean style and an elaborate plasterwork ceiling. At the far end of the room, in front of a roaring fire which seemed to have been built as high as possible to banish the horrors that lurked outside, two small boys were playing quietly with a train set. 'How is Teddy?' Penrose asked, easily identifying Virginia Moorcroft's son by the rich, chestnut brown hair that he had inherited from his mother.

'It's hard to say. He was very upset when he got back to the house – they both were – but he's calmed down now. I guess I'll find out how he really is when he tries to go to sleep. I haven't worked out yet what I'm going to say to the other parents. Finding a dead body isn't the sort of activity we usually plan for a visit to Angerhale.' She gave him a faint smile. 'Anyway, I brought you in here because I thought you might need to speak to the boys?'

'No, not at the moment. It looks as if their minds are on other things, at least for now, and I don't want to remind them unnecessarily. I'll look at the scene first, and save any questions for later.'

'Then I'll show you to the old mill.' She seemed grateful for his sensitivity, and they left the boys in peace. 'You know who that poor wretch in the cellar is, don't you?' she said as they walked through the staff quarters to the other side of the house.

'Obviously he'll need to be formally identified, but I think his name is Rufus Carrington. He was a professor of medieval history at Oxford who was supposed to be here on a research sabbatical. He was also at King's with your husband. They were in the choir together.'

'Like the other men who've been killed? The ones you asked me about when you were last here?'

Penrose nodded. 'Where is Mr Moorcroft now?'

'Upstairs, sleeping it off. He passed out in his study so I got a couple of the staff to put him to bed.' She stopped by a window which looked out across a kitchen garden, and he knew what she was going to ask. 'Is Robert the next to die? Is that why he's so frightened?'

Penrose hesitated, but there was little point in keeping anything from her now. 'There are only two men still alive from that particular group of choral scholars,' he said. 'Your husband and a civil servant in London called Richard Swayne.' The name obviously meant nothing to her, so he carried on. 'Four of the others have been murdered, one was killed in the war, and another – Alastair Frost – died very recently from cancer. I spoke to Dr Frost just before his death, and he told me that these men are being murdered because of something they did during their time at King's. Do you have any idea what that might be?'

She shook her head. 'No, I don't. I was telling you the truth when I said that their names mean nothing to me. Robert never talks about them.'

'And do you think you could persuade him to talk to me now?

Until I know what happened all those years ago, I can't even begin to work out who might want to punish them for it. It could be the difference between his living and dying.'

'That might be quite a dilemma if I really thought I could change his mind. Fortunately, I can't. Robert never listens to me.' She gave a short, bitter laugh. 'You must think very badly of me, Mr Penrose.'

'No,' he said quickly. 'No, I don't think badly of you at all. On the contrary.' She smiled and they walked on in silence as far as the rear porch. 'Just give me directions from here,' Penrose said. 'You don't need to come with me – you've seen more than enough already.'

She put a hand to his cheek and he felt himself flush like an adolescent. 'You're very kind,' she said. 'I don't suppose you have any idea how terrifying kindness is when you're not used to it.'

'Why?'

'Because there's always a chance you'll come to depend on it – and then you really are lost.' She opened the door abruptly, saving him from the problem of knowing what to say. 'The mill is a five-minute walk from here. Follow that path until you get to the river on the edge of the estate, then you'll see the mill and the ruins of the house up ahead. There's a trapdoor down to the cellar. It's been covered over for as long as I've been here, but I suppose whoever did this uncovered it.'

'Probably. I'm expecting some colleagues from Scotland Yard – perhaps you'd be kind enough to point them in the right direction when they get here?' She nodded and began to close the door but he stopped her. 'Mrs Moorcroft, is there somewhere you can take the children until this is all over? Somewhere safe, perhaps with your family?'

'I don't have any family here – they're all in America. Anyway, I don't want to frighten the children. It's best if we keep things as normal as possible – and surely we'll be safe here? It's Robert who's involved in all this – have any of the other men's families been harmed?'

'No,' Penrose admitted. He could understand her preference to stay, but still it bothered him. Perhaps he was simply allowing his liking for Virginia Moorcroft to cloud his judgement, but it seemed to him that her husband was the odd man out in this story, taunted and frightened while the men around him were ruthlessly eliminated; it was as if even the cruellest of deaths was too merciful a punishment, and he wouldn't have put it past the killer to use Moorcroft's family against him. 'Please reconsider,' he said gently. 'I can't guarantee your safety here, but I'd be happy to arrange somewhere for you all to stay if you don't want to go to America. Will you at least think about it?'

She agreed reluctantly, and he set out down the path she had shown him without any great hope of her changing her mind. The gardens at Angerhale showed the same flair for beauty and comfort as the house. Even at this time of year, it was easy to see a design of skilfully judged contrasts: the formal and the flamboyant; the wild and the managed; precise, geometric lines and sweeping, open landscapes. Under different circumstances, the walk would have been a delight. He was soon at the river, which formed a natural boundary to the north of the estate, and the long, straight ribbon of water led his eye to the mill in the distance. As he drew closer, he saw that the house and outbuildings which formed a courtyard to the side were blackened by fire and derelict. Perhaps it was the knowledge of what awaited him inside, but the scene in front of him seemed to hold a tangible melancholy, as if the fire had simply finished a natural process of waste and desolation which began in the human spirit.

He showed his warrant card to the officer standing by the bridge, then crossed the river to the old mill gates. The spot was isolated, hidden from the Priory by a thick band of woodland and approached from the opposite direction along a cart track through open fields. The killer had chosen shrewdly: as well as its proximity to Angerhale and similarity to the location in James's story, the spot was eminently suited to the disposal of a body – unused, private, remote. Its selection was deliberate, and suggested a familiarity with the area. He glanced through the open door of the mill, where the shafts and grinders were still in place, then walked over to the derelict house. The trapdoor led down from the room which had obviously once been a scullery. Penrose pulled it back, and saw a set of wooden steps leading into the blackness. A musty smell rose up to greet him – the stale, bleak smell of neglect – but the intense stench of death which accompanied the earlier stages of decomposition was mercifully absent.

He took a torch from his pocket and began to descend the steps, weighed down by an uncharacteristic sense of dread. The room was desperately cold, lined with brick and about twelve feet square. In the limited light, he could see that the dead man was sitting with his back towards the steps at what looked like an old school desk. The black parson's cloak which the corpse in James's story wore had been replaced here by a college gown, and the effect was surreal; the man's head lolled slightly to one side, but otherwise it would have been easy to believe that the figure might stand and turn at any moment. Penrose's torch picked out dark stains on the floor under the chair, and the sheer volume of blood told him that Rufus Carrington – if this *was* Carrington – had been killed where he sat. The cellar was, quite literally, a chamber of horrors, and he couldn't help but contrast the comfortable thrill of a ghost story with the brutal reality in front of him.

He walked slowly towards the body and forced himself to direct the circle of soft yellow light at the dead man's face, remembering the description he had circulated for the missing academic: of medium build, with wavy dark brown hair and brown eyes, and a beard worn to cover a distinctive strawberry birthmark on his left cheek. But what Penrose saw before him was barely recognisable as human, let alone identifiable. Most of the soft tissues on the face and neck had been eaten away by scavengers, leaving the sinews and tendons exposed and the mouth pulled back in a sinister rictus grin. The victim's eyes were long gone, and the wide, empty sockets joined with a gaping jaw and prominent teeth to create an impression of surprised amusement, as if his fate had proved so absurd and so unexpected that the only response left to him was to laugh. His hands were tied to the arms of the chair, and Penrose noticed that the skin was heavily discoloured and leathery, where the process of mummification had begun. Suddenly, he longed for the innocent horror of James's dry, cobwebbed skull, and he could only begin to imagine the pictures which would haunt Teddy Moorcroft and his friend in their dreams.

He turned his attention to the items on the desk: an old briar tobacco pipe, a tin of Sun Dew tobacco, a whisky bottle and a soda siphon – so incongruous in their current setting. There was a blank, unsealed envelope propped against the bottle, labelled simply 'To whom it may concern'. Penrose picked it up and took out a small slip of paper. The only thing written on it was a series of five punctuated numerals: '11.3.34'. They looked like a date of birth, and had he not read 'The Tractate Middoth' – in which a series of numbers also appeared – he would never have considered that they might be the library reference number for a book. In the story, the book in question had been found on the shelves of the University Library and held the key to the whole mystery; with a surge of excitement, Penrose wondered if the volume to which these numbers belonged would do the same.

He made a note of the five digits and put the envelope back by the bottle for the scene of crime photographs, then turned to look again at the body. There was a natural order to everything, Alastair Frost had said: assuming that this was Rufus Carrington and that the murder had taken place shortly after his disappearance, then his death was the second in the sequence, after Giles

Shorter and before Stephen Laxborough. Why was the pattern of killing so important? Penrose wondered. And what sort of person was behind it? These murders were among the most audacious crimes that he had ever come across. The systematic elimination of four men would, in itself, require nerve, discipline and careful planning, but there was another layer to every death: the symbolism and the careful staging of each crime scene, the confident taunting of the police along the way – this was the work of someone highly intelligent, someone driven to the point of obsession by hatred or by an acute sense of injustice and retribution.

When he was sure that he had noted everything, Penrose climbed back up towards the light, pleased to be breathing fresh, clean air again. In the distance, he could see Fallowfield and Spilsbury turning on to the river path and he raised his hand in greeting. 'I'm sure it's Rufus Carrington,' he said, when they were close enough to talk. 'But we'll have to rely on dental records to prove it.'

Fallowfield raised an eyebrow. 'That bad, eh?'

'Oh, he's surpassed himself this time,' Penrose said with feeling. 'There's a whole stage set in there. The floor's covered in blood, Bernard, so my guess is that his throat was cut, but I'd be grateful for a time and cause of death as soon as possible.'

'When wouldn't you, Archie?' Spilsbury said wryly. 'So a relatively swift death compared to our Hampstead friend?'

'Yes, although there's no way of telling how long our killer might have played with him before using the knife. Whatever happened, the rats are finishing what he started.'

'Have you spoken to Moorcroft?' Fallowfield asked.

'No, only his wife. He's upstairs, sleeping off a heavy session.'

'And we believe her?'

The comment wasn't meant to be accusatory, but Penrose realised suddenly that he hadn't so much as questioned what he had been told and Bill was right: he should have checked for himself. He had only his instincts to prove that Virginia Moorcroft wasn't playing a very clever game, pretending to be frightened of her husband while actually protecting him – and Penrose was honest enough to admit to himself that his instincts were unusually biased where the lady of the house was concerned. For all he knew, Moorcroft might have left the country days ago. 'Of course we believe her,' he snapped. 'Why would she lie?' Fallowfield said nothing, but exchanged a 'what did I tell you?' look with Spilsbury, and Penrose guessed that his ears should have been burning during their drive up from London. 'I'll go and see him on my way out,' he added defensively, 'and we'll question him formally tomorrow, when he's sobered up. By then, I'm hoping to have a bit more information to play with.'

Fallowfield looked at him curiously. 'Right-o, sir,' he said, as good-naturedly as ever, 'but where are you going?'

This time it was Penrose's turn to look smug. 'I'm off to the library, Bill,' he said. 'I think at last we might be getting somewhere.'

19

Penrose stood in the foyer of the University Library, waiting impatiently for the attendant to return with the book he had requested. According to the library's files, the numbers found with Rufus Carrington's body belonged to a publication called *Byways in British Archaeology* by Walter Johnson, which dated back to 1912. The title was unpromising, but Penrose had never expected the book's significance to lie in its subject matter; Walter Johnson was, no doubt, a greatly respected authority on archaeology, but he was far more interested in any recent additions that might have been made to the book – something tucked inside its pages, perhaps, or annotations to the printed text added by a second, anonymous author. He looked for the umpteenth time at the vast clock behind the desk, which told him that he had been waiting for nearly fifteen minutes, and caught the attendant's eye. 'Is the archaeology section in a very distant part of the library?' he asked, worried now that the book might be missing. 'If the volume I need is on open shelves, I'm more than happy to go and fetch it myself.'

'That won't be necessary, sir,' the attendant said, glancing behind him to the first-floor corridor which ran past the catalogue room. 'I think I can hear Mr Duncan coming now.'

Sure enough, the librarian soon appeared at the top of the steps, his modest frame burdened by a pile of eight or ten books. Quite reasonably, he had collated a number of requests together on a round-trip of the book stacks, but Penrose could cheerfully have strangled him for every wasted moment. 'Here you are, sir,' Duncan said, handing him the larger of two volumes bound in red cloth. '*Byways in British Archaeology*.'

'Thank you.' Penrose tried not to snatch the book from his hand. He took his prize over to one of the leather chairs by the library's revolving doors and set about examining it. In the story of 'The Tractate Middoth', the secrets which the book held – a missing will – were inscribed on the flyleaves, so he looked there first but they were blank. He flicked slowly through the five hundred or so pages, but there seemed to be nothing tucked between them except dust and a comprehensive exploration of burial customs, churches built on pagan sites and the folklore of yew trees. Convinced that he must have missed something, he repeated the process and then, in frustration, held the book by its outer covers and shook it up and down to see if anything fell out. The carpet at his feet remained obstinately bare, and he noticed that the librarians were beginning to stare at him as if he were a lunatic shaking a defenceless child. He smiled apologetically and turned back to the book. Had someone got there ahead of him, he wondered? Walter Johnson's particular brand of scholarship seemed to be out of fashion – the dates on the title page showed that *Byways in British Archaeology* hadn't been borrowed for five years – but anyone consulting the book in the library could have tampered with it. Or had he misread the situation completely? Perhaps the piece of paper was nothing more than a reference to the story, an empty stage prop left there for one reason only – to send anyone investigating the murders on a wild goose chase. If that was the case, it had worked to perfection.

Bitterly disappointed, he decided to borrow the book anyway. He might have missed something, and after his earlier excitement – not to mention his smugness with Fallowfield – he couldn't bear to leave empty-handed. 'I'd like to take this out, please,' he said to the librarian who had fetched it for him. 'Thank you for your help.'

'Do you have borrowing rights, sir?' Mr Duncan asked politely, and Penrose didn't know whether to be charmed or irritated by the institution's insistence on protocol, even in the face of a police investigation. He gave his college and year of matriculation, and waited while the register was consulted; when his request was deemed to be in order, the volume was duly stamped and given over to his custody for a period of two weeks.

Penrose went back to his car, tossing the book onto the passenger seat with a lack of ceremony which would have sent the librarian to new heights of indignation. He sat there for several minutes, fighting the despair which had begun to overwhelm him when he realised that the clue on which he had briefly relied – the first possibility of moving forward with the case – was nothing of the sort. He had hoped to have something new to put in front of Robert Moorcroft when he next sat down to question him, but he was back where he started and he needed to clear his head. On a whim, he drove to the nearest telephone box and dialled Josephine's number.

Five minutes later, he saw her walking down St Clement's Passage to meet him as he parked his car near Jesus Green. Perhaps it was the sober, dark coat or the resonance of the poppy pinned to its lapel, but she looked thoughtful and reflective, scarcely more content than he was himself, and he felt the weight of a day which held sadness for them both. 'I'm sorry not to be more hospitable,' she said as he got out to open the door for her, 'but we can't talk properly in the house at the moment. In fact, the house is turning into a bit of a nightmare. I've managed to hire Marta the daily woman from hell and the decorators are currently building to some sort of crescendo on the first floor. They'll be leaving soon, but until then I can't even hear myself think.'

'You'll be glad to get back to Inverness for some peace and quiet.'

Josephine looked sceptical. 'That rather depends on the daily woman. Just my luck to end up with someone who's got relatives in my home town. She's determined to get to the bottom of me, but

I'm afraid it's a rather doomed effort.' She must have seen his look of bewilderment, because she smiled. 'I'm sorry, Archie – it's a long story and it's not why you're here. Shall we go somewhere in town and talk there?'

'Do you mind if we just stay here? It's been a bit of a day already and I'm at my wits' end with people. I came close to hitting a librarian earlier, and a waitress might send me over the edge.'

'That's not like you.'

'A lot of things aren't like me at the moment, but I still seem to be doing them.' He wound down his window and rummaged for a packet of cigarettes in the glove compartment. 'I'm sorry, Josephine. The front seat of a car on a drizzly November evening isn't very glamorous.'

'Oh, I don't know. It's got a B-movie charm.' She took a cigarette and waited for him to light it. 'What's the matter, Archie? Why are you so unsettled?'

He hesitated, scarcely knowing how to answer such a straightforward question, or to explain that he had simply wanted to see a friendly face on a day when nothing – least of all his own feelings – seemed to make sense to him. 'It's this case I'm working on,' he said eventually. 'Four people have been killed and two are still in danger, and I'm no wiser now than I was five weeks ago.'

'Is that all?' Josephine looked surprised, as if she had been expecting him to say something else. 'I don't mean it isn't important – it sounds terrible and you must feel completely helpless – but I thought there was something more personal troubling you. You seem . . .' She paused, trying to put her finger on it. 'Well, you seem unhappy. Unhappy, and angry with yourself.'

'Do I?' He smiled at her, comforted by how well she knew him. 'I'm not really unhappy. Disappointed, perhaps – in myself, you're right about that – but even that's not quite the right word. To be honest, Josephine, I'm not sure *how* I feel.'

'So what's happened? You were distracted like this the other night, too. Is it about Bridget?'

'Yes, I suppose it is – indirectly.' He stared out of the window, watching families trying to make the best of the weather at the Armistice fair. The light had faded, replaced by flickering dots of yellow and orange as the stallholders brought out lamps and torches, adding a warmth to the scene which had so far been absent. In the distance, he could hear the first, nostalgic notes of a brass band. 'She's been away a long time now. We speak on the phone, but sometimes we're strangers to each other – and I think Bridget feels that, too.'

'She's back in Cambridge, Archie. I bumped into her this morning.'

'Is she?' He stared at her in surprise. 'I wasn't expecting her for another week or so. She must have finished her work early.'

'But she didn't tell you she was coming home.'

Any curiosity that he might have felt about Bridget's silence was lost in a sudden, overwhelming surge of relief which took him completely by surprise. 'No, she didn't, but that's wonderful. Now things can get back to normal, without all these distractions.'

He began to regret ever starting the conversation, but Josephine seemed reluctant to let it drop. 'What distractions?' she asked. 'I've never known you to think of work as a distraction – just the opposite – so what else has been getting in the way?' He felt himself flush, and she noticed immediately. 'Or should I say *who*?'

'It's nothing, Josephine, and it probably doesn't matter now.' She didn't argue, but waited patiently for him to decide how much he wanted to say. 'Can I tell you something without your thinking badly of me?'

'I'd say there's a good chance you can, yes.'

'I blamed the case for unsettling me, and that's true – but not just professionally. There's a woman involved. Her name's Virginia Moorcroft, and she's married to one of the men being targeted.'

'Yes, you told me. You were with her the other night.'

'That's right, and I saw her again this afternoon. Another body's turned up, this time at the Priory where she lives. Her son found it, and she telephoned me for help.' He blushed again. 'Bill thinks she's wrapping me round her little finger, and he's got a point.'

'Because you like her?'

'Yes, I like her, and I can't keep pretending to myself that I don't. Moorcroft's a brute, Josephine. He treats her appallingly, and I don't know why she—'

'Hang on, Archie – don't confuse attraction with sympathy.'

'Is that what you think I'm doing?' he demanded, daring her to say yes.

'I can't answer that. I'm just saying that you're a kind man who hates injustice – and Bill's usually a very shrewd judge of character.' Archie laughed and she looked at him curiously. 'What have I said that's so funny? Bill knows you as well as I do.'

'It's not that. It's something *she* said. She told me that kindness frightened her because she might come to depend on it.'

Josephine lifted an eyebrow. 'Gosh, she *is* good.'

'So *you* think I'm being stupid as well. I wish I'd never mentioned it. Virginia's not on trial, Josephine. I don't remember being this judgemental when you were dithering about Marta.'

In all the years that he and Josephine had been friends, he had rarely been able to get the better of her in an argument, and today was no different. 'As I recall, you refused even to talk about Marta at the dithering stage.' She smiled, and took his hand. 'I don't think you're being stupid, but it sounds as though both of you are vulnerable at the moment and whatever you feel for her might be tied up with your frustration at not being able to solve the case.' She sensed his resentment, and tried to explain what she meant. 'You know they arrested a man for the rapes this morning?' Archie nodded. 'I was in the market square when it happened and I saw it all. The only thing I could think of afterwards was Mary – my young neighbour who was attacked – so I went to the hospital to tell her. I thought if she could look forward to some sort of justice, it might help.'

'That was kind of you.'

'I couldn't do it, though, because she'd already been discharged. But the nurse on duty told me that Mary's decided to go back to the town she came from and marry the boy next door. I think she saw it as something to celebrate but I was horrified. It's Mary's choice, I know that, and perhaps I'd feel exactly the same in her position, but it just seems such a waste. She'll have to give up everything she's worked for. I can't believe it's 1937 and women are still having to make those choices.'

'I agree with you, but what's that got to do with Virginia?'

'Perhaps nothing, perhaps everything. I was thinking about Mary's fiancé, too, as I walked home. I don't doubt that he asked her to marry him for all the right reasons, but he can't possibly save her now from what happened to her – the horse has bolted on that one. And when they finally realise that, I think it will destroy them both.'

'So you're casting me as the boy next door?' Archie asked, his irritation returning as quickly as it had left. 'Anyway, I *love* Bridget, and I can't believe we're even having this conversation.'

It was to Josephine's credit that she refrained from pointing out who had raised the subject in the first place. 'I know you love her, but as someone said to me recently, love isn't always enough in itself.'

Now it was Archie's turn to look concerned. 'Is everything all right between you and Marta?'

'Oh yes. It wasn't Marta who said it. Marta will have "love for love's sake" engraved on her tombstone – at least I hope she will. But we were talking about you, and "getting back to normal", as you put it just now, isn't always the best thing to do. Sometimes it means settling for less than you want, and only you can look into your heart and decide whether or not that's what you and Bridget have been doing.'

He nodded, reluctantly acknowledging the sense of what she said. 'The trouble is, I don't trust my own judgement about anything at the moment, personal or professional. And you're right, I suppose – I am letting the hopelessness of this case colour everything, but it's hard not to. I've never felt so out of control. Whoever's behind these killings is always one step ahead.'

'How many times have I heard you say that?'

Archie smiled. 'Yes, but this time it's true. I really thought I was getting somewhere today, but it turned out to be yet another dead end.' She listened, intrigued, while he outlined the connection between the four murders and M. R. James's stories, finishing with the clue that came directly from 'The Tractate Middoth'. 'So I'm no closer to knowing who's doing this, or even why.'

'But surely when James wrote that story, he set it in the *old* library, not the new one. That's only been there a few years.'

'Yes, I know it has, but the books are the same – and it's the books that matter, not where they are.'

'Are you sure about that? What's the old building used for now?'

'It's a law library.' She just looked at him and Archie realised how stupid he had been. 'Bill's right, isn't he? I really am losing the plot.' He looked at his watch. 'Five to six – it should still be open. Thanks, Josephine – I'll telephone you later to let you know if you were right.'

He leaned forward to kiss her and she stared at him in amused disbelief. 'You're surely not expecting me to get out of the car? I'm coming with you to the law library. The least you can do is give me the satisfaction of seeing the look on your face when the key to the whole case comes fluttering out of that book.'

'I suppose it is,' he admitted sheepishly. 'Sorry.'

A sequence of side roads surrounding St Clement's Church

brought them back to the main thoroughfare. Trinity Street was almost too narrow for two lanes of traffic, and Penrose had to pull over once or twice to make room for delivery vans coming the other way. 'I don't know why they can't bring the bloody groceries in at a more convenient time,' he muttered as the driver of a Matthew's lorry gave him a cheerful wave of thanks. 'We'll be lucky to get there before Christmas at this rate.'

But when he reached the end of the street, lights were still blazing from the neoclassical building next to the Senate House. 'I'll wait here,' Josephine offered as he parked at the corner of King's Parade. 'I think the simultaneous presence of a police officer *and* a woman might be a little too much for them.'

'All right. I'll be as quick as I can.' He was back at the car in less than ten minutes, carrying a heavy, leather-bound book. 'The fact that they were about to close rather played into our hands,' he explained. 'I thought I was going to have to jump through hoops to borrow this, but one flash of my warrant card did the trick.'

'So it should when you're in the law library. And?'

'I don't know yet. I thought we'd look together.' He gave her the torch from the glove compartment to enhance the efforts of the street lamp, and opened the book – an exhaustive study entitled *Law and the Practice of Criminal Appeals* which made Walter Johnson's archaeological insights seem daring by comparison. Again, there was nothing taped to the flyleaves, but it didn't take him long to see that there was something tucked inside about halfway through the book. He turned the pages carefully in case the placement itself was important, cursing the clumsiness of his gloves, and took out a small, dog-eared photograph of a gravestone. 'Ellen Jane Cleever,' he said, reading the inscription on the stone. 'Beloved daughter of Alfred and Maud Cleever. Why is that name familiar?'

'Because it was in the list of news items I gave you the other day. Do you remember? There were two young women who had drowned, one not long after the other, and one of them was called Ellen Cleever. I can't remember if it was the one who was missing for a month or the one who was found soon after she disappeared, but I'm sure she's one of them. Do the dates on the stone tally? I can't read them in this light without my glasses.'

'Born 3 July 1896, died on Christmas Eve 1913. And there's an inscription: "To live in hearts we leave behind is not to die".' He looked at her, his eyes shining with excitement. 'We might not be any closer to the "who", but I think we've just found the "why". Can you remember what the newspaper said about her death? Was there any suspicion of foul play?'

'Not that I can remember. I think I'd have taken more notice if there had been – but I can go back to the library tomorrow and check if you'd like me to? As far as I recall, it sounded like a tragic accident and there wasn't any connection to King's or the choir, so I didn't follow it up, but there might have been an inquest report later on. What do you think happened, Archie?'

'I have no idea, but I intend to find out and the first person I'm going to ask is Robert Moorcroft.'

'I suppose there's no chance that he might be killing his fellow choristers to prevent them from revealing what happened?' She gave him a sly half-smile. 'That would solve one of your problems, at least.'

'Don't think I haven't considered it. But no, I still think Moorcroft is a target rather than a killer. If revenge for Ellen Cleever's death *is* the motive for these murders, then I suppose we should be looking for someone close to her – someone in the family, perhaps.'

Josephine looked again at the photograph, and her face held the sadness he had noticed earlier. 'She was just seventeen,' she said. 'Born a couple of weeks before I was. I wonder who she'd be now, if she'd lived?'

'And I wonder who she was then? *Will* you go to the library for me tomorrow and see what you can find out? I'll check the police files, obviously, but the newspapers might have more background about her and her family.'

'Yes, of course. There might even be a few more details in the notes I've made already – where she lived or what she did. If I find anything in the news reports that I think you should know, where can I get hold of you?'

'At the local station – leave a message for me there. And if there are any developments in the meantime, I'll give you a ring.' He switched on the headlamps, then noticed that she was smiling at him. 'What's that for?'

'Nothing. It's just nice to see you more optimistic. Perhaps getting back to normal isn't so bad after all.'

She opened the car door, ignoring his objections. 'Please, Josephine – let me take you back to St Clement's Passage.'

'No, don't worry. You've got work to do and it'll only take me a minute or two. At least I can put the key in the door now without worrying who might be waiting for me.'

'All right, but be careful until they're sure they've got the right man.'

'I will, I promise. Where will you stay tonight?'

'I think the hospitality of the local nick is about the best that I can hope for. I'm waiting for some forensic reports and I want to go through all the victims' files again, just in case I've missed something. I hope I'll have time to go and see Bridget, though. You're right – we do need to talk.'

'Well, you know where I am if you want anything.'

He was touched to see the concern on her face as she got out of the car and walked away. With one more glance at the photograph, he went to start the engine but stopped when he saw Josephine change her mind and turn back to him. 'Archie?' she called from the other side of the street. 'You take care, too.'

20

The notes from Josephine's first visit to the library were more comprehensive than she remembered. Ellen Cleever had been found on Christmas morning by a middle-aged couple walking along the Cam, en route to spend the day with their daughter's family in Newnham. Her body was caught up in mud and weeds on the river's east bank, a little way out of the town centre near a place called Hodson's Folly, and the girl was identified by her father, Alfred, a butler's assistant at Jesus College, who had reported her missing late on Christmas Eve. Ellen's mother, Maud, was a bed maker, also at Jesus, and at the time the family had lived in a college house in Park Street, just around the corner from St Clement's Passage.

Was it feasible that they still lived there, Josephine wondered? Ellen had died twenty-four years ago at the age of seventeen, so, if her parents had had her when they were young, there was a good chance that they would still be of working age and entitled to their college-owned house. She longed to talk to the couple personally about their daughter rather than relying on second-hand accounts, but had no way of confirming their address: she could hardly knock on every door in Park Street without arousing suspicion, and it was unlikely that they would have a telephone, so looking them up in the local directory would be pointless. In any case, they might well have moved away after the tragedy or died themselves in the intervening years; perhaps Alfred Cleever had gone to war, leaving Maud to cope with the loss of her husband as well as her daughter. Archie, of course, would be able to check all of this much more efficiently than she could, but Josephine wanted to have more information to hand before bothering him, so she packed her glasses and a notebook and set out for the library.

It was a bitterly cold morning, but the grey skies and drizzle of the day before had been replaced by a crisp brightness. Shopkeepers were raising their blinds and unlocking their doors, and, as she turned into St John's Street, the newsagent – who had had an earlier start than most – was mending a puncture in between customers. She crossed the cobbles and he leant the bicycle against the window, anticipating her daily visit for sweets or magazines. 'And a copy of last night's newspaper if you haven't sold out?' she asked, looking in vain for the *Cambridge Daily News* on the counter. 'I expect everybody's keen to read about the arrest now he's safely behind bars.'

The newsagent gave a scornful laugh and Josephine looked at him in surprise. '*If* he's safely behind bars,' he muttered. 'Five hundred to one they've got the wrong man.'

'Why do you say that?'

'Robbing a jeweller's in the middle of the day with the police milling around for the Armistice? Someone who's been as clever as he has until now would never take a risk like that. It's asking for trouble.' At the time, Josephine had also thought it an odd change to the rapist's established pattern, but she assumed that he had been provoked by the recent police press statements accusing him of cowardice. 'I'm afraid I *have* sold out of last night's edition, but you're welcome to my copy free of charge,' he offered, reaching under the counter for a newspaper which – in spite of his disdain – looked remarkably well read. 'It seems to me that the police are so desperate they'll arrest anyone. We'll just have to wait and see if the real man strikes again, I suppose. In the meantime, I'm telling all the girls who come in here to keep their wits about them.'

'Yes, I suppose you're right,' Josephine said. It was a chilling thought, and she wondered how many women around the town would – like her – be dropping their guard prematurely. She accepted the paper gratefully and paid for the other items, waiting patiently while the newsagent went through to the back to fetch more change. There was a pile of empty news bags in the corner, left there after the morning's delivery, and it gave her an idea. 'I suppose you deliver to Park Street?' she asked, and the newsagent nodded. 'You must know all the locals – does a family called Cleever still live there?'

'Alf and his lady? Oh yes, they're still about. I don't see much of her, but he's in here two or three times a week for his Amber Leaf.'

'I don't suppose you have their address to hand, do you?' He looked at her suspiciously, and she offered the first explanation that came to mind. 'My brother was at Jesus College before the war, and he always says that Mrs Cleever was the kindest woman he'd ever met. He was so homesick, living on his own for the first time and the rest of us miles away in Scotland, and she was his bed maker. I promised him I'd look her up while I was here if I had the chance.'

She must have been convincing, because the shopkeeper took an enormous ledger down from the shelf behind him and began to flick through the pages. 'It's Park Street, as you say, but I couldn't tell you the house off the top of my head. Ah – here it is,' he said, stabbing the line triumphantly. 'They're at number ten. *Cambridge Daily News*, *Radio Times* and a *Woman's Weekly*.'

He closed the ledger and Josephine thanked him. 'I'll call round to see them later, so can I take one of those as well?' she asked, pointing to a box of Terry's Thistle Chocolates with its expensive-looking packaging. 'And a couple of packets of Amber Leaf.'

'Generous chap, your brother.'

Josephine smiled. 'If I'm honest, they're as much a thank you from me as from him. He once told me that if it weren't for Mrs Cleever, he'd never have stayed at Cambridge – and the last thing I wanted when I was thirteen was to have him back at home and stealing the limelight.' She paused, then spoke more seriously. 'And it was a terrible thing, the way they lost their daughter. I don't suppose you were here back then? Just before the war, it was.'

'No, I've only had the shop a year or so. What happened to their daughter? Alf's not much of a talker, except about his roses.'

Josephine hesitated. 'Please don't say anything to Mr Cleever – I'm sure it's not something he'd want raked up again – but she drowned in the Cam on Christmas Eve. I gather no one knows quite what happened.'

She waited hopefully, in case he recalled some lost fragment of gossip that had passed across his counter, but he just shook his head sadly. 'The poor bloke. You never know what some people have to carry, do you? Give them my regards when you see them.'

'I will.' She left the shop with more than she had hoped for, and, instead of turning right towards the library, retraced her footsteps and headed for Round Church Street, named after the distinctive Norman building on the corner. Park Street was at the bottom of the road, and she could already see the row of Victorian houses which bordered the grounds of Jesus College – uniform brick and slate cottages with sash windows and dormer attics, pleasant to look at but neat rather than memorable. Number ten was identical to its neighbours except for its front garden; whereas the houses on either side had attempted nothing more ambitious than a tidy square of lawn and a privet hedge, the Cleevers had transformed their small patch with a number of carefully planted flower borders which must have looked glorious in spring and summer. Even now, there was a flash of startling colour here and there in the acid-yellow of the winter jasmine and a clutch of red dahlias by the door.

Josephine lingered on the other side of the road, torn between a curiosity to know more and a reluctance to force her way into a family's grief under false pretences. In the end, the decision was taken out of her hands: the Cleevers' front door opened and a frail, grey-haired woman peered curiously out at her from the shadows of the hallway. She was dressed entirely in black and Josephine guessed that the clothes she wore were the uniform of her college work, but the length of the skirt and the fullness of the sleeves seemed to belong to a different age. She smiled awkwardly, guessing that the woman had been watching her for some time from inside the house, and Maud Cleever half-raised her hand in a gesture of recognition, then let it fall to her side.

Knowing that any more hesitation on her part would look suspicious, Josephine walked briskly across the road and opened the gate. 'Mrs Cleever?' she called brightly, in what she hoped was the manner of someone about to fulfil an agreeable obligation.

'That's right.'

'My name is Josephine Tey. We've never met, but my brother was at college here over twenty years ago and you were once very kind to him. He's never forgotten you, and he asked me to look you up while I was in Cambridge.' The look of joy and gratitude which suddenly transformed Maud Cleever's face tugged at Josephine's conscience as much as it moved her, but she was committed to the lie now whether she liked it or not. 'Homesickness is a terrible thing,' she continued, 'but not everyone is as sympathetic as you were. You helped him settle in here and make friends, and he's always been grateful for that.'

'How lovely. I do miss those boys, dear. I'm not at the college any more, you see. It's hard work, up and down those stairs a hundred times a day, and arthritis got the better of me in the end. My husband's still there and he keeps me up to date with things, but it's not the same.' Her voice was gentle, with the softest hint of a West Country accent, and Josephine realised that she could not have chosen a more credible scenario if she had had all the time in the world to think of it; Maud Cleever might never have made her brother feel at home in this strange new world, but there were surely scores of men all over the country who had found comfort in her kindness. 'What was your brother's name?' Mrs Cleever asked.

'Colin,' Josephine said quickly. She had taken her own name from her mother, so it seemed reasonable to assume that her fictional elder brother – had he ever existed – would have been named after her father. 'He came up to Cambridge to read history – 1913, it must have been. I always remember that because it was the last Christmas before the war.'

Mrs Cleever's face clouded over, and when she spoke again her interest in the conversation was more forced. 'And he was from Scotland, obviously.'

'That's right. From Inverness.'

'Ah, yes. I remember him now. A sweet boy he was, always so polite.'

The words were bland and unspecific, and Josephine knew that she was trying not to cause offence by admitting that the name meant nothing to her; Mrs Cleever didn't remember young Colin from Inverness, and why should she? 'These are for you,' she said, holding out the chocolates, but the woman surprised her by ignoring the box and instead raising her hand to touch Josephine's cheek.

'You look a little like her, you know. For a minute there, when you were standing across the street, I thought . . .' She left the sentence unfinished, but shrugged the moment off before Josephine could press her on it. 'You mustn't take any notice of an old woman, dear. I'm just talking nonsense. Come in and have some tea.'

'Oh no, I wouldn't want to put you to any trouble.'

'It's no trouble. You'd be doing me a kindness. We don't get much company these days, and I miss having young people around me. Sit yourself down in there. I won't be long.'

Josephine did as she was invited, the gift suddenly hollow in her hands. She tried to tell herself that she was merely trying to right an injustice, but, as she took a seat in the Cleevers' sitting room, the deception felt shabby and unnecessary, and she wished in hindsight that she had been honest from the start. The room was at the back of the house and looked out over a small courtyard garden and then – through an arched gateway – to the playing fields of Jesus College. The roses which were Alfred Cleever's pride and joy took up every inch of growing space and she noticed how meticulously tended they were, their stems neatly cut back for the winter and straw scattered around the roots to protect the plants from frost. Somehow, the care and attention suggested more than a professional habit, and she wondered if she was reading too much into the Cleevers' need to surround themselves with beauty and colour.

Inside, the house spoke of a quiet, companionable marriage. This was obviously the room where the couple spent most of their time, and Josephine warmed to the fact that Mrs Cleever had felt no need to show her unexpected visitor into the formal, little-used room that they had passed on their way down the hall. There was an armchair on either side of the fire, with a *Woman's Weekly* on her cushion and a seed catalogue on his, and small patches of long, dark fur on the sofa where Josephine was sitting testified to the presence of a cat. A wireless stood on the mantelpiece, and someone had obviously been looking through the *Radio Times*: the magazine lay open on the sofa, marked up with programmes not to miss, and Josephine noticed that the couple had a preference for dance music and comedy. Otherwise, the room was unusually free of clutter: there were no books, very few ornaments, and – most annoyingly of all – not a single photograph anywhere to be seen.

Mrs Cleever came in with a plate of biscuits, a little short of breath and obviously in pain. 'Can I bring something through for you?' Josephine asked, standing to help her.

'You're very kind, dear. The tea's ready but you'll need to put the milk and sugar on the tray – if you're sure you don't mind?'

'Of course not.' She went through to the kitchen and was rewarded with more than the promised cup of tea. The dresser was dotted with photographs and Josephine's eye was immediately drawn to an attractive, dark-haired girl who appeared in several of the pictures at different stages of her life, and who must surely be Ellen Cleever. In one of them – taken shortly before her death, Josephine guessed, because she looked to be sixteen or seventeen

– she was surrounded by a group of small boys dressed in top hats and Eton suits. The boys were far too young to be the choral scholars Archie was interested in, but the building in the background was unmistakably King's College Chapel.

'Can you find everything you need?' Mrs Cleever called.

Josephine hurriedly picked up a jug from the dresser and filled it with milk. 'Just coming,' she replied, adding two cups and taking the tray through to the sitting room. 'Sorry to be so long. I was looking everywhere for the sugar, then I found it right in front of me.'

'Don't worry, dear. Set it down there and have a biscuit. I'll pour for us.' The shortbread was delicious, even though Josephine had very little appetite for it, and her obvious enjoyment seemed to please Mrs Cleever. 'The college boys always appreciated my cooking, but I expect you know that already. Colin loved his chocolate if I remember rightly?' Josephine nodded, playing her part in the mutual charade that they had both settled into. 'Ah, yes – it's all coming back to me now,' Mrs Cleever added, encouraged by her success so far, 'and he can't have lost his thoughtfulness if he asked you to come and see me. What's he doing with his life?'

'He's a teacher at a school in Edinburgh,' Josephine said, and spent the next half an hour giving Colin the sort of life that she thought a history graduate with a background like hers might have. She told Mrs Cleever about his war service and the long battle with a shoulder injury that had marred his return to England; about the joy he eventually found in his work and the chance meeting with the woman from Ireland who would become his wife; about the twins who had come along soon afterwards, giving her own parents the grandchildren they had always longed for. She took her inspiration from Archie's life or from the anecdotes passed down within her family, occasionally adding traits from the characters who peopled her books, and in the end the picture was so convincing that she began to long for the brother she had never had.

It was strange, but she found herself desperately wanting to repay this kind, generous woman with a story which would please her and make her proud of all the lives she had touched, but, when she finally ran out of ideas, Maud Cleever's expression was a complex muddle of satisfaction and sorrow.

'It's lovely to know the whole story,' she said quietly, 'and it means a great deal to me that you bothered to come here today. When you do the sort of work that I did, you watch your boys go off into the world but you never find out what they made of themselves – for good or bad. Sometimes I can't help wondering what might have been. I shouldn't, perhaps, but I do.'

Josephine knew that she was thinking about her daughter and the life that would – for a very different reason – always remain a blank page, a series of unanswered and unanswerable questions. The older woman stared into the fire, lost in her own thoughts and oblivious now to her visitor. 'Who did you think I was when you came to the door?' Josephine asked gently. 'Was it your daughter? Was it Ellen?' Maud looked at her, brought back to the present by the name. 'Colin was so shocked by what had happened,' Josephine explained. 'He wrote home about it when he came back here in January for the new term, and I remember him telling me later that you'd never got over it – but why would you?'

'I didn't see her, dear – not after she died. They wouldn't let me. Alf identified her, and I know in my heart that she's gone, but that's not enough somehow. It never has been.' Josephine moved to the other end of the sofa and took her hand. 'They didn't have to protect me like that. Nothing could have been worse than the moment when they came to the door on Christmas morning and we'd been up all night worrying about her – but they said it would be better if I didn't go to her. They said it wasn't for a woman to see. Men don't understand, though, do they? Not even Alf. They meant well, I know they did, but they don't understand what's here between a mother and her daughter.' She touched her heart and Josephine listened sadly, wondering what sort of injuries Ellen had sustained to make her body unfit for her mother to see. 'It's the same with fathers and sons, don't you think? I expect you're closer to your mother and Colin's his father's boy?'

'Yes, I suppose that's true.'

'But I didn't go to her when she needed me, and I let her down.'

'No, you didn't. They let *you* down. As far as Ellen was concerned, you'd cared for her since the moment she was born and yours was the love she'd always known. Her suffering was over by then, but someone should have thought more about yours.'

Maud Cleever smiled gratefully and squeezed her hand, but Josephine knew that nothing anyone could say now would numb her pain or her sense of guilt. 'It's kind of you to say so, but I still wonder what Ellen would have made of her life – who she would have loved, where she might have gone. And I was hoping for grandchildren, of course, like your parents. Sometimes . . .' She hesitated, and Josephine waited patiently for her to continue. 'Sometimes I miss her so much that I can't believe she's gone. I think she'll come back, and I start to imagine how it might be – Ellen standing across the road, just like you were this morning.' Plagued with remorse now for all the suffering she had resurrected, Josephine wondered if she should think of ways to divert the conversation, but Mrs Cleever – who obviously didn't have much opportunity to talk about the daughter she had lost – seemed to find comfort in voicing her grief. 'Did Colin come to Ellen's funeral?' she asked suddenly.

For the first time, Josephine was thrown. 'I'm not sure,' she admitted. 'He was probably still at home for the Christmas holidays.'

'Oh no – we had to wait to bury her because there was a heavy fall of snow shortly after she died. Term had started again before the thaw, and lots of the boys came to pay their respects to the family – from Jesus and from King's.'

Had Archie's murder victims been among them, Josephine

wondered? Had those young choral scholars had the nerve to join the mourners for the girl whose death she was now convinced they had been involved in? 'That must be why I don't remember Colin mentioning it,' she said. 'The weather was terrible in the Highlands that winter and he couldn't travel in time for the start of term.' She pictured the gravestone with its unconvincingly hopeful inscription, and imagined how desperately bleak that January funeral must have been. 'Where is Ellen buried?' she asked.

'Over at the cemetery in Mill Road. We go as often as we can, but it's harder to get to the other side of town now we're older.'

'And did you ever find out how she died, Mrs Cleever?'

'Not to *my* satisfaction, no. The police didn't put themselves out, I must say. I suppose it was very inconsiderate of Ellen to get herself killed at Christmas, when everyone was off enjoying themselves.'

Remarkably, it was the first hint of bitterness that she had shown. 'So she *was* killed?' Josephine said. 'Her drowning wasn't an accident?'

'No, it wasn't an accident. I was too ill to go to the inquest, but the verdict was murder by person or persons unknown. Alf told me that Ellen had been hit on the head and knocked into the water, but that was only half the story, I'm sure, and I didn't force him to tell me what else he'd heard – for his sake, and for mine. There were a lot of beggars in town that Christmas – they come up from London every year – and the police put it down to them. They decided that whoever had done it would have moved on to another town.' How convenient, Josephine thought. She would have liked to tell Mrs Cleever that times had changed, that someone now cared enough about her daughter's death to look again – but that would have given her away and, in any case, it was only partly true; she had heard enough of Archie's monologues on the shortcomings of Scotland Yard to know that his dedication to justice was by no means universal. And of course there was another reason for discretion on her part; if it turned out that someone *did* care enough about Ellen's death to kill several times, then the escalation of violence would, she knew, bring very cold comfort to someone as gentle as Maud Cleever.

'I went to Hodson's Folly after she died,' the woman said. 'I thought that if I couldn't see Ellen I could at least see where she'd died, but I wish I hadn't. Godforsaken, it was. I've never been back since.'

'Why was she there?' Josephine asked. 'Was it somewhere she often went?'

'In summer, perhaps, but not on a winter's night.' She shrugged, like any mother whose adult child has become a mystery to her. 'I've thought and thought about it over the years, but I don't know why she was there. The police asked me if I thought she'd gone with some boys but I soon put them right about that – Ellen wasn't that sort of girl. No, dear – I can't explain it. The last time I saw her was on the morning of Christmas Eve. She was excited about the carol service in the afternoon, and she told me that she was going out to the pictures with a friend afterwards. She promised her father and me that she'd be home by eight, in time to dress the tree, and we waited up all night for her. Then that poor couple found her the next morning.'

'Was Ellen your only child?' Josephine asked, remembering what Archie had said about finding the killer among Ellen's relatives or friends.

Mrs Cleever shook her head. 'No, we've got a son. Ernest is six years younger than Ellen and he was always a good boy, but he went off the rails when we lost her. Hit him hard, it did, because he worshipped the ground she walked on. He drank a lot and got into fights, and then he started to steal from us so Alfred had to tell him to go. It broke his heart – and mine – but we didn't know what else to do. That was towards the end of the war and we haven't seen him since.'

So one way and another, the Cleevers had lost two children in those terrible days of 1913, Josephine thought. 'Is that Ellen in the photograph on your dresser?' she asked. 'The one with the little boys?'

'Oh, you saw that, did you? Yes, she was a maid at King's College School. She could have come to work at Jesus with me, but she wanted to go her own way and have her independence, and I was just the same at her age. She made a good job of it, too. She was kind, you see, and all the boys at that school loved her.'

'Kindness must run in the family.'

Maud Cleever smiled. 'It was even more important there. At least by the time they got to college most of my lads could look out for themselves if they had to, but those little ones were so young. A lot of them had parents abroad and they hardly ever went home. Ellen used to spend a lot of time with them – far more than she was paid for, but she'd had plenty of practice with Ernest and she was always good with children. It's such a shame . . .' The regret ran too deep to be spoken aloud, but Josephine knew how the sentence would have finished. 'I've talked far too much, dear,' Mrs Cleever said, leaning forward to pick up the box of chocolates. 'You'll have to forgive me, but I don't see many people these days and I miss the company. Now – let's have one of these as Colin has been kind enough to send them. Do thank him for me, won't you? And for the tobacco – Alf does love his pipe.'

Josephine took one of the chocolates she was offered. They chatted for a little longer, and then she stood to leave. 'Please don't get up,' she said. 'I can see myself out.'

But Mrs Cleever insisted on showing her to the door. 'Thank you for coming,' she said, clutching Josephine's hand again. 'You will give my regards to your brother, won't you? It was such a long time ago now and it means the world to me that he remembers.'

'Of course I will,' Josephine promised. It was scarcely surprising that a woman whose daughter's death seemed to have been forgotten by the world would be touched by the idea that something far more ordinary still mattered to someone, and she was pleased to have brought that gift, even if the person concerned had never actually existed. 'And may I come back and see you again?' she asked. 'A friend of mine has just moved here and I'll be coming down from time to time. It's been a pleasure to meet you and it would mean a great deal to me to get to know you better.'

'You'll be welcome any time,' Maud Cleever said, and Josephine left her to her memories. She walked back to St Clement's Passage and wrote down everything that she had learned while it was still fresh in her mind, then telephoned the police station, only to be told that Chief Inspector Penrose was unavailable and unlikely to be free for some time. Disappointed, she left a message for him to call her urgently, then thought about what to do with the rest of her day. There seemed little point in going to the library now; other than the full inquest report, which Archie could easily access for himself, she doubted that the newspapers would tell her anything which she didn't already know. On the other hand, she was too restless to sit around and wait for Archie to telephone when it might be hours before he was able to. In the end she decided to leave a note for him at the police station, detailing everything that was most important from her morning's work, then check the map and walk along the river to Hodson's Folly. Although it would tell her nothing, she was keen to see for herself where Ellen Cleever had died.

It was one of the things that she had come to love most about Cambridge during her time there: everything was in walking distance, and there were very few walks that weren't beautiful. Within a few minutes of leaving Regent Street, she found herself strolling across common land with cows grazing peacefully on either side, and it astonished her that a landscape as pastoral as this could be found so close to the heart of a town. She crossed the road which cut through the fen and picked up the towpath on the other side of the bridge, forgetting for a moment the tragedy that had brought her here and enjoying the sights and sounds of a river walk in winter – the harsh cry of a pheasant startled out of the undergrowth, an unexpected blaze of white as a swan settled on the bank. Through the trees Josephine could see a group of wooden bathing huts, deserted now but with signs of recent use by someone much hardier than she was. She paused to look at her map, and saw that Hodson's Folly was marked nearby, on the other side of the river.

And then she glimpsed it up ahead – a small stone shelter, built in the classical style and standing in a walled garden like a Cambridge college in miniature. The folly was accessed by a footbridge and she crossed the river slowly, struck by the peculiar nature of the building and the remoteness of its location. It was deathly quiet, and branches snapped loudly under her feet as she followed the wall round to a narrow, arched gateway. The folly itself was built sideways to the river with open windows looking downstream, and the grass in front of it was blackened in places where someone had lit a fire. Obviously the building still provided shelter or a meeting place for those with the nerve to use it, but even now, in daylight, Josephine found its atmosphere unsettling. She remembered the description that Maud Cleever had used – godforsaken; perhaps it was because she knew that a young girl's body had been found here, but she couldn't have described it better herself.

She stepped forward to take a closer look at the coat of arms which had been engraved into the stone above the entrance, careful to avoid the nettles that threatened to overwhelm the folly on the woodland side. It was an interesting motif, a swan swimming beneath a rain cloud, and she wondered who Hodson was and why he had chosen to make his mark in such an incongruous way. The French inscription – translated as 'fare well' – told her nothing about the folly's creator, but she found a certain irony in the motto and in the image of a knight's helmet which was elaborately carved above it; whatever had taken place here all those years ago on

Christmas Eve, she doubted that it could ever be described as chivalrous.

Inside, the small building was open to the sky but it was hard to say now if it had been designed that way or if the roof had simply fallen in over time. To her surprise, someone had left a sprig of winter jasmine on the window ledge, tied at the stem with a red ribbon. She looked at the flowers with interest, recognising the plant as something that grew in the Cleevers' garden and wondering if Ellen's father secretly came out here with flowers to remember his daughter, or if someone else had left them. Either way, their presence could hardly be a coincidence.

Beyond the window, the river was still and murky, a dirty dull green which Josephine shivered just to look at. No wonder Maud Cleever had regretted coming here, she thought: standing on the spot where her daughter had died, it was impossible not to imagine how bleak and lonely those final moments must have been. What had brought Ellen here, she wondered? And could her death really be connected to a group of men whose lives seemed so far removed from hers – a barrister and a Home Office official, a respected musician and the owner of a substantial country house? Josephine took a final look round, wishing that the stone could talk, then headed back to town to wait for Archie's call.

21

Penrose walked away from Little St Mary's Lane in the early hours of the morning, feeling a strange mixture of sadness and relief. Although he and Bridget had come to no decisions about their future in the brief time they had spent together, he had seen in her a mirroring of his own uncertainties. A mutual awkwardness was natural after such a long absence, and it had been unfair of him to arrive at her door unannounced, but there was very little joy in the reunion, just the guilty, bittersweet alliance of two people who had acknowledged – to themselves, if not yet to each other – that they were happier on their own. The sense of regret and failure hovered over everything they said and didn't say, and when Bridget suggested that they meet to talk properly as soon as his case was over, Penrose gladly took it as his cue to leave.

He walked the streets for a while, having little appetite for company, but they felt too much like a map to his past, forever leading him back to those early days with Bridget, so he dozed in his car until the church clock woke him at eight. The police station was quiet when he walked through the front door and a subdued George Clough stood by the enquiries desk in a crumpled suit, apparently having had very little sleep. 'You look like you've had a long night,' Penrose said. 'Have you charged him yet?'

'It's not the right man,' Clough said through gritted teeth, taking Penrose to one side. 'It turns out this one's a petty thief up from London, chancing his arm during the silence when he thought everyone was looking the other way.'

'So the attack on the shop girl—'

'Was just to shut her up when she screamed, yes. That's all we can lay on him – assault and attempted burglary. He's got a cast-iron alibi for at least three of the rapes, and I don't think he'd even set foot in Cambridge before this week. So we're back to square bloody one.'

'I'm sorry to hear that. Webster must be taking it badly. He'd worked so hard to get his man, and he deserved a bit of luck.'

'Taking it badly? That's an understatement. I thought he was going to punch this bloke's lights out for *not* being a rapist. Anyway, I've sent him home for a few hours to pull himself together. This will look bad enough in the press as it is, and I can do without Webster's temper making things worse.'

'The papers haven't got hold of it yet?'

'No, but it's only a matter of time and I want to get a statement out before they do, otherwise we won't just be accused of incompetence – they'll say we're encouraging women to take risks by withholding information. I don't suppose anyone will remember for a moment that it's the papers and not the police who decided publicly that this man *was* the rapist, but that's all par for the course.' He patted his jacket pocket and scowled when he found it empty. 'Got a cigarette on you?' Penrose obliged, happy to stem the rant for a second or two. 'With a bit of luck, your body at the Priory should distract them for a while,' Clough added with a glint in his eye. 'Very considerate of you, Penrose.'

'Always glad to be of service.'

'Is there any news on that since last night?'

'No, but I'm expecting Spilsbury's preliminary report to be here soon. That should confirm identity and an approximate time of death, but there's still a long way to go.'

Clough nodded sympathetically, more serious now. 'Well, if you need anything from us you only have to ask.'

'Actually, I was hoping to look through some old files. Are they kept here?'

'How far back are we talking?'

'Christmas 1913.'

'Yes, they'll be downstairs in the basement. Tell me what you want and I'll get my secretary to look it out for you.'

'Anything relating to a girl called Ellen Jane Cleever. She died on Christmas Eve – I think it was a drowning. Does the name mean anything to you?'

Clough shook his head. 'No, but it was before my time. I'm just short of twenty years here, although forty feels closer on days like today. Make yourself at home upstairs and I'll ask Penny to bring you the paperwork and a cup of coffee. You look bloody awful.'

Penrose smiled, grateful for the professional camaraderie which was always at its strongest when things were going equally badly on all fronts. 'Thank you, sir. I'll keep you informed of any developments.' He headed up to the first floor and found an empty desk, then put a call through to Fallowfield in London to bring him up to date. The sergeant had very little news of his own, except to report that someone from the Home Office had telephoned and grudgingly given the details of Richard Swayne's country home in Sussex, which he was following up with the local force.

Penrose's next priority was Robert Moorcroft, but there was little point in speaking to him until he knew as much about Ellen Cleever's death as the local police records could tell him. While he was waiting, he took his own files out of his briefcase and began to read through the details of each murder in turn to see if anything new occurred to him. Stephen Laxborough's tortured final hours came back to him now in ruthless detail as he looked once again at the scene of crime photographs from St John's churchyard, and he laid the images of Westbury's body and Carrington's out next to them on the desk. Taken together, the photographs bore witness to an extraordinary catalogue of suffering and punishment, but the later murders answered many of the questions which had puzzled him about Laxborough's death. He knew now why the killer had risked returning to the graveyard to reveal the musician's body when he could easily have let it lie there undisturbed and undiscovered: getting away with murder wasn't the sole objective of these crimes; it was just as important to the killer to make an exhibition of his victims, to present in public an intensely private course of justice. As he got closer to the end of the list, he was also beginning to reveal his reasons, and Penrose wondered what he would do if – God forbid – he was allowed to complete the task.

He put the photographs away and began to look through the post-mortem reports and his own notes from the scene of each crime. A familiarity with the details of Laxborough's murder had not made them any easier to read, and he turned with relief to the rest of the report. It included a transcript of the words carved on the tomb where the body was found, and Penrose glanced through it: 'Here Lyeth the Body of Mr James McArdell, Metzotinto Engraver of London, who departed this Life on the 1st of June, 1765, aged 37 years. A native of Ireland and the most eminent in his Art in his time.' He read the inscription again and the same word – 'Metzotinto' – jumped out at him. Until now, he had always assumed that the grave was chosen for its secluded position and distance from the public paths, but now – with a greater knowledge of the killer's preoccupations – he saw instantly that the bones buried there were in themselves a clue. There was a story in M. R. James's first collection called 'The Mezzotint' which he hadn't yet read and he took the book eagerly out of his briefcase to see what it might tell him. The setting was familiar – a Cambridge college and an antiquarian collector who acquired an object of great interest – but as he read on, the significance of the story chilled him for reasons entirely different to the ones that James had intended. The object in question was a mezzotint engraving of a manor house, ordinary enough until the picture began to change over time, showing a sinister figure crawling across the lawn, then an open window and the figure – horribly skeletal – fleeing from the house clutching a baby who might have been alive or dead.

For the first time, Penrose understood that the murders followed the pattern of this story, with everything gradually closing in on Angerhale and Robert Moorcroft: the photographic fragment of a manor house found with Laxborough's body; the open window at the Priory, forced by an intruder who had stolen nothing; the photograph sent to Simon Westbury with the threat of someone coming; and finally the body at the edge of the Priory grounds. He wondered if Moorcroft had made the connection, and skipped to the end of the story with a mounting sense of dread. It was just as he feared: the changing mezzotint told an ominous tale of revenge in which a landowner's son – the last of his line – was stolen by a ghost as a reckoning for the evils of the past. So was that to be Robert Moorcroft's punishment, he wondered? The abduction of a much-loved child and his only male heir, but this time by a very human form?

More concerned than ever, Penrose picked up the telephone and asked to be put through to Angerhale Priory. 'Mrs Moorcroft?' he said, trying to keep the panic out of his voice. 'It's Chief Inspector Penrose. Where's Teddy?'

The question sounded more blunt than he had intended. There was a pause and then he heard her voice, confused and a little anxious. 'Teddy? But Teddy's with you, or he should be by now. I sent him to make a statement, just as you asked.'

'What do you mean? I didn't send for Teddy.'

'But a policeman came to fetch him first thing this morning. He apologised for arriving unannounced, but he said you needed a formal statement about yesterday. I wanted to go with him but Evie was crying about something and Robert was nowhere to be found, and the policeman promised to have him back with us as soon as possible. I knew Teddy would always be safe with you, so I let him go.'

Penrose felt a sudden wave of fury that his name should have been used to deceive her, but the anger was swiftly followed by guilt at not having acted quickly enough. 'Please try to stay calm when you hear what I'm about to tell you,' he said, 'but the man who came to your house this morning *wasn't* a policeman. He might have said he was, but—'

'You're wrong about that,' she insisted. 'He showed me his warrant card and I telephoned the police station to check with them. The man I spoke to confirmed that he worked there. You surely don't think I'd let my little boy go off with someone without making sure that he was who he said he was? Inspector, you're as bad as Robert. He was furious with me when I told him Teddy was at the police station, but what was I supposed to do?'

Her tone was increasingly defensive now because she knew that something was wrong and blamed herself. 'What was the policeman's name?' Penrose asked.

'Wait a minute – I wrote it down.' She put the receiver down and he heard her footsteps moving away and coming back across the Priory's stone floor. 'Webster. Detective Inspector Thomas Webster. Do you know him?'

Obviously not at all, Penrose thought. He gave a brief description of Webster, and Virginia Moorcroft confirmed that it tallied with the man who had taken her son. 'What's going on, Inspector?' she asked. 'What have I done?'

'You're not to blame and I promise to get Teddy back, but first you need to tell me exactly what happened – every small detail, as quickly as you can.'

'The housekeeper came to fetch me just after seven and told me that there was a policeman at the door. That didn't surprise me after yesterday, and Robert had gone out early with the dogs so I went downstairs myself. I suppose if I'm honest I thought it might be you. He introduced himself and explained what he wanted, and I had no reason to doubt him but obviously I checked with the station before agreeing. Teddy was downstairs by then, full of bravado about his big adventure, and this man was good with him.

I watched them together while I was making the call, and Teddy obviously liked him because he was chattering away about the choir and the school and the music he loved.' She paused, and Penrose could only imagine the effort it took for her to remain calm; there could be nothing worse than the moment when you realised that your child was in danger. 'Anyway, when I had my confirmation I asked Inspector Webster not to keep him out too long and he agreed. He gave me a note for my husband and they left straight away.'

'And the car?'

'Just an ordinary dark-coloured saloon. Teddy was disappointed it wasn't a police car with a bell, but Webster said that plain clothes officers didn't drive those.' She took a deep breath, and he could hear that she was fighting back tears. 'I waved them off down the drive, for God's sake. How could I have been so stupid?'

Penrose's mind was racing as he tried to connect Webster with the events of the last few weeks, but somehow he forced himself to concentrate on the urgency of Teddy's disappearance. 'There's no reason to assume that Inspector Webster will harm your son,' he said, praying that he was right. 'I suspect that Teddy is being used to get to your husband. Where is Mr Moorcroft now? You said he was angry with you for letting Teddy go.'

'Yes, he was. He went crazy when I told him what had happened, and there was nothing I could say to pacify him. He said he was going to get Teddy back, and then he left. I assumed he was on his way to the station.'

'Had he read the note by then?'

'Yes, I left it in his study.'

'Do you know what it said?'

'No. Webster told me that it was just a formality to do with the body found on our land.'

'Will you go and see if it's still there?'

'Yes, of course, but aren't we wasting time?'

'It's important, Mrs Moorcroft. Please look for me.'

'All right. I won't be long.' She was as good as her word, returning in just a few minutes. 'It's a postcard, not a note,' she said. 'I found it in the wastepaper basket, but I don't understand what it means. It looks like a quotation from something.'

'Read it to me.'

'It says: "The evidence of the man at the Martello tower freed us from all suspicion. All that could be done was to return a verdict of wilful murder."'

'Is that it?'

'No, not quite. There's a line underneath that says "A Warning to the Curious".'

Penrose recognised the title of the story immediately. 'Is it a picture postcard?' he asked.

'Yes, from somewhere called Aldeburgh.' She pronounced the name of the seaside town with three syllables and a strong American inflection. 'Do you know where that is?'

'It's on the Suffolk coast, about two or three hours from here. Listen, Mrs Moorcroft – I haven't got time to explain everything now but I need you to trust me. I think that's where Inspector Webster has taken Teddy, and he wants your husband to follow him. That's what this is about. I have no idea how Webster is connected to these men, but I think his ultimate goal is to get your husband to confess to something he did many years ago. As it says in the quotation, he wants the verdict of the man in the Martello tower.'

'You think Robert killed someone?'

'I think Robert and the men who have died were all involved in a girl's death when they were at King's, and one by one they're being made to pay.'

'By this man Webster?' She was quiet for a moment, and when she spoke again there was a new determination in her voice. 'Get Teddy back for me. Please. I don't care what happens to Robert, but I want my son.'

'I will – I swear I will.' It was the second promise that Penrose had made and he had no idea if he could keep it, but it was the only comfort he had to offer. 'Is your little girl with you?'

'Yes. I'm not letting her out of my sight.'

'And Teddy's friend from school? Where is he?'

'His parents came to collect him last night as soon as they heard what had happened. Thank God they did. Why on earth didn't I listen to you when you asked me to take the children somewhere safe? If I had, Teddy would still be with me.'

'Don't be too hard on yourself. If I'm right, Teddy has only been taken to lure your husband to the Martello tower, nothing more than that.'

'And if you're wrong?'

'I'm going after them,' he said, ignoring the question, 'but in the meantime I want you and Evie to stay where you are and I'll send some officers out to stay with you until we know it's safe.'

'Thank you – I mean that. And Inspector?'

'Yes?'

'Tell Teddy I love him, and I'll be waiting.'

Penrose put the telephone down and went to make George Clough's day. 'Sorry, Penrose. I know you're waiting for those files but we've had a call from the *Daily News* and I've had to come clean about the man we've got in custody. As soon as Penny's finished typing up the statement, I'll send her across to you.'

Penrose waved the apology away. 'It's not important now,' he said, shutting the office door behind him. 'What do you know about Thomas Webster?'

'Webster?' Clough looked at him in surprise. 'He's been with us for about five years, I suppose. He transferred from Bristol as a sergeant and was promoted eighteen months ago. He can be a bit hot-tempered and he takes himself and his work far too seriously, but he's a damned good copper. Why?'

Penrose explained, and watched the superintendent quite literally age before his eyes. 'But he can't possibly be involved in any of this,' Clough objected. 'He's been working flat out on the assaults.'

'Which could easily have given him the perfect cover,' Penrose argued, thinking back to the time that he had bumped into Webster at the Evelyn Nursing Home. 'And *because* he's been flat out, can you honestly say that you always knew where he was?'

'No,' Clough admitted. 'Like I said, he's a good man and I gave him a free rein.'

'Exactly.'

'Jesus, Penrose, I might as well hand my card in now. What the hell am I going to do if you're right?'

Clough's head was sunk in his hands and Penrose looked at him with sympathy. 'Let's make sure first. I'm going to drive over to the Martello tower now and see—'

'I'm coming with you.'

'But sir, there are things that need to be done from here and surely you don't want to let anyone else in on this before we're sure? Think of the consequences.'

'Webster is *my* officer, Penrose. If anyone has a right to understand why he's doing this, I do. You're in charge of this one and that's understood – but I want to be there. All right?' Penrose nodded reluctantly. 'Good. Now tell me what else you need.'

'Some reliable officers out at Angerhale to look after Virginia Moorcroft and her daughter. Someone needs to alert the Suffolk force and get them out to Aldeburgh as back-up. Ask for Detective Inspector Donovan if he's available – he attended Westbury's murder in Felixstowe, and he seemed to know what he was doing. It'll take us a while to get out there, so I want that tower watched in the meantime – but only from a distance. On no account is anyone to approach the building unless Webster shows signs of leaving. And most importantly of all, I want every scrap of information you can find me on Webster. He told me once that he was brought up in Cambridge as a boy, so I need the details on that and his career record since. We need a check on his house, too, just in case I'm wrong and he's taken the boy there. Is there someone you can trust with that?'

'Yes, I think so. Give me five minutes to brief him and then we can go.'

'While you're doing that, I'm going to call my sergeant and ask him to come up here.'

Clough nodded and Penrose left him to it. He brought Fallowfield up to date for the second time that day, then waited impatiently at the front desk for the superintendent to join him. 'A lady left this for you, sir,' the man on duty said, handing him a note. He opened it immediately, recognising Josephine's handwriting, and quickly read the results of her morning's work in Park Street. The letter had reached him just in time, and the information about Ernest Cleever gave him an idea.

Clough appeared, shaking his head. 'You'll have to go without me, Penrose. The morning paper's just come out and all hell's broken loose. People are already causing trouble in the market square and I can't leave anyone else to deal with it. Will you keep me posted on Webster, though? I want to be the first to know.'

'You will be.'

'And I'll make sure everything else you asked for is covered.'

'Thank you, sir. One other thing . . .'

'Yes?'

'Ellen Cleever, the girl whose file I asked for – I think she might be at the bottom of this, and she had a brother called Ernest. He'd be about Webster's age. Would you do some digging on him for me?' He gave Clough Josephine's note. 'This will help with the background.'

The superintendent glanced through it, struggling to read the unfamiliar hand. 'You think Webster and this Ernest Cleever might be connected?' he asked.

'More than that, sir,' Penrose said on his way out of the door. 'I think there's every chance that they might be one and the same person.'

22

Aldeburgh had changed very little since the days of M. R. James's story: the long sea front and charming red-brick cottages; a handsome flint church and two white windmills on the horizon; wind-beaten fir trees and heath land to the north, then, to the south, the distant Martello tower. And at the margins of it all, the heaving, dirty, life-affirming North Sea, tugging at an ever-changing shoreline with ruthless deliberation. Penrose had only been here once or twice before, but the town had made a strong impression on him with its combination of the tamed and the wild, and today the latter had the upper hand; an easterly breeze – always present on this coast, even on the mildest of days – stirred the dry grass which lined the sandy road and sent iron-grey clouds scudding across a pliant sky.

The old Martello tower was about a mile out of town, separated from the last row of houses by a long stretch of sand and shingle. It was one of several tiny forts built along the coast during the Napoleonic wars to protect England from an invading French army, and although the towers had never been tested for that purpose, many of them had gone on to be used by coastguards as an excellent foil to smugglers. Penrose guessed that this one had been allowed to fall derelict, and Webster had chosen well: regardless of its presence in James's story, the Martello tower gave him the perfect private stronghold in which to play out the final stages of his plan – remote and protected, and with an uninterrupted view that made it impossible to approach without being seen. He recognised Moorcroft's Jaguar and the dark saloon car among a small clutch of vehicles parked where the road began to dwindle, and left his

Daimler at the end of the row. Webster's car was locked and a quick glance through the window told him nothing, so he walked over to the nearer of the two police cars, glad of the fresh air; the last few days and another long night were beginning to take their toll, but the sharp sea breeze and open skies revived him a little. 'Have you seen anyone?' he asked, getting into the back seat.

'Not yet, sir, but there's definitely someone in there. Every now and again you can see a torch or a lantern moving about inside.' Donovan handed Penrose the binoculars, and he trained them eagerly on the building. 'We can't have been far behind them because the bonnet on the Jag was still warm when we got here, but there's been no sign of anyone on the move.'

'So you don't know if the boy's all right?'

'No, sir. I haven't set eyes on him.'

Penrose paused, trying to second-guess Webster's objectives. There was no doubt in his mind that what Webster wanted most of all from Moorcroft was a confession, but it was impossible to calculate what he might do if and when that was achieved. Until now, his actions had been cold and deliberate, with each of the four murders planned and executed to ruthless perfection, but Penrose knew what it was like to care desperately about a case and be thwarted in its investigation – and he was convinced by their brief meetings that Webster *had* cared about catching the rapist in Cambridge. The false arrest would have been a bitter blow, and that, coupled with a lack of sleep and the emotional strain of abducting a child and confronting Moorcroft, would surely make him volatile and unpredictable. Penrose was no longer as confident as he had been that Teddy was safe, and waiting for Webster's next move seemed too big a risk to take. 'I'm going over there,' he said, having dismissed the alternatives. 'If I try to talk to him before this goes any further, I might just be able to get the boy out. Wait here, but be ready to come if I signal.'

'But he'll spot you long before you get there,' Donovan objected.

'What if he's armed? You're a walking target across that sand.'

'I know, but have you got any better ideas? The longer we leave it, the worse it'll be for the child.'

Donovan nodded reluctantly and Penrose got out of the car. It was mid-afternoon now and the air was damp, with only a pencil-thin line of light between the sea and the grey pall of sky. The squat, brick-built tower sat menacingly on the horizon and he began the long walk towards it, choosing the most overt approach across the sand. The tide was receding, but the sea had done its work and the going was heavy and damp underfoot; when he glanced back towards the town, the marks he had left on the broad stretch of beach were deep and meandering. As he drew near to the tower, an ever-decreasing spit of shingle parted the sea on the left from a river on the right, and after that there was nothing of comfort – just a vast expanse of water which, on a bleak November day, could easily have marked the edge of the world. The unassailable sense of solitude which exhilarated Penrose whenever he walked on a windswept beach was entirely absent now, and all he was left with was a profound unease.

Aldeburgh's Martello was of a quatrefoil design, four smaller towers joined together rather than the single cylindrical forms found at Felixstowe and elsewhere; even without any knowledge of the tensions inside, Penrose would have found its quiet hostility forbidding. He walked round the building, sensing more acutely than he ever had before that his every move was carefully watched. The only way in was through a narrow doorway on the landward side, about fifteen feet up from beach level and accessed across a dilapidated bridge which connected the tower to a raised cliff path. He clambered up the bank and set foot on the fragile wood, expecting at any moment to be stopped or challenged, but nothing hindered his progress and he began to fear what might already have happened inside. The walls of the building were several feet thick, designed to resist cannon fire, and once through the door he was faced with a choice: to continue into a warren of rooms on the same level, or to follow a dark stone staircase down to the ground floor. There was a flicker of light from below so he headed towards it. The steps were slippery, the air fetid with damp and decay, and he was pleased to emerge into a wide open space which must originally have been used as a storeroom for provisions and ammunition.

But there his relief ended. When his eyes grew accustomed to the dimly lit room, he was aware of someone standing just a few feet away from him. A powerful torch was suddenly switched on, blinding him for a moment, and he heard Webster's voice from behind the glare. 'Afternoon, sir. I was hoping you might be able to join us.' He shone the beam obligingly round the room, and Penrose took everything in. A series of iron rings was set at intervals into the curved outer wall and Robert Moorcroft was tied to one of them, his face cut and bruised, a rag stuffed into his mouth. His body was slumped on the floor but his eyes were frightened and watchful; he stared pleadingly at Penrose, seeing an ally now in the man he had always regarded as his adversary.

On the other side of the room there was a makeshift camp bed, and Penrose saw the small form of a child, covered entirely by blankets. 'Teddy?' he said, his voice echoing round the hollow chamber, but the boy on the bed lay ominously silent and still, and Penrose prayed that he was drugged rather than hurt. The room was bleak, and the few lighted candles did little to offer any cheer. In the lull that followed each distant wave, he could hear the steady drip of water from the ceiling. 'I need to know he's all right,' he said, turning back to Webster.

'That's up to his father.'

He gestured to his captive and Penrose saw the gun for the first time, an old Webley revolver, cradled in Webster's left hand. It was no surprise to him – he had expected Webster to be armed – but still the weapon sent a shiver of recollection through him, a stark reminder of those moments a few months before when he had lain on the ground, watching the blood drain from the wound in his shoulder, honestly believing he was about to die. As Moorcroft strained ineffectively at the ropes which held him, trying to get to his son, Penrose signalled to him to stay calm. 'What do you want?' he asked. 'Why have you brought them here?'

'I want him to acknowledge what he did,' Webster said calmly. 'The truth has stayed buried for too long, and I want it out in the open. I want Robert Moorcroft to say sorry for the life he destroyed back then, and all the lives that have been ruined since.'

'You mean the truth about Ellen Cleever?'

'About Ellie, yes. The girl he raped and killed.'

'Was she your sister? Is your real name Ernest Cleever?'

Webster smiled, but shook his head. 'No. Ernest was just the poor bastard who could never get over losing the sister he worshipped. He's in Pentonville now. I went looking for him, and found him doing a stretch for burglary. *Another* stretch, to be more accurate. Like I said – all the lives that have been ruined since then. That really was one hell of a Christmas.'

The bitterness in his voice was so acute that Penrose could almost feel it as a physical presence in the air between them. 'So what was Ellen to you?' he asked. 'Who *are* you in this story?'

'That's just what I was explaining to our friend here.' He took a photograph from his pocket and held it up to Moorcroft's face, and Penrose saw confusion there followed swiftly by recognition. 'I was ten years old,' he said angrily. 'That little boy from the choir whom you all bullied and pushed around – unless you wanted something, of course. And that Christmas you wanted her.' He let the photograph fall to the floor and Penrose bent to pick it up. In the light of one of the candles, he looked down at an attractive girl with long dark hair and pale skin, pictured with a small, blonde chorister and laughing into the camera as she borrowed his top hat for the photograph. There was something in the girl's spirit which reminded him of Bridget when they first met, and he could see from the expression in the young Tom Webster's face that he had adored her.

'Lovely, wasn't she? I thought she was the most beautiful thing I'd ever seen, but it wasn't just that. She was kind to me, and I wasn't used to that. All the older boys used to flirt with her whenever she brought us across from the school to sing at the chapel, and she was flattered – why wouldn't she be? She'd been brought up to think those young men walked the Cambridge streets like gods. And you had your eye on her from the beginning, didn't you?' He kicked Moorcroft hard in the ribs and the man on the floor groaned. 'You used me as your little go-between, taking her notes or presents, asking to meet her. And then came Christmas.'

Slowly, Penrose began to guess at the truth which he had struggled for so long to find. 'What happened that day, Tom?' he asked gently. 'Moorcroft might know but I don't, and I need to understand.'

'I'd been at the school for over a year by then,' Webster said, 'so I knew how wonderful Christmas there could be. Monty would take us to the pantomime as a treat or put on a play himself, and there'd be lots of parties. And then there was the music – always the music. We practised so hard for that service, and I loved every minute of it. And best of all, because most of the boys had gone home by then, Ellie had more time to spend with those of us who were left behind.' Penrose let him talk, trying to marry the killer in front of him with the innocent little boy he was describing, and wondering how one could be born from the other. 'By the time Christmas Eve came, we were beside ourselves with excitement.'

'You all took part in the carol service?'

'Yes. For a while it was the happiest day of my life. I waited with the rest of the boys in the vestry on the north side of the chapel, and the men were in the chantry opposite. Those last few minutes of waiting seemed to go on for ever, but the choirmaster signalled to us just before the clock struck the hour and out we went. The chapel was dark but you could feel how crowded it was, how full of expectation. There was a faint hum as the choir took up the note – and then the choirmaster pointed to *me*.' Penrose looked blank. 'To sing the solo, the first verse of "Once in Royal David's City". No one knows who's been chosen until the very last moment, and that year it was my turn.' He shook his head, as if scarcely believing that the moment had ever really belonged to him. 'I always loved that carol – its innocence, its hope. Now I can't bear to listen to it.' His words reminded Penrose of the deep, inescapable melancholy that Stephen Laxborough had apparently experienced at Christmas. 'The men joined in with the second verse as we walked up the aisle,' Webster continued. 'I can't expect you to understand how important that sense of belonging was to a little boy who had been lonely all his life. I remember Westbury giving me a wink as we sang, as if he was as proud of me as I was of myself, but I realised afterwards that they were only using me. They'd planned it all, you see.' He put the torch down on the floor while he looked in his coat for a packet of cigarettes, and the room was plunged briefly into darkness. 'I can honestly say that was the last time I was ever truly happy.'

Penrose stared at Webster's face, illuminated by the lighter cupped in his hands, and saw that he was in a world of his own, reliving every moment as if it were happening all over again. 'Where was Ellen?' he asked.

'At the service. There's a choristers' tea afterwards and she helped with that, then she told me she was going to meet a friend outside the Empire.'

'But she never got there.'

'No. Moorcroft took me to one side and said that he was planning a surprise for her and he needed my help. He said I was the only person he could trust and he promised me a present if I brought her to Hodson's Folly to meet him. He knew how to make me feel grown up, you see – and after the excitement of the service,

I thought I could do anything. He also told me that Ellen would be so grateful to me once she found out what the surprise was, and I didn't doubt that. As I said, she was flattered by Moorcroft's attentions. She'd never have gone to meet him on her own – she wasn't like that – but going with me made it safe.'

'And you knew Hodson's Folly?'

'Yes, we used to swim there all the time. There'd be school picnics on the river and they were always happy days, so I really thought I was doing something nice for Ellen. That's all I ever wanted, you know – to please her. Instead, I led her to them like a lamb to the slaughter.'

'But how were you to know?' As true as that might have been, it made no difference now and Webster didn't answer. Penrose looked over at Moorcroft, wondering how he could have allowed anyone to witness whatever he had planned. 'Did you see what happened, Tom?' he asked.

Webster nodded. 'I watched while they killed her.' There was a muffled noise as Moorcroft tried to speak, and Webster tore the rag from his mouth. 'Oh, I know – you sent me away when you had what you wanted, but I didn't go and you were too preoccupied to check. I wanted to see Ellie happy, so I stayed behind and watched from the footbridge across the river. I saw everything you did to her, and I knew it was my fault.'

The story was taking its toll by now. 'Tell me what you saw,' Penrose said gently, hoping to get the whole story before Webster's own recollections drove him to turn on Moorcroft.

'The folly looked beautiful from the river,' he said, struggling to hold back tears. 'They'd filled it with candles and lanterns, like a tiny chapel, except there was nothing sacred about what they had planned. Moorcroft was standing by the entrance and he held out his hand to her – but then the rest of them appeared, one by one out of the shadows. When Ellie saw how many of them were there she tried to run, but Moorcroft grabbed her and forced her against the wall. He was hurting her. I didn't really understand then, but I do now. She cried out when he forced himself into her, and I could hear her sobbing. Do you remember what you said when she gasped like that?' he demanded, turning to Moorcroft, and Moorcroft shook his head. 'Well, I do. You said: "See? The little bitch is enjoying it."'

Penrose looked for the slightest trace of shame in the accused man's eyes, but there was nothing. 'The others lined up to take their turn,' Webster continued. 'It's hard to be sure now what I actually remember and what I've imagined since, but there was a fleeting moment of bewilderment on Ellie's part. She couldn't understand what was happening to her. They weren't strangers or monsters, and they weren't even drunk – just privileged young men who should have known better, but who felt they could do what they liked. They mattered, and she didn't. It was as simple as that.' Penrose listened, understanding exactly what Webster meant. He had seen it himself, at school and in the army – never a rape, and never violence this extreme, but the bullying and peer pressure which lay at the heart of it. One day – he could only have been about five or six – he remembered stumbling across a group of older boys in the woods on his uncle's Cornish estate; they had a young fox cornered and were beating it to death, and even though he would have been powerless to save it, the fact that he was too frightened to try had haunted him for years. The guilt had stayed with him, and he could only begin to imagine how Tom Webster must feel. 'She struggled at first, but Moorcroft and Frost held her up against the wall while Carrington wedged a plank of wood between her feet so that she couldn't close her legs. After that, I think she gave up. Shorter was next, although he looked almost as frightened as she was, then Carrington. Laxborough couldn't do it, and the more the others laughed and jeered at him, the more impotent he became. In the end, he gave up and took his anger out on her.'

'You mean he beat her?'

Webster nodded. 'Yes, within an inch of her life. And a bit of rough seemed to do the trick for him – he was quite a man after that.'

Alastair Frost's words about the order of things made more sense to Penrose now; Frost had realised that the sequence of murders followed the order in which Ellen Cleever had been raped, but there was more to it than that. Each victim seemed to have been killed in a manner which reflected their part in the assault: a simple push down the stairs for Giles Shorter; hours of torment for Stephen Laxborough; and for Robert Moorcroft, the instigator of the crime and undisputed ringleader, a living hell which was not yet over. 'Weren't you frightened of being seen?' he asked Webster. 'God knows what they'd have done to you.'

'They were far too busy to worry about me. I didn't know *what* to do, if I'm honest. The folly was far too remote to run for help, and anyway I didn't want to leave her. I suppose I thought they'd stop eventually and then I could go to her, so I left the bridge and hid in the woodland. I wish I hadn't, because I could see so much more from there. Ellie was barely conscious by now. I watched her sink to the floor and still they didn't stop, and all the time they were laughing and joking. It was Bairstow's turn next, then Westbury and Frost, and then Swayne, but the thrill was beginning to wear off. I'll never forget it, you know. The sudden silence when all the anger was spent and each man began to realise what he'd done – but it was too late by then. Ellie had stopped moving and Swayne dragged himself off her and looked at the others as if they'd tricked him in some way, but they were all as horrified as he was – all except him.' He jabbed the gun at Moorcroft, who flinched with fear, sensing now that he was running out of time. 'I thought Ellie was dead and so did they, but then she tried to speak. Just one word. "Please." Like an animal begging to be put out of its misery. And gentleman that he is, Moorcroft obliged.'

'You saw him kill her?'

'I saw him drag her towards the river and push her in with his foot. The others had run off across the bridge by then, but Moorcroft stayed behind to clear up. By the time he'd finished, there was no sign that they'd ever been there.'

Penrose looked again towards the boy in the corner and began to hope for Teddy's sake that he *was* drugged and unconscious; to make him listen like this to what his father had done was unbearably cruel, no matter how convinced Webster was that he had right on his side. 'And what did you do?' he asked.

'I waited until I was sure they were gone and then I went to Ellen. I tried to pull her out but she was too heavy, so I sat with her for as long as I could bear it. After a while, I went back to the college to tell someone what I'd seen.'

'And *did* you tell anyone?'

Webster shook his head. 'No. I lost my nerve. When I got there, I saw Moorcroft and Westbury coming out of their staircase as if nothing had happened, and I knew then that no one would believe me. I had no proof, and there were eight voices against mine. Anyway, in my heart I knew it was my fault. Ellie would never have gone to them if I hadn't taken her there. I'm just as guilty as they are, but at least I admit it.'

'Teddy isn't guilty, though,' Penrose said. 'Let him go, Tom. I can see why you want Moorcroft to suffer, but don't make Teddy pay for his father's sins. You're better than that. Whatever you think, and however responsible you feel, you're *not* the same as those men.'

He took a couple of steps towards the camp bed but Webster stopped him with the revolver. 'Did you get a chance to look at Ellen's police file?' he asked.

'No.'

'Well, I did. I've looked at it a lot since I've been at the Cambridge station, and I don't know what sickens me more – the details of her injuries or the fact that no one really bothered about her after she died. I joined the police because I thought I could make up for everything I should have done for her back then and didn't, but we're no better than anyone else, are we? We still allow filth like him to walk the streets, destroying lives whenever he feels like it, and there's not a damned thing that any of us can do about it. How can that be right? Ask him, Penrose – did he ever think about Ellie after that night? Did any of them?'

Penrose glanced at Moorcroft, hoping that he would have the sense to stay quiet, but there was a defiance in his eyes, an expression of arrogance which did as much to confirm Webster's accusations as any spoken confession could have done. 'No,' he said brazenly. 'No, I didn't think about her. If you hadn't reminded me, I couldn't even have told you her name.'

Before Penrose could say anything, Webster walked over to the camp bed and pointed the gun at Teddy's head. 'I've blamed myself all these years,' he said. 'The life I could have had was taken away from me just like Ellen's, and now I'm going to destroy yours.'

'Wait!' Penrose shouted, at the same time as Moorcroft let out a howl of rage and fear. 'Wait, Tom – please. It's not just Moorcroft you're punishing. That boy has a mother who loves him, just like Ellen's mother. Don't put her through the same pain that Maud Cleever has suffered all these years – that's not justice.'

Webster paused, and Penrose walked over to Moorcroft and forced him to his feet. 'If he had the gun at your head I wouldn't be standing in his way,' he said, shocked to find that he was actually speaking the truth. 'But you've already ripped one woman's heart out and I won't let you do that to your wife. Tell him what he wants to hear. Admit what you did all those years ago and take the consequences properly, in a court of law.' Moorcroft remained stubbornly silent and Penrose tried the only argument he had left. 'If you think he's bluffing, ask yourself what it takes to shut a living man in a tomb and walk away. I don't think I ever told you how much Stephen Laxborough suffered, did I? I work with a pathologist who's seen every sort of torment that one man has seen fit to inflict upon another, and he told me that Laxborough's death was the most agonising he's ever come across. Hours shut in another man's grave, knowing there was no escape, so mad with fear that he tore the skin from his own face and gnawed his fingers – those beautiful musician's fingers – quite literally to the bone.' He watched with satisfaction as Moorcroft's confidence began to drain away, and hammered home his advantage. 'So don't ever underestimate what Thomas Webster might do. That child's life means nothing to him compared with making you suffer, and pulling a trigger is easy. If you have any love for your son, give Webster what he wants. Is he telling the truth? Was Ellen Cleever's death your fault?' Moorcroft nodded, but Penrose still wasn't satisfied. 'Say it out loud,' he insisted, shaking Moorcroft hard. 'It's the only thing that can save Teddy now.'

'All right – it was my fault. I killed her. I killed Ellen Cleever.'

Penrose let him go and he slumped to the floor. For a moment, Webster's expression was hard to read as he took in the four small words which meant so much to him, but eventually he let the gun fall to his side. 'You heard that, sir,' he said, 'and I want you to make sure he hangs for it. Now untie him and let him see his son.'

Penrose did as he was told, but something in Webster's words made him fear for the tiny form which lay so still and lifeless beneath the blankets. Oblivious to the expression of triumph on his captor's face, Moorcroft ran over to the bed and began to tear off the covers, but all that he found was a pile of crumpled linen and sacking, shaped to look like the body of a boy. Desperate now, Moorcroft continued to search for his son, calling Teddy's name again and again, even though the trick was painfully obvious. 'Where's my son?' he cried, throwing himself on his knees in front of Webster. 'I'll do anything you want. Just tell me where he is.'

Webster watched him for a moment, then simply turned and

left the room. Fearing what was still to come, Penrose took Moorcroft's wrist and handcuffed him to one of the iron rings. 'I'm going to look for your son,' he said, 'but don't think for one moment that I'm doing it for you. And make no mistake – you *will* pay for this now it's out in the open.'

'Don't be ridiculous,' Moorcroft said, a trace of his old arrogance returning. 'There's no proof, and that confession was made under duress. You wouldn't even get me to court.'

'Your confession might be inadmissible, but Richard Swayne's isn't.' Penrose let the lie sink in, enjoying Moorcroft's surprise. 'Didn't I mention it? We've got him in custody now and his lawyer is advising a full confession – in exchange for leniency, obviously. I'm afraid you won't come out of it very well, sir.'

Sooner or later he would have to admit to the deception, but for now Moorcroft's uncertainty was reward enough and he set off up the steps after Webster. There was no sign of anyone on the first floor, so he continued on to the roof – a flat, open space with a high parapet and a raised platform in the centre where the original artillery had been mounted. It was dark now, and a mist was coming in with the approaching tide, deadening the roar of each successive wave. Webster sat on the wall with his back to the sea, smoking a cigarette and nursing the revolver. 'What have you done with Teddy?' Penrose called, stopping by the central platform. 'It's time to end this now, Tom. He's just a little boy. Don't do to him what those men did to you.'

Webster looked at him and calmly stubbed the cigarette out on the wall. 'Teddy's at the college school,' he said.

'What?'

'I dropped him off there before I left Cambridge. They'd heard about the body at the Priory, so it was quite understandable that his parents would want him to be taken care of until all that was cleared up. One flash of my warrant card and they were very happy to oblige.' He smiled and Penrose could have wept with relief. 'You don't honestly think that I could hurt a child after what I went through, do you? And he's a nice lad – loves his music, just like I did. I hope no one takes that away from him.'

'So that charade was entirely for his father's benefit?'

'It worked well, didn't it? For a moment there, that bastard knew what it was like to be afraid, just like she was.'

Penrose walked over to the wall and sat down a few feet from Webster. 'Why now, Tom? Why after all these years?'

He ignored the question and stared back towards the lights of the town, faint and indistinct against the mist and the past. 'Monty talked about this place a lot,' he said. 'His grandparents lived in Aldeburgh and he spent a lot of time here as a child. He once told me it gave him so many of the things he most loved – the first stained glass he ever saw, the first organ he ever heard, the first voices raised in song. He came back every year, right to the end of his life. For me, the only place that was ever that special was Cambridge. I'd never been happy with my family. My father was a military man and my mother was a military man's wife, and they moved about a lot. When they sent me away to school, I felt as if I'd finally come home. It was the first time I had friends, the first time I knew kindness, and when you're a little boy and you walk into that chapel and hear the music – well, you think you'll never want to be anywhere else.'

'But you had to give all that up after what happened to Ellen. You felt you couldn't stay.'

Webster nodded. 'Suddenly all the good memories disappeared. That's the difference between what Aldeburgh meant to Monty and what Cambridge meant to me. He wrote the stories he wrote because his own ghosts were happy ones. Mine were malevolent to start with, so I ran away from them.'

'But you still went back. George Clough told me that you'd asked to be transferred to Cambridge.'

'Yes. I never stopped missing it, and – like you said – so many years had passed. I thought I could put it behind me. It worked for a while.'

'So what happened to change that?'

'Two things, really. Monty died and I went to his funeral, and that's when I saw them all again – Moorcroft and Westbury, Frost and Swayne. All important men now in their own right, and yet I watched them and they hadn't really changed. They were still spoilt little bullies who got their own way, no matter what it cost.'

'Did they know who you were?'

'No, not at all. I shook Moorcroft's hand and looked him in the eye, but he brushed me off like a college servant. It's funny, isn't it? One moment that changed my whole life and they had no recollection of me at all. Even so, I probably could have coped but then the rapes started in the town and it was like living through that night all over again, each and every time it happened. All those poor girls – the shame and the violence and the fear, and still no one really cares. It's more than twenty years later and we've come through a war, yet nothing's changed. The men I work with don't take it seriously, any more than the men in the Cambridgeshire force bothered about Ellie. They wrote her off as if her death counted for nothing, as if she'd asked for it. And perhaps in hindsight Ellie was the lucky one – she didn't have to live with the shame. These women do. Their lives are destroyed.'

'And what about all the lives *you've* destroyed? You're a decent man. You can't think that was right.'

'Of course it wasn't right, but it was necessary. How else would they have paid?' Penrose had no answer, so he let Webster continue to talk. 'I went to see Monty when I heard he was dying.'

'He must have meant a lot to you.'

'He meant a lot to everyone. I doubt there were many boys or undergraduates who passed through King's during his time and didn't think of him as a father or a friend. He'd been back at Eton for years by then, and he was confined to his rooms and very weak, but he remembered my name immediately. And he remembered that he'd found me crying on the steps of the chapel one Christmas Eve. That's why he didn't finish writing a new story that year – he was looking after me.'

'The current Dean told me that Monty had tried to help you. He was chaplain at the time and Monty wanted you to talk to him about what was troubling you.'

'Yes, but I couldn't. I was too frightened, and too ashamed.'

'And too grief-stricken. You'd lost the first person you loved. That's hard at any age.'

'Yes, I suppose it is.'

'Did Monty have any idea why you were so upset?'

'No. I told him I was missing my family at Christmas, but I don't think he believed me. He took me back to his rooms to cheer me up. It would have been such a treat at any other time, because only his friends and a handful of undergraduates normally got to hear him read a story, but it just made things worse. All the choral scholars were there, and I had to face them. It was only a few hours after Ellie had died and already they were behaving as if nothing had happened, drinking Monty's whisky and enjoying the story. He chose an old one to read – "The Story of a Disappearance and an Appearance", I remember that. It's the only one I can never bring myself to read. Moorcroft and his friends lapped it up, as if terror were something to relish, something that only happened in stories.' He looked Penrose in the eye for the first time since he had begun talking, and the sadness in his face was replaced fleetingly by a steely determination. 'I wanted to show them that it wasn't.'

'How long did you stay at the college school after that?' Penrose asked.

'I left on Christmas Day. My parents came to collect me after the morning service, and I never went back. That was the last time I saw Monty until I went to Eton last year. He'd hardly changed at all, you know. He still had that sense of fun. Some friends of his had sent him a gramophone to cheer him up during his convalescence, and it was all a great adventure. I told him then what I should have told him twenty-four years ago, but I wish I hadn't. It wasn't fair to burden him with so much sorrow at the end of his life.'

'What did he say?'

'He told me that I knew what I had to do. He said I was a man now and not a boy, and I had to find the courage from somewhere to do what was right.'

'But he didn't mean . . .'

'No, of course he didn't. Monty didn't have a violent bone in his body. He wanted me to go to the police – to my colleagues – and tell them what had really happened.'

'So why didn't you?'

Webster stared at him scornfully. 'Why do you think? There wasn't a shred of evidence, and look what those men had become. No one cared about Ellie when they thought she'd been killed by a beggar off the streets, so why would she suddenly be more important than the lord of the manor or a barrister like Westbury? You know I'm right.' Penrose conceded the truth of his words with a nod. 'Monty never understood evil, not really. He liked to keep horror at a distance, even in his stories, and he certainly couldn't cope with it in human form. He would never have turned a blind eye to what they did, but he was naive. He always thought that things worked out for the best, and he never once lost his faith – in this world, or the next.'

'I envy people like that, but I'm afraid I've never been one of them.'

Webster smiled. 'No, nor me. I haven't forgotten what he said to me, though, when he was trying to comfort me about Ellie's death. He was talking about a friend of his who died suddenly of a perforated appendix, and he said that it had been such a relief to him at the time to know that there were people there to meet him. He said it as matter-of-factly as if his friend had simply gone to stay with friends at an unfamiliar house, and I so desperately wanted to believe like he did that Ellie was somewhere better.'

'But you couldn't.'

'No. I argued with him, but he just smiled at me as if I were still a child who had so much to learn, and then he said: "What is all this love for if we have to go out into the dark?" They were his last words to me, and for a while they made me feel better.' He took his warrant card from his coat pocket and looked at it for a long time before throwing it over the wall into the water. 'I joined the police because I wanted to do some good,' he said, 'but it's really just made it easier for me to be as evil as everybody else. I ran out of time, sir. I failed those women in Cambridge just like I failed Ellen. I suppose you know I caught the wrong man?' Penrose nodded. 'So I'm still that helpless little boy, standing on the sidelines watching, never saving anyone.'

He picked up the gun, and there was something both chilling and inevitable in the way that he handled the weapon, as if it were the only answer to his pain. 'That isn't true, Tom,' Penrose said firmly. 'Those women you say you've failed – don't you see that each and every one of them finds it easier to cope with what she's been through because you've made her feel that it matters, that someone is taking her story seriously and doing all he can to help? This isn't finished yet. Don't just give up.'

'I hope you never know what it's like, sir, this rage that won't go away. All I've ever wanted since I was ten years old was to make those men suffer. I told myself it was for Ellie, but it was more selfish than that. I hated them because they destroyed my life, as well as hers. I know what I've done, and so do you. You've seen it for yourself. I'm just like them.'

'But what about Swayne and Moorcroft?' Penrose demanded, desperate now to prevent a final tragedy. If he had sensed a bond growing between himself and Webster, he knew now that it was slipping away. 'They still haven't paid for what they did, and they never will if you're not here to testify.' Webster hesitated, and then – to Penrose's huge relief – threw him the revolver. 'I'll help you, Tom,' he promised. 'I'll do everything I can to get justice for Ellen. Let's go back inside.'

He held out his hand, but Webster just smiled. 'That's not how it ends, sir. Remember the story.'

In that split second, Penrose knew exactly what he was going to do but it was already too late to save him. Like James's doomed protagonist, Webster let himself fall back over the edge of the parapet and Penrose heard the sickening thud of his body hitting the ground forty feet below. He ran to the wall and looked down from the tower, but in the darkness and the stress of the last few hours, the reality of the scene fused with images from that prophetic story until he found it hard to separate fact from fiction. Webster's body lay smashed and broken on the rocks. He only glanced once at his face.

23

The pleasure of Mrs Thompson's company on a Saturday morning was something that Josephine could well have done without, but, when she heard the clatter in the hallway just after nine o'clock, she resigned herself to the fact that this must be 'every other weekend' and hurriedly pulled on some clothes. 'What a dreadful situation,' the daily woman said, picking up last night's paper while she waited for the kettle to boil. 'Fancy arresting the wrong man. Now everyone will start to panic all over again, and I'll never see my husband. He'll be out at all hours, making sure those girls stay safe. You'd think the police would have more consideration.'

Josephine doubted that they had made a mistake deliberately to inconvenience the Thompson household, and she didn't quite understand why fitting locks was suddenly a nocturnal business, but she was too worried about Archie to argue. She had telephoned the police station repeatedly the night before, but no one would tell her anything except to offer a half-hearted reassurance that the inspector from Scotland Yard was 'perfectly all right', and in the end she had given up. Perhaps she would have more luck this morning.

As if on cue, the telephone rang in the hallway. 'I'll get it,' Mrs Thompson said, and the peal of the bell was duly cut off in its prime before Josephine had a chance to argue. She hovered in the doorway, feeling like an eavesdropper on her own conversation, and listened while Mrs Thompson tried to make sense of whatever was being said at the other end. 'Hello? What was that? I *beg* your pardon? Who is this, please?' There was a long silence, and then Josephine heard her voice again, clipped to the point of rudeness.

'I see. Just one moment.' She held out the receiver, her face scarlet. 'Miss Fox would like to speak to you,' she said.

Josephine took the telephone and waited while her messenger went upstairs. 'Who the hell was that?' Marta asked, her words distorted by distance and a bad connection.

'Your new daily woman. I did explain in one of my letters, but you obviously haven't got it yet. What on earth did you say to her?' She listened while Marta repeated her greeting. 'Well, I suppose there's only one way to interpret that,' she said, scarcely knowing whether to laugh or cry. 'At least it's so explicit that she's unlikely to repeat it to her aunt in Inverness.'

'She hasn't really got an aunt in Inverness?'

'So she says.'

'God, Josephine – I'm sorry, but this line's bloody awful and I never dreamt it wasn't you. All I could hear was a Scottish voice saying hello. And I have missed you. Is it any wonder that I was a little enthusiastic about where I'd like to be right now?'

'The feeling's mutual, but I'm not quite sure how either of us is going to assert any domestic authority after that. Anyway, what are you doing up at this time? It must be the middle of the night over there.'

'It is, but I couldn't sleep without talking to you.'

'Why? Is something wrong?'

'Not wrong, exactly, but there's something I need to ask you. The Hitchcocks are staying on longer than planned – will you come out and join me?'

'What?'

'Just for a couple of weeks. We could spend Christmas here and then travel back together.'

'Marta, I can't just drop everything and leave for Los Angeles.'

'It would be New York, not Los Angeles. That's why the trip's been extended – to fit in some meetings there.'

'Even so . . .' There was a loud knock at the door and Josephine waited to see if Mrs Thompson would come downstairs to answer it, but there was no sign of her. 'She's probably had to have a lie down. I'll just ignore it.'

The banging came again and Marta's sigh almost rivalled it for volume. 'Go and answer it. I'll hang on.'

'Are you sure? I won't be long.' She opened the front door and found Archie standing outside, looking exhausted. 'Thank God – I was getting worried about you,' she said.

'I'm sorry I couldn't speak to you last night, but everything happened so quickly that there just wasn't time to call.'

'Don't worry about that. You're safe – that's the main thing. Come in. I'm just on the phone to Marta.'

'I don't want to interrupt. If now's a bad time, I can come back later.'

'Don't be silly. Go up to the sitting room and make yourself at home, but don't upset the daily woman – she's had enough shocks for one day.'

He looked bemused but did as she suggested, and she went back to the telephone. 'Sorry about that. Archie's here.'

'Does he know yet?'

'No. Things have been a bit busy, and Bridget's only just got back.'

'Well, you obviously can't talk about that in front of him, but you *were* about to tell me all the reasons why you can't spend a fortnight in America.'

There was an edge to her voice and Josephine hesitated. Marta was right: she *had* been about to give a list of habitual excuses, the list which tripped automatically from her tongue whenever it suited her to turn down an invitation. But this was different, and she was surprised by how desperately she wanted to go. 'Give me a couple of days to think about it,' she said instead. 'I'd love to come, but I'll need to make some arrangements here first.'

'Really?'

The surprise in Marta's voice gave Josephine pause for thought. 'Yes, really. It's about time I stopped saying no to things just because I've always said no to them. And I can think of worse places to spend Christmas than with you in Central Park.'

Marta laughed, and Josephine felt the double-edged miracle of a telephone line which made her seem so close. 'You might not have any choice after the domestic's phoned her aunt. I love you, Josephine.'

'I love you, too. Now go and get some sleep.'

She rang off and took Mrs Thompson's abandoned tea tray up to the sitting room, where she found Archie waiting discreetly like a doubtful suitor. 'Sorry about that. Just let me go and give the daily the rest of the day off and we can talk properly.'

'She's obviously upstairs. There's been a lot of banging.'

'That doesn't surprise me.' She found Mrs Thompson in her bedroom, holding a duster and a photograph which Josephine could have sworn had been tucked away in a drawer. 'Is there a problem?' she asked, determined not to be intimidated.

'I'm really not comfortable with this,' the daily woman said, gesturing towards the bed. 'I'm not comfortable with this at all.'

'I was rather hoping you'd make it, not sleep in it.'

'That's not what I meant, and you know it. I meant I'm not comfortable with this . . . well, with this *arrangement* you seem to have, for want of a better word.'

Whether it was tiredness, the exhilaration of speaking to Marta, or simply irritation, Josephine found it impossible to keep her temper. 'Try love,' she said angrily.

'I beg your pardon?'

'The word you're looking for – it's love.'

'Don't be ridiculous. You're two grown women and you ought to know better. I've never heard anything so—'

'Mrs Thompson,' Josephine said, holding up her hand to interrupt. 'I really don't give a damn about what you may or may not be "comfortable" with. From the moment you walked into this house, you've been fumbling around in my life, putting two and two together to make five and jumping to conclusions based on nothing but your own unpleasant prejudice. You have no understanding of who I am, and you never will have. How I choose to live is *my* business – it has nothing whatsoever to do with you, with your aunt in Inverness, or even with my own family.' She snatched the photograph from Mrs Thompson's hands and pointed to the door. 'Now get out.'

'What? You can't possibly speak to me like that.'

'I think you'll find I just did. Go and pick on a house you're more comfortable with and leave the rest of us in peace.'

Mrs Thompson opened her mouth to argue, then thought better of it. She turned and hurried down the stairs, and Josephine took great satisfaction from the expression of uncertainty that crossed her face when she turned back and saw Archie on the landing. 'The agency will hear about this,' she offered as a parting shot.

'They certainly will – and if they really *do* pride themselves on their discretion, I doubt they'll take kindly to slander from any of their employees.'

The door slammed behind her and Archie gave a round of applause. 'I think she's gone for more than the day, though,' he said. 'What on earth did she do to rile you like that?'

'It's not even worth mentioning,' Josephine said. 'Come down to the kitchen. I'll make us some coffee and you can tell me why you look so awful.'

She led the way back downstairs, relieved to have the house to herself again. 'I've just come from the Cleevers,' Archie said when they were settled round the kitchen table. 'All those years and they finally know who was responsible for their daughter's death.' Josephine listened while he told her everything that had happened since they last met. 'There's a part of me that thinks it might have been kinder to leave them in ignorance,' he admitted, 'but they're not the sort to shy away from the truth. You were right, Josephine – Maud Cleever is remarkably brave and remarkably dignified. So is her husband.'

'They've lost everything,' Josephine said. 'A son as well as a daughter.'

'Not necessarily. Webster managed to trace Ernest Cleever and found him in prison. He's coming to the end of a six-month stretch for burglary and I've arranged for them to go and see him. They're keen to get him back on the straight and narrow when he gets out. I think it's given them a sense of purpose which they haven't had for years. It won't be easy – for any of them – but something might be salvaged. Let's hope so.'

'I can't get Hodson's Folly out of my head,' Josephine said. 'I went to see what it was like after I dropped your note off, and it's desolate. Now I know what really happened there, I can't stop imagining that poor girl's face in the water. God, Archie, how she must have suffered. And Webster, too. That explains why he seemed so driven when he came here that night. It was as if each and every rape was personal to him, and in a way I suppose it was. I know it's an awful thing to say, but I completely understand why he did what he did.'

'Yes, so do I. I only wish I could have saved him.'

'No one could have done that.' Archie was quiet, and Josephine could tell how badly he had been affected by Webster's death and the hours that had led up to it. 'You can try and do as he asked, though. Do you think you'll be able to charge Moorcroft? Have you got enough evidence?'

'It's looking hopeful.'

'Then why do you look so *un*hopeful?'

'Because it's filthy, Josephine. The whole damned thing is corrupt from start to finish, and I'm part of that now. To get Moorcroft, I have to make a compromise.'

'With whom?'

'With the only other man from that group who's still alive. When we were in the tower, I told Moorcroft that Richard Swayne was about to give a full account of what had happened that night in exchange for leniency. It was a lie, told in the heat of the moment, and I shouldn't have said it, but I wanted to wipe the smirk off his face. It gave me an idea, though. Swayne was complicit, but he didn't instigate anything and he didn't kill Ellen. From what Tom said, he could also argue that he didn't actually rape her, so he's in an ideal position to corroborate the evidence against Moorcroft. And of course the Home Office will do everything they can to push it through. Swayne's one of theirs, and we all look after our own. I expect he'll be pensioned off when a discreet amount of time has passed – a generous settlement if he goes quietly. Tom was right. Nothing's changed.'

Josephine took his hand. 'Don't, Archie,' she said gently. 'Don't tarnish yourself with someone else's bitterness. Sin-eating is a fool's game at the best of times and these *aren't* your sins, whatever you might think now.' He looked doubtful and there was obviously no point in pressing the matter. 'Do you think there's any chance that Moorcroft might be the rapist the police are looking for?' she asked.

'Leopards and spots, you mean?'

'Something like that. But I was also thinking about the night of the rape next door – you came here because you were looking for Robert Moorcroft, so he was obviously out there somewhere and not at home.'

'Yes, his wife told me that he often disappeared for nights at a time. The thought had crossed my mind, actually. I tried to speak to Clough about it, but it wasn't the right moment. He's so shocked and devastated by Webster's death that he couldn't take anything else in.'

'But you've still got Moorcroft in custody?'

'Oh yes. He's not going anywhere for the time being.'

'That must be a relief for his wife. I imagine she's very grateful to have her son back safe and sound.'

'I haven't spoken to her.'

'Why not?'

'It didn't seem right while I'm trying to hang her husband.' He gave a wry smile and poured them both some coffee. 'I went to see Bridget the night before last,' he said, apparently oblivious to the telling train of thought. 'I can't believe it was less than forty-eight hours ago. It feels like a lifetime.'

'Did you have a chance to talk properly?'

'Not really. We were both conscientiously polite.'

'That's only natural. You've been apart a long time.'

'It was more than that, though. We can't go on like this and we both know it. It's always a mistake to go back. Bridget and I have a past, but there's nothing to connect us to that now, nothing to link the people we are to the people we were then.'

He was wrong about that, but now wasn't the time to discuss Bridget or what the future might hold. 'You're too tired to think straight about anything,' she said. 'Let me make up a bed for you. You can't go back to London until you've had some sleep.'

'What would your daily woman say?' He grinned, and she was pleased to see the clouds lift, if only briefly. 'Don't bother to make the bed up, though. I'll be out like a light wherever you put me.'

He went off to the spare room and Josephine settled by the window to work, but all she could think about was Ellen Cleever and the last, torturous night of her life. The gardener was busy in the churchyard below and she watched him for a while, still not able to shake off her earlier suspicions entirely but struck more forcefully than before by the danger of judging what you could never really know. As she watched, a young woman opened the gate to St Clement's and sat down on the bench by the church wall, shoulders hunched against the cold. She looked up towards the houses, her face visible now beneath the brim of her hat, and Josephine was surprised to see that it was Mary Ennis. Wondering what the girl was doing back in Cambridge, she took her coat from the rack and went out to speak to her.

Mary raised her hand in acknowledgement, and Josephine walked through the gravestones and sat down on the bench next to her. 'It's nice to see you,' she said. 'I didn't expect our paths to cross again, but I've often wondered how you are.'

'We've just come back to collect my things,' Mary explained. 'I so badly wanted to do it myself, but in the end I just couldn't bring myself to go back into that room.'

'That's hardly surprising. What happened is still very recent.'

'Even so, it would have shown a bit of spirit, a bit of fight.' She smiled sadly, and looked again to what had once been her window. 'It seems that fight is something I don't really do any more.'

'Would you like me to get your things for you?'

'Thank you, but my father's in there with Peter. They shouldn't be long now.'

'Peter?'

'He's my fiancé.' She hesitated over the word, as if it didn't really belong to her, then took off her glove to show Josephine her engagement ring.

'Congratulations.'

'You don't really mean that.' She looked at Josephine, defying her to argue. 'I know what you must think and you're right, but nobody really understands how lonely it is. I've always liked my own company, but not like this. It's so hard to realise that people can only help you so far. Peter tries, though, bless him. He's always loved me, right from when we were children.'

'And do you love him?'

'No, but I'm grateful to him. I was astonished when he asked me to marry him after everything that had happened – flattered, I suppose. *I* might feel second-hand, but Peter still wants me – not out of duty or pity, but out of genuine love. And I care for him. That's a start, I suppose.'

'But is it enough?' It went against Josephine's surest instincts to interfere in anyone's life, particularly someone who was a virtual stranger to her, but there was something in Mary's wilful sacrifice of her own future which was as tragic in its way as Ellen Cleever's death.

'It's enough that Peter knows,' Mary said. 'That means the world to me somehow. If I met someone new, no matter how well suited we were, I'd have to start from the beginning and I really can't face that. And I have to think about my parents, too. None of this is their fault and they've tried so hard to look after me. I remember my mother standing at the gate when I was a child, worrying herself half to death if I was so much as a few minutes late home from school – and I know now that she's tearing herself apart because she wasn't there to protect me when it mattered. My father's so upset that he hasn't once looked me in the eye since it happened.'

'I can understand how hard it is for them, but what about your job? What about—'

'My freedom? Don't, Josephine – please. I know what you're going to say, but it's hopeless and I'll send myself mad if I think about it. It's better that I just accept what has to be and make the best of it, for my own sake as well as for Peter's. That life is gone.'

The door of Mary's former lodgings opened and two men came out into the street, burdened with suitcases and a couple of large picture frames. 'Looks like it's time for you to go,' Josephine said, giving the younger woman a hug. 'Good luck.'

'Thank you. And thank you for everything you did that night. I'll never forget it.'

Which was, of course, the trouble, Josephine thought as she watched her walk away. Peter put an arm protectively around his fiancée's shoulders as they headed back down St Clement's Passage to the waiting car, and she wondered how Mary would cope with all that desperate devotion. The girl in the nurse's uniform who had cycled off to her shift with such energy and joy was a different person altogether.

*

Archie slept through lunch and afternoon tea, and Josephine was just beginning to think about a supper for them both when the telephone rang. 'Miss Tey? It's Bill Fallowfield here. I'm sorry to disturb you but is the Chief still there?'

'He's dead to the world, Bill. Is it urgent, or can I get him to call you when he wakes up?'

'I'm afraid it *is* urgent, miss. He'd want to know about this. Would you get him for me?'

'Yes, of course.'

She woke Archie and left him to discuss whatever developments his sergeant had to report in private, but he came to find her almost immediately. 'I'm sorry, Josephine – I've got to go.'

'What's the matter?' she asked, taking one look at his ashen face.

'There's been another attack, and it looks like Bridget's involved.'

'*Bridget?*'

'Yes. The woman who called the police gave her name as Foley. She's not the victim, thank God, but she's at the scene and I need to go to her. They say it's serious.'

'Where did this happen?'

'In a theatre on Newmarket Road. Bill's meeting me there.'

'The Festival Theatre?' Josephine asked, realising to her horror that the Miss Foley Archie was expecting wasn't the one he was going to find. 'Are you sure it's Bridget? Shouldn't you check before you go rushing off?'

'Foley isn't a very common name outside Donegal.'

'But what would Bridget be doing in a theatre?'

'Seeing a play? Painting scenery? For God's sake, Josephine – how do I know? And I can't waste time arguing with you about things that hardly matter. I need to make sure she's all right.'

'Well, at least let me come with you—'

But he grabbed his keys from the table in the hall and left without another word. Josephine telephoned Bridget, hoping to warn her, but of course there was no answer – if Bridget had been contactable, she would surely have left to be with Phyllis by now. Horrified by the impending disaster, she tried to think of some way of averting it but her mind refused to help her. Archie didn't know Phyllis, of course, so if Bridget *wasn't* with her, there was a small chance that he would leave without making the connection. And then she remembered the painting. Archie wouldn't recognise Phyllis, but there was no way that Phyllis wouldn't recognise the man she had been told was her father from Bridget's poignant and sensitive portrait; how on earth would she feel when she saw him walking into the Festival Theatre alive and well? A war hero perhaps, but certainly not a war casualty. Feeling guilty at her part in the deception played on both of them, Josephine hurried out into the street to find a taxi.

24

One glance at the small yard in front of the Festival Theatre was enough to fill Josephine's heart with dread. Three police cars and an ambulance fanned out from the foyer doors, parked as a barricade to a growing crowd of spectators, and she could only begin to imagine what horrors they heralded for those still inside. The taxi dropped her across the street and she joined the throng on the pavement nearby, a motley assortment of theatre-goers arriving early for the evening performance and ordinary passers-by, drawn to the ominous group of emergency vehicles. Police officers stood outside both entrances, solemn and tight-lipped, and, in the passageway which ran along the side of the building, Josephine could see the dark, forbidding outline of a mortuary van. There was no sign of Archie.

She pushed her way to the front of the crowd, heading for a man with a notebook whom she assumed was a reporter from the local paper. 'What's going on?' she asked, trying not to listen to the alarming speculation taking place on either side. 'How bad is it?'

The journalist shrugged. 'No one's come out to talk to us yet, but there are rumours that this one's fatal. It was always going to happen sooner or later. The police have been running round like headless chickens from the moment that this bloke first struck, and now it looks like some poor girl's paid the price for it. The golden boy hasn't even put in an appearance yet, as far as I can see. Perhaps he's done the decent thing and resigned.'

If the reporter was referring to Detective Inspector Webster, then he was more accurate than he could ever have imagined. Clearly the scandal of the murders hadn't reached the press yet, and for Archie's sake Josephine was relieved. She waited impatiently for something to happen, sharing excitements with the crowd as sporadic flurries of activity by the front entrance stirred false hopes of a more tangible development, but eventually the side door opened and an ambulance man emerged, supporting a young woman wrapped in a blanket. Her head was covered and it was impossible to see her face, but a murmur of hope and relief rippled through the crowds when they saw that she was well enough to walk. As Josephine watched, searching for the slightest confirmation that this was Phyllis, she thought of Mary Ennis, walking down St Clement's Passage on the night that she was raped, and of all that she had given up since; there was a certain 'least of all evils' element in praying that the girl climbing into the ambulance was Archie's daughter, that the fatality was a colleague or a friend, but the alternative was unthinkable.

And then the door opened again. Two men bearing a stretcher walked out into the passage, and everyone fell silent as they carried their burden – shrouded entirely in a blanket – to the waiting mortuary van. There was something profoundly sad and shocking about the scene, Josephine thought, as if the body leaving the theatre carried with it the fear and sorrow of a whole community. The stretcher was loaded gently into the vehicle and the crowd parted in a respectful silence to allow it out into the street. As it drove away and the babble of conversation returned, Josephine found herself wondering if the last few days could have been anything other than a surreal, hideous dream.

Such was the commotion now that it took her a few moments to locate the voice calling her name. Bill Fallowfield was walking down the side passage with a scene of crime photographer, and she waved in acknowledgement, relieved to see someone who might tell her what was going on. The sergeant nodded to one of the uniformed men who had been stationed at regular intervals to keep the public at a distance, and she was allowed to pass through unchallenged. The reporter glared at her, realising that he had missed an opportunity, and apparently blaming Josephine for not offering up her connection to events more readily. 'Thank God you're here, miss,' Fallowfield said as he escorted her over to a quiet area by the door. 'I had half a mind to telephone you.'

'What's happened, Bill? Is Archie all right?'

'No, not really. He had such a shock when we got here, and I blame myself for that. I assumed the Miss Foley who'd made the emergency call was *his* Miss Foley, but it wasn't.'

'It was her daughter.'

Fallowfield stared at her in astonishment. 'You knew she had a daughter?'

Josephine nodded, too shamed by the tone of his voice to listen carefully enough to his words. 'Yes. I found out recently – by accident, really. Bridget swore that she was going to tell Archie, but she obviously didn't do it quickly enough.' Fallowfield looked sceptical, and she knew he was imagining some sort of feminine conspiracy which had never existed; his loyalty to Archie was unswerving, and he wouldn't look kindly on anyone who served him badly. 'Does Bridget know what's happened yet?' she asked. 'She'll want to be with Phyllis.'

There was a pause, then Fallowfield put his hand on her arm, all traces of hostility gone. 'Miss Tey, you obviously don't understand. Bridget – Miss Foley – was killed this afternoon.'

'*Bridget?*' Josephine steadied herself against the wall as the ground seemed to shift beneath her. She looked at Fallowfield, trying in vain to make some sense of what he was telling her. 'No, Bill, that can't be right. Are you sure?'

'I'm afraid so. She was supposed to be having supper with her daughter in between the matinee and the evening performance, but when she got here to meet her she walked in on the attack. The bastard just lashed out at her. There was nothing that anybody could do. She died before the ambulance got here.'

Josephine closed her eyes, but the images which played out in her mind were too horrific to contemplate. 'What about the rapist? Did he get away again?'

'Yes, he ran as soon as he realised what he'd done.'

'And Phyllis? Did he . . .?'

'Get what he came for? No. Miss Foley got there in time to save her.'

But at what cost, Josephine thought. 'Could Phyllis tell you anything about him?' she asked.

'Only that his voice sounded familiar, but she couldn't place it. She didn't see his face.'

'And where's Archie now? Can I go and see him?'

'Yes, I'll take you in. We'll have to use the front entrance, though. The backstage area is still out of bounds.'

So that was where it had happened. Josephine imagined Phyllis alone there, carrying out the final checks for the evening performance, calmly making sure that everything was in place for the opening scene. She would have taken those precious, ordinary moments for granted, never thinking that they were the last she would ever have, oblivious to the fact that a stranger was about to cheat her of everything that mattered: her independence; a job she adored; her mother's love – all tarnished or destroyed in the blink of an eye. 'Did Archie see Bridget's body?' she asked.

Fallowfield nodded. 'I'm afraid so. The local boys would have stopped him if they'd known, but they had no reason to think he was connected to the victim.'

'No, of course not,' Josephine said, trying to imagine the shock he must have suffered. 'And did Phyllis see Archie?'

The sergeant looked at her curiously. 'Yes, she did. Only for a moment, but it was very peculiar. Forgive the cliché, but she seemed completely bewildered, as if she'd seen a ghost.' Bill Fallowfield had thirty years' experience of talking to witnesses, and Josephine's lack of surprise now didn't go unnoticed: 'Do you know something else, Miss Tey?'

'Yes, Bill, I'm afraid I do, and I honestly can't decide if it makes things better or worse – if worse is possible. I'll have to tell him, though,' she added, as much to herself as to the sergeant. 'I'll have to tell them both.'

He escorted her into the building, through the foyer and into the auditorium. The stage lights were full on, flooding the area beyond the proscenium arch with an artificial radiance which bled out into the stalls below, depriving the area of its customary, consoling darkness. Archie was sitting in the front row, staring straight ahead. Josephine hesitated when she saw him; a cliché it might have been, but Phyllis's response to seeing her father was appropriate – it was like looking at a ghost. His face was gaunt and pale, a colour she had only ever seen in those who were seriously ill; he shrank into the seat as if trying to withdraw completely from the world. In the hour since they parted, it seemed to Josephine that Archie had lived at least another twenty years of his life.

The echo of her footsteps sounded unnaturally loud in the empty theatre, but still he didn't turn to her. 'I'm so sorry, Archie,' she said, sitting down next to him. 'I can't even begin to imagine how you must feel.'

She took his hand but he withdrew it immediately. 'He cut her throat – did you know that?' he said, his voice tight and bitter. 'The girl says Bridget was trying to pull him off her and he just turned round and lashed out.' Knowing all she did, the impersonal way in which he referred to Phyllis jarred with Josephine's conscience. 'He had a lucky strike, you might say.'

'Archie—'

'She bled to death, Josephine. He cut through her windpipe so she wouldn't even have been able to cry out or—'

'Archie, please – don't do this.'

'Why not?' he demanded angrily, looking at her for the first time. 'This *is* what I do, isn't it? I'm a policeman. I waste my life trying to understand how and why people die – and they're strangers, all of them. Who are Tom Webster and Robert Moorcroft to me? Or even Ellen Cleever, for that matter? And yet I put them first. I was asleep in your house when Bridget died, and I should have been with her.' Josephine felt the sting of his words, and knew that the sorrow of Bridget's death would, for Archie, be amplified beyond measure by the doubts and half-decisions of the weeks preceding it. She wished with all her heart that he and Bridget had been able to come to some sort of resolution before the tragedy, to some sort of peace; there was no way now that Archie would ever be able to grieve without guilt, if such a thing was even possible for anyone who loved. 'I let Bridget drift away and become a stranger, too,' he continued quietly. 'I'm mourning her now but I have no idea who she was.'

'Bridget wasn't a stranger.'

'How do you know? Why are you even arguing with me, Josephine? She was a mother and she never told me. Why would she keep something like that a secret? And that girl obviously didn't know anything about Bridget and me. Clearly whatever we had wasn't even important enough to mention.'

It was the moment that Josephine had been dreading, and the growing silence between them only made the choice she was faced with more momentous: she could say nothing and protect their friendship, telling herself that it was Archie she was shielding, safe now in the knowledge that her complicity with Bridget's secret needn't be revealed; or she could be honest with him and risk all that they meant to each other. 'You were *too* important, Archie,' she said, before the first option became too tempting. 'That's why Bridget didn't tell you.' He stared at her and she watched the implication of her words sink in, but she was too committed now to change her mind. 'That's right. I found out about Phyllis a few weeks ago, and I talked to Bridget about it as soon as she got back from Devon. I tried to—'

'How?'

Josephine hesitated, reluctant to admit that Marta had known Bridget's secret for months. 'Does it really matter now?' she asked.

'Of course it matters. How did you find out?'

'By accident. Marta bumped into them together at the station.'

'But Bridget hasn't been in Cambridge since August. You must have known this for a damned sight longer than a few weeks.' Loyalty to Marta prevented her from denying it; there was no point in trying to appease Archie's anger by pretending she was as much a victim as he was. 'So that's why Marta was so odd when I met her in Hampstead,' he said, getting up and walking over to the stage. 'She knew what I'd find if I came to Cambridge. My God, Josephine – you women really are beyond belief. Who *do* you think you are, sticking together like that and keeping me in the dark? What has a man ever done to *any* of you that you can have so little faith in his understanding?'

She saw in the remark all the long-held resentment of her love for Marta, all the feelings of exclusion from something with which he could never compete, and while she tried to tell herself that it was his grief talking, she felt another piece of the trust between them shatter with every word he said. 'Please, Archie, come and sit down,' she begged. 'There are other things I need to tell you. At least let me try and explain.'

He turned to face her, but stayed where he was. 'Go on. I want to hear you justify Bridget's secret. Why didn't she tell me she had a daughter? Why was that something she felt she had to hide?' Josephine waited, hoping that his own reasoning might lead him to the answer which she found so difficult to speak aloud, but he simply stared at her, daring her to rise to the challenge. 'Well?'

'Phyllis isn't just Bridget's daughter. She's yours, too.' She watched the astonishment turn to disbelief, and hurried to fill the silence before Archie could argue. 'After you'd gone back to the Front, Bridget found out she was pregnant. By then, you'd both agreed that the relationship was over and she thought she'd never see you again, so she decided to bring Phyllis up on her own.'

'Without even trying to contact me?'

Josephine stood and walked over to him. 'Believe me, Archie, I don't agree with what Bridget did all those years ago, but I do understand it. She didn't want either of you to be forced into a marriage that you wouldn't have chosen, and you'd made no effort to pick up where you left off when the war was over, so she did what she thought was best.'

'You're saying this is my fault?'

'No, of course not, but it certainly isn't Phyllis's. She's the one who's suffered most here, and she's the one who needs help now. Don't let whatever you feel about Bridget blind you to that.' She put a hand to his cheek, forcing him to look at her, and this time he didn't move away. 'Bridget loved you, Archie. When you found each other again by chance and she realised how much she still cared for you, she was in an impossible situation.' The memory of that meeting on Armistice Day came back to her, the single-minded determination in Bridget's eyes, but Josephine put it from her mind: there was no need to hurt Archie now with the harshness of those decisions; better to salvage comfort wherever she could. 'She was frightened of losing you – that's why she waited. She didn't think you'd ever be able to forgive her, and the longer she put it off, the harder it got.'

'But what about the child?' Archie said, and Josephine noticed that he still could not bring himself to use her name. 'She must have thought that I didn't want her. What sort of father would go twenty years without even picking up the telephone or trying to make contact? She'll never forgive me for that. I wouldn't, in her position.'

'But in her eyes, there was nothing to forgive,' Josephine said, wishing that there was some way of avoiding the confession which was still to come. 'Bridget told Phyllis that her father had been killed in the war. Phyllis had no reason to doubt that, and certainly no reason to think that you'd abandoned her.'

'My daughter thinks I'm dead, and you say it as if it's a blessing.'

'That isn't what I meant.' She looked intently at him, willing him to realise that she wasn't his enemy in this, but so much damage had already been done. He turned away from her and she realised that she had never seen him cry before – not even during the darkest days of the war, when he had been so badly injured. 'But she knows you're alive now, Archie – at least I think she does. She knew as soon as you walked in here today.'

'How?'

'Bridget's portrait of you – the one in uniform. Phyllis knows that the man in that picture is her father, and you haven't really changed.'

She was crying herself now, and he walked over to hold her. 'Why didn't you tell me, Josephine?' he asked softly, and there was something defeated in his voice that made her fearful. 'I thought we were better than that.'

Sadly, Josephine pulled away from him, knowing in her heart that there could be no way back from this, no matter what she said now. 'Bridget wanted time to tell Phyllis,' she explained. 'I promised her I wouldn't say anything before she'd had a chance to do that.'

'So was that why she came here today? To break the news to Phyllis?'

Josephine shrugged. 'I don't suppose we can ever know that for certain. Come back to the house with me,' she offered tentatively. 'You can't stay here, and we need to talk.'

He shook his head. 'I honestly don't see what more there is to say, and anyway I've got to go to the station. I can't forgive Bridget, she was right about that, but I *can* get justice for her.'

'Surely you're in no fit state to work.'

'What else do you suggest I do? What else is left?'

'Phyllis, of course. Don't you even want to talk to her?'

Archie hesitated, and for a moment she dared to hope that he might change his mind. 'It's too late, Josephine,' he said, 'and I think Phyllis will tell you the same thing if you ask her. I can't deal with this now. Everything I thought I was sure of is a lie.'

It was meant as a parting shot, but Josephine grabbed his arm. 'Don't you dare include me in that,' she said, her guilt finally giving way to anger. 'You and I have been telling each other lies for twenty-five years, but every single time has been because we love each other and this is no different. Yes, it's a mess, but life is – and this was never some conspiracy dreamt up by harpies to hurt you.' He opened his mouth to argue, but she was too incensed to give him the chance. 'You can't stand there and decide what's too late for Phyllis just because *you're* feeling guilty – and if you really want to know what guilt is, think about her. Bridget *died* because of her. She didn't ask to be saved, but that's what a mother does and now Phyllis has to live with that for the rest of her life. I think that rather trumps anything you and I are feeling, don't you?' She stopped, unable to trust herself not to go even further and suspecting that she had already said more than she would ever be forgiven for. 'We all do what we think is best at the time, Archie, but we can never see the consequences. How was Bridget to know that you'd meet again and have something more than a wartime affair? And how was I to know that she'd die before she had a chance to put things right?' He turned away, but she tried one last time. 'Please, Archie – go and see Phyllis. Let her decide if it's too late.'

There was no answer and Josephine watched him go, feeling the emptiness and desolation close in around her, a tangible presence which she knew would be with her long after she left the theatre.

25

My dear Phyllis,

Please forgive a letter from a stranger, particularly one which must open with another deception. When we met at the Festival Theatre in the week of Night Must Fall, *I wasn't, as I told you, looking for tickets – I was looking for you. I had, by chance, discovered that my oldest friend is your father, and – call it curiosity or meddling or concern – I wanted to meet you. It wasn't my place then to say anything to you or to him; that was for your mother to do, and you may find some comfort in knowing that she had every intention of doing so. But the opportunity of telling you everything, of trying to make you understand why she did what she did, has been stolen from her. This letter – if and when you feel ready to read it – is no substitute for the conversation you were never allowed to have, but it does at least contain some of the information that I know she would have given you.*

Your father's name is Archie Penrose, and he and Bridget met during the war – in the autumn of 1915, to be precise. Archie had been badly wounded at the Front, and they sent him to a makeshift hospital here in Cambridge, set up in one of the college courts. He told me once that his earliest recollection of your mother was like a dream: he awoke to find her sitting on the end of his bed, sketching him as if it were the most ordinary thing in the world, and they grew to love each other while he was convalescing. She gave him that first drawing and he's kept it ever since; it was, he says, the reminder of peace and sanity that got him through the horror of returning to war. In time, it became the portrait painting which you know so well; one day, I hope he'll show it to you.

Your parents both loved this town. The weeks they spent together here were among the most precious of Archie's life – although of course he had no idea until now quite how precious they had been.

Archie never knew that he had a daughter; if he had, he would have loved and cherished you every single day of your life. He went back to war before Bridget discovered she was pregnant, and they lost touch, like thousands of our generation. You were born into a world of chaos, a world which had lost sight of every human value and instinct to love, and yet your parents did *love each other – one of those small, ordinary miracles that save us from ourselves. Their time together back then might have been brief, but it was no less important for that. A love that begins in darkness has a habit of lasting.*

You may already know something of your parents' history. What you won't be aware of is the man your father has become in the intervening years, the man that he is today. He trained as a doctor, but gave up medicine after the war and joined the police force instead. Now he is a detective chief inspector at Scotland Yard, and – like your mother – he is devoted to his work, perhaps at the expense of other things in his life. A policeman and an artist might seem an odd combination, but, in very different ways, both your parents set out to improve on the messy, muddle of a world that we make for ourselves, or at least to shine a light on all that is good about it. I've often thought that this is what bonded them so strongly. Archie is a fine man – compassionate and brave, warm and intelligent, with an unflinching sense of right and wrong that can sometimes prove his downfall. He has a genuine interest in others, and a talent for finding common ground with people from all walks of life; until I met you, I assumed that this was a necessity of his job, but in hindsight it seems to be a natural gift, and one that he has passed on. It's hard to know how much to tell you, and, in any case, the things that are important to me about Archie won't necessarily be the things that speak to you. He loves theatre, though, which will please you. And you have his smile.

There is nothing I can say that will numb the pain of your mother's death, or change the fact that she left you with so many questions unanswered. I don't presume to know how you must feel, except to guess that your grief for her is blurred by a sense of betrayal because she kept something from you which it was always your right to know, and for twenty years you have loved and mourned a father whom you believed to be lost to you. Make no mistake, Phyllis – she regretted that decision bitterly, for your sake and for Archie's, and she was about to put it right – but war has much to answer for. She had no reason to believe that she would ever see him again, and you were always her priority. When I saw her a few days before she died, she told me that you were the best thing about her, that you were strong enough to forgive each other anything. In time, I hope you'll realise that she was right.

Archie once said that your mother helped him to see the beauty of the world more often. His day-to-day landscape is brutal and bleak, a world full of hate, and his job expects him to understand why we do the most terrible things to each other. Now, while his heart breaks, his answer is to seek justice for Bridget – but he knows, too, that the other answer is love. At the moment he's afraid to trust in it, and perhaps you are, too. But you are the only two people in the world who can truly understand each other's pain, and I hope that will bring you together. As I said, a love that begins in darkness has a habit of lasting.

Yours very sincerely,

Josephine Tey

Josephine sealed the letter, which had been her one salvation in a night of sleeplessness and regret. Her confrontation with Archie had left her numb, but, as the shock wore off, the rawness of his anger came back to her and – selfish as it was when so much else had been lost – she found herself in mourning for their friendship. In her heart, she had known from the moment of Marta's revelation on Garret Hostel Bridge that the bond of trust between them was under sentence, but she could never have predicted the tragedy which had made every lie less redeemable. Now, she felt more isolated than at any other time in her life, and she longed to be with Marta. In the morning, she would make arrangements to go back to Scotland, and then to America. Archie was unreachable, and there was nothing else she could do here; her absence was the only thing which might begin to heal the rift.

She dressed and set out for Little St Mary's Lane to deliver the letter. Phyllis would probably still be in hospital, and Josephine had no idea where she lived, but she would have to go back to her mother's house sooner or later to begin the heartbreaking process of dismantling Bridget's life. As soon as she turned in off the main street, she hoped for Phyllis's sake that it was later: a small but intrusive clutch of newspaper reporters was gathered outside Bridget's front door, obviously waiting for someone to return there, and, as Josephine watched, she saw a photographer put his camera to the downstairs windows and take pictures of the rooms inside. There were too many men for this to be purely a local story, and Josephine felt a rush of helpless rage on Bridget's behalf as she imagined her murder splashed all over the national papers, making an insufferable situation even worse. She lingered by the church railings, knowing that she couldn't approach the house and put something through the letterbox without being photographed; the letter would have to go in the post.

As she was turning to go, the bells of Little St Mary's began to ring out, calling worshippers to early morning mass. Josephine hesitated, drawn to the complex, tuneful sound which she had begun to take for granted in a town of ancient churches. There was something clean in this call to the heavens, something pure and unchangeable, and for the first time in her life she found herself tempted inside a church by something other than curiosity or a love of its earthly beauty. The church was aisle-less, with no division between the nave and the chancel, and she wondered if it might at one stage have been intended as part of a larger college chapel. Light flooded through a beautifully decorated east window and Josephine slipped into a pew at the back, breathing in the pungent smell of incense and hoping that something in the service would bring her comfort. But she wanted it too badly: the words and the music failed to touch her, and she left the church as far from peace as she had entered it.

She found a stamp in her bag, posted Phyllis's letter, and headed home. It was after nine o'clock now, but the newsagent's on the corner of St John's Street was still in darkness. A handful of delivery boys hung about outside, late to collect their allocation of the Sunday papers, and a few disgruntled customers were standing in small groups on the pavement, waiting impatiently for the shop to open. Josephine joined them, scarcely having to guess at the main topic of conversation; she tried not to listen as she glanced through the advertisements in the window to pass the time. A card caught her eye in the bottom left-hand corner, different from most of the others in that it wasn't offering or asking for accommodation; it was an advert for a stage-hand at the Festival Theatre, poignant in light of what had just happened there but innocent enough otherwise, and Josephine tried to put her finger on why it troubled her. She looked at the other cards, thinking back to the very first time that she had entered the shop and recalling the conversation between the newsagent and a young girl looking for a flatmate; back then, she had assumed he was being friendly, but in hindsight the exchange seemed more probing. What better way to identify young women living alone than in a seemingly harmless conversation about their domestic arrangements while he wrote out their card? She imagined Phyllis placing the advert, drawn into a conversation about how busy she was at the theatre and how much time she spent on her own there, then dismissed the idea as fanciful. But something nagged at her sufficiently to scour the rest of the window, and there it was – an advertisement for rooms to let in St Clement's Passage, rooms in the house where Mary Ennis had been raped.

Josephine walked away, stunned by the thoughts that raced through her head with such seductive logic. Why would the shop be closed without notice on a busy Sunday morning? Surely the newsagent would try to make capital of yesterday's shocking events – unless, of course, he had something to do with them and wanted to keep a low profile. She remembered the scorn with which he had discussed the police investigation, his indignant dismissal of the false arrest on Armistice Day – almost as if he knew better. She remembered the rattle of an old bicycle that Mary Ennis had heard and the one that often stood outside the little shop. And then she thought about the state of Mary's bedroom, the violence and the hatred with which everything safe and familiar had been destroyed. Suddenly she knew what the filthy black staining on the sheets was because she had washed it countless times from her own hands. It wasn't dirt and it wasn't coal dust. It was newsprint.

When she got home, she sat in the kitchen and tried to talk herself out of her conclusions, but now that the seed of suspicion was planted it refused to go away. A newsagent was perfectly placed to know all the things that the rapist had needed to know: where a girl lived and with whom; when lodgings were empty; when a landlady cancelled the newspapers, signalling her absence from the house. And it would be very easy for the police to find out if the other victims had frequented the shop, innocently chatting away while the man behind the counter selected his next target. Eventually, she went into the hall and picked up the telephone. There was no point in asking for Archie: he wouldn't take the call, and in any case her accusation would be safer in the hands of someone less involved. But if she was right, if the newsagent was the man who had terrorised the town for months and taken Bridget's life, then perhaps Archie would see that she had done all she could to put things right. Perhaps he would forgive her.

26

Josephine looked down over Times Square from her window at the Hotel Astor, and marvelled for the thousandth time at its spectacle. From the moment she arrived in New York, she had behaved like a small child at a fun fair, desperate to experience everything, and the city hadn't let her down. More than anything, she had come to love this part of Manhattan, with its clutch of theatres and music halls – stoically battling an influx of peep shows and vaudeville – and the faded splendour of the grand, turn-of-the-century hotels. Each night, the square came miraculously to life, lit by brightly coloured billboards and huge electrified signs which made Piccadilly Circus seem like a quiet backwater; she and Marta returned together to their temporary home in this hotel of a thousand rooms – tired, anonymous, happy.

But now it was morning and a heavy fall of snow had muted the colours of the unlit billboards even further, transforming her view of the street into a movie played out slowly in monochrome. Few people had ventured outside on foot, and the roads were deserted except for a handful of cars which had been abandoned on the pavement and were now covered by a delicate film of white. The glare was so intense that even the light seemed to freeze in tiny shards on the buildings opposite, and she opened the window a little to breathe in the sharp, exhilarating air. It was early on Christmas Eve, and the city which seemed to offer everything had delivered the perfect gift: a clean, white day, as hopeful as a blank sheet of paper.

'Beautiful, isn't it?' Marta put a cup of coffee in her hand and kissed the back of her neck.

'Yes, it is. I'm not remotely interested in going home.'

'We've got a few more days yet, so don't even think about it.' They watched as a solitary bus inched its way nobly down Seventh Avenue for the benefit of one or two passengers. 'I can't believe you didn't come here when your own play was running on Broadway,' Marta said. 'I'd have gone every single night, but then I've always had a shameless lack of modesty.'

Josephine laughed. Her biggest stage hit, *Richard of Bordeaux*, had transferred to the Empire Theatre shortly after its West End run, but she had resisted all the invitations to come over and promote it. 'No, it was stupid of me,' she admitted, 'but I'm glad now that I didn't. I would never have wanted to see New York for the first time with anyone but you.'

Marta smiled. 'Well, I think we've seen just about every inch of it by now. And it's been nice to hear you laugh again.' She took Josephine's face in her hands, and drew her into a long, intense kiss. 'It *will* be all right, you know. He called, didn't he? The ice is broken, and Archie made the first move.'

'Yes, he did.'

'It was never going to be easy, and believe me – I rue the day I ever walked into that station buffet and met Bridget and Phyllis, but what's done is done. Archie's not stupid enough to sacrifice your friendship, and it's thanks to you that he caught Bridget's killer. Neither he nor Phyllis will ever forget that. You'll have a relationship with both of them, but you just need to give it time.'

Josephine stood up and walked over to the vast art deco wardrobe on the other side of the room. 'You're right, but I don't even want to think about that now. I want to savour every moment of the time we've got left here.' She threw Marta a bundle of warm clothes and scarves. 'And I think you promised me Christmas in Central Park.'

*

Archie stood in the Front Court of King's College and watched as the myriad lights from inside the chapel grew stronger against the encroaching darkness. It was bitterly cold, although the winter hadn't yet seen fit to offer snow, and he pulled his coat around him as he waited for the end of the service. The opening bars of 'Hark! The Herald Angels Sing' gave him hope, and within a few minutes the choir and clergy were proceeding out of the chapel, followed by the various officials of the college and their guests.

He moved a little closer to the south door, trying to remember the last time he had felt so nervous. A woman who seemed familiar was walking towards Wilkins' Building, and, as she passed a lighted college window, he recognised Virginia Moorcroft. She looked surprised to see him, then pleased, and took a different path to speak to him. 'Have you been in for the service, Chief Inspector?' she asked.

'No, I'm afraid I couldn't face it after everything that's happened.' It was hard to explain, but it wasn't just the tragic history of this particular day which had prevented him from entering the chapel; since Bridget's death, he had been too angry to step inside a church, even for her funeral, and although it made little sense to rail against a God in whom he had never believed, he couldn't help himself. 'What about you?'

'I wouldn't have missed it for the world. Teddy sang the solo. He'll be insufferable now, of course, but I'm pleased for him. Pleased for us all. It felt . . . well, it felt cleansing.' She stared past him across the court, and he waited for her to continue. 'I'm so ashamed of what Robert did,' she admitted, 'and I can't thank you enough for saving Teddy.'

'There's no need. As it turned out, Teddy was never in danger.'

'But you didn't know that. You went to look for him, regardless of the consequences, and things could have been very different. I owe you a great deal.'

'Then there is one thing you can do for me.'

'Just name it.'

'You can accept that you have nothing to be ashamed of. We can't be responsible for other people's decisions, whether we love them or not. You have to look to the future now – for Teddy's sake, and for Evie's.' She smiled, but he knew from personal experience that it would take more than logic and wise words to convince her. 'What will you do now?' he asked.

'Pray that the divorce goes through as quickly and as quietly as possible. There's bound to be a furore in the press when Robert goes to trial, but I'll grit my teeth and look after the children as best I can. Then, when a decent amount of time has passed, I'll sell the Priory. It was always my husband's home, not mine.'

'Do you know where you'll go?' Archie asked, surprised by how much he cared.

'Not yet. My father wants me to move back to Chicago, but I'm not sure about that. Teddy loves England, and I don't see why the children should suffer for any of this.' By now, the general congregation was spilling out from the chapel, their Christmas well and truly under way, and Archie looked over to the crowd. 'Are you waiting for someone?' she asked.

'My daughter.'

He still felt no ownership over the words, and Virginia Moorcroft looked at him in surprise. 'I didn't know you had a daughter.' Archie gave a wry smile, and her surprise turned to curiosity. 'But then why would I know that? I really don't know very much about you at all.'

'It's a long and complicated story. I'm not sure I understand it myself yet.'

'Then perhaps you'll tell it to me someday. I'd like that.'

They said goodbye and he watched her walk away, then turned back towards the chapel. Phyllis was heading towards the porters' lodge, where they had arranged to meet, and Archie longed for the day when everything about her that reminded him of Bridget would be a cause for joy rather than resentment. She waved when she saw him and he quickened his step, feeling the bewildering muddle of awkwardness and pride which was still so new to him. They greeted each other hesitantly, and then, as they headed out into King's Parade, she smiled and took his arm.

Acknowledgements

Nine Lessons had two very different inspirations – a love of M. R. James's ghost stories, which remain among the finest ever written; and a real-life haunting, the period in the early 1970s when the Cambridge Rapist terrorised the streets of a quiet and beautiful university town.

Peter Cook assaulted at least nine women in a series of increasingly violent attacks, but his crimes affected the whole town: removing the freedom that women had fought so hard for; casting suspicion on to innocent men; and humiliating a local police force which worked under pressure at a time when even Scotland Yard still had no specialist methods of investigating rape. Cook was arrested in June 1975 and given two life sentences; he died in prison in 2004. *The Cambridge Rapist: Unmasking the Beast of Bedsitland* by Paul G. Bahn gives a full account of the case, and I'm grateful to the staff of the Cambridgeshire Collection for access to extensive national and local press coverage.

The events of that time are still tangible today, in the barred ground-floor windows that you can see as you walk around the city, and in the memories of those who lived through the fear. Like many women, my partner, Mandy, unwittingly met the Cambridge Rapist several times in the course of her everyday life; her recollections of those months – the sense of shock and vulnerability – have made a vital contribution to the novel.

It's taken me a long time to set a book in the city I live in and love. Writing this has left me with a terrible sense of nostalgia for the 1930s Cambridge which I never knew, but also with a much greater appreciation of all that remains precious and unchanged.

My thanks go to Peter Monteith, Assistant Archivist at King's College, for information about the Chapel and College during M. R. James's time; and to the Cambridge Buddhist Centre for preserving so beautifully the fabric and history of the Festival Theatre. Sheila Mann's history of the Evelyn Hospital and *Down Your Street* by Sara Payne provided invaluable Cambridge research, and Gaynor Griffiths gave life to 10 Park Street. Anyone with a love of snowdrops and Jacobean architecture will recognise the inspiration for Angerhale Priory, but its inhabitants are entirely fictional.

Of the many books on M. R. James and his work, those by Michael Cox and Peter Haining were particularly helpful.

It's true that James failed to finish a new story for Christmas 1913, but his reasons were far less sinister than those I've given him, and the glorious tradition that he started is still honoured in Cambridge to this day. I hope that King's College Chapel will forgive me for bringing the shadow of an imaginary horror to its door, but like Portmeirion, the BBC and London's West End, I suspect its reputation will easily withstand the attentions of a crime writer who loves it.

Love and thanks, as always, to my mum and dad, whose support and encouragement is more important than they'll ever know. I'm indebted to Walter Donohue at Faber, and Véronique Baxter and Laura West at David Higham Associates for their continued support; to Sandra Duncan and all at W. F. Howes for giving the series a wonderful audio life; to Mick Wiggins for his beautiful cover illustrations; and to the growing band of librarians, booksellers and readers whose enthusiasm for the series ensures that Josephine's adventures will continue.

And to Mandy – not just for the conversations, insight and ideas this time, but for making Cambridge more special than anyone else ever could. Thank you.

Also by Nicola Upson

ff

An Expert in Murder

An Expert in Murder is the first in a new series that features Golden Age crime writer Josephine Tey as its lead character, placing her in the richly peopled world of the 1930s theatre which formed the other half of her writing life. It's March 1934, and Tey is travelling from Scotland to London to celebrate what should be the triumphant final week of her celebrated play, *Richard of Bordeaux*. However, a seemingly senseless murder puts her reputation, and even her life, under threat. *An Expert in Murder* is both a tribute to one of the most enduringly popular writers of crime and an atmospheric detective novel in its own right.

'Highly original and elegantly written . . . The first of what promises to be a distinguished series.' P. D. James

'Upson's plot is cunning and she skilfully recreates 1930s theatreland . . . This is entertaining stuff.' *Observer*

'A satisfying array of backstage jealousies, betrayals, long-buried family secrets, adultery, illegitimacy and the tragic consequences of the First World War.' *The Times*

ff

Angel with Two Faces

Inspector Archie Penrose invites Josephine Tey down to his family home in Cornwall so she can recover from the traumatic events in *An Expert in Murder*. Josephine welcomes the opportunity, especially since Archie's home is near the famous Minack open-air theatre perched on the cliffs overlooking the sea. However, Josephine's hopes of experiencing a period of rest are dashed when her arrival coincides with the funeral of a young man from the village who has drowned when his horse inexplicably leapt into the nearby lake.

When another young man disappears and the village's curate falls from the cliffs onto the rocks below, Josephine and Archie begin to suspect the involvement of a cold-blooded murderer.

As Josephine and Archie try to unravel the mystery, they begin to see death as an angel with two faces – one gazing at the violence of the present, the other looking back to the crimes hidden in the past.

'[Gives] new life to a classic murder setting . . . Upson is chillingly effective at showing how good intentions may lead to evil consequences . . . A fine addition to a promising series.' *Spectator*

'Carefully plotted, full of historical information, local colour and meticulous psychological analysis.' *Literary Review*

ff

Two for Sorrow

London, 1903. Two women are hanged in Holloway Prison for killing babies. More than thirty years later, Josephine Tey sets out to write a novel about Amelia Sach and Annie Walters, the notorious Finchley baby farmers. Meanwhile, her friend, Inspector Archie Penrose, is investigating the sadistic murder of a young seamstress, found dead in the Motley sisters' studio, amid preparations for a star-studded charity gala.

The girl's death seems to be the result of a long-standing domestic feud, but Archie is unconvinced; and when a second young woman is involved in a horrific accident soon afterwards, the search begins for a vicious killer who will stop at nothing to keep the past where it belongs.

'With a well-made plot and fascinating cast of female characters, both haves and have-nots, this is an assured addition to an excellent series.' *Guardian*

'A heartfelt account of the condemned prisoner, a vivid picture of London life in the thirties and a cleverly plotted mystery.' *Literary Review*

'Touching and psychologically compelling.' *Sunday Times*

ff

Fear in the Sunlight

Summer, 1936. Josephine Tey joins her friends in the holiday village of Portmerion to celebrate her fortieth birthday. Alfred Hitchcock and his wife, Alma Reville, are there to sign a deal to film Josephine's novel, *A Shilling for Candles*, and Hitchcock has one or two tricks up his sleeve to keep the holiday party entertained – and expose their deepest fears.

But things get out of hand when one of Hollywood's leading actresses is brutally slashed to death in a cemetery near the village. As fear and suspicion take over a setting where nothing – and no one – is quite what it seems, Chief Inspector Archie Penrose becomes increasingly unsatisfied with the way the investigation is ultimately resolved. Several years later, another horrific murder, again linked to a Hitchcock movie, drives Penrose back to the scene of the original crime to uncover the truth.

'The best of the series . . . The novel injects new life into the serial killer genre, as well as offering an elegiac commentary on Tey's sadly truncated life.' *Sunday Times*

'A class above the usual crime fiction . . . A novel that charms until the dagger strikes and then, as Hitchcock once explained, it provides the public with beneficial shocks.' *Independent on Sunday*

ff

The Death of Lucy Kyte

When Josephine Tey inherits a remote Suffolk cottage from her godmother, it came full of secrets. Sorting through the artefacts of her godmother's life, Josephine is intrigued by an infamous murder committed near the cottage a century before. Yet this old crime – dubbed the Red Barn murder – still seems to haunt the tight-knit village and its inhabitants.

As Josephine settles into the house, she knows that something dark has a hold on the heart of this small community. Is it just the ghosts of the Red Barn murder, or is there something very much alive that she needs to fear?

Trapped in this isolated community and surrounded by shadows of obsession, abuse and deceit, can Josephine untangle history from present danger and prevent a deadly cycle beginning once again?

'A highly literate page-turner is something you don't see every day. Nicola Upson is a new discovery for me, and this novel is so interesting, so well-crafted, so engaging and so genuinely creepy.' *Sydney Morning Herald*